Mark's Strength

BOOK TWO
of the

TRILOGY

Endorsements for

Mark's Strength

by Skye Elizabeth Wieland

"This is another fascinating story by Skye Elizabeth of good versus evil in a wonderful South African setting. Characters from Book One, *Sarah's Gift*, continue in their journey of learning to trust God through life-threatening dangers as they seek to know and try to obey His direction for their lives. I fell in love with a new character, the boy Kwanele, and look forward with keen anticipation to reading more of his journey when Book Three, *Kwan's Choice*, is released. This is a series not to be missed!"

Mary Hawkins
Multi-published Christian Fiction author
www.mary-hawkins.com

"What an inspiring book, it is for everyone who have lost hope, passion and trust. It teaches someone to be strong in all situations. It is with this book that I discovered that one can do all things through Christ who gives strength."

Lerato Khoza
Letaba Elephant Hall SANParks

"Skye Elizabeth has once again crafted a gripping story of adventure, romance and faith set within the magnificent Kruger game park. Sarah and Mark face new challenges, reconnect with old friends and must face an old adversary. Their destiny becomes intertwined with Kwanele's as the orphaned Zulu boy seeks to escape his troubled past. *Mark's Strength* is a poignant and inspiring tale well worth reading."

Jeanette O'Hagan
Campus Crusade for Christ

"Be strong and courageous.

Do not be afraid or terrified because of them,

for the Lord your God goes with you;

He will never leave you nor forsake you."

Deuteronomy 31:6

KRUGER NATIONAL PARK
Zimbabwe
Limpopo
Eastern Transvaal
Mozambique
South Africa
Border Gate
Shimuwini Bushcamp
Jacob and Martha's Bushcamp
Phalaborwa Gate
Letaba
Olifants
Hoedspruit
Timbavati
Orpen Gate
Paul Kruger Gate

PROLOGUE

Dust choked up Sarah's lungs. She clawed her way across the hot dirt. Grappling at tufts of lowveldt grass, she tried in desperation to ease herself to her quaking knees. The distressed squeal of a nearby elephant calf and the echo of gunshots reverberated through her eardrums. She clamped shut her eyes against the sight of bloodshed and slaughter. She needed to move—to get to safety. Injured in the middle of the fray, she didn't relish the thought of death by elephant trampling. Queasy, she heaved herself off her stomach again, propping herself up onto one foot. Confused, she stared at the dirt. It was the wrong color. She lifted her palms and turned them to herself with vivid fascination. Blood! Recoiling, she wiped her hands against her jeans, trying to remove the offensive liquid. Elephants fell, brutally murdered all around her. She felt as if she were in some kind of a vortex. The sounds. The heat. The pain! Why was she not dead? Why couldn't it all just end? She scanned the fog of swirling dust. A rush of hot wind rose from her left—stinging her eyes. A gasp escaped and she raised her arm to her face, trying to ward off the wind and dust. Then she felt it. Watching her. A sudden wave of panic constricted her throat and she struggled to get up. The pain was unbearable. Sarah spun her head, her eyes wide with fear. Where was it? Without warning, a dark shape flew out of the gloom and knocked her back to the ground with a forceful thud. Sarah cried out as sharp pain shot up her spine. She sensed the presence of the figure before it was seen. A man? Sarah's gaze shot from left to right, squinting through the haze. Shadows darted everywhere, but she knew something...someone, still lurked there, stalking her. Her breath came in rapid short bursts as she tried to rub her eyes with her sleeves. He was here! Sarah realized somewhere in the blinding dust and noise of elephants, horses, and people, her assailant stood, waiting. She couldn't see.

Blinking against the grit boring its way into her eyes, she tried to move. She needed to get somewhere—anywhere—away from here. Panic rose in her throat as she scrambled mentally to get her bearings. Suddenly he made his move. She sensed him approach, with the litheness of a leopard. Cruel laughter echoed somewhere close. Behind her? She craned her head, but saw nothing. No! With horror, she realized it was above her— looming over her. Sarah froze—she knew that laugh. Hated that laugh! All at once, images flashed in her mind of a distant past. She had been disarmed by the charm of an inviting Irish voice, chiseled features, and the false promises of help.

The sudden hot tears stung her eyes as her head snapped up and she focused on the face of the man who had shattered everything important to her. Declan. The one who had deceived her—pretended to help her—pretended he loved her, and then tried to kill her.

"No, you're supposed to be dead!" Sarah stammered. The Irishman's lip curled; his once-handsome features appeared warped and angular. He shook his head.

"Look at what you've done, Sarah!"

Sarah looked down at her bloodstained hands and saw she was holding a rifle—her Winchester. The wood was smeared with blood. Her heart beat hard as the dust around them started to settle. Then she spotted her. A few meters in front of her was the still form of her beloved horse, Honor.

"No," she whimpered. Declan strolled in catlike prowess to the beast and cocked a heavy booted foot upon the horse's shoulder. He cradled an elephant rifle, irony in his expression as he smirked at her. Sarah's face flushed red. She opened her mouth to speak, but stopped as his hand shot up with authority. His arrogance smoldered to a cold, hard stare— hatred bore down on her.

"It's your fault! Everything! You risked everything for a bunch of elephants, and what good did it do you? More culls will happen. What will you do then? You don't have a gift, Sarah!" Declan's face twisted as he spat her name. Sarah narrowed her eyes. This man was not Declan. It was the devil in

Declan's form—condemning her, undermining her gift from God. Sarah threw the rifle aside and clamped her red-streaked hands over her ears, doubling over in grief. She didn't want to hear anymore. Leering at her, he ground the heel of his boot around on the body of her horse. Squeezing her eyes shut, she curled into herself and wept as she tried to shut him out.

After a moment, Sarah only heard the sounds of her own sobbing. Tentative, she lifted her head. The scene had changed. Was she in a dream? Was she dead? Kneeling in the open lowveldt, hot wind coursing through her loose black hair, Sarah noticed the gun had gone and her hands were clean. The sky loomed a rich sapphire above her, light wisps of clouds flicking across the expanse. The soft, long grasses swayed around her. It was pleasant. Heaven? The thought vanished as a deep foreboding sank into her. The sound of a heartbeat, slow and steady, began to echo in Sarah's ears. It wasn't her own. Fear swept through her as she scanned the grasslands. Realization struck and her hands ran down over her belly. It was swollen. She was with child! Panic seized her. No, not this! Not again! A sharp pain struck her. She clutched at her abdomen.

"No!" Clenching her teeth, Sarah moaned. Not again! The pain intensified, until all of a sudden it ceased. The sound of the heartbeat softened, slowing until the sound was silenced. Sarah stayed hunched over on the ground; her eyes squeezed shut. A dull emptiness replaced everything. Grief washed over her as she clutched her stomach. She became aware of another presence. Flinging her eyes open, she looked around. Declan crept from behind her, like a cat stalking its prey. He leaned close to her ear—his voice a sinister whisper. "It's all your fault! Everything! It's your fault you lost your first child."

"No!" she screamed. Ripping out fistfuls of dirt and grass, she flung them at the form of Declan. "Get away from me!" Her face contorted as she lunged toward him. But in an instant, he was gone.

CHAPTER ONE

Polokwane, South Africa, 1994

"Hey. Hey. Sarah? Wake up...Sarah!"

Sarah sat up with a start. She was in her bed, trembling and sweating, though the night air was cool. Her vision began to focus. Dust, squeals, blood, and pain were still so vivid in her waking mind. The baby! The grief! She blinked and gazed up into a rugged face. Warmth emanated from his eyes, but concern was etched into his rough features.

"Wha..?" Placing her hand to her head, she looked around in confusion. Cold sweat trickled down the back of her nightshirt. A violent shudder racked her slender form. Husband of three years, Mark, was quick to her side, pulling her into himself. His warmth enveloped her, thawing the darkness of her dreams.

"Shhh, it's okay. It's over...shhh." He moaned and kissed her hair, rocking her like a wounded child. Melting into his strong embrace, Sarah allowed him to hold her head to his bare chest. His fingers pushed up through her dark tendrils of thick hair. His steady heartbeat thrummed in her ears as his fingers worked their magic on her scalp, easing the tension. She was safe. She was here, with her man. Sarah was grateful for his strength and comfort. It was needed and she couldn't seem to function without it. She was helpless, like a child.

"I'm sorry...I..." Sarah said, but he covered her lips with his fingertips.

"I know—you don't need to explain," he murmured, his cheek resting on her head. "You were dreaming again." His voice trailed off before changing. "Come on." He adjusted his position and guided to her into the thick comfort of the duvet. Sarah allowed her head to sink into the pillow. "It's over now, try to get some sleep." He positioned himself facing her. Slipping his arm under her head he draped his other arm around her waist. She shivered and let him pull her in close. Her back nestled into his warm embrace. Relaxing, Sarah felt protected, like a dove cradled gently in strong hands.

She had lost more weight from her already slim figure over the last year. Mark was clinging to a wisp of the woman he used to know. But he loved her regardless and prayed every night that she would come around—praying they would be safe in this volatile town. The nation was reshaping and many white South Africans were moving overseas to escape the violence, in particular to Sarah's homeland of Australia. They said it was the land of opportunity. Would Sarah have left, too, if they hadn't married? He dismissed the thought, focusing on her immediate needs. Was she settled into sleep yet? Easing back from her, he watched the soft rise and fall of her diaphragm, listened to her deep, steady breathing. He ran his fingertips down her arm. It was smooth and cool. She didn't stir. He pulled the duvet up over her shoulders.

Rolling onto his back, Mark gazed at the ceiling. The moonlight streamed in through the window. He listened to the irregular buzz of the traffic and the distant sound of music as it played at the nightclub a few blocks away. Sounds echoed off the apartment building, carried south on the cooling breezes of May. Things were different here in the city of Polokwane. It was so different from the quiet tranquility of Brennan's Safari Trails. He missed the unassuming chorus of crickets and the mournful hoot of the owl. Even the low-toned roar of the lionesses as they called to their prides after returning from a kill. The city had always been a large place, but to Mark and Sarah it seemed to engulf them, drown their spirits in its magnitude. People, traffic, noise everywhere. And the crime. News of daily rapes, car-jackings, and the like had turned Sarah into a hermit, never wanting to leave the building. Had he made the right choice? Bringing his young wife to live in this city after the trauma of what had occurred in the Kruger? They were under a witness-protection program. Stay hidden. Stay anonymous. Stay safe. How long would it last? There was a price on Sarah's head. Police weren't taking any chances. She was the girl who opened the doorway and stopped the culling. Provided a hope for conservationists in South Africa to make a difference, had closed one of the biggest doorways to the underground ivory smuggling businesses that took advantage of culls. Once Brennan's Safari Trails was sold, they were told to give up their identity. Stay hidden, in one of the many violent towns in South Africa. And to top it off, the changes occurring in the nation were making matters worse. Changing the national flag hadn't brought peace. This year alone had seen too much bloodshed, especially in KwanZulu-Natal, where last month, a state of emergency was declared. A new president was sworn in earlier this month. Mr. Nelson Mandela—the first black president. Mark could only hope and pray that under his leadership, the unrest in the country would start to dissolve. In light of their current predicament, the success with the elephant translocation seemed like a lifetime ago, not just three years. Depression settled on Sarah in the years that followed. She lost her drive. A year into their marriage, Sarah insisted on bringing children into the world. Mark had tried to put her off, worrying they needed to wait until they were safe. They needed to lie low. All his rationalizations had fallen on deaf ears, however, and he finally agreed. He wondered if falling pregnant might give her new hope, a new purpose. But it was not to be.

It was then that something inside her broke. Try as he may, Mark couldn't think of how to pull her out of it. Catatonic. For months, she barely spoke, barely ate. He felt like he was losing his wife, but he refused to give up. She was the love of his life.

A police siren in the distance followed by gunshots pulled Mark from his reflections. He rolled his head toward Sarah. She tossed and turned in response, causing the springs in the old mattress to protest under her meager weight. Mark frowned with concern. He couldn't even provide what she deserved, like a new bed, a decent home. Sitting up, Mark looked out the window, his strong, bare shoulders flexing in the moonlight. He glanced over at Sarah, and brushed his hand lightly across her head. Slipping from the saggy mattress, he padded to the window and peered at the empty street below. In just a pair of cotton briefs, he shuddered at the cool air, sliding shut the window against the breeze. He tried in vain to rub the sleep from his eyes. Deep down, he knew they were still not safe. Not all the poachers were accounted for. Their old boss, Johnno Brennan, was now in jail for his involvement in ivory smuggling, and the business had been sold. The horses and gear were all sold, apart from Mark's horse, Sniper, and another horse, Buster. But the real fear was that there were still others out there, stalking them, wanting Sarah dead. As he focused out the window, a movement caught Mark's attention down on the street below. He narrowed his eyes as he noticed a black man in a tartan golfer's cap, standing outside of the pawn shop. He was leaning against the light post, a cigarette poised between his fingers. Mark shook his head. What was becoming of him, suspicious of everything, everyone? As if feeling Mark's piercing scrutiny, the man glanced up at the window. They locked eyes for a moment, before the man glowered, flicked his cigarette butt on the footpath, and shuffled away. Mark stood watching him leave—would the man turn around for one last look? He didn't. Mark snorted as the man disappeared around the building. He rubbed his face with annoyance. Was he paranoid? Slipping back into the bed next to his wife, Mark sighed. She was suffering now—suffering with recurring nightmares over the ordeal—suffering with depression. He toyed with the idea of calling the lieutenant in the morning, finding out where they stood. He dismissed the idea. What good would that do? Mark was tired. He'd had enough of having to report to the police—enough of other people running their lives. When were they going to be free? His brows pulled together as he rolled toward Sarah. She had moved onto her back, her face falling toward him. Mark watched her sleep—her dark hair forming into ringlets, framing her face, which at this moment seemed at peace. Her full blush lips were parted a little as she breathed lightly. They looked too big on her sunken face. He ran the back of his index finger down her smooth cheek. She needed to stop stressing—needed to eat, to put on weight. She wasn't anorexic, but stress was eating her to the bone. Mark was helpless as he watched his wife dwindle away. Her gentle sleeping form gave no hint to the turmoil that lay beneath. He was tired of waiting—tired of watching her suffer.

Blast it!

Mark got up and wandered into the kitchen, scratching the three-day growth on his chin. He flicked on the light and poured himself a glass of water. His eyes came to rest on a framed photo mounted on the wall. It showed the lowveldt of the Kruger. The silhouette of an elephant, Sarah's favorite game animal, depicted in the still image, frozen in time as it meandered along, searching for mopane. Mark clunked the glass down on the bench, causing water to splonk from the vessel onto the laminex. He wiped it away with one hand, running his other hand through his thick, wavy brown hair. It was getting long again. He tried to remember when he last got it cut. What would happen if they took a vacation? Work wouldn't miss him. If they snuck out for a few days, he wouldn't even need to tell the police. He cringed, knowing how angry Lieutenant Tim Naicker would be if he knew what Mark was thinking. His heart quickened. What harm could come of just a few days? So what if they slipped out from police protection a bit? If they stayed with friends, nobody would notice. Then they would be safely back in no time. Right? Mark looked over his shoulder toward the bedroom. He grimaced. Setting his jaw, he tossed his head back, finishing the water in his glass, and placed it in the sink with care. He would ring his workplace in the morning, and tell them he needed to take time off work for personal reasons. It was only a fill-in job at a travel agency anyway—they wouldn't care much. He wasn't where he should be in life. His profession should be on the field, not behind a desk. His passion. The wilderness of Africa. Mark glanced over at the pile of half-unpacked removal boxes in the corner of the room. It was funny how long they'd lived here, but not settled. Balancing on top of the haphazard pile were two empty suitcases. Taking care not to wake his wife, he hauled them down onto the couch, flopping them open. His eyes flicked to the clock—3 a.m.

CHAPTER
TWO

A travel mug of steaming coffee was placed into Sarah's unsteady hands. "What are you up to?" She felt alarm as she blinked back the sleepiness.

"It's okay, it's okay...don't worry. It's nothing bad." A secretive smile lit up Mark's face. Arm about her waist, she allowed him to wheel her toward the apartment door. She had dressed in her favorite pair of jeans, shirt, and boots. They left the apartment, went down the steps, into the underground car-park, and into their battered, old white Land Cruiser. Finally settled into the passenger seat, Sarah glanced over her shoulder, spying the bloated suitcases. She gave her husband a sly look.

"So...?"

He turned to her, tilting his mouth. "Trust me."
He took her hand and gave it a quick squeeze. Using the coffee as a ruse, she took back her hand and clasped the travel mug. Mark was quiet as he turned the key in the ignition. Dazed in the passenger seat, Sarah surveyed the street scene emerging through her sunglasses as Mark pulled up and out of the secure underground car-park.

"So, where are we going?" She looked at him sideways, studying his profile. "Why aren't you going to work?"

The car was braked at the stop sign. Mark turned to look straight into her eyes. The warmth and love she saw emanating from them filled her with pleasure. She was way too hard on him. He loved her unconditionally and she returned it with ice. Did she take his love for granted? She didn't deserve him. He chose not to answer her questions, but pulled a silly face instead. Sarah felt a smile tweak at her lips. He seemed satisfied as he pulled back into first gear and drove off. She loved it when he did things like this. He used to do it a lot…before they were meant to be incognito. Planning secret surprises for her. It didn't happen much anymore. Hiding had dragged the life out of their relationship. Her smile lingered on as she gazed out the window. Watching the crowds had become a habit of self-preservation. She frowned as she caught herself doing it again and glanced back at her husband as he drove. He must have felt her look, because he beamed at her, his expression full of mischief. Sarah scowled at him. "What?"

"I just know what my girl needs." He laughed. She smiled, worrying about the safety side of whatever he had planned. She sipped her coffee, trying not to think about it. She needed to be grateful for some glimmer of sunlight in the daily grind of their current existence. That's all it had been, mere existence. There was no joy, no excitement in their life anymore. No purpose. She would make the most of whatever Mark had planned. Perhaps they were off to the pictures, or a swish restaurant? No. There were suitcases packed. Maybe he had booked a posh hotel somewhere nice in town, to escape life a bit. Surely that wouldn't hurt. It might hurt the budget, though. They had struggled financially since they had married. Sarah realized the worry lines had become visible in her twenty-nine-year-old features. How would they cope with whatever he was doing? Her heart rate went up a notch just at the thought of it. She needed to relax. What did the doctor say? *Not to let myself get stressed.* Sarah took a breath, forcing herself to calm down. Mark was just trying to help. She needed to reassure him.

"Well, you already got me coffee." She giggled lightly, taking a deep, shuddering breath. His lips tweaked in a small smile. Returning her gaze out the window, Sarah saw how the thick clutter of buildings started to thin out. They were moving away from the commercial center and were now in the outer suburbs. Was he taking her out of town? They passed a mopane tree, and her thoughts rolled back to some distant place. A place filled with mopane trees and thick shrubs. The Kruger.

The smile faded from her face and her thoughts shifted back to darker realities. She sighed, trying to push back the memories, both good and bad—memories that filled her with dread and a deep ache. Shoving the dark images aside, she focused on the good memories—for a place she loved so dearly—a place that seemed to be etched into her very soul. She was heartsick. The sight of a baobab tree on the side of the road didn't help matters.

She lay back against her seat and closed her eyes. Her hands still clasped the half-full beverage. It was lifted from her grasp, and she heard it clunk into the drink holder. Her eyes flickered open just as Mark slipped his hand over hers, intertwining his fingers into hers. He squeezed gently. Sarah returned the action and allowed him to return his hand to the gear stick. He glanced sideways and she tried to read his thoughts. Was that concern? She knew she was depressed. She knew he worried about how to help her. But nobody thought about him. Was she living up to the standard she felt a good wife should be?

Opening her eyes, Sarah sat upright. How long had she been asleep? The digital clock on the dash of the Cruiser indicated they'd been on the road for about an hour. She looked at Mark apologetically and was greeted with a warm smile. "*Goeie môre...*again." He chuckled.

Being married to Mark and having lived here enough years now, Sarah had learnt to pick up a little Afrikaans. She smiled at his "good morning," stifled a yawn, and watched as they passed the entrance to Wolkberg Wilderness Reserve. "*Koppie koffie?*" He waved his hand towards her travel mug in the holder. Sarah glanced over at him, her eyes narrowing when she saw a travel mug protectively clutched in his left hand.

"I refilled them when I fueled up." He answered her unspoken question.

"Really? You don't need more coffee." Sarah shifted, nervous. She sat up further, a frown marring her features. They were fast approaching Phalaborwa—the town they had avoided for years. This was the closest town to Brennan's Trail riding Safari Park. The place she'd called home when she first moved from Australia to South Africa. They were very close to Kruger National Park. She ignored the gourmet-smelling coffee.

"Mark, I don't think we should be going..."

"It's okay, love. I'm not stopping in town, okay? We're just passing through." His deep blue eyes rested on her a moment, reassuring her.

"Hmmm." Sarah slumped into the passenger seat of the old Land Cruiser, unconvinced. After they had traveled along the R71 for another hour or so in silence, Mark turned to her, concern in his eyes. "We need to do this, okay? I need you to trust me." The intensity in his eyes made her do a double take.

"What are you up to?" she asked in a low voice, sensing the tension etch its way across her face.

"Just...please, don't panic." Mark set his jaw. He fixed his sights out the front windscreen. Sarah looked around the countryside with growing dread. It was unsafe to travel. People could follow. What about their friends? Evil people would do anything for leverage, even hurt their friends. Mark touched his hand to her arm, breaking her from darker thoughts. She attempted a smile, although it didn't reach her eyes. Through the outskirts of Phalaborwa, Sarah surveyed the view as they passed the industrial estate and the mines. She shrank into her seat, unsettled by the proximity of a town that could contain so many people who wanted to see her dead. They were too close to what used to be Brennan's. Sarah felt her blood chill.

Before they got to the property, Mark took a turn, back onto the R71 highway. They were headed to the Phalaborwa gate. They were heading into Kruger National Park. The Kruger! Sarah shuffled in her seat, sinking lower. Absently, she tugged at a loose thread on the hem of her shirt. Maybe he wouldn't go through the gate. The Cruiser slowed down as they approached the gate.

"Mark?" She gasped, as though the wind had just been knocked from her. "Of all places, Mark! Are you mad?"

He looked down at her, now slunk way down into the passenger seat. His eyes sparkled with amusement.

"It's not funny, Mark. We haven't been into the Kruger...since...since, the muster across the border...into

Mozambique."

"I know." He shrugged. The chug of the engine grew louder as Mark lowered his window to pay the conservation levy toll. Warm air flooded the air-conditioned vehicle. Mark inclined his head toward the dark-skinned man who took his money. He nodded, taking the toll. Then he stopped. His expression was hooded as he stepped closer to the Cruiser, peering in through the driver's window at Sarah. She curled up in a ball nearly on the floor of the vehicle, blinking back at the guard with wide green eyes. He frowned and hesitated. Mark forced a chuckle. "She's afraid of lions."

The man's shoulders dropped with relief, and a slow grin spread across his face. Amusement danced in his dark eyes, and white teeth flashed in a broad smile. "You're a cruel man taking her on a safari, then." He stepped back with a laugh, and waved them through the boom-gate. Mark nodded his thanks and drove through into the Kruger.

"Relax, Sarah. Don't you think you're overreacting just a bit?" Mark brushed his hand across her hair as he began to drive down the narrow dirt road.

"Overreacting? We shouldn't be here!" She hissed. "Tim would kill us if he knew we were here." Or someone else.

"Ahhh, but what the good Lieutenant Tim Naicker doesn't know won't hurt him." Mark pressed his lips together as he continued down the road. Sarah gazed back up at him from her position on the floor. She had slipped out from the seat belt now, which still held her form in its place. Mark shook his head. "You sure you won't come up? Look...I can see zebra!" he coaxed in a singsong voice.

"What if someone finds us?" She swallowed, hard.

"Nobody knows this Cruiser. Nobody realized we were going, anyway...except for work...but they don't know where we're going. Sarah...please." The sincerity in his voice started to melt her fears. "We'll be out into the middle of the Kruger, the last place anyone would expect to find us. We're safe, Sarah. You need this. *We* need this."

There was a moment's silence. Little by little, she started to creep back up onto the seat and peer out the window. The scene was just as her memories had preserved. Beautiful, dense mopane as far as the eye could see, ochre dirt roads, wildlife hidden among the foliage, waiting to be sought out—like a gift, waiting to be unwrapped. In some sections of the Kruger, they would come into more open areas of lowveldt with waterholes, where they would see small herds. She gazed at a dense section of shrubs. What else lay hidden in there? Did it expect them? Sarah's fear was beyond the wildlife. In the wilderness, she was at one with the animals. It was the poachers she feared. Poachers who were out for blood—her blood. It had gotten way out of hand. She thought of all those American films that depicted people being hunted down by the mob. They would hire assassins to do the job. They rarely missed. She was like one of those targets. Nowhere was safe.

"Sarah, we're safe." Mark caught her gaze. He cleared his throat and looked pointedly at her belt. "Well, somewhat."

She tilted her head, puzzled. Then realized. "Oh!" Unclipping the belt, she lifted her bottom, pulled it out from under her, and strapped herself back into the belt.

Mark turned his gaze toward her, and his blue eyes melted her heart. "It'll be fine. I promise." He rested his hand on her jean-covered knee.

She sighed, dropping her shoulders and attempting to smile. It was funny how well he knew her. He once said she wore all her feelings on her sleeve—that she was an open book. Sarah had taken it as a challenge to try and mask her thoughts even more. Every time she tried, he'd just look at her in that funny way and she'd burst out laughing. Laughter. She could probably count on one hand how many times she'd done that in the last few years.

"Do they know we're on our way?" She leaned forward in her seat. Squinting into the sunlit bushveldt beyond the gates, she scanned the mopane, scrutinizing every movement.

"Who?" Mark feigned ignorance.

She shot him a sarcastic look, knowing full well he knew who she meant. A smile tickled the side of his mouth, and she wanted to jab him in the ribs. She thought better of it and turned her gaze back to the landscape.

Mark glanced sideways, his eyebrows pulled together. "No, the poachers don't know we're coming." A comical look flashed deep in his blue eyes. That was it! She jabbed him hard in the ribs and he crowed in mock pain, clutching his ribs between bouts of laughter.

"That...was not funny!" she growled and shrank back down into the seat. The mirth died on his lips as he looked at her.

"Just trust me, please."

"They don't know we're coming, then." She turned her attention back to the landscape. Jacob and Martha were the caretakers of one of the bush camps out in the Kruger. Over the years Mark and Sarah had worked at Brennan's, they had used Jacob and Martha's as a stop for overnight trail rides into Kruger. Their bush camp was set up like a mini resort with luxury rondavels, tents, and a large pool. They even had wooden kraals set up for the horses. To Sarah and Mark, Jacob and Martha were like parents. Sarah didn't doubt they would be happy to see them, but would it be safe?

Mark cocked his right arm on the open driver's side window ledge and inhaled the fresh air. He cast her a smile. "Wind down your window."

She paused before complying, sitting up and winding down the old window. She groaned as it caught. An extra pull saw it squeak loose, and it eased the rest of the way down. She lifted her nose into the breeze as it coursed through the window, picking up the scent of mopane that occupied the majority of the bushveldt of Kruger. Sarah closed her eyes and savored the smell; she allowed the sensation to flow over her weary soul. She was home.

A lone tear slid unhindered from her eye, and she turned toward the window to hide it from Mark. She was no stranger to depression. It had haunted her for many years when she was growing up. But when she'd found God in 1990, she'd thought it had been banished forever. She'd found peace, hope, a destiny. She'd found love in Mark. The fact that depression could still affect her as a Christian had paralyzed her with uncertainty. She'd recognized it as it crept upon her, powerless to stop it as it ravaged her emotions, her life, her destiny. Did she even have one anymore? A destiny? She'd had a destiny at first—to move the elephants. Now translocating them was completed—did this mean God was finished with her? Would

He take her home now in some tragic way? Would He discard her, as she was now doing to herself, by allowing depression to take over? What did God do with people who had fulfilled their purpose? Deep down inside, she identified her misconstrued view of God as false and fell on the fact she had isolated herself from the church. She needed to pick herself up and find God in all her chaos. But for now, her comfort zone was depression. She knew it. It knew her. Within its dark confines, she was safe and comfortable. Paired with depression was the ever-increasing reliance on Mark to look after her. Was she codependent on him? Did he realize? Was this healthy? Loose questions circled in her mind, like vultures waiting for her hope to shrivel up and die. Didn't they realize, it already had? She didn't even care for horses anymore, couldn't stand Mark's pleas to go out and ride again. What was the point of it all now? She pushed God aside. He wouldn't want what was left of her. She slunk away to the recesses of her mind, catatonic, unable to be reached. She was there now, watching as the vultures circled overhead.

The scents of bushveldt drew Sarah from her tormented thoughts. She looked out the window in concern. The hot-scented wind resounded with remnants of her dreams she'd been harassed by of late. Dreams reminding her of the horrors that had led her down this spiral of self-guilt and condemnation to the place where she now slumped. She needed to escape. Her muscles tensed and her breath quickened. The Cruiser slowed down.

Sarah snapped back to reality. She questioned Mark with her eyes as he moved over onto the dirt curb, pulled the vehicle out of gear, and wrenched on the hand brake. He turned to her, grave concern in his eyes. "Hon?" Reaching out, he brushed a lock of hair from her face and tucked it behind her ear.

She stared back, blank.

Mark began to choke up with emotion. The sound drew Sarah back to him, and she opened her mouth to apologize, but no words issued forth. Mark jumped in. "It'll be okay. I promised. Remember? I'm here for you. Nothing will happen. I promised I would protect you." He dropped his hand to her jean-covered thigh, giving it a light squeeze. A remorseful smile touched the corner of her mouth as she took his hand away from her leg and clasped it between her hands. His hand was strong and warm compared with her trembling, cool fingers. She tried to draw warmth from him as she ran her thumbs over the back of his hand.

"I know," she murmured.

"We have God on our side, remember?" He took one of her hands and brought it to his lips.

"I know." She repeated, her gaze shifted back out the window. Did they really have God on their side? Then why did she doubt it so much?

Kwanele examined the image of the white woman with the thick, wavy black hair who leaned against a massive elephant. She had tanned skin and bright green eyes. He couldn't work out what nationality she was. He tilted his head, obediently drinking in the image. She was very pretty. He shrugged and slipped the tattered segment of newspaper into his pocket.

"So, are we clear on what you need to do?" The white man in the clean, white business suit and the shiny shoes leaned down toward him. Warning flashed in his ice-blue eyes. His eyes didn't look natural to Kwanele. Were they fake? He'd heard of rich people who bought glass slips to go over their eyes to see better. Were they called contacts? Some contact lenses were colored to make eyes look different. These just looked creepy. He shouldn't stare, he could get beaten.

Darting his eyes to the ground, Kwanele stared at the shiny white shoes against the filth of the cramped alleyway. How did they stay so clean? He flicked his gaze over toward Joseph, the man who had taken him in when his parents had died. He had only been a toddler and couldn't remember anyone else in his life except Joseph. Scrunching a tattered old tartan golfer's cap in his hands, Joseph nodded toward Kwanele, a warning in his old eyes.

"The boy will do as you say," he assured the businessman, before turning back to Kwanele. Self-conscious, the boy gazed at his dirty clothes. "Don't lose that newspaper, it will show you what she looks like. You need to find her," he growled. Kwanele nodded at both Joseph and the white man in the suit. His throat was dry. He longed for water, fresh air, anything but to be here with this powerful man, who could so easily crush him if he so much as soiled that starched white suit. Joseph rubbed his dark hands together, as he addressed the man with the piercing blue eyes. He looked nervous to Kwanele, more so than usual.

"Tom, it will be done as you say."

The man in the business suit straightened up, dusted invisible dirt off his jacket. He regarded the older black man, eyes narrowed. Kwanele wondered if the white man hated being in this place as much as they did. Did standing in this dirty alleyway make him feel like the filth was leaching into his skin? Kwanele shifted from one foot to the other, willing the man to leave. Finally, with one final pause, he stared at Kwanele, his eyes two pinpoints of ghostly aura piercing right into the bone. The boy shuddered and looked down.

"Right! Well, see to it, Joe. You know what happens with those who screw up."

It wasn't a question. With that, the man waved them on ahead of him.

Joseph pulled the old cap snugly onto his head. The muscles in his neck tightened, as he moved over to Kwanele and placed his hands on his shoulders. He steered him from the dank walls, into the fresh air. Tom followed He slipped past them without the slightest acknowledgment and strode from the area to his companion in the Mercedes Benz at the end of the street.

When the soft hum of the engine started up and the vehicle disappeared down the road, Kwanele turned to Joseph in confusion. The old man's hands were shaking as he lit up the fresh cigarette that hung from his lips. They had never done a job like this before. It was unfamiliar territory. Kwanele prepared to break the ultimate rule. He questioned Joseph's judgment. "Why are we doing this?"

Joseph spun and raised his hand as if to swipe him across the mouth, but then stopped himself. Kwanele waited as he slipped his cigarette lighter back into his pocket and, closing his eyes, took a deep drag from the tobacco. His whole countenance relaxed as he inhaled.

"Because it's what we do. We're getting paid a fortune from these people. Now the woman has left Polokwane, and we need to follow. It's our job." The cigarette started to calm him. Kwanele frowned. Joseph treated this like any other job they'd done. But it wasn't. This was no heist of the till in the local news agency. "But why do I have to talk to her?"

"Because we want to get her to trust you, that's why. People trust kids!" Joseph stopped speaking as a police car turned into the street. "Stop asking questions about it now, okay?" He growled low in his throat.

Joseph became absorbed with his cigarette. Pushing his hand into his pocket, Kwanele checked that the newspaper was still there and pushed it deeper. He kept his eyes lowered as they began to work their way up the street. Ever since he'd known Joseph, they'd been involved with crime—it was all Kwanele knew. But something about it always made his stomach churn. Why was he uncomfortable every time he did what he was told? Wasn't that what kids were meant to do? He scratched his grime-filled hair. What he wouldn't give to swim again, or at least stand in the rain for a while. Let the cool, clean water wash down his forever dirty body. He wouldn't mind even a bucket of water thrown at him. They didn't own anything. They didn't live anywhere particular, but moved from place to place—based on work and the need to hide. What money they gained from the jobs Joseph regularly acquired, fed them from day to day and paid for Joseph's smoking and drinking habits. Kwanele's stomach rumbled as he thought about where they were heading now. Would there be much food? Where would they sleep tonight?

They slowed at the corner of a block of shops. Stopping right outside a news agency, Joseph leaned against the window and savored the remainder of his cigarette. Kwanele moved close to his guardian, wary of the crowds. People dressed in fine, clean clothes, looking preoccupied and stressed, avoided eye contact with them as they went about their business. They were in their own spheres, disdainful of the out-of-place pair against the window. Kwanele shuffled his feet. The end of his shoe was bust open, and he could see his big toe jutting out. He'd be better off barefoot. He snuck another peek at the people strutting past them.

A white woman holding a little girl by the hand stopped at the stand of newspapers. The girl peered around her mother, eyeing Kwanele. She looked to be about five years old. Kwanele risked a small smile at the girl, whose large hazel eyes lit up. She giggled. Her mother glanced down at her, and then followed her line of sight to Kwanele. Her expression hardened. Without a second glance, she grasped her daughter's arm and pulled her in the other direction, then moved down the street.

Kwanele glanced up at Joseph, but the man seemed not to have even seen the exchange. Wasn't the nation meant to be changed now? Kwanele reasoned that with a new flag telling the world that South Africa was the rainbow nation, and with a black man as the new president, they would see change. No more racism. Yeah, right. White shoppers refused to even acknowledge them.

Joseph grunted beside him, pushing him back against the wall and out of the way of the crowd. A couple stopped and scowled at the pair, before moving on. Kwanele sighed. He thought back to last time they'd been in this district. This was the busy part of Polokwane, a part Kwanele preferred to avoid because of the strange glances they always drew. Looks of disgust aimed at Joseph, and then pity aimed at Kwanele. He hated the pity. But more than that, he hated seeing the indifference—the people who would choose to deny his very existence rather than face him.

Kwanele shrank back against the wall as the crowds grew larger. Down the path, the bus stop congested with commuters waiting for a ride. The government had changed the system of segregation that had separate black buses and white buses, but people's habits die hard. There were still two distinct lines. In this part of town, though, even the Zulu and Sotho people wore clean clothes, some fancy even. Joseph and Kwanele didn't look or smell the part. With their unwashed clothes, Kwanele detected an invisible bubble around the pair against the wall. People would skirt around them, trying not to seem impolite as they held their breath. Others would screw up their noses.

Kwanele looked himself and Joseph up and down. At least Joseph's clothes were finer than Kwanele's, whose clothes were ripped in places and becoming too small. The boy looked up at Joseph, about to ask about why they stopped here, but the man's stern gaze warned him not to speak.

Soon enough a new blue 4X4 pulled up on the curb next to them. Joseph opened the back door and motioned for Kwanele to slide in before him. Kwanele sniffed the fresh new-car smell like a frightened animal as he sidled into the middle seat.

"Move over," Joseph scolded under his breath then smiled at the men in the front seat. Kwanele scooted over to the window seat and clipped up his seat belt. They often relied on other people to transport them places when they had jobs to do, but usually they had to manage with public transport. This was the most luxury the two had ever experienced for a job. It reeked of danger.

"Thank you." Joseph removed his golfer's cap and inclined his head to the men in the front, who continued to look forward. One of the men turned to the other and muttered under his breath, "Turn the air-con up." The driver did so and adjusted the fragrance device that was clipped onto the air vent. Kwanele looked down at his hands folded in his lap, feeling his face grow hot.

"We'll drop you off before the National Park Gate at Phalaborwa. The rest is up to you."

Joseph nodded his understanding to the broad-shouldered man in the passenger seat with the dark, reflective sunglasses. "What about the bait?" Joseph's tone held respect.

"There are men on the ground in Kruger. They will meet you near Olifants River. It's just a few miles from the gate."

Kwanele sighed and glanced at his shoes with the busted-out soles. They would have to walk again, but this time in the wilderness. The thought of lions made him shudder. He'd lived in the city most of his life, but he had heard stories of the wilderness and it turned his innards cold.

"And then they will show the boy where the bush camp is, take him back to the bait, and leave him to it," continued the broad-shouldered man. Joseph nodded and looked severely at Kwanele, his silence warning him not to argue. Kwanele looked away and out the window, his eyes wide with fear as understanding sank in. What were they saying? They were going to leave him in the wilderness? Kwanele understood better than to argue with Joseph. In the past, when he had questioned, he was beaten ruthlessly. Joseph had also trained the boy that in the company of others, he was not to utter a word or the beatings would be double. Kwanele knew that he had already crossed the line once today by asking too many questions. The look on his guardian's face now proved he'd better just keep to himself.

As he watched the world pass by through the cool, tinted windows of the 4X4, a deep fear grew in the pit of his stomach. Would this be it for him? Would he die before he even completed his job? The large man in the passenger seat flicked on the radio and scanned through as he tried to pick up a station. Failing, he sat back. Silence. A deep throb pierced Kwanele's stomach. He wondered when he had eaten last. Despair and terror gripped his gut. He tried to conceal the hungry sounds rumbling from it.

Chapter Three

"Sarah, look!" Mark ushered her from the Land Cruiser as Jacques—Jacob and Martha's resident cheetah orphan—lazily padded his way over to them. Past attempts to release the cat had failed, and the cheetah now spent his days skulking around the camp looking for scraps and photos from tourists. The large orange and black beast was aged, white fur showing around his muzzle, and he walked with a slight limp. Sarah knelt to greet the animal.

Studying her profile, Mark thought he spied her cheeks lifting in a slight smile. The cat rubbed himself into her slender, tanned hands and maneuvered so Sarah could ruffle him around the neck. Sarah knew just what he liked and she obliged without hesitation. They spent a moment there, Mark standing over them. Tenderness flooded him.

A reluctant Sarah straightened as Martha burst from her house and came hurrying out to them.

"Sarah, Mark! How are you both? Come here." The large African woman gathered them into her arms as one, sobbing. "You have no idea how much we've prayed, how we worried! Are you okay? Is anyone following you? It's been so long. Is it safe for you to come?" Tears of joy welled as she scolded them, and beneath her large floral dress she quivered with delight.

Mark scratched his head, guilt and discomfort at their predicament reminding him. "We don't know." His words caught in his throat and Martha continued on with her appraisal.

"Mark, what is wrong with this girl?" Martha held Sarah at arm's length, staring, searching her face. "Sarah? This is not like you."

Mark watched, knowing the worry that was not so apparent earlier must now be carved into his features. Martha nodded with sympathy. She seemed to understand everything that had occurred, without the passage of a single word. Martha was like that. You couldn't hide anything from her.

Sarah looked away from the woman she loved, tears in her eyes. Martha was an expert at both reading people and taking control of a situation—something Mark found both unnerving and comforting. At the moment, though, he welcomed it. The dark-skinned woman who was larger than life stood for a moment, savoring the joy of seeing them after so many years in hiding. Mark noted she looked more alert, more formal. Had she bought new clothes? Martha, who preferred the practical, wore a generously sized, brilliantly colored African floral dress with a matching scarf over her head. Something else was different, though—something in her demeanor that had shifted since they saw her last. What had happened to them?

Mark followed Martha's sudden change of focus, looking over their shoulders to the gate. Guards in khaki uniforms were changing shifts. Mark frowned at the addition to the bush camp. "Ahh, Martha... When did you come to need this level of security?"

Eyes wide, she shook her head and ushered them on toward the house. "Come inside, we will have us a lovely catch-up...but, shhh...Jacob has a broken leg, he is asleep."

Warning bells set off in Mark's head. He tried to smile, as they followed her to the house, but it was stiff and halfhearted. "How did he...?"

"Inside." Martha reinforced with a firm gentleness. The bush camp was quiet tonight, no tourists or visitors camping out, just the new security patrolling the parameter. Mark glanced around and noted other changes that had occurred since they were last here. The large communal campfire was still in the same place, but more logs were around it for people to sit on. They had a bar/café area set up nearby. The accommodation was also different with the permanent outdoor safari tents being replaced by new rondavels. The perimeter fence was strengthened with more barbed wire curled at the top, and extra foliage had been planted to make it appear natural. But the biggest change was the new guards posted around the property. He stepped up through the doorway of the house behind Sarah, careful to keep his emotions in check. What had happened out here? He was torn in two directions. His main concern was Sarah—he needed to keep her safe. But he also needed Jacob and Martha's help to snap her out of this depression. He needed his wife back, but if this place was not safe, he needed to know. Now.

Martha sat them down in the kitchen and immediately switched into hospitality mode, her greatest gift. She buzzed about the kitchen, flicking on the kettle, pulling out her best mugs, and rummaging through the fridge for food. "Wait till you see the horses. They look fine and fit at the moment." Failing to find what she wanted in the fridge, Martha pulled a plate from the cupboard and proceeded to pile various biscuits onto it from the pantry.

"I don't ride anymore." Sarah's tone was flat.

Martha stopped to regard her. "I don't mind."

She assured her host, taking a deep breath. Mark could see Sarah try to force a smile as she fought back the tears. She was losing the battle as the corners of her mouth twitched. "I'm sorry..." Embarrassed, she pushed herself up from the table. "Can I go and lie down?"

Martha nodded, her eyes clouded as his slender wife hurried past her to the guest room. As soon as the door clicked shut in the next room, Martha continued to prepare herself and Mark a hot beverage as if nothing had happened. "You still drink coffee?"

The question shook him from his thoughts. "Pardon? What? Coffee, *ja! Dankie.* The same as always."

"Two sugars?"

"Three."

Martha shook her head, making a *tsk-tsk* noise. "Too much sugar!" She measured the three level teaspoons into his mug and stirred in the milk. She slid his coffee across the table and settled into the seat opposite him with her own mug of tea. Taking a tentative sip, Martha leaned forward, a hush to her voice.

"What's happening? Have you been looking after her properly?" She held his gaze. Mark realized the woman only asked out of love for them and he knew her enough not to take offense. Emotion rushed into his eyes. He'd been through a lot with his young wife. Could Martha see that? She waited, looking upon him with kindness.

"Are people still harassing you?"

He gave the older African woman a telling look. "*Ja*...that's the trouble." He sighed. "We don't know...I don't know...but we can't live like this. Sarah can't...we can't keep living in hiding." Mark put his mug down and rubbed his face. Martha stared at her drink. Tracing her finger over the rim of her mug, she nodded in thought.

"It's not easy." Mark pressed his lips together then went on. "There's more..."

Martha looked up sharply, a frown crossing her face.

"Sarah can't...I mean...we can't have kids," he murmured, lowering his gaze to his beverage. He twisted the mug in his hands and the heat seeped into his fingers. He grimaced and took a sip. "We found out, but then we were hopeful enough to try anyway...or stupid..." He looked over his shoulder toward the hallway where Sarah had disappeared. "I don't know. I wanted it, too. But Sarah wanted it more. I worried about her. Then we did it. According to the doctors, it was a miracle. Well ... it was." His voice trailed off and he turned toward the open window, his mind going numb. Mark sipped his coffee, avoiding eye contact with Martha. He could feel her regarding him. Looking toward her, he saw sympathy.

"I'm truly sorry to hear that," she offered in a quiet voice. They sat in silence for a moment. Mark didn't have to spell it out to Martha, and for that, he was grateful. She was sharing his pain—words were not needed. They focused on their drinks a while longer before Martha looked up.

"What about you, Mark?"

Uncertainty crossed his face. "Me? What about me?" He exhaled.

"You've stayed strong for Sarah..."

A muscle twitched in his jaw, though he continued to stare down at the half-finished coffee.

"...but you haven't really come to terms with it all yourself, have you? You haven't grieved."

That was the straw that broke the camel's back. He locked eyes with Martha, his blue eyes large and growing glassy. "I can't," he stammered. "Sarah needs me." He pressed his lips together, angered with the level of emotion in his voice. He looked toward the open window. "I can't let her down."

Martha reached her hand across the table, resting it lightly on his arm. "Mark, you just lost a child. You've just discovered you can't have your own children. You can't be a daddy."

He stiffened, felt the deep crease marring his forehead. "There are other ways to be a daddy, Martha." He got up from the table and finished his coffee in quick gulps as he strode across to the kitchen bench. It burned his throat, but no more than the emotion lodged there. He placed the mug in the sink. "Is Sniper in the kraals?"

Martha rose from her seat to block his escape, "Mark, you can't keep running from this. You'll have to face it—let it out."

He looked at her, incredulous. That was what he was trying to do. He shouldn't need to explain it to her. He thought she knew him. Had Martha changed, too...or was it him?

"I just need time to think, okay, Martha? Let me ride my horse." He hesitated when she wouldn't move. "I'm sorry. Maybe it was wrong for us to come out here." His words had an instant effect on the African woman, who folded her arms across her chest, pain in her eyes. A thumping noise echoed from down the hallway. Mark stopped in his tracks. He turned to see Jacob, entering on wooden crutches.

"What's going on? Who's here, Martha?" Jacob entered the kitchen, the whites of his eyes flashing.

Mark blinked in surprise as he saw how aged and weathered the man appeared. Jacob limped in with his broken leg, and as Mark looked closer, he saw he appeared scuffed up, too...and was that a black eye?

Jacob's fierce expression melted as he looked Mark up and down. "Mark van der Merwe?! What are you doing here? Thank You, Jesus!" He then stopped and shook a crutch toward Mark, squinting out of his good, beady dark eye. "Why do you raise your voice at my good woman here?"

Mark felt a lump in his throat, and lowered his head.

"Why are you so angry?" continued Jacob. It was as if his steely gaze penetrated Mark's soul. His voice was firm but full of love.

Mark's defenses slipped away, and he found himself wrestling to control the grief that rose from the pit of his stomach. "I can't do this anymore, Jacob...Martha...I don't know what to do. It wasn't supposed to turn out like this." He ran his fingers through his brown hair. "I just want to keep her safe...and I feel like I'm failing..."

Mark gestured at Jacob's cast-stricken leg. "What happened here?"

The room went still. What weren't they telling him? Surely he would get answers from Jacob. Martha jittered, breaking the silence as she fussed over her husband. He waved her away as he eased himself onto one of the chairs at the kitchen table.

"A few months after your wedding..." Jacob sighed deeply. Martha cut him off.

"Tea, Jacob?"

"Martha, I know what you're trying to do. We owe him the truth." He glared at his stricken wife, before the frown lessened into weariness. Mark considered their exchange. They had changed. Something had happened.

"Yes, please, my love. I would like a tea." The old man gave her a warm smile. He reached out a hand to her and she took it, somewhat sheepishly. Releasing his hand, she set about fussing in the kitchen. "We started getting visitors," Jacob continued as he bent to scratch the top of his cast. Jacob's words sank in. Visitors? He got the instinctive feeling Jacob meant they were being harassed, in the same way he and Sarah had been. Were none of their friends safe?

"Why didn't you say something?" Mark said, his voice rising.

"How could we? You have been isolated, out of contact. We didn't know they meant any harm. At first...they would come and say they were from the newspaper, and that they wanted to ask questions about the elephant muster and Sarah. We didn't tell them anything. They kept coming at unusual hours. We kept sending them away. Once we threatened to call the police."

Jacob looked at his wife. Martha poured boiled water into a mug, glancing over her shoulder at him. Her smile was tight.

"It's been unbelievable out here in the Kruger, Mark. The amount of poaching has increased dramatically. Just the other day, an elephant was found dying...not dead...dying. They had tranquilized it—cut off its whole face—just to get the ivory. Then they left it to die. It's awful! That's been all too common of late." Jacob shook his head with sadness.

Martha cut in as she stirred her husband's drink. "And the rhinos! The new trend is to go after rhinos rather than elephant. Eleven in the last month found dead, their horns cut out. Bled to death. It's getting so violent out here."

"Sickening." Mark shook his head, bewildered by it all. Clearing his throat, he indicated Jacob's leg again. "So, what happened?" Mark seated himself opposite Jacob.

"Our visitors? Oh yes. The last time they came was three weeks ago. They came late in the night. I knew it was them, because I recognized the fluro blue jacket one of them was wearing—extremely eighties. I heard a commotion at the horse kraals and I went to investigate—I didn't have any weapons, so I picked up a large stick. When I got there, they were attempting to saddle up the horses. They had broken open the tack shed and were going to steal the lot."

Mark's eyes went wide as he thought about Sniper, his reliable old gelding.

"And?"

"I rushed at them. They hadn't got all the saddles on the horses yet, luckily. Martha had already called the police. They attacked me. Beat me up, left me in the dirt with a broken leg, and fled. I heard their cars take off in the distance. They left the horses spooked and gear all over the ground, but the gates were still shut, thank goodness."

"Did you get a number plate?" Mark rocked back on his chair.

"No, they parked too far away, outside in the mopane...besides, it was dark and they left me in the dirt. I could barely see." He indicated his black eye, still swollen, a pinkish-purple hue. "Somehow, they cut off the power to the electric fencing, and jumped the fence."

Anger rose up—anger that people could be so cruel, so evil.

"Mark, there's nothing that can be done now, except for what we've already done. We don't have to pay for the protection outside. It's supplied by the government, because we live in the national park. Anyway, God is much bigger than them."

"That's not the point!" The injustice rose up like a broiling mass. "Just because we stand up for what is right—just because Sarah follows a dream and does what God asked her to do. Why do we all have to suffer for it?" He looked at the concern, love, and grace in the couple's faces, and it extinguished his flame in a snuff.

"I'm sorry..." He paused, his voice teetering off. "I hate seeing people we love getting hurt by this. Sarah will be so devastated...please, pray for us. Pray for me! This makes me so angry, and I need to learn to calm down. Do you mind if I go and see Sniper?"

Jacob nodded "Son...your saddle is still in the tack shed. Take my rifle—that pride of lions still lives on the east side, so avoid them if you can." Martha ducked down the hall, keys jingling in her hand. She returned soon after, handing Mark the rifle and ammunition. Crossing back to the key hook, she replaced the gun safe key and took the tack shed key, handing it to Mark. "Give him a good ride. He hasn't seen you for a couple of years. Don't go far, though, and please...be careful. It's not the same out there. Crime in Kruger is at an all-time high." Martha wrung her hands.

Nodding with understanding and gratitude, Mark took the key and strode out the door. He needed to get outside. He needed to vent. As he stepped away from the house, he overheard Jacob speak to Martha. "So where's Sarah?"

The thunder of hooves reverberated through the ground as Mark and his brown horse, Sniper, galloped across the open lowveldt. He shouldn't have gone this far. It was Sarah who used to be the reckless one—rushing off into lion country alone, getting herself in trouble. People once called her suicidal. Not

Mark. He was supposed to be the sensible one. But he was the one who was now so confused in the head, he was doing what he used to preach against.

The hot wind whipped at his hair, and the blood coursed through his veins. It had been too long since he'd been on his bay gelding. He hadn't dared ask Sarah permission to ride, out of respect for her since the loss of her beloved Palomino mount, Honor. Sniper snorted with pent-up adrenaline as they tore their way up a small bluff, jumped a fallen log, and flew their way down toward Olifants River.

Mark altered his seat and pulled Sniper back to a short trot. They eased their way down an embankment toward a waterhole close to the river, but one known not to be infested with crocs. The horse, overweight from lack of work and thick with sweat, stood panting. He was so worked up, the sweat had created white foam between his back legs and down his shoulders. Pausing by a tree, Mark slipped the rifle from its sheath on the saddle. Catching it up by the shoulder strap, he arranged it to hang on a low branch. Task completed, Mark nudged his horse onward, and together they surged into the cool green water. Sniper dipped his head down through the lily pads and began to slurp the water with greed. Mark felt the cool penetrate into his submerged socks and boots and leach up his jeans. He stared absently at a heron across the pond, standing on a branch, surveying the water for prey. He had been so preoccupied with life, with survival, he had neglected to go to the One who could fix everything first. God. He was filled with so many emotions that he didn't know where to start to deal with them. Anger over the injustice against the people he loved, fear for their safety, grief over the loss of a child and the prospect of not ever having any more. He had been brought up with a culture that deemed emotions a feminine thing. The male heart was not to be displayed, nor were men to show weakness. Mark thought of Jacob and the difference in their cultures. Jacob didn't understand the western culture and how it treated men who showed their emotions. He was lucky in that sense—lucky and blessed to have the freedom to know how to release them.

Jesus, what am I doing? I need Your help, God! Help me to

rely on You, help me to be free...just...help me, Jesus.

The horse shifted in the water before it moved forward into a deeper section. A cool surge of water moved farther up Mark's jeans. He leaned back, checking the leather on his saddle. It was semi-submerged—he would need to re-oil it later on when it dried. His gaze fell onto the small leather saddlebag, which was attached to the back of the saddle. It hadn't been opened for years and he wondered if it contained anything of value that could get damaged by the water. Working loose the stiff buckles, Mark reached his hand into the hard, cracked leather, bracing himself in case he put his hand into a spider nest. He fumbled through the satchel—his fingers caught onto something. He pulled it loose and lifted it up in front of his face.

Emotion caught in his throat as he looked upon the leather necklace that his longtime Sotho friend, Koto, had given him several years ago. Hanging from the cracked leather was a delicately carved wooden figurine of an elephant. Koto had told him the elephant represented "strength," and that strength came from God, not himself. It had been given to Mark to remind him. Why had he left the precious item in his saddlebag? He couldn't remember. It didn't matter, though. What mattered was that God was speaking to him now, at a time when he needed it. Quickly slipping the leather over his head, Mark touched the elephant to his chest.

God, You are my strength. I need to rely on You!

A sudden wave of grief took hold of the strong man—like an electric shock it shot up his body. He bent over his saddle as heaving sobs took over. Eyes half-closed, Sniper stood and loafed under Mark, soaking in the cool of the water, seeming to obey an unseen, greater Master than the one he now carried.

"I'm so sorry, Lord!" Mark looked into the sky as tears ran down his cheeks. "I'm sorry that I've drifted away from You. I repent for trying to do things my way. I'm just...sorry. Please help us, Lord!" He blinked against the tears that continued to course from his eyes. Without another thought, Mark slid off his horse and into the water. The cool, opaque-green liquid enveloped him up to his chest as he took the reins over Sniper's head. Taking a breath, Mark submerged himself beneath the water and allowed the peaceful silence to envelop him. A rush of cold water surged from beneath as his long legs and heavy boots churned up depths. It seemed to refresh him, wash him clean. Heal his weary soul. Bending his knees, he allowed his body to sink deeper, where the cooler waters resided. The murky reeds that had pulled loose began to sway and tickle the skin on his arms and face. Loss of oxygen cut short his retreat. Rising slowly back through the sun-warmed surface water, Mark burst to the surface and threw his head back. Water arced from his thick hair toward his horse, baptizing the animal in silver droplets. Sniper shook his head with irritation. His ears swiveled back and forth in question, before finally settling still again. Mark ran his hands over his face and back through his wet hair. Emotionally and spiritually, he felt as if a weight had just been lifted—like the welcome freshness that washes over the land when a storm breaks after a suffocating, hot summer.

Sniper exhaled with fluster, causing Mark to grin. It would be okay. He would find a way to help his wife.

"Dankie Jesus!" He squinted through the trees into the vibrant sky. Pulling Sniper's reins back into position, Mark hauled himself onto his horse. Water rushed over the leather saddle as he found his seat. His khaki shirt clung to his muscled torso, and he shuddered at the cool breeze. Guiding the horse's head back toward the shore, they waded up and out onto the bank with lazy steps. Sniper paused on the dry shore, and Mark steadied himself, knowing what was coming. Dipping his head low, the gelding did a full body shake in attempt to remove water from his coat. Mark leaned down, patting the horse's neck. He glanced back at the heron he'd seen earlier. It had abandoned his branch to now stalk through the shallows of the water that had been churned up by the pair. Spotting easy quarry, the heron struck the water and brought up a small fish. All things work for good.

Mark turned away from the scene with satisfaction. He retrieved Jacob's rifle and trotted Sniper up into the hot grasslands. He'd be dry in no time if they cracked on a good pace. Onto open track, Mark squeezed Sniper into a soft canter, following the track along the river they used to frequent when they worked at Brennan Safari Trails. He often missed his old job, where he had met his wife years ago. They had both taken tourists out along these routes by horseback. They had delighted in showing off the vast beauty of the Kruger to foreigners, who came to get R&R. Funny how it was now Mark who needed it. The self-made structures of his life that used to make him feel so secure—now as fragile as grass-seeds blown away by every wind of chance. He was so grateful through growing to love Sarah, he had also met the One with whom security was as solid as a rock. Why had he allowed emotion to pull him back to the uncertainty that came with self-reliance?

He slowed his horse to a walk, noting his clothes were already semi-dry. An urge hit and he began to pray as he meandered his way along the riverbank track under the shade of the acacia trees.

Chapter Four

The sweet stench of rotten meat filled Kwanele's nostrils. With distaste, he stared at the large male rhinoceros carcass, which lay sprawled in the sun. Where its majestic horns had once stood was now a cartilage-bare cavity, oozing with caked blood, dried black where it had run down upon the tough hide. Bloated flies buzzed around the putrid flesh, drunk with gluttony. Dizziness and nausea swept him, and Kwanele began to lose his footing, staring at the beast. He swayed dangerously, tasting bile as it rose up his throat, but dismissed it as he began to black out.

"What the hell? Catch him!" Strong black arms gripped Kwanele roughly and dragged him to a sitting position in the dirt against the tire of one of the 4X4s. "You said he could do it!" a deep voice demanded.

Kwanele strained to open his eyes. He had already been so starved of food in the last two days, and then there was the long walk into Kruger with Joseph. His strength was all but gone. He was barely able to stay awake as his body coped the best way it could. The wrenching of hunger that had assailed his stomach in the past couple of days was fading—replaced with the ominous cloud of sleep that dragged him down, offering respite from the pain. He turned groggily and saw Joseph, who looked fatigued himself. He stood in the sun, slightly hunched over—his palms upturned as he pleaded with the tall dark man in mismatched army khakis. Over his khakis, he wore an old leather jacket, left open. Confusion crossed Kwanele's eyes as he drifted in and out of consciousness. It was too hot to wear a jacket like that.

"What? You bring us this starved kid and expect to get

paid? When did you feed him last?" the man growled at Kwanele's guardian. Joseph tried to stutter a reply when the man stepped forward and slapped him across the mouth. "I've heard enough!" Kwanele watched Joseph shrink back, a hand to his lip. He glanced toward the boy, indecision lining his face.

"Use what we've got…bring him," the Khaki-man barked. Kwanele felt himself hefted into someone's arms and carried toward the back of a truck, where he was laid with little care on a bundle of rancid old blankets. A man propped him up, gripped his chin, and held a bottle of warm water to his lips, tipping it up.

Kwanele's eyes flew open and he sat bolt upright, spluttering and coughing in desperation as the water hit his windpipe. He looked into the eyes of his assailant, narrow and dark, as the man wiped the spray of liquid from his chin and neck. The man jutted the bottle of water toward Kwanele, who gingerly took it and drank.

Slowing as the water soothed his parched throat, Kwanele's senses began to prick up and he gazed around the inside of the truck. The smell of rotted flesh was just as strong in here. The man still stood at the back of the truck, scrutinizing him.

"Here." He threw a plastic bag with a few slices of white bread into Kwanele's lap. The bag was hot from sitting in the sun—droplets of condensation clung to the inside, soaking into the limp slices. The boy greedily snatched it up, reefing his hand into the bag and consuming the few slices in a matter of moments. He looked into the bottom of the bag and wiped a finger around the inside, collecting up every last crumb. His stomach awoke with a strangulated growl, and Kwanele looked up at the man with hope. Behind the burly man who had given him the water and bread, stood Joseph and the Khaki-man.

"See?" Khaki-man turned to Joseph, triumphant. "You starved the kid! How's that going to do any of us any good?" He strode to the back doorway of the truck, examining Kwanele. Jutting his chin at the burly man, he dismissed him. The man glanced once at Kwanele before he shuffled off.

"Now listen here, boy." Khaki-man leaned on the back of the truck. His eyes bored into Kwanele's. "You eat now. Get your bearings. Then—" He was interrupted as the burly man returned with a half-eaten apple. He offered the browned fruit to the irritated Khaki-man, who snatched it from his hand, tossing it to the boy. Kwanele grappled for the fruit as it hit the side and rolled along the filthy blankets. Gripping it, he brought it swiftly to his mouth and sank his teeth into it. It was hard to concentrate on the man's next words as his mind filled with the sweet sensation of the natural sugar in the fruit. "When you are done, we'll leave you here and you need to find your way to the bush camp, okay?" Kwanele stopped chewing and stared at the man with the piercing black eyes, his mind awhirl.

"You hear?" the man barked with sudden intensity. Kwanele startled, his wide eyes locking onto the man's. What had he just said? The man's face twisted with impatience, and his hand rose as if to strike Kwanele.

He broke out of his stupor and spoke up quickly. "*Yebo!*" he confirmed in his Zulu tongue, sure they saw the fear in his eyes. Satisfied, they left him to suck at the rest of the apple core that was in his hand. Kwanele jumped as another full bottle of water and another apple were tossed into his lap. Eager, he snatched the water up, cracked the seal, and tipped his head back. The bottle was empty in seconds. For the first time, he was left alone in the truck. He overheard the adults somewhere outside, their voices muffled and subdued. Turning the new apple in his hands, he slowly bit into it, this time savoring the sweet taste as he rolled it around on his tongue. He could sense his strength slowly returning, and he sat up taller, examining his surroundings with a little more interest.

It was dusty, covered in dirt—even the windows. Piles of dirty old blankets occupied most of the space in the trunk. They smelt musty, covered in dirt and blood. Sticky, bloated flies buzzed in and out, infiltrating the small space, landing on Kwanele's skin. Flicking them away in disgust, he narrowed his eyes. What were they chasing in here? Twisting to look behind him, he watched as the black intruders would land intermittently on the bulk of blankets, darting to and fro as they sought something.

Taking another bite of the apple, Kwanele flicked his empty hand toward the flies. Curious, he began to explore the lump of blankets behind him with mild curiosity. *What is that? A horn?*

His hand froze on the shape in revulsion. Tasting bile rising in his throat again, Kwanele peered out the clouded side-window toward the still form of the decimated rhino. He withdrew his hand, wiping it on his trousers. Trembling and trying to control his heaving stomach, he took the half-eaten apple and bottled water and slid out of the back of the truck. He settled himself onto the dirt, back leaned against the tire as he had been earlier. His heart beat loud in his chest like a tribal drum, daring him to muster some semblance of bravery—but reminding him he had none. He needed to be strong—to be brave—to do what was required...but was it possible? Never before had Joseph gotten them caught up with this kind of job. It filled Kwanele with despair and fear. His musings were interrupted as he overheard Joseph continue to argue with the man in khaki.

"I don't understand how you want us to play this out. Why not just kill her outright?" Joseph reasoned.

"She can't be just killed, man! She is high profile in the media, plus she has some sort of creepy voodoo protection over her. She's un-killable outright! She must be lured—her defenses worn down. It has to be planned to look like an accident."

"Nobody is un-killable!" Joseph glowered. After a pause, he glanced over his shoulder at Kwanele sitting on the ground. Relief filled his face as Kwanele sat up and regarded him. The man in khaki followed Joseph's gaze, gesturing toward Kwanele with one hand and touching his other to his leather jacket.

"That's why we need the boy. Get her defenses down, make her trust him...then he can lead her to the place."

Joseph scratched his stubbly face. "Why is this woman so dangerous to you again?"

Two of the other men who had been cleaning their knives looked over. One cleared his throat.

"Boss? You telling too much?" He turned the statement into a question so as not to infuriate his superior. Khaki-man whipped his head around to stare at the man. He spoke through gritted teeth. "It doesn't matter...okay?" Kwanele shrank against the truck tire. A chill swept over him despite the heat of the day. The knife cleaners looked at each other, realization dawning and their faces twisted into cruel smirks. The burly man who had fed Kwanele stood up and snapped at them harshly in Sotho. They all obediently returned to their tasks, casting dark looks at each other.

Khaki-man turned back to Joseph, pacing with importance, his hands folded behind his back. "If this woman keeps saving elephants, rhinos, and other animals, then others will start to copy her. Then we have a problem. Lots of problems. We lose our white gold, man! Rhino horn is worth fifty thousand pounds per kilogram. Do you understand? That's more than gold! That's more money than you and I would ever see in a lifetime! I know she's been hiding in town with that husband of hers for the last few years, but now she's back on the reserve. Who knows what she has in mind. She can put traders and poachers like us out of business."

Joseph nodded his head slowly. As if reacting to a silent command, the men all packed up their work as one and began to pile into the vehicles.

"Boss," the burly man announced, "...something on the radar, a car...someone headed this way." Khaki-man turned back to Joseph, his eyes like sadistic, thin shafts of light.

Kwanele missed the exchange, getting up and dusting himself off as best he was able. Khaki-man heard the movement and swung his piercing gaze toward the truck.

"Okay, boy. Listen up!"

Kwanele stepped toward Khaki-man with obedience, fearful of making him angry.

"See that ridge over there?" He pointed, and Kwanele nodded. The man leaned down, his hands braced on his knees as he spoke slowly. "...over that ridge is a bush-camp...a camp...Okay? You need to find the woman in the newspaper photo and be her friend. Someone will contact you when the time is right...then...you bring her to them...do you understand?"

Kwanele stood dazed, his mind reeling over the information. Did he hear earlier that they were going to murder this woman? It would be his fault that she died... his fault for leading her into a trap. He felt sick all over again. This wasn't what he was used to. He was a thief, not a murderer. The dust cloud on the horizon was growing larger as a vehicle approached.

"I said, *do you understand?*" the man bellowed, close to Kwanele's face, causing his ears to ring. He blinked in shock, taking several steps backward and nodding with vigor.

"Aye, Boss," Burley-man called out with mild curiosity. Khaki-man spun to face him, glowering under his brows. "What about lions, Boss?...that skinny kid wouldn't last two minutes ..."

"Shut up!"

The burly man slunk back into his truck. Kwanele's head flicked between the adults in turn. His body stiffened in panic. He locked a pleading gaze onto his guardian. Joseph opened his mouth, and Kwanele hoped he was about to negotiate backing out of the plan.

Joseph cast Kwanele a penetrating look before turning back to Khaki-man. "Won't they be suspicious that there is a boy in the middle of the veldt by himself? Wouldn't they wonder why he doesn't have an adult with him?"

The men in the vehicles pulled their heads out the windows—mordant grins on their dark faces. Khaki-man barked at them and they grudgingly disappeared back into the trucks. Thrusting his hand into his open jacket, he answered Joseph's questions in a cool manner. "There will be an adult with him." Joseph raised a brow in question, which turn to horror as the man pulled a handgun from his jacket. With calculation, he took aim and shot Joseph square in the chest. With a grunt, Joseph fell to the ground—dead.

Kwanele cried out raggedly, stumbling backward away from Joseph and Khaki-man. He tripped upon the leg of the rhinoceros carcass, falling onto his backside. Whimpering, he froze in terror as the dark man wheeled his focus on him, gun still in hand. "You get it done, boy, or your fate will be the same as his!"

Kwanele's eyes were wide as he watched the smoke curling from the muzzle of the weapon.

Keeping his cold stare on Kwanele, Khaki-man jerked his head toward Joseph's body to emphasize his point. Swallowing hard, Kwanele's eyes were round as he stared for the last time at the body of the man who had looked after him for as long as he could remember.

"Boss! Quick!" Burly-man called. Khaki-man's attention was drawn to the approaching vehicle on the horizon. The engines of the 4X4s and truck roared to life as Khaki-man launched himself into one.

Kwanele caught a glimpse of him slipping the gun back into his jacket as they sped down the dirt track, a cloud of dust following them. In a short time, they were out of sight—headed in the opposite direction to the oncoming cloud. Shaken and running on adrenaline, Kwanele turned his gaze toward the second cloud of dust, speedily approaching from the direction of the ridge. Panic-stricken, he spun, unsure where to run. Desperate to hide, to gather his thoughts, he tried to figure out what to do next. He turned toward the river. Would the steep inclines and foliage offer protection? What wild animals were out here, and would he outsmart them long enough to live? He needed to get to safety. The sound of the approaching vehicle grew louder and without looking back at the rhino carcass and his guardian, Kwanele ran. He ran as fast as he could toward whatever shelter the river could offer. Without Joseph to look after him, the job no longer mattered. He needed to just escape, go anywhere, somewhere safe. Terrified, Kwanele kept running, blind to what he was going to do, where he was going.

"Where did he go?" Sarah walked into the unsettled quiet of the kitchen. She had been in the guest room listening to their conversation with Mark, and she'd finally mustered the courage to enter. Apprehension flooded her as she realized he had left. Where was he? Why would he go out into the Kruger on his own? Especially if it was as bad as they said it was? She was fuming at him—and irate at them for letting him go.

Martha looked up from the book she was reading and smiled warmly. The way she smiled told Sarah she was hesitant to tell where Mark had gone. Sarah worked to unfurl her balled fists, trying not to lash out at the couple as soon as she saw them.

Setting down a screwdriver, Jacob looked up from where he

was fiddling with a broken two-way radio. "Did you have a good rest?" He looked her up and down.

Sarah could tell he saw straight through her façade, and she felt her cheeks burn at his scrutiny. She finally ventured a tight tone, knowing full well the answer. "Where's Mark?"

Jacob jerked a thumb toward the door. "He went out on a ride...come...come sit and talk to us."

Sarah grimaced with indecision. Martha put a bookmark in her page, placing the thick volume in her lap. She sighed as she studied Sarah's movements.

"What's going on, Sarah? You seem so far away. Far away from us, far away from yourself, far away from God."

A defensive knot balled in her stomach as she sat at the kitchen table with them. She struggled against the surge of anger that threatened to explode from her—an anger against two people whom she loved dearly. She leveled a cool gaze at them, unwilling to let her thoughts show. She had known them so long, did they see through all that? Why was she angry at them—for letting Mark go? Would they have stopped him? She doubted it. Sarah realized her anger was misguided. She was angry at Mark—angry at herself for being angry. Perhaps she was the problem after all.

Sighing in defeat, she felt her face soften. Sarah looked at their concerned faces and offered her own silent plea. She wondered if she was going bipolar. Moisture sprang to her eyes.

"Oh honey!" Martha rose from her chair. Crossing to her in an instant, she pulled Sarah's small frame off the kitchen chair and into her embrace. At the old woman's embrace, the tears exploded, her face crumpling as she heaved deep sobs.

"I'm so sorry. I don't know how I got to this...I'm supposed to be a Christian. I'm meant to have it all together now. I'm so cranky at everything all the time. I'm so afraid!"

Jacob's gaze was patient from under his white, bushy brows. "Being a Christian doesn't mean we have it all together, Sarah. It means that we have Someone to go to for guidance because we *don't* have it all together."

Sarah attempted to smile, to blow her nose neatly on the tissues that Martha pressed into her hand. She regarded the elderly man. His once black, wiry hair was now speckled gray and white. Here he sat, broken leg, black eye, trying to run a business, and talking like nothing ever bothered him. He had peace. She wanted that peace again. She sighed, a frown crossing her face as she regarded his injuries. "Ever since I found God and rescued those elephants...it's as if I have no purpose anymore. What if that's it for me? I can't keep being like this for Mark...what if he leaves me?"

Jacob leaned forward, rubbing his chin. "Sarah?...the real question is, how much time have you been spending with God?"

Sarah blinked at the unexpected question, then lowered her gaze.

"I thought as much. Girl, you have much fear in your heart, about many things. It's as plain as the nose on your face. If you don't go to God with your fears, they will eat you alive. They'll be the end of you."

Martha stepped back and sat once more. Sarah folded her hands together in her lap. She wanted to dissolve into the furniture. The last thing she needed was a lecture, but deep down, she knew he was right and it made her pride squirm. Martha brushed a tendril of black hair from Sarah's face. Sarah noticed her hesitate as she decided on her next words.

"...Mark told me about your..." The older woman cleared her throat.

Sarah leaned back in her chair, staring at Martha in confusion. What on earth had Mark told her? She felt the color drain from her face. No!

"Mark told us about the baby, Sarah." Martha moved again, this time to sit in the chair beside her.

Sarah snapped her gaze from Martha to Jacob. How dare he tell them without asking her first? Her jaw tightened, but she said nothing. Jacob lowered his eyes, picking up the radio and the screwdriver again. Martha bravely continued.

"It's not an easy thing, Sarah. And you both had to deal with it all without your friends and family close by to support you."

Sarah moved her hands under the table and balled them into fists till her nails dug into her palms. She liked the feeling. She couldn't endure their pity. It made her feel worse. Martha leaned closer, trying to look into her eyes. Pain screwed up her face, and she looked away in shame.

The older woman shook her head with deep regret. "I know how you feel, Sarah. Really, I do...I've been there."

Sarah's frustration melted into shock. She locked eyes with Martha's searching face. "You...you lost a baby?" Her eyes went wide with disbelief.

"Two, actually." Martha smiled warily—a distant pain crossing her features. "I was pregnant with twins once. I lost them three weeks before the due date. They might have lived...but circumstances..." Tearing her eyes away from Sarah, she looked out the window absently. It was a familiar expression to Sarah, but one that she had never seen on Martha's beautiful face. How could she have been so blind to think that Jacob and Martha were above pain? They were just as human as she was.

"Oh Martha, I'm so sorry," Sarah whispered, her voice hoarse.

"It's okay. I got through it. I had my loving husband, just like you have Mark." She smiled at Jacob, a twinkle in her eyes. "And I had God. I prayed every night. I spent lots of quiet time alone—praying and reading the Bible. I recovered. I was renewed and refreshed and healed...and God gave me other children to love." Martha looked into Sarah's eyes before she gave her a playful wink. Sarah stared at the floor, her disillusionment was still there.

"Don't get me wrong!" Martha went on. "I didn't do that at first...I blamed God. I became angry, I didn't eat for weeks—I tried to punish myself for not doing everything right—thinking I should have done more—that I could have. Sarah, it was lies. I couldn't have done anything else to save them. I just had to accept it."

Sarah inhaled sharply and looked away as her eyes grew moist. Accept it? How could anyone accept it? She continued to stare at the dining table. Martha and Jacob were right. She'd been going about this all wrong. She needed to pull herself from this pit of despair that she'd found herself in, but she couldn't do it alone. She needed God, and she needed Mark. Sarah thought of him in alarm. She needed to appreciate him more.

He'd been so attentive and loving toward her. What did she do for him? He must be suffering, too. Guilt crept into her conscience, but Martha stopped it in its tracks.

"I know that face! Do not listen to the devil. He came to kill, steal, and destroy. There is now no condemnation for those who are in Christ Jesus," she quoted from the Bible.

Sarah wiped at her burning eyes. How long had it been since she'd opened her Bible? Martha cut into her thoughts, her soft voice a balm on her raw spirit.

"It's a process, Sarah. Don't expect everything to come good in a heartbeat. You need to give your heart time to heal...on many accounts. You'll go through many emotions. We did. But remember, you are never alone." Martha's eyes shone with love as Sarah met her gaze.

She smiled, but she knew it didn't reach her eyes. She was suddenly grateful to Mark for bringing her here. She'd needed to hear these words...had needed it for a long time.

"I know you're both right. I know you're both always here for us." She stood. "Do you...do you mind if I go and find Mark now?"

"He headed down toward the Olifants River track, I think." Martha glanced at her husband. Jacob's head lifted to regard them both.

"Are you sure?" He frowned slightly at his wife. "He knows that's a dangerous trail."

"I saw him head in that direction when I looked out the window. I can't be sure he went that way." Martha's eyes darted back and forward.

"I knew I should have given him a radio," Jacob muttered. "Here." He stood and hobbled across the kitchen, pulled another radio from its charger on the wall, and passed it to Sarah.

She murmured her thanks, grabbed up the keys, and exited the house. She trotted down the back steps and jogged over to the cruiser. Yanking open the door, Sarah slumped into the driver's seat and ran her hands over the wheel. She pushed the keys into the ignition, turning the engine over. The Cruiser rumbled to life under her. Letting out a sigh, Sarah pulled out of the gateway as the guards held it open for her. Just outside the gates, she stopped, looking down that ominous dirt road that she hadn't been near since the accident. Did she have what it took to face that place again? Sarah exhaled deeply and pushed the Cruiser into gear.

CHAPTER
FIVE

As Sniper trotted along the river track, Mark sensed that something was wrong. He pulled up his mount and swiveled in the saddle to look back up the track—nothing but the stillness of the midday heat greeted him. He'd been unaware of how much time had passed since he'd left the bush camp. He scanned the track, unable to shake the unease in his gut.

There were no other sounds but the chorus of birds, flitting away the afternoon, swooping for small insects as they were stirred up from the horse's passage. Mark touched his hand to Jacob's rifle, perusing the mopane shrubs for signs of a big cat ambush. He was good at reading the signs of the wilderness, sensing danger. The birds seemed unperturbed, which was a good sign. Mark shrugged and resolved it was high time to return back to the bush camp. He urged his gelding into a light trot. The shrub-lined track opened up out to his left, revealing a snippet of the golden lowveldt. Mark smiled to himself as he noticed the numbers of zebra, meandering closer to the waterhole. He heard the distinct shrill whinny as two of them got into a tussle over their rank in the herd. Mark knew, as soon as he left the spot near the water, they would feel safe enough to come drink. He trotted onward as several zebra stopped and turned their heads to watch him. He was almost back to the original track—veering away from the river and up the road toward Jacob and Martha's.

Mark gasped as Sniper stumbled. Recovering his balance and pushing his horse onward, he looked around with sudden suspicion. The hairs on the back of his neck rose. He pulled Sniper up short, eyes narrowed at the shrubs. *Is that You, God? Are You trying to tell me something?*

Mark attempted to urge his horse into a walk, but Sniper stopped again, gazing around with nostrils flared. Mark touched the hilt of the rifle again for reassurance. Something was amiss. Turning Sniper's head back onto the road, he shortened his reins and booted the reluctant animal into action—something his wife would not have approved of. Sniper grunted and leapt toward the crossroad in the track. They nearly overstepped the spot as Mark pulled his horse up a little too roughly. Mark grimaced as he eyed each track. Which direction held the danger he felt? Was it a danger? It felt like something was out of place. Should he go back to the bush camp, or continue up the river trail?

Mark squinted, shielding his eyes against the glare as he gazed down through the trees towards the waters of the river. A huge embankment lay between him and the churning waters. Was it coming from below? Mark scanned the rushing surface, well aware it was inhabited by large numbers of Nile crocodiles. From the safety of the track above, Mark noticed several of the large reptiles, sprawled in the heat of the sun on the muddy banks. They were big enough to take down even the powerful wildebeest if it dared venture to cross the winding green waters of the Olifants.

Mark rationalized that the crocs were not cause for concern. "What is it, God?" He peered through the branches of an overhanging acacia to the sapphire sky. No answer. He turned back toward the bush camp track. He was still uneasy. Perhaps God would answer him tonight as he slept. A hornbill called out noisily somewhere close by, causing Sniper to shy with fright. Mark snapped his gaze above and spotted the mottled bird as it spread its huge wings and took off. Patting his restless horse on the neck, Mark turned to regard the river trail again and felt heat rise up his neck. "Come on, boy. Let's go a little farther down and check it out." Pointing his horse's nose back toward the unexplored river trail, Mark squeezed his mount onward toward the direction of his unease.

They had been working their way down the trail for a while when Mark's disquiet eased up. There was nothing here. He exhaled deeply, releasing the tension. Pushing Sniper into a soft canter, they covered the ground quicker, until they reached an overgrown section. Mark eased Sniper around the overgrown mopane shrubs and was about to push him back into a canter when a dark shape burst out in front of them. The blurry object caused Sniper to rear in terror. Commotion ensued as Mark fought to regain control of the animal. The blur now stood frozen in its tracks.

Mark looked up and stared with disbelief at a small dark-skinned boy. The boy stood in front of him, small chest rapidly heaving from exertion. He stood poised, as if ready for flight, indecision apparent in his wide eyes.

Mark surveyed the boy. Where had he come from? He was not from around here, in his tattered clothes. Most of the people who lived on the outskirts of town wore traditional clothes or they were better looked after. This boy appeared homeless—perhaps from one of the Zulu slums in town. "*Praat jou Afrikaans?*" Mark breathed, trying to control his nerves. The boy gave him a blank stare. "You speak English?" Mark asked slowly, frowning.

"*Yebo*—yes," the boy answered. He peered back over his shoulder and a look of terror crossed his features. Mark followed his gaze.

"Are you alright?" He considered getting off Sniper to speak with the boy, but the wariness had returned, so he thought better of it. What if this was a trap? Mark studied his small face. "Are you okay?" He watched for the boy's reaction. Large brown eyes locked on to Mark's. The child didn't answer, but threw a look over his shoulder again. Trouble was brewing for sure. Mark tilted his head with indecision. "What are you running from?" He shifted his gaze to the shrub, trying to peer through the densely packed foliage. He pushed Sniper a few steps in that direction.

"Please." the boy gasped, his tongue suddenly loose. "Please. You do not want to see it. It's horrible. Please, how do I get out of here?" He jumped in terror as another bird flew from the trees above.

So there was something. Mark raised an eyebrow and dismounted Sniper. The boy's eyes widened and he tensed, as if ready to bolt.

"Hey, hey. Why are you so afraid?" Mark knelt down to the

boy's eye level. He hung an expression of sympathy—careful not to crinkle his nose when he smelt the foul odor wafting from the boy—rotting garbage. Mark saw him tremble, the whites of his eyes growing bigger. His mouth was clammed shut again.

Mark frowned and looked again toward the shrub. "Well, if you're not going to talk, I guess we'll have to check it out." He turned and remounted his horse. "Come on." He held out a tanned, well-muscled arm toward the boy, open palm ready to help him mount.

The boy's eyes grew wider and he backed away from the animal, shaking his head.

"He won't hurt you," Mark assured with a calm voice.

The boy continued to shake his head, quivering as he backed against the shrub. Mark wondered if he was going to make a break for it and run. He grew impatient with the lad. Dismounting again, Mark willed himself to stay calm. "I want to help you. What's your name?"

A muscle tightened in the child's jaw.

"Listen, if you want me to help, I need to know what happened." Mark took a step closer. The boy pressed deeper into the shrub. Stepping back to take the pressure off, Mark scratched his chin. The stubble had long since begun turning into a short beard, which itched. He needed to shave. Desperate to return to the bush camp and have a shower, Mark's impatience grew. It was past midday and he was hungry. The thought struck him. This boy looked starved, in more ways than one. "Are you hungry?"

Seeming to consider the question, the child's shoulder's drooped, but his glinting eyes still carried an edge. "I...I just want to get out of this place." He kept his eyes lowered.

"And you are hungry?" Mark pressed again, suspecting he saw the hint of a nod in the boy. "I can help you get out of here, but it's a long way. You need to ride with me. You look sick."

The boy raised dubious eyes at the large brown horse, which stood with its head lowered.

"I promise, he won't hurt you." Mark watched the boy seem to weigh things up. "Here...put your hand out like this, so he can smell you." Mark demonstrated. The dark child shook his head vigorously, staring in horror as Sniper nudged Mark's hand. When the horse did nothing else, he let out a sigh. After a moment of waiting, the boy began to edge forward.

Mark took a different approach. "Look, if you stand here"—he indicated next to Sniper's shoulder—"you can stroke him on the neck without being near his mouth. He likes that."

Appearing to muster up some degree of courage, the boy stepped next to Sniper. He reached out his hand. Mark noticed how delicate his long, tapered fingers were under the grimy skin. Mark thought he was about to pat Sniper's shoulder when the boy stopped, moving instead to the saddle. He looked back at Mark, his dark eyes large. Was he going to let Mark help him after all?

"Please, help me get out of here." The boy looked up at the saddle. Feeling a rush of relief, Mark slipped past the boy, grabbed up the reins, placed his foot in the stirrup, and stepped with ease onto the saddle. He held out his hand once more to the boy. This time he took it and allowed Mark's strong arms to pull him up onto the horse. Settling the child in front of him on the saddle, Mark sensed the boy freeze with fear as the large animal swayed beneath them.

"It's okay. We'll take it slow at first." Mark held the reins in front of the slight boy, effectively cradling him and preventing him from slipping off. At Mark's direction, Sniper stepped forward and sidled his way around the shrub. With each pace, Mark felt the boy stiffen up further. Was it the fact he was on a horse, or the direction they were taking? They were headed down the track the boy came from, beyond the mopane scrubs.

"Please, sir...is there a different way?" The boy spoke up boldly as he looked up at Mark, terror in his eyes.

There it was. The answer. Mark narrowed his eyes. "I'm sorry, kid. Things aren't adding up here. I want to know why you are running." Mark gripped the boy tightly, who yelped in alarm as Mark kicked Sniper into a canter.

"No." The child held the front of the saddle, his knuckles stretching white. Ignoring the protests, Mark continued on, the suspicion in his heart turning to anger. What was this kid hiding? Soon enough, the boy's whimpers settled to silence. They rounded a bend and the child sucked in his breath. The carcass of a rhinoceros came into view. Mark's heart fell. Poachers! He looked down at the boy, accusation in his eyes.

"What's this?" He trotted Sniper over to the beast. Mark sucked in a sharp breath as something else came into view. The body of an elderly black man lay crumbled in the dust. Boy forgotten, he vaulted from the saddle to check for signs of life. The man was still beneath his touch and his eyes stared sightlessly into the sky. Running his hand over the crinkled shirt, Mark paused at the gun wound in the man's chest. He felt the color drain from his face.

He looked toward the boy, alarmed. Turning back to the body, Mark carefully brushed his hand down the man's face, closing his eyes forever. He knelt there for a moment, unsure of what to do. A slight yelp behind him alerted Mark to the fact he'd left the child on his horse. He craned his neck around, just in time to witness the boy tumble from the beast in an attempt to dismount. The kid fell with a grunt onto the dirt. With little care, Mark turned back to the body, a cold lump in his gut. The soft footfalls of the boy behind him brought him back to the present.

"This was Joseph." The boy dragged in an unsteady breath as Mark turned to regard him. Tears seemed to be fighting their way from the boy's livid eyes. "He had looked after me as far as I can remember." He choked up, falling to his knees before the man. Mark could see the inner turmoil. Perhaps it wasn't a trick after all. He stood and flipped out his cell phone. Scrolling through the numbers, he located the local police.

"Wait," the boy cried out in anguish. "Are you calling the police?" Finger paused above the button, Mark looked at the boy.

"They said they will kill me..." Mark watched as the child stopped midsentence, biting his lip as a new terror appeared to overtake him.

"You don't want me to call the police?"

The boy shook his head. Mark raised an eyebrow as he lowered the phone. "Who said they'd kill you? The police?"

"No, the men who did this." Struggling with words, the boy paused, seeming fearful of revealing what he knew. Mark could sense the child's mind whirling. What was he thinking?

"They said they would shoot me, too...please...just drive me to town, drop me off in town."

"They said they will shoot you if you call the police?"

The boy shuddered and didn't reply, but shuffled from one foot to the other.

Exhaling deeply, Mark approached him and crouched at eye level. "There's nothing more we can do here. I have to call the police to tell them about this. This is a crime scene. I can't leave it and pretend I didn't see it. They will help you."

The boy shook his head. "You don't understand. I cannot go to the police."

Uncertainty swayed him. "What is your name? Who are you? Why would you and this man be out here with poachers anyway?"

The child shook his head again. This was getting them nowhere. Mark gagged as the breeze changed direction and he turned his head away from the smell of the rhino carcass. The flies swarmed about the cavity on the rhino's face and were thick and sticky in the midday heat. They were also starting to swarm around the gun wound on the man, making Mark sick to his stomach. He stood and swayed slightly as he dialed the number on his cell phone.

"I have to call them." His stern gaze came to rest on the wary child. As Mark listened for the dial tone, he saw the boy spin about in sudden panic, eyes locked onto the horizon. Mark followed his gaze. A distant dust cloud showed an approaching vehicle. Mark grasped the collar of the boy's shirt as he was about to make a quick escape. Holding the squirming boy firmly in one hand, he pressed the phone against his ear with the other. The dial tone clicked off and connected to an automated answering service. Sniper lifted his head toward the dust cloud, his ears pricked forward. Mark narrowed his eyes, trying to make out the vehicle.

Relief flooded his heart when he saw that it was his and Sarah's own white Land Cruiser. Just as he began to speak into the phone to leave a message, the boy wrenched himself free of Mark's grip and hurtled toward a tree, skittering up it as fast as he could. Within moments, all Mark could see was one of his wide eyes just visible among the foliage. Shaking his head with frustration, he hung up the cell phone. He'd call back in a moment.

"Boy! Come down. It's okay. It's just my wife. She can drive you to town. We'll get you food." The boy continued to look wary, shaking his head. Mark grimaced and waited for Sarah to arrive.

He heard the boy's meek voice from the tree. "You promise?"

Growing tired of the child's games, Mark ignored him and waved toward Sarah as she slowed the vehicle. He grimaced as he prepared for her reaction to the scene. Halfheartedly, he turned toward the tree. "Come down, boy. We want to help you."

The youngster hesitated, eyeing Sarah behind the wheel of the vehicle. After a moment, he eased himself from the thick safety of the branches above. Just as his feet found the ground, Sarah stepped from the old Cruiser.

A look of pure anguish reefed upon her face as she saw the rhino. "I came this way earlier, but I didn't see you and I certainly didn't see this." She waved her arms with dismay as the flies assailed her.

"How could you miss it?" Mark frowned. "I veered off down the track."

Sarah pointed behind her as she stepped closer to the scene. "I went up river—" She stopped short, spotting the body of the boy's guardian. "Mark," Sarah's voice rasped. "Have you called the police?"

Scrambling into the dust beside the man, Sarah repeated Mark's earlier actions, checking for signs of life.

"Forget it, Sarah. He's gone." Mark began to pace, refusing to look at the man in the dirt. "I was just doing that...ringing the police...but..." He indicated the boy who stood off to the side, staring at Sarah. Mark did a double take at the boy. What now? Color was draining from his young features.

"Hey?" Mark approached the kid, putting his hand on the boys shoulder. "It's okay. I said we can help you."

Sarah and the boy regarded each other for a moment before the boy snapped out of his trance as if he'd been whipped.

"I have to go," he shrieked and went to run.

Mark caught him again, just in time. "No, you don't." Hand

gripping the collar of the child's tattered shirt, he held firm as the dark-skinned boy thrashed.

"Mark, don't hurt him." Sarah rushed forward, kneeling before the frightened child. She touched his hot arms and searched his face with concern. Mark watched with amazement as his wife calmed the frightened child with just a look. "Okay, I don't know who you are...or what has happened here...but you look like you need help. We came from a bush camp...a campground...we have friends there who can help. Do you understand? They will be putting together a huge meal now for lunch. You are welcome to come with us, have some food, maybe have a wash, and then we'll sort out what you want to do next." Sarah looked to Mark for his consent.

"That's what I've been trying to tell him." Mark rolled his eyes as he released his grip on the boy's collar. Mark looked to Sarah. "I have to call the police now." He pulled his cell phone back out and walked away from the pair.

The boy stood motionless, as if transfixed by some thought.

Sarah returned her gaze to him. "Do you know this man?" She indicated the body on the ground.

The child nodded, a tear slipping from his eye. Expression hooded, he smeared it away with the back of his hand.

"Someone special to you?"

The boy's face wrenched with anguish. Sarah nodded, his expression confirming both her questions and that she'd pushed it too far. "They killed him, didn't they? The only person you've ever had to look after you." His eyes welled with moisture at her soft words.

Mark turned away to make his phone call, but not before he overheard Sarah begin to coax the boy about coming back to the bush camp. He hoped that she would have more luck than him. Flies were annoying Sniper, and he snorted in annoyance. Mark heard someone on the other end pick up, and he led the horse away from the carcass and tied him under the shade of a nearby tree.

Mark finished his call and slipped his phone back into his pocket, striding back to the pair. "They're on their way. Did you want to take him back to Jacob and Martha's and I'll wait here for them?"

Kwanele, white dust smeared with tears painted across his dark face, nodded faintly. "I want go with you in that." He pointed at the Cruiser. "Not on the horse." He blinked fearfully at Sniper.

Mark saw his wife about to say something, but she hesitated then changed the direction of her thoughts. "Sure, I can do that...he says he's not going on Sniper again, that's for sure." Sarah pressed her lips together.

It was the first time in months Mark had seen fire in her eyes. What was she thinking? The boy climbed into the front seat of the Cruiser and waited for Sarah, who regarded her husband with concern. "Please be careful. It's dangerous out here. Come back soon," she cautioned him in earnest.

"I know, I will—as soon as the police allow." Placing his hands firmly on her shoulders, he kissed her lightly on the forehead and they parted. They needed to speak many more words. "I'll get Martha to put your lunch in the fridge," she called back as she leapt into the Cruiser's drivers' seat.

"*Ja...dankie!*" he thanked her in Afrikaans, and turned to run his stirrups up.

Kwanele looked back out the window as the Cruiser sped off down the track, the last image of Joseph burnt into his mind. Sighing, he slumped down in the seat. He didn't want to do the job. He didn't want to be with this woman. Out of all the people in Africa who could have stumbled upon him, why did it have to be the woman from the tattered picture in his pocket? Neither did he want to stay out here and starve again. The landscape whooshed past them at a steady pace as words Joseph had spoken to him flooded into his mind. Joseph had always taught him that food, shelter, and comforts were few and far between; you had to take them when you could. The thought of more food made his stomach ache. What he'd eaten earlier hadn't even hit the bottom, not to mention his stomach felt uncertain holding it in.

He looked ahead, his eyes dark. He would accept this Sarah taking him somewhere and feeding him. After that, he might enjoy a good wash, and then he would be out of there—far from this woman whom the poachers were stalking, far from the job, farther from danger. Would he be safe? The words of the Khaki-man rang through his mind. *You get it done, boy, or your fate will be the same as his.* Would they find him if he ran? Pushing the nagging thoughts aside, Kwanele settled deeper into the passenger seat, setting his thoughts on oncoming comforts.

CHAPTER
SIX

Kwanele eased himself into the bath, hot and frothy with soap and bath salts. Never in his life had he enjoyed a bath like this. After years of the occasional wash in cold rain, or showers and basins—the idea of lying back in deep, clean, hot water was Kwanele's idea of heaven. Was this how rich people lived? Kings?

Kwanele felt like a king right now. Taking up the long-handled body brush, he scrubbed years of filth from his skin. He took up the facecloth and scrubbed at his weary-worn face. A face that had seen way too much horror in the past few years. The innocence of his eight-year-old frame had long since dissipated with the years of crime Joseph had subjected him to. He'd been forced to grow up too fast. What was it like to live as normal children did? To bathe and eat regularly, to not relive the nightmares of life each night in fitful dreams? He sank back and allowed his weary body, filled with good hot food, to sink deeper into the luxurious waters.

Mark watched as Martha hunched over, bustling through a deep chest of old clothes. "I know they are here somewhere!" She continued her search.

"What are you looking for?" Mark leaned against the doorway, arms folded against his chest.

"My sister's clothes she sent here ages ago. Her son outgrew them and she sent them here for me to donate to the Sotho village."

"What happened?" Mark smirked. "They obviously didn't make it to the village."

"Oh, I just forgot all about them." She turned, producing a zipped-up storage bag from the chest. Propping it on the edge, she unzipped it and tossed the first pair of child-sized trousers at Mark.

"Hey!" He caught them just before they hit his face.

She threw a grin over her shoulder, and then went back to her rummage. She pulled out some fresh underclothes and a checkered boy's button-down shirt. She also produced some socks and shoes. "I don't know if these will all fit him. He's so skinny!" She studied the shoes.

"Nothing a belt won't fix...or string." Mark tucked the trousers over his arm. "It's better than what he had on." He tilted his head. "Hey, how old do you think he is?"

Martha straightened up, a thoughtful look on her face. "Seven...eight?"

Mark examined the size on the tag. "I doubt these will fit then, maybe too small."

"Mark!" Sarah's voice was heard from the kitchen. "Your lunch is ready."

Mark laid the trousers over an ornament by the door and left Martha to her task without another word. He went to find his lunch.

Martha swept back into the dining area soon after, a grin pasted on her face. Mark lifted his gaze to her as he ate his late meal. He shook his head and swallowed a mouthful of reheated roast chicken before he spoke.

"How you got a name out of that kid, I'll never understand."

Martha tapped her nose as Sarah swept past and set a glass of fresh juice down for Mark. She took a seat next to him, her face full of worry. "What do we do with him?" She collected a drop of condensation from Mark's glass on her finger. "I don't want to just turn him over to the police. He is so scared of them. He's been through way too much already." They sat in silence awhile, and the question hung in the air. Mark glanced over at Sarah, who stared back.

"What is it?" He swallowed a hunk of food. Sarah's smile reached her eyes, and she reached out to him. Warmth flooded his heart at her touch. He'd missed her.

"What's this?" She reached toward his shirt and pulled the

elephant pendant from under his collar.

"Don't you remember it?" He raised a brow, forking in another mouthful of food.

Her eyes widened with recognition. "This was from Koto. Where was it?"

"I found it in the saddlebag. As I was praying." He marveled out loud. "Isn't that something?"

"It certainly is. I thought it was lost."

"So did I...but then, so was I..." He eyed her, cryptic for a moment before taking a swig from his glass of juice.

"Hmmm." Sarah sat back in thought. Mark soon finished his meal and took his plate to the sink, just as Kwanele silently padded around the corner and into the room.

"Oh, the clothes! You look great and they fit perfectly." Martha beamed.

"Now, what you need is some rest," his host insisted. The boy shrugged wearily and tried to hide a yawn. He nodded and followed Martha from the kitchen.

"He has new ones, he doesn't need them. Look at them, perished—full of lice. I'm going to just burn them." Mark wrinkled his nose at the soiled clothes on the bathroom floor. "He won't even miss them."

"That's not the point, Mark. They're not yours. Wait till he wakes up." Sarah ushered her husband from the putrid-smelling bathroom. "But I need a shower and I'm not doing it with that...smell in there." Mark screwed up his nose.

"You're such a baby." Sarah pulled his arm and dragged him out of the room.

"What's this about, you pair?" Martha bustled into the hallway.

"Whether or not to throw away Kwanele's old clothes." Sarah let go of Mark's sleeve. Their hostess shrugged. "They didn't fit; they're too small and rotten. He has new ones. I would just make sure he has nothing valuable in them and then throw the rest on the fire."

Sarah sighed and moved aside for Mark, who smirked as he

picked up the gray mass of rags. "It's fine." He held the pile away from him. As he passed Sarah, he planted a chaste kiss on her lips. He headed outside to where Jacob was starting a campfire.

Kwanele burst out from the guest room into the kitchen, where Sarah was cutting up onions. "My clothes! Where are my clothes? Did someone take them away?"

Sarah pointed to the back door. "Mark was going to burn them. They were ripped and ruined." Panic caught in Kwanele as he burst into a run and headed for the door. What if that man checked his pockets? What if he found the newspaper photo of his wife? What would he think then? Dread filled Kwanele's heart as he looked around the twilight. He searched for signs of the fire. He saw a soft red glow from behind some buildings and sprinted toward it.

"Wait!" He was nearly out of breath as he stumbled into the area.

Mark halted in surprise.

"My clothes! I need them back." He reached out to take back the clothes from Mark, who pulled the rags away. He searched the pockets and frowned as he produced a tattered bit of folded-up newspaper. Mark held it out in question. "This?"

Kwanele snatched it back and stepped back as Mark arched an eyebrow.

"Anything else in there I should know about?"

"No, you can burn them now." Kwanele turned without eye contact and returned to the rondavel. He placed the newspaper in the inside pocket of his new shirt.

"It's a bit cooler out there tonight, Kwanele. We'll still eat outside, though...so here," Martha greeted him at the door with a small boy's jacket. The near new fabric was a brilliant red, thick and comforting. Kwanele hung his head at the amount of comfort these people were already lavishing on him.

"But...I have no money to pay you for all of this." He looked up with sad eyes at the large African woman.

Martha folded her arms. "Now listen here. Nobody is expecting you to pay for anything. This is a gift. It's free."

Kwanele looked at her for several moments. "Nothing is free."

"Well, this is. Many things in life are free. Many things in life are also a gift, a blessing. We are surrounded by them." Martha eased herself down onto the porch steps next to him, compassion in her face. She looked out toward the rich colors of the twilight horizon.

"But...that's not what you have learned, is it?" Her voice was soft. Kwanele looked down at the ground again and kicked at a tuft of grass. "Come, have a seat with me, young man." She motioned toward the steps beside her.

Kwanele sat and Martha slid the red children's jacket over his thin shoulders. "You don't owe anything. We're blessed when we give to you. All we ask is that one day, when they no longer fit you...and you are blessed again with more clothes, that you pass them on to someone who needs them."

Kwanele sat in silence and looked out upon the deep colors of the sky. It looked so dark beyond the gates, he wondered if it would be too dangerous for him to leave in the night. A lion called out in the distance. Its rhythmic bellow resounded off the buildings as it called to its pride. Kwanele jumped, and then stiffened, his eyes flying wide open.

He looked at Martha, who laughed.

"It's just a lion, you'll get used to it." She rubbed his back. Kwanele shook his head. How could he feel safe?

"So, you want to go back to the city? I take it you have never been in the wilderness..." Martha interrupted his thoughts and he shrank back. "It's okay, Kwanele. It's just a lion. He's looking for his pride. He won't harm you...you're safe in here. Most are more afraid of you than you are of them. But you just have to respect their territory. Lions can be testy, though. You need to be careful in lion country." Apprehension flooded him.

"Are there any other towns or villages out here?" he asked. Martha laughed despite herself.

"What, between here and Phalaborwa? Boy, you're in a

National Park. It's huge. Between here and Phalaborwa is wilderness."

"Oh."

"Kwanele, relax and enjoy being here. You are safe now. I don't know what kind of life you've lived before now...but we will look after you. The police will come and talk with you tomorrow about the men who want to kill you, and it will all get sorted out. For now, we will look after you."

Kwanele shook off Martha's arm and stood up in shock. "I can't talk to the police! I need to get away from here." His voice rang with panic as he leapt from the steps onto the dirt in one motion. He needed to get out of here. He didn't know how, or where to, but he had to get far away, now! He spun on his heel and ran blind. Straight into Mark.

"*Ommpf!* Hey? We've got to stop meeting like this." The tall Afrikaans man grinned.

"I have to get away; I..." Kwanele shoved him to the side and ran.

"Hey! I didn't mean..." Mark looked at Martha, seriousness in his eyes. "You'll never win him over. He's a con. He's involved with smugglers. They would have trained him to lie and cheat...and run. It doesn't matter how much we play the nice guy. It's all he knows. We can't keep him locked up. He'll feel like a trapped animal." He shook his head. "I don't trust him."

Martha stood and wiped the dust off her hands onto her dress.

"Mark. How can you talk like that? You don't even know his full story. Besides, what witness are we to him if we don't show him Christ's love? Christ's hospitality? He's got nothing, Mark, he needs to know love." She moved to find Jacob at the fires, but paused. She looked him in the eye. "He is only a child!" She walked off.

Mark stepped after her but stopped, his hand on the rondavel door handle. The Holy Spirit knocked at his heart. She was right. Where would any of them be if not for the love of Christ? He was exhausted from hiding from those types of people. Trying to keep his wife safe. How could Sarah ask him to now accept one of them? The whole point of coming out here was to try to help her out of her depression. Mark realized that deep in his heart he was annoyed that this boy would turn up and make life even harder. Allowing his hand to slip off the door handle, he knew it was time to go and pray. He needed to ask forgiveness for being so selfish. How many times did he need to go through this? Surrendering his fears over to God, surrendering the control of life that he kept trying to take back. Mark slinked into the shadows behind the rondavel for a moment to again ask God for help.

CHAPTER
SEVEN

Running around the whole parameter fence of the bush camp, Kwanele sank onto his bottom against the cool bricks of one of the buildings. He wiggled back more and nestled in. Good and hidden among the ferns that landscaped the base of the building, he hugged his knees to his chest and wondered what he would do. His keen eyes lifted and traced the line of the perimeter. Darkness enshrouded the entire landscape beyond the fence like a beast in hiding, waiting to pounce upon all that entered its domain. Even if he could crawl under or scale through the curled barbed wire at the top, he doubted he would survive the wilds of out there. Even if the fat African woman was right that the wildlife was more scared of him, his heart wouldn't take the fear of it. For the second time today, Kwanele was alone. Hugging his knees tighter to himself, he buried his head into his knees and wept.

What was he going to do? Trapped with a job, or certain death, maybe both...he didn't know where to turn. Would he spend his whole life running from poachers? He heard someone call his name. Tense, he lifted his head. Someone had called him to dinner. His body relaxed again. He had already eaten today, more than he'd usually eat in several days. He didn't need to show himself. He slunk himself deeper into the cool dirt and arranged the ferns to cover him more. Satisfied with his camouflage, he kept very still. After a while, the voice stopped. He sighed and closed his eyes against the raging thoughts within and listened to the unusual sounds of the wilderness outside the fence. The rhythmic *chirrup* of the crickets lulled him, and soon enough, the tension ebbed, released from his body.

A shuffling noise startled Kwanele from an uncomfortable doze. He rubbed his eyes, adjusted to the darkness as he scanned his immediate surroundings. *Schhh, schhff.* There it was again, a shuffling, sniffling noise. He sat up in panic and looked around. What if it was a lion outside the fence? Could it smell him? Could it get in? He leaned out of the ferns and peered toward the fence line. There was nothing, except for the floodlight on the post that bathed the dusty ground beyond with an eerie blue circle of light. Not a sound, except the chortle of the crickets and an owl hooting in the distance. Kwanele turned back to the ferns and was faced with a strange creature.

Kwanele yelped with fear and jumped to his feet, taking on a defensive pose. He faced the curious beast head-on. The old cheetah blinked with surprise and sniffed the air toward the boy. "Stay back!" Kwanele warned, a low growl in his throat. A nearby stick caught his attention and the boy grabbed and held it up at the ready. It was the adopted cat they called Jacques. He didn't care. It could still eat him.

Adjusting his hands on the stick, he stared as Jacques yawned. The large orange spotted cat then turned and padded away, the tags on his collar clinking into the darkness. A squeak of relief issued from Kwanele. He dropped the stick and looked around to see if anyone had heard him. Cautious, he stepped out from the foliage, and peered around the corner of the building as he dusted himself off. He looked toward the sky. Bright stars blinked back. Surely it was too late for people to be out now?

Kwanele stepped farther out. Now what? His gaze was drawn once more to the darkness outside the fence. A shudder ran down Kwanele's spine as he decided on a course of action. The darkness beyond the gates beckoned him, like a sinister predator trying to lure its prey. Would freedom come at the ultimate price? His heart quickened as he spotted a small hole at the base of the fence. Could he squeeze under that? Crouched, he tensed his muscles, ready to fly, his eyes fixed on the goal. A twig snapped somewhere close and Kwanele swiveled his head around in alarm.

Someone's coming! He'd lingered too long in the one spot. Maybe it wasn't as late as he'd supposed. Footsteps crunched on the gravel footpath close by, and Kwanele dove back into his spot near the ferns. His heart hammered in his ears from the pent-up surge of adrenaline. He shrank against the cool wall of the building. The sound was now right here, along with the soft pad of the cheetah. A man's legs came into view, boots visible from beneath the fern where Kwanele hid. Scowling, Kwanele spotted the cheetah's oversized clawed paws come into view beside the boots.

"I see you've met Jacques." A male voice spoke. Kwanele's scowl deepened. It was that man who had tricked him on the horse and burnt his clothes! Was his name Mark? He didn't want anything to do with any of these people, least of all Mark. He sensed that the man didn't like him. Wary, Kwanele watched as Mark moved to the opposite side of the path, leaned against the other building, and spoke, as if into the air.

"Look...I owe you an apology."

Kwanele blinked. *What does he want now?*

"I mean, I need to say sorry, okay? I was afraid...afraid for Sarah." Mark sighed and Kwanele saw him look into the night air as if thinking. His brows creased as he edged forward.

"People have been chasing us, you know...for many years. We are..." Mark cleared his throat and went on. "We're tired of it."

Silence sat in the air as Kwanele processed what was said. Looking up through a gap in the ferns, he watched the stern man's jaw set as he shook his head. Jacques the cheetah flopped over onto his side at Mark's feet, panting lightly despite the cool night air. Kwanele watched with mild interest as Mark crouched to rub at the soft orange and cream coat with its distinctive black spots.

"Nothing ever worries you, does it, Jacques?" The man chuckled. Face now level with where Kwanele sat hiding, Mark looked into the ferns and locked eyes with him.

How he managed to even see him in the dark, Kwanele had no idea. Perhaps the distant floodlight glinted off his eyes. They both remained frozen, seeming to measure each other up before Kwanele squirmed with discomfort and looked away.

"You said the police would help me," Kwanele murmured. A muscle in Mark's mouth jerked as he focused on the cheetah again. Kwanele emerged with caution from his hiding spot and fixed his eyes on Mark, who looked up from the cheetah.

"*Ja*, I did. And *ja*, they can." He held Kwanele's gaze.

Kwanele's eyes darted from Mark to the cheetah. Jacques continued to lie on his side, soaking in the attention from Mark's hand. "But...if they can help me...why have they not helped you? Why are you still scared?"

Mark's eyes flashed for a moment as Kwanele fully emerged. "Touché." He rubbed the back of his neck.

Kwanele tilted his head to the side, not understanding.

"I meant, *ja*... Okay. You got me." Mark looked uncertain. "I don't know..." He sighed and scuffed Jacques's fur around the neck. "I don't know." His voice trailed off. There was an awkward silence as Kwanele stood and shifted from one foot to the other.

"Then...you will help me get to town and stay away from the police?" Kwanele edged closer, hope in his voice. Mark's vision refocused on the boy.

"And then what will you do?" His voice was low. "You have nowhere to go, do you? What if you lead those people straight back here to us?"

"Please, sir! I promise you, I have no one to go to!"

"Then why are you so eager to get away from us?" Mark raised a brow. Kwanele stepped back a pace. "If you have nowhere to go, no one to look after you...then what's wrong with being with us? Or the police? What difference would it make? You are only a child. You can't just go and live your own life. You need to be looked after!" Mark spat the words.

Jacques lifted his head. He looked disappointed that the pampering had stopped. He yawned, stretched out his hind leg, and scratched behind his ear like a regular cat. Kwanele jumped back. Mark's expression softened at his fear, but his eyes danced with amusement.

"Come here." He motioned to Kwanele.

"What?" He shook his head, backing away. "Why?"

"He won't hurt you." Mark ushered Kwanele closer. "Come on, come and meet him. He loves people."

Remembering how Mark had tricked him with the horse filled Kwanele with apprehension. "He will not...bite me...will he?" His throat constricted.

Mark scuffed Jacques up around the neck again and rubbed his hands over the cheetah's muzzle. Jacques opened his jowls, his long, shiny teeth visible around his black lips. He then caught the taste of salt on Mark's skin and licked his hand.

Kwanele watched with avid interest as the cat didn't maul the man.

Mark chuckled. "It's fine. I doubt you'll do what I just did...so here..." He straightened and patted his thigh to call the cheetah.

Jacques stood, the loose skin on his belly quivering as he stretched out into another long yawn. Kwanele waited until the animal stood still with his mouth shut until he crept over behind Mark. The boy stretched out his hand and gave the cheetah a quick rub on the shoulder. He then shot his hand back to the safety of his barricade.

"See? You lived!" Mark looked over his shoulder at Kwanele, frozen still. He sighed and jerked his head toward the light coming from over the buildings. "Hungry?"

Mark turned to regard Kwanele as Jacques sauntered past.

He made sure to stay away from the cat and skittled behind Mark. The cheetah ignored them and headed in the direction of food. Kwanele released the breath he'd been holding.

"Are you hungry?" Mark repeated, his expression hooded as he looked down.

Kwanele shook his head as he realized with horror that he was still gripping the man's shirt. Throwing his hands away, he backed up.

Mark shrugged and began moving toward the campfire. At a distance from Mark, Kwanele edged into the open area. Everyone sat around the fire. They had already begun to eat. Sarah's eyes lit up as she saw Mark accompanied by Kwanele, who stayed a few meters behind. Mark took his place next to Sarah and nodded with appreciation as Martha handed him a fully burdened plate.

Kwanele found a space on the logs a little away from the

others and gazed into the warmth of the fire as he sat. Martha appeared in front of him and placed a plate of food in his lap. She stood waiting, hands on her hips. They exchanged looks before Kwanele picked at some of the food in front of him. He was reluctant to waste such an offering, especially when the African woman stood over him like that. When she saw he ate, she nodded and left him to it.

"Mark, Sarah says she wants to go back to that rhinoceros carcass tomorrow...you both know I believe in divine protection, but you don't go inviting trouble upon yourselves. I told her you wouldn't let her anyway. You need to tell her no." Martha bustled over and filled two cups with fruit juice, serving them out to Mark and Kwanele.

He looked up toward Mark from his food, his eyes wide. "I still want to go to town," he spluttered through a mouthful of juice. Mark put his hands up in defense.

"Whoah. Everybody stop. I thought you wouldn't want to go anywhere near there, Sarah? And Kwanele...what were we just talking about earlier?"

He stared at his plate and frowned, but not before he saw Mark turn to Sarah, a deep scowl etched into his face.

"You want to go back there? Why?" Mark's eyes rested on Sarah and she held his gaze for a moment before she looked away into the fire.

"This kind of stuff has been tormenting you for years. It led you from success and your destiny in God...to what? Pain and depression. The enemy has been having an absolute field day taunting you over this." Mark rubbed his hands over his face. To Kwanele, he looked weary. Sarah continued to gaze into the fire. Jacob looked from one to the other, lines of sadness in his face.

"Mark. It's not your job to keep Sarah safe either..." Jacob's words fell onto the ground and with it a hush came over their meal.

Awkward, Kwanele looked at his plate then back up at everyone. He could feel the tension as it filled the circle of friends. Martha was busy packing her own plate full of food in the corner, while Mark and Sarah refused to look at anyone. Jacob looked Kwanele's way, then back at the couple. He adjusted his cast, scratching at the red skin on his foot with the tip of one crutch as he continued.

"A few years ago, you both learned of Jesus and what He has done for you both. You both received supernatural revelations that led you down His path. You found a loving community of believers in the church at Phalaborwa. But somewhere, something went wrong. You have become comfortable with the routine of hiding, of isolating yourselves from those who love you…and you don't rely on God.

"Mark, you cannot do God's job in Sarah's life. Sarah, you need to stop listening to the enemy's lies. Both of you are being rendered ineffective in God's Kingdom. Mark, Sarah, we've needed to talk to you about this for a long time. When coal is taken from a fire, it loses its heat. A branch cut off from the vine, well, it shrivels and dies."

He paused, waiting for their response. He turned back toward Kwanele. As soon as they locked eyes, Kwanele felt awkward again and returned to his food. Mark glowered as he lifted his gaze to the older couple. Before Mark could speak, Martha took over from her husband, a look of pure love in her eyes.

"I know the police told you that you both needed to hide…but has that helped, or has it made it worse for you both?…emotionally and spiritually, I mean?"

Mark clamped his mouth shut and reached out to clasp Sarah's hand. She regarded her husband for a moment, and Kwanele wondered what was going through her mind as Martha spoke again.

"You both need to come back and be around God's family, the people who love you, pray for you, and support you."

Sarah shook her head. "No, that will lead poachers to our friends. We want to protect them from that…you from that."

Jacob patted his leg, a sad look in his eye. "You think staying away will stop that?"

A muscle twitched in Mark's jaw. Before he could object, Jacob continued.

"Mark, Sarah. Many people you love have been affected by all this. But your friends in Phalaborwa, well, they have each other for support. They stay accountable to each other and are closer to God through all trials and tribulations because of that. They know they are never alone. They pray for you both every day, and they are no longer threatened by dangers. They are strong, they have no fear, they live in faith. They are more protected inside the community of believers than they would be if they isolated themselves. Think of the lion when it selects easy prey from a herd. Which animal does it select, the strong ones in the middle, or the stragglers on the outskirts?"

There was a long moment of silence. Kwanele squirmed, and kept his focus on his food.

Jacob chewed on a bone and repeated his earlier thoughts. "Mark, you cannot keep Sarah safe. Only God can. Rely on Him."

Mark put his half-eaten plateful of food on the ground in front of him. Staring at the ground, he sat in silence. Kwanele peered at the couple. Sarah smiled at her husband, her fingers intertwined with his. Mark lifted his gaze to meet her eyes. They both then turned as one to regard the older couple beside them, gratitude in their eyes. Jacob smiled warmly, inclining his head.

Kwanele stared at each person in turn. Moments before, the air had been hostile. With no spoken words, the air cleared and it was as though everyone understood one another. He blinked and twirled a piece of potato on his fork. He was confused. Who was this Jesus whom Jacob had spoken about? How did they all resolve their differences and problems, just like that?

Martha beamed as she polished off the last of her meat. Placing her plate on the ground, she slapped her thighs and got up. "Who wants dessert?" She collected their dishes and disappeared off to the rondavel.

Kwanele raised his head. "What's dessert?"

Sarah chuckled. "It's the best thing you'll ever taste!" She squinted across the fire trying to make Kwanele out through the flames. His small frame probably resembled kindling. And he knew it. He snuck around the fire and appeared in an instant beside her. He was timid as he moved to sit next to her. All three adults smiled, and he was glad that he had changed his mind and sat with them.

"I just want to take some photos. Send them in to the media. Something has to be done." Sarah moved toward the Cruiser. Mark followed, exasperation in his face when she looked over her shoulder at him. "Trust me!" She grinned. "Once word gets out about what's happening in Africa, people are bound to get behind it and support efforts to stop poachers."

"You sound so sure, Sarah."

"I'm not, but we've got to try."

"That's assuming the photos even reach all of South Africa, let alone beyond." Mark snorted.

Sarah blinked and was about to speak but shook her head instead. Mark stifled a chuckle as she pushed past him and jogged back to the rondavel. She was dressed in the jeans and boots she used to ride horses in. Mark was pleased to note she also wore the lovely western-style pink button-down shirt he'd bought her. He smiled at the messy way she'd pulled her wavy long black hair into a ponytail. He loved her. To him she looked beautiful, and Mark thanked God that she was climbing out of the hole she'd crawled into.

Returning with her Digital SLR in hand, Sarah practically vaulted into the passenger seat. Mark turned to her in question and she held up the device.

"Ahh, so you nearly forgot the most important thing, huh? Now...are you sure, absolutely sure?" He secretly hoped she'd change her mind. "We might not be allowed there anyway. It's a crime scene now and all."

He grumbled as he turned the key in the ignition. The last thing he wanted to do was visit a rhino carcass, and knowing that it was also the scene of a murder didn't lighten his spirits.

Sarah waved a hand. "Bah! They have to clean up crime scenes out here fast, remember?"

Mark looked sideways as he pulled out of the bush camp gates. He remembered all right, but why was she so indifferent about it now? This was the stuff her nightmares had been made of. Climbing the gears into fourth, he worried that she might break down later on. She'd been a totally different person since their arrival out here, and for that, Mark was grateful. He was also grateful for some time alone with her. "So, what exactly are we photographing, then, if they would have cleaned it all up?"

"The rhino, silly. They wouldn't have moved that."

"Hmmm." He wasn't convinced, but hoped that the police had blockaded the way.

"Mark?"

He glanced at her. The doe-eyed look she gave him flooded his heart with warmth. "Hmmm?" He was intrigued with her tone and deep green eyes. But it soon gave way to concern.

She bit her lip as she gazed from under her thick lashes.

A smirk tickled Mark's face and he gave her as much of his attention as possible while driving. "I know that face. What are you up to?"

"Well...I was thinking that while you have time off work..." Her voice took on a singsong tone.

"Hmmm?" He returned his focus to the road.

"Well, maybe we could go for a longer drive on another day or so..."

Mark flicked his eyes back to her, laughing now. "Come on, woman, out with it!"

"You know...over the border to Mozambique?"

Silence filled the Cruiser for a moment as Mark digested what she had asked. "You want to go see your elephants, don't you? You want to see Maggie?" Mark's voice came out quiet. He knew the special connection she'd had with the old matriarch elephant and her herd. This was the herd that Sarah had led across the border several years ago. From the corner of his eye, he saw her lean forward and search his face. Her large green eyes distracted, and he tried to keep his eyes on the road.

"What do you think?" Her lips pulled into the start of a pout.

He made her wait a few beats too long before he turned to her. He could see she had held her breath. A broad smile crept across his features. "I think it's a great idea." He reached over, grasped her hand, and squeezed it a little too hard. Sarah yelped with joy, squeezing it back.

"Thank you!"

Silence filled the Cruiser again, and his smile dipped at the corners. He could tell there was more. They were close to the site of the kill. He stole a glance and saw the struggle in her face. Then she said it.

"We could take Kwanele with us and teach him about how special our wildlife is."

Mark's dream of spending more time alone with her ended abruptly. He blinked. "Kwanele?"

"Well, yeah, it would be good for him. Good for him to have decent role models and learn there is much more to life…" She frowned at his sigh.

He flicked on the indicator with one hand and steered left onto another dirt track.

"I know you don't trust him," Sarah started. "But he needs us."

Mark felt her insistent grip on his hand grow tighter, and he pulled it away to change gears. "Wait and see what happens with the police, Sarah. We don't know what will need to happen with him."

"But it would be great for him."

"He's not our child!" His voice was more forceful than he'd intended. Sarah pressed her lips together and looked out the window. He'd hurt her now. "I didn't mean it like…"

He stopped and his brows drew together. He did mean it. He just didn't mean to hurt her. "I'm sorry, honey, but he is not our child." Mark's voice softened and he looked at her. He reached out and tried to find her hand again, but she kept it away. What if she latched on to this boy as her own? It could be the undoing of them.

"I know that." Sarah continued to look out the window, her body stiff.

Glancing at her hands balled together in her lap, Mark let his own hand slip back to the steering wheel. Silence ensued and he scolded himself for stepping in it again. As they came over the ridge, the line of trees in the distance marked the line of the river edge. There was no police tape, no other vehicles. Then the dark form of the rhinoceros came into view. Mark groaned inwardly. It was just how Sarah hoped it would be. He braced himself for the smell they would be hit with when they arrived.

"You know, the police will have fresher photos." He moaned as they pulled up and they opened their doors. The stench was almost unbearable.

"As if they would release those photos to us." Sarah rolled her eyes and then gagged as a fly nearly flew in her mouth.

"We need our own." Sarah covered her mouth and nose with a scarf and secured it in place. She stepped out into the sea of flies and started to shoot snaps of the rotted carcass. Already scavengers had cleaned up much of the beast, but the head still remained intact, showing the grisly wounds given by the poachers. This was what Sarah wanted to snap. Any other evidence that had alluded to it being a different type of crime scene was all but cleaned up by the police.

Mark remained in the Cruiser, windows up, engine running and air-conditioner cranked to full blast. He sat in bewildered silence as his wife danced around the site in an energetic fashion, swiping at flies and snapping images. He silently prayed she would hurry along. This place filled him with dreadful memories—memories of other corpses, memories of nearly finding her that way. He swallowed back the lump in his throat and thumped the windscreen with the back of his fist to get her attention.

Sarah turned and raised her brows in query. He waved her to hurry up. She held up a finger and scouted around the rhino for more angles. Several shots later, she jumped back into the four-wheel-drive next to Mark.

"Done!" She beamed. Mark caught the tension in her announcement. They sat in silence for a moment and stared at the stripped beast.

"It's awful, isn't it?" She shuddered.

He nodded, feeling numb. "It is..."

"But"—she patted her SLR—"this will help. We'll send them to the Parks Board and also to the media and see if we can't rally some support." Mark smiled at his wife.

"This means a lot to you, doesn't it?"

Her eyes sparkled in response. Mark's reserve slipped away. At least it was done now. What harm could come of it?

"I had no idea that the way to cure you of your fear was to throw you back into the thick of it." His mouth tilted as he struggled to work out his wife. Perhaps she would be a mystery he continued to unravel for the rest of their lives. Pulling the Cruiser into gear, Mark reversed away from the carcass, turned the vehicle around, and headed back down the track.

"As long as we are going through to Mozambique..." Mark paused midsentence. He wondered if it truly was safe to rely on God and safety in numbers. If what Jacob said was true, then they should reach out to their friends again. Sarah looked at him, full of expectation. He shook aside his thoughts and continued.

"Did you want to stop in at Lebowa village first and see if Israel or any of the others want to come along, too? After all, they did help move the herd over the border." Mark tilted his head toward her, waiting for an answer. Lebowa village housed the Northern Sotho tribe's people and some people they had come to know as dear, close friends. Many of these people had also helped in the translocation of the D-12 herd of elephants across the border. Sarah held his gaze.

"This isn't a plot of yours to fill the Cruiser so Kwanele can't fit, is it?"

Mark frowned and she held up her hands in defense.

"Okay, okay. Just checking." She looked out the window in thought. "I think that would be great...if you think it's safe."

He looked at her. She was trusting his judgment. A warm glow spread in his chest.

"And they can tell us what's happened with tourism at their end of the park," Sarah went on. "We know it's low at the moment already, but it will be more obvious in the village. They depend on it. I hope Koto and his family are okay."

At the mention of Koto, Mark went quiet, concentrating on the track ahead. Mark owed his salvation to the beautiful Sotho family in the village. They'd introduced him to Jesus. He felt a brotherly connection to Koto he couldn't explain. He and his wife, Lerato, had held no judgment, no resentment toward Mark and his racist heritage. They just saw him as him, proud and lost. He missed them. He missed Israel, who had been an African shaman, but who was now one of the most respected spiritual leaders in the village. They deserved a chance to travel with the couple and see how the elephants over the border had fared.

CHAPTER
EIGHT

"Come on, there you go." Kwanele placed another small cut of meat on the ground, before he shuffled backward. With care, he placed another piece on the dirt, and stepped back. He looked up and took a deep breath. A small smile tilted his lips as he saw Jacques pad along the meat trail, delicate as he licked up each morsel with his large, rough tongue. The aged cheetah got to the last piece and swallowed it down. He licked his chops, sniffed the air, and glanced up at Kwanele with expectation. When he realized there was no more, he flopped onto his side and began to groom himself. Kwanele giggled, producing another piece of meat from a hidden pocket in his clothes. He held it out with triumph, and then threw it to the cat. Jacques stretched out from his spot on the ground and hooked it up into his mouth. Kwanele rubbed his sticky hands together, regarded the cheetah one last time, and walked off around the side of the building. He paused out of view of the cat and pressed his back against the wall of a building. Soon enough, Kwanele was rewarded with the sight of a curious amber head, dotted with deep black spots, that peered around the corner at him. Jacques regarded the boy for a moment through his golden eyes. Kwanele giggled and moved off again, disappearing a second time around the building. He glanced over his shoulder with glee and picked up the pace as he spotted the cheetah trot after him. Kwanele could sense his heart thump in his chest. He should be terrified of being chased by this hunter, but beyond all rational reason, he wasn't. He trusted the cat. He liked the company of the cat. It was fun. And what was better, he knew that Jacques enjoyed his company also. Heat rose in his cheeks as Kwanele ducked around a different building and changed direction to throw Jacques off the trail. He jogged past the guard at the main gate and felt the man's gaze upon him. He heard the guard chuckle as the cheetah, seeming to enjoy the game, padded after him, ears pricked forward. He led the way over to the seat logs in the communal campfire area and sat dramatically. A smile of triumph lit up his face when Jacques joined him. The cheetah sat at his feet, his head tilted as he waited for more meat. The lanky cat's thin frame heaved in and out as they both caught their breath. Finally, Jacques settled onto the cool dirt. Kwanele sighed with contentment as he kicked a stick toward the unlit campfire.

He didn't make any effort to touch his new friend, simply happy just being with the animal. A quiet moment passed between the boy and the cat, before Kwanele sensed that he was being watched.

"He likes you." Sarah was leaning against the building behind them. Kwanele jumped with surprise at her presence.

"He does," she assured him again. "Look. See how he sits now? He's relaxed and wants to be with you. If he didn't like you, he would walk away." Kwanele pondered this a moment, then offered.

"But I just fed him meat I found in the kitchen. He only followed me for the meat." Sarah's face appeared to tighten.

"Kwanele...did you ask Martha for the meat?"

He tore his eyes away from her gaze.

"Kwanele, you know...you don't have to steal here. You can ask, and we'll just give it to you, if we can. If you had asked Martha for the meat, she would have happily given it to you. She might have even shown you where Jacques's food was."

Kwanele looked up at Sarah, uncertain.

"It's true." She approached him. "You try and ask her tomorrow." Turning to Jacques, Sarah pressed her lips together and nodded. "So, back to Jacques. He likes you. The meat is gone. He is still here. What does that tell you?"

"That he thinks I have more, or that he is too full to move," Kwanele reasoned. His serious words sent a fit of laughter to bubble up from Sarah, and when she looked upon him, her eyes were genuine, warm, and loving. Kwanele felt the tension seem to ebb away, and his face lit up so that he, too, began to chuckle. Jacques let out a loud yawn and flopped over in the dirt.

A couple of days passed and Kwanele grew less afraid of Jacques. He also became more curious about Sarah and Mark's obsession with the dead rhino and all the talk of elephants. One afternoon, Kwanele was on his knees rubbing the cheetah with care around the back of the neck when Mark strolled up to him with a toothy grin. Kwanele looked up at the man, curious. But after a moment, Mark shook his head and continued on.

That night, Sarah, eyes bright with a light the boy had never seen before, told Kwanele about the elephant muster and how they had saved the elephants after she received a special call from God. She told him about the dangers, the adventure, and how God had saved them. She then said they were going to Mozambique to visit the herd in the next day or two. She also asked if he would like to come along and meet them. Kwanele's eyes lit up with delight.

He lay in bed awake later that night, his heart filled with excitement. He really liked it here. He was shocked to discover that he really liked these people, too. Could they really care for him forever? Would they really protect him? But then, just as he would get his hopes and dreams set to soar, doubt and fear would cloud his vision. Who would want him? He was worthless, a criminal. And then there were the poachers—they would try to contact him. They would want him to lead Sarah to them. They would want to hurt her. Would their reach extend as far as Mozambique? Confusion and fear flooded his mind. So much had happened in such a short time and he felt powerless to stop it. One thing he knew for sure, he could continue to live by Joseph's rule: Take comforts when they are offered. This had indeed been a season of plenty for Kwanele. When would he finally wake up from this dream? He stared at the ceiling in the bush camp guest room and decided that he wanted to go with Mark and Sarah across the border.

Kwanele was ready. He was all packed and ready for an adventure in another country. Mark and Sarah stood at the kitchen bench and prepared food and water for the trip. Martha bustled about to ensure they had enough. The room was awash with motion and excitement. Jacob alone stood still in the corner of the room, phone pressed to his ear, while his other hand shielded his other ear. He appeared to strain to understand the voice on the other end. Kwanele pushed a hat into his bag and watched Jacob, curious. The old man's face was downcast and Kwanele wondered what was wrong. Jacob ended the conversation and hung up the receiver. He glanced over his shoulder, and caught Kwanele's eye. There was a bleak sadness in his eyes.

"They need to interview Kwanele. They need a statement."

"What...today?" Sarah's brows creased as she turned to the older African man. Jacob nodded, his gaze falling back to Kwanele.

"I am not going to the police!" He threw his pack on the floor and ran from the room. He reached the sitting room, slid behind the sofa, and hide among the curtains. He held his breath as he heard the adults enter the room.

"You don't have to go to the police, Kwanele." He heard Jacob's voice. "They will come here, talk with you, and then go. You don't have to go anywhere you don't want to." Kwanele grunted.

"Today, you say?" It was Mark's voice now. He sounded cranky. Kwanele shrank back further as he sensed Mark begin to pace the room. "When exactly do they want to do this interview? We were just going to go to Lebowa village now."

There was a pause in the conversation and Kwanele was tempted to poke his head out when he suddenly spotted Sarah. She was crouched down in front of him, brushing the curtain aside.

"Kwanele"—she smiled at him with compassion—"it won't take you long. You can still come on the trip with us...we'll go to Lebowa today, and then be back here by tonight. We'll all leave for the border in the morning." Kwanele shook his head.

"Mark." Kwanele looked past Sarah as he heard Martha's voice. "How are you going to take that boy across the border without papers, eh?"

"Same way we got the Lebowa guys across the border for the muster. Special immunity," Mark shot back. Martha glared at him. The tension in the room grew, and Kwanele resolved to stay behind the couch.

"It's okay, Martha!" Mark puffed with exasperation. "Sarah has rung the National Park border security and explained what she wants to do." Their voices trailed off as Kwanele returned his focus on Sarah. They heard Jacob clear his throat and poked their heads out from behind the sofa as one. "They're here." Mark pulled a face and ducked down near the sofa. He spoke low to his wife.

"Keep talking him through, honey." Kwanele saw the corner of Mark's mouth twitch upward in amusement.

Mark moved into the kitchen and sighed at the inconvenience of it all. He grabbed some crackers from the kitchen cupboard, went to the fridge, and snatched up some carrots for Sniper. He headed out the back door, munching on the crackers as he went. He needed some fresh air for a bit. As long as they were delayed, he was going to take some time out. Mark paused on the porch and noticed that Jacques was asleep under the back steps. It was odd behavior for the cheetah. He flicked the rest of the cracker into his mouth and headed toward the horse kraals. It was nice to be able to go and see his horse every day. He'd taken it for granted when he worked at Brennan Safari Trail rides. He knew it would take a while for his wife to coax the boy out, and even longer for him to give a statement. He had time to burn now. Mark sauntered out toward the kraals and breathed in the fresh air of the African morning. This was what he missed, the fresh scent of the blossoming shrubs, the smell of adventure. This was what the smog and noise of the city could never offer. What beauty was there in car fumes and hard geometric landscapes? Sniper stood in his kraal, head lowered, eyes half-closed, back hoof cocked. He was backed into the corner of the kraal under a low-hung tree, still except for the occasional flick of his tail. Mark kicked at a clump of dirt and clucked his tongue as he approached. The animal flicked his head up and gazed Mark's way.

"Hey, buddy." He cooed and leaned on the fence. He held out the carrot, waving it around. The horse lifted his head in Mark's direction, but made no other move to respond. Sighing, Mark rested his arms against the rail as the horse regarded him. Finally, stretching first, Sniper lifted his head toward the neighboring paddock, where he called out with a soft whinny to Buster. Buster nickered an answer before Sniper meandered over to greet Mark. The crunch of the carrot soon echoed in the morning air. Mark began to stroke the soft fur along the animal's face as it ate. He could feel it through his fingers as Sniper ground up the vegetable with his strong back teeth. Mark frowned as his thoughts strayed back to their current situation. What were they going to do with their lives? They couldn't stay locked up in Polokwane forever. They belonged out here, in the wilderness of untamed Africa, with its beauty, its tranquility, and its dangers. At least the dangers of the wilderness were preferable to the dangers of the city. Mark breathed heavily and looked heavenward through the swaying trees. He began to murmur his concerns to the only One who could really help them.

Later that morning, a police officer nodded his thanks to Kwanele, Sarah, Mark, Martha, and Jacob, pulled on his hat, and took his leave. Kwanele sat on the sofa and held a mug of hot chocolate like it was the only comfort left in the world. He looked up as Sarah let out a sigh of relief.

"See? That wasn't too bad, was it?" As strong as she was, Kwanele still caught the quaver in her voice. It had been a long interview, with lots of strange people. Kwanele remembered the sight of Mark's face when he returned to the room and saw all the people. He frowned into his cup; it had been the hardest on him. He still felt sick. It had taken Sarah every ounce of effort just to keep Kwanele from either jumping out the window or passing out with stress. At Sarah's insistence, all parties agreed that it would be in Kwanele's best interest to allow him to remain in the care of the bush camp for the time being. Kwanele had almost cried with relief. He'd been through enough. He needed to feel safe. The group of professionals all trailed out to their cars, leaving the police officer at the rear, who paused on the porch to speak with Mark and Sarah in private. It was then that Martha had brought Kwanele into the kitchen to fix him a drink and the boy overheard the adult conversation at the door.

"Do I know you both?" The police officer narrowed his eyes at Mark and Sarah, crinkles forming on his weather-beaten skin. Mark rubbed the back of his neck, and looked at Sarah.

"I don't know." He shrugged. The officer squinted and rubbed the back of his neck.

"Hmm, okay. I just thought you both looked familiar, that's all. Are you sure it's not going to be a bother watching the boy?"

Sarah shook her head. "If you please, Officer, he is frightened of everyone. We have worked hard to get him to trust us. We don't live here, but we are more than willing to look after him while we're here and...also at home later on if needed." Mark shot her a look, the muscles in his face tight. Kwanele's heart dropped at his expression.

The officer narrowed his eyes at them. Martha's hands grasped Kwanele's shoulders and she steered past him and approached the group at the door.

"He can live here at the bush camp. When Mark and Sarah return home, he can stay here with us." Her expression was hooded as she regarded Sarah. Kwanele turned away, awkward.

There was a long pause and the officer appeared to be in thought. Sarah shuffled from one foot to the other.

She opened her mouth to speak, but he held up a finger as the radio on his belt crackled to life. Turning away, he spoke to into the mouthpiece. His conversation was easy enough to overhear, and Kwanele turned back to listen with interest. He finished the conversation and turned back to Mark and Sarah.

"That's fine." He looked through the adults to nod at Kwanele, and then focused back on the others in turn. "We'll review it again in a few weeks' time." Nodding his thanks, the officer departed. Mark turned to Sarah

"We can't get too attached." He held her gaze. "We just lied to a police officer. Isn't that an offense? I remember him. He helped with the Brennan investigation! We're meant to be in Polokwane. If he figures it out, we'll be raked over the coals by Naiker!" Sarah lifted her chin, her face pulling as she glanced at Kwanele before she left the room. She tossed a look over her shoulder at Mark.

"You didn't lie; you just omitted the truth, Mark."

"Same thing!" Mark mumbled through gritted teeth. They all trailed into the room.

"I said I didn't want to talk to them." Kwanele glowered, as he sat and cradled the hot drink Martha had given him.

"It's over now, Kwanele. You can relax." Mark's tone was flat as he collapsed into a soft couch. "Now, drink up…then we'll go to the village."

Sarah shot Mark a cranky look, to which he shrugged. "What? We need to get going."

"You did so well, Kwanele. All those people." Sarah sat next to the boy and wrapped her arm around his shoulder. He stiffened under her touch and she removed her arm. Jacob sat opposite the pair and looked squarely into the Zulu boy's eyes, his dark brown eyes penetrating from under his thick brow.

"It had to be done, son, and it may have to happen again. For now, though, they said that you can stay with us." Kwanele's eyes shot around the adults in the room.

"They were going to take me away?"

"We don't know. Maybe…it may still happen yet." Jacob continued to look at the boy, his eyes full of compassion and wisdom. Kwanele held his gaze.

"Will you let them?"

Jacob broke his gaze, cleared his throat, and looked around at the others.

"We have to pray about what will happen. It may not be up to us. We need to think about what's best for you." He frowned.

"That means yes." Kwanele stared them all down in turn.

Anguish filled Sarah's heart. "We don't want you to go, Kwanele." The boy gazed up at her, and then at Mark, who lowered his eyes to the floor. Kwanele drained his mug of hot chocolate.

"Are you sure you want me to come and see the elephants?" He looked at Mark and Sarah in turn. Mark sighed. He looked impatient as he stood up in front of the boy.

"Of course we want you to come. Now come on, let's put your cup away and get going." He took the mug from the boy and disappeared into the kitchen. Kwanele turned to Sarah, and she smiled. "Come on. Let's go."

The drive out to Lebowa village was quiet. Everybody was still shaken from the interview and the whirlwind of emotions that followed. Once the Cruiser pulled up at the Sotho village, everyone sat in silence and watched the small but busy life of Lebowa pass by. Women carried baskets of crafts to sell at the markets to the tourists. Children ran past laughing gleefully, with skinny dogs that bounded alongside, tongues hanging from their mouths. They smiled as a young girl produced a clump of rags that had been wound into a tight makeshift ball, bound with knots. She tossed the ball over the head of a brindle-colored dog and cheered with joy as the dog went into a frenzy skittering after it. Mark opened his door. A rush of warm air whooshed into the air-conditioned vehicle. He stepped out and trotted up to Koto and Lerato's home, rapping his knuckles on the door. Sarah and Kwanele left the Cruiser and stepped up behind him.

"You'll love these people, Kwanele." Sarah placed her hand on his shoulder. "They have two children. Moses and Kagisoy, who are about your age. They would love to play with you." Mark rapped on the door again, harder this time. His eager smile faded to confusion as he peered into one of the nearby windows. He wiped away the buildup of dirt from the glass. Brushing his hands together, he peered through again. Nothing. The curtains were drawn. Sarah continued to speak to Kwanele in quieter tones. "We haven't seen them for about three years or more. Not since we moved the elephants. Koto is one of Mark's closest friends."

Mark checked another set of windows. He cupped his hands

around his eyes to block out the glare as he peered inside the dirt-streaked glass. He stepped down again, wiping his dirty hands on his jeans.

"Sarah...they're not home. Maybe they're in town." Mark peered in the first window again. By this stage, several people had gathered to observe them. A couple of women murmured to one another and then walked off in a hurry. Mark, Sarah, and Kwanele were about to the turn back to the Cruiser when Sarah felt a tap on her shoulder. She spun and her eyes lit up as she saw Kgomotso. This was the man who used to work at the bush camp before he moved back to the village to look after his aging cousin, Israel. He was another of their longtime friends.

A brilliant white smile lit up his dark face as he hugged them warmly in turn.

"It's been too long!" He grinned. "You must come. Israel will be much happy!" Mark noted how his stunted English had gotten worse since he'd been away from the bush camp. Reluctant, he followed, casting a final look behind at Koto and Lerato's home. Pain clouded his eyes. What had happened to them?

"Motso!" Mark caught up to the tall Sotho man at a jog and his hand swept back toward the humble home. "Are they out? Koto and his family?"

Kgomotso rocked to a stop, looked at the home, then back at the Afrikaner man, a strange sadness in his eyes. It was more than Mark could bear. "What happened, Motsu?"

"They left," the Sotho said and turned to leave again. Mark grasped his shoulder, turning him back around.

"Whoah! They left? What do you mean, left? When? Why?"

Kgomotso paused again and looked at the ground. "I do not know. Koto say...no money. No work, no money. They left." He shook his head sadly. Sarah frowned.

"But they have nowhere else they could have gone. Do they have family somewhere else? Maybe they just got more work elsewhere." She looked up at Mark to verify.

"Maybe." Mark stuck his hands in his pockets and followed them toward Israel's place. Perhaps Israel would have more answers. Israel had once been a great Sotho shaman, or witch doctor. Now he was a man of God. He changed his name to Israel and ran a small rondavel church in Lebowa. People respected him, and many people had come to know Jesus because of him. Even in his old age now, Israel was a man full of the Lord's wisdom.

Kgomotso threw open the door to the rondavel, calling out in English. "Israel! Come see who is here!" Mark and Sarah peered into the dark home. Soon enough, Israel limped out into the open front door, his eyes wide with excitement as he recognized his guests.

"Sarah! Mark! Come in, come in! And who have we here?" He leaned down on his walking stick and examined the boy. "Zulu, eh? *Ngiyakwemukela! Unjani?*" Kwanele's eyes lit up at the Zulu welcome.

"*Ngikhona, ngiyabonga!*" he replied with respect. Mark and Sarah exchanged looks, not understanding the exchange.

"What is your name, boy?" Israel went on, his voice croaky with fatigue.

Kwanele looked back at Sarah before he stepped forward.

"Kwanele."

Israel nodded in thought and looked at the others.

"Well, come in. My guests do not stand outside." They all entered, and regarded the home with mild interest. His home was simple, but elegant. A large artwork hung on the main wall depicting the Lion of Judah. He sat majestically, paws crossed over and wearing a crown of thorns over his large mane. Mounted on another wall was a large shiny Kudu horn. Sarah blinked in surprise.

Israel followed her gaze and frowned in deliberation. "Sarah." She turned to regard the man, her brow lifted in query. "What has happened to you, Sarah?" She paused, unsure what he meant. His gaze penetrated into her soul, and in an instant she realized that she couldn't hide from this man. He could see everything. He had seen into the spirit realm when she was protected by angels in the past, and he could see something was amiss now. It was the power of God within him. "You do not glow as you used to." He tilted his head, his eyes never leaving her face. "You have not spent time in His presence...have you?"

Sarah sighed and sat heavily on an old, weathered couch. She was close to tears. The Holy Spirit was tweaking at her heart, and it filled her with regret. Israel was right.

"Please, Israel." Mark cut in, directing the old man's scrutiny away from Sarah. "We came to see if you wanted to journey with us to check the elephant herd over the border. You helped us so much in the past, and we thought it would be an honor to invite you to come see them with us. Of course, we had wanted others to join us, too." His voice trailed off as he looked toward the doorway. Israel rubbed his stubbly old chin. He appeared to regard the proposal, not taking his eyes from Sarah.

"The weight of this world sits heavy on you both. Why? It is not yours to bear." He tore his eyes from Sarah and regarded Mark.

"Pardon?" Mark looked uncomfortable. Israel cleared his throat and sat down, indicating for everyone to join him.

"There is more to this than the herd over the horizon." Eyes wide, Kwanele sat meekly beside Mark and Sarah. The boy shrank into the creases of the old couch.

"I am old." Israel sat back, deep into the couch, pushing his back into the heavy blankets that covered the fabric. He examined them all in turn. "It is so easy, in this world, to forget who gave you what you have. To forget what He paid for."

Sarah leaned forward in earnest. "We haven't forgotten, Israel. It was only by God and His Son, Jesus, that we did what we did. It was by His supernatural protection that we survived it."

Israel smiled knowingly, compassion in his eyes. "But you have forgotten, Sarah...and you, too, Mark. Why do you think He would protect you any less now?"

"But we are not afraid to go over the border, Israel." Mark looked at his wife, then back to the others.

"I am talking about more than that. You fear being caught, hunted down." His eyes flicked to the boy, and then back to Mark. "Mark...you live by your own strength, not God's."

Mark's face dropped. "That's what Jacob and Martha said, too..." He lifted his eyes to meet Israel's. "But I am dealing with that. I am handing it over to God, daily."

"And so you must Mark. Daily! It is still written on your face...it is not yet done."

One of Kwanele's eyes was visible as he attempted to cloak his presence behind Mark. Israel regarded him strangely.

"What is your story, Kwanele?" The boy slunk deeper into the couch.

"We found him in the Kruger. His guardian was murdered by poachers and they left him for dead." Sarah leaned over Mark and squeezed the boy's hand.

"It's okay, Kwanele. This man won't hurt you. Why are you so afraid?"

Cautious, he peeped out from the back of the soft couch.

"It's true...sir." The boy's voice was barely above a murmur. Israel turned to look long and hard at Kgomotso. It was as though they communicated without words. Finally, Israel spoke.

"I will not go with you this time. This is a journey you must take on your own. But beware! You must find your reliance"—he looked at Mark—"and your strength from God alone."

Mark and Sarah nodded in union before Israel continued on. "Mark and Sarah. It is time to grow up in your spiritual walk with God. You cannot keep living on milk. It is time to move on to solid food. Meat. You must learn how to fight."

"We will." Sarah stood and ushered Kwanele.

"You didn't hear me, Sarah." Israel's voice rose and she blinked with surprise.

"Fight what?" Mark stared at Israel, his interest piqued. "Poachers?" The old Sotho man's face stretched into a genuine toothy grin, revealing rows of jagged teeth and gaping gums. He spoke to Mark as if to a child.

"You need to read the Word of God more than you do, Mark van der Merwe. You cannot live on yesterday's manna."

Mark was taken aback at the abruptness of his words. Sarah grasped his arm. "Thank you, Israel." She gave him a genuine smile. "We really must be going." The others stood and they all headed for the doorway.

"Wait! I need to know about Koto and his family." Mark stopped in his tracks. Israel grimaced as if remembering a painful event.

"I am tired. Don't forget what I told you." He turned to head back into the old home, but stopped, turning once more. "Oh…and Mark?" Mark regarded him, a frown of frustration apparent in his eyes.

"Teach the boy the Way." Israel jutted his chin out. His ancient eyes bore into Mark's with an unspoken challenge. Mark looked toward Kwanele, who was now heading away with Sarah, his brows raised in confusion. As if on cue, Kwanele peered over his shoulder toward Mark and Israel, the perfect picture of innocence etched in his small face. "The way…" Mark murmured. Kwanele turned back to Sarah and jogged to catch up with her. Mark shook his head and turned toward the old man. He stepped close.

"Please. I need to know what happened to them. To Koto and his family!" His brows knitted together with worry. Israel regarded him for a long moment.

"I cannot say, Mark, but I pray that you will find a way." With that, the old man turned and walked back into his home. Kgomotso nodded at Mark, then followed his cousin back into the rondavel. Mark stood alone, emptiness in his stomach as the dust swirled about his jeans.

CHAPTER NINE

The familiar hum of the Cruiser engine kept them company as they headed toward the Mozambique border the next day. After a restless night back at the bush camp pondering all that Israel had said to them, neither Mark nor Sarah were in the mood to talk. Kwanele sat quiet in the backseat, observing the scenery as it drifted past. Thick mopane dominated most the landscape with its hidden gems of wildlife. Prides of lions lazily dozed under the acacia trees. Elegant giraffes meandered toward a watering hole. But most of all, Kwanele loved to spot the small herds that dotted the lands. Herds of wildebeests, zebra, gazelle, sometimes intermingled with each other. Mark glanced in his rearview mirror and smirked at the way the boy was fixated onto the glass. A storm could be seen in the distance, unusual for the start of the dry season. Soon, many of the water holes would be dry and the herds would have to move on to greener pastures for the cooler months.

"Look!" Kwanele's shrill voice pierced the hum of the engine. Sarah turned in her seat to follow his direction out toward their left. Three cheetahs stood regally on a knobby crest, on guard as the vehicle passed by. "Just like Jacques." He laughed with delight.

"You don't want to cuddle those ones, though." Mark chuckled. The cats watched, tails flicking in agitation. A small springbok strayed a little from its herd, and one of the cheetahs left the other two, its attention now engaged elsewhere. Within seconds, the scene seemed to ebb away from Kwanele's vision as the Cruiser continued on its journey down the dirt track toward the border.

"Fastest land animal alive. If you ever get to see a hunt, it's pretty spectacular." Mark slipped back into his trail guide mode. Kwanele looked with regret over the backseat and out the rear window. A silent flash of lightning lit up the dark clouds on the horizon before them. It was in stark contrast to the sun that beat down on them from above. Sarah eyed Mark and bit her lower lip.

"It is darker out there, isn't it? Don't worry. We'll be there soon...look! There's the east gate now."

Soon enough, they were stopped at the border gates. The guard stepped out from the small shed to check their clearance papers. "Not good weather for sightseeing," the man observed. Mark nodded, took back his paperwork, and drove through. It didn't take long before he pulled the Cruiser into one of the empty spaces at the park warden's rondavel. Killing the motor, the three of them stepped out into the cooling air.

"Wow. That looks like one fierce storm on its way." Sarah wrapped her arms about herself as she shut the Cruiser door. A flurry of dirt eddied its way around their legs as they moved toward the building. Low rumbles in the distance answered Sarah's comment as they made their way up to the door. It opened just as Mark was about to knock, and there stood the warden, a broad smile on his face.

"My name is Abasi. I am the new management here. I've heard so much about you and what you did to save the D-12 herd. Amazing work!" The man extended his hand to Sarah and Mark. "And this little fellow...welcome." Abasi released Mark's hand and shook Kwanele's slender hand firmly.

"What happened to Thomas de Jager?" Sarah raised a brow as she saw strain cross his face. "He was here with his family several years ago when we moved D-12." She tried to rub the goose bumps from her arms, but to no avail.

"Ahh! Yes, yes. The de Jagers. They, er...had a transfer. Moved on. Like I said. I am new, but I trust that we'll be able to work together as well if not better than you did with the last people. Follow me. I'll take you to see the elephants." He looked toward the storm, doubt crossing his eyes. "We'd better get a move on, though." Mark and Sarah were quick to nod their agreement as they jumped back into the Cruiser. Abasi jumped into a government bakkie with the Mozambique National Park logo painted on the side.

The convoy set off down a track, which led to a thicket of dense foliage where elephant damage was clearly evident. When they weren't at the water holes, or enjoying dust showers, elephants liked to meander through the foliage picking the choice greenery that was to be found at their leisure. When doing so, elephants were known for being destructive, which left an obvious trail for everyone to follow. The vehicles pulled up at the edge of the foliage. "We'll have to continue on foot from here." Abasi approached the Cruiser as they all stepped out and gazed into the thick underbrush. In the distance, there was commotion. Mark and Sarah grinned at one another and set off in the direction of the sound. Kwanele trailed behind them all, nervous as he drank in his surroundings. He glanced at the trees above and wondered if there were animals in here that would attack from above. The sound of the wind began to whistle through the foliage. Flickers of lightning lit up the broad leaves of the foliage as Kwanele scuttled to catch up and walk close to the adults. Abasi glanced behind at the boy. Soon enough, they saw the elephants, pulling down branches and snapping them with their great trunks. Then they pulled other branches down from higher up with their strong trunks and pushed the leaves into their mouths. The sound of loud chewing echoed in the clearing. Some of the herd had moved into a quiet bunch, their rumps turned toward the storm in preparation to weather it out. The company all hid behind a nearby shrub and watched in hushed quiet until Sarah broke from the group and pushed forward through the underbrush toward the elephants. The warden grabbed her by the arm.

"You mustn't," he hissed. "They are wild animals." Sarah pulled her arm away and glared at the man.

"It's okay," Mark whispered, putting his hand up to stop Abasi. "She knows to be careful. She knows this herd and they know her."

Abasi shook his head, unconvinced.

Before they could stop her, Sarah had already slipped over to the herd. In clear view of them now, several of the younger ones retreated deeper in the underbrush, while some of the older elephants stood inspecting her. Sarah frowned as she turned back to the others.

"This is D-12, isn't it?" She turned to check again. When she returned her silent gaze to the warden, he just nodded from his hiding spot.

"Where's Maggie?" Pain crossed Sarah's face. Abasi shook his head with confusion, stepping out from the foliage.

"Who?"

"The large matriarch elephant. She was massive. A great tusker!" Mark explained, keeping a wary eye on his wife. Recognition appeared to strike the young warden.

"Oh yes. I know that one." His gaze fell.

"What?" Sarah returned to the group, a frown at the warden's expression. "Unfortunately, she has passed on."

"What? She died?"

The warden nodded.

"Take me to her!" Sarah choked up.

"You want to see her?" He blinked. Sarah nodded, her face set.

"I'm not sure it would be a good idea to see..."

"I want to see her." Sarah repeated firmly. Abasi regarded her for a moment, seeming to fight within himself. Finally he nodded.

"It's not far from here. We can get there before this storm hits." Abasi looked at the dark sky. They trudged through the undergrowth, down another track that led away from the vehicles, until they came onto a very large clearing. Only a few spindly dried-up bits of grass covered the dusty ground. Mounds of dirt dotted the area. As Mark stepped onto one of the mounds, he realized the mounds covered over the large bones of deceased elephants. Years of eddying wind had blown through this spot, burying what remains were left with years of dirt. After a quick survey, they recognized an elephant's graveyard. Beasts of intelligence, the dying preferred to take themselves to a common spot where other elephants had previously died, thus forming a remarkable natural tradition among their kind. Kwanele snorted and held his nose as he gazed over at the monstrous carcass of a large female elephant. The cool wind front came from the storm, doing nothing to deter the flies, which still clung to what was left of the great beast. Sarah pushed back the loose strands of hair that blew into her face as she approached the fallen beast.

"Why were her tusks removed?" She turned to Abasi, hurt in her eyes. Hands on her hips, she circled the carcass, her body rigid. Sarah glanced up and locked eyes with Mark.

"Surely no one knows where this place is. It's protected, so why take her tusks?" Sarah glared at Abasi. Shifting uncomfortably, the warden explained.

"No...nowhere is safe, miss."

Kwanele looked at the man as he watched Mark and Sarah examine the carcass. A muscle in Abasi's jaw twitched as his narrowed eyes turned from the couple to the boy. Kwanele caught his odd expression and looked away. He stepped up next to Mark and Sarah. A chill swept over his body as the wind picked up speed, howling through the mopane.

"Can we go now?" he whimpered at Mark's side. Sarah was unresponsive as Mark put his hand about her waist and wheeled her back toward the track. A rumble caused them to pick up their pace. Their long legs cleared the ground in no time, leaving Kwanele behind with Abasi. As the couple walked ahead, Abasi suddenly closed the gap and grasped Kwanele by the arm. The boy stumbled and cried out in shock. Abasi's stare was cold as he gazed into the boy's eyes. Fear rose up in Kwanele's throat, threatening to choke him, but when he opened his mouth, he couldn't make a sound. Mark and Sarah unexpectedly turned in unison to witness the odd scene. Seeing their confused expression, Abasi broke into a broad smile toward the boy, lifted him gently back to his feet, and then shrugged at the couple. Turning back to the boy, he started to brush the dirt off his back.

"You alright, little man? Lucky I caught you. You have to watch for holes out here or you'll trip." He dusted the boy off down his back. Kwanele lurched forward to free himself from the man's touch, but Abasi tightened his grip on the boy's arm. Mark shrugged and continued to guide Sarah down the track. When their backs were once again turned, Abasi glared into the boy's face, his grip tight on Kwanele's arm. The man's thick, dark brows shot up in question, waiting. When Kwanele blinked, the man jutted his head, demanding an answer from the boy. Eyes growing wide with fear, Kwanele was quick to nod, unsure of what else the man wanted. Abasi released his strong grip on the frightened boy's arm, his fingers leaving marks for a moment. Straightening up, he walked past the boy as if nothing had happened.

"That storm is nearly upon us. Come! Back at the bunker I'll put on the kettle. It is most unusual to get storms this time of the year, let alone this time of the day. But it is okay. We can eat some lunch while the storm is blowing over and come back out after. What do you say?"

Sarah looked back at the warden, her features tight. They returned to the vehicles just as the first large drops of rain began to splat their way upon the dry ground.

"Hey, boy. Did you want to go for a ride in a park warden's bakkie?" Abasi called out in a friendly tone toward Kwanele. The boy hesitated, looking at Mark and Sarah, a plea for help in his eyes.

"If I may, Kwanele is really shy. I don't know if he'd like that terribly much," Sarah offered. The boy's shoulders dropped with relief and he was quick to slip into the safety of the Cruiser. His relief was cut short when he saw the look the warden flashed him as he peered out the back window.

"See you back there," Mark called as their engine started.

"What was all that about?" Sarah leaned toward Mark as they followed the park vehicle back to the bunker rondavel. Mark shrugged as he adjusted the rearview mirror, looking at Kwanele. Something unusual had passed between the two, but he just couldn't work out what, or why.

Tom Dawson narrowed his icy blue eyes.

"You're sure it's them?" He adjusted the receiver in his hand irritably.

"Yes, sir. The same girl and her husband."

"What about the kid? Is he with them?" There was a pause on the other end of the phone. "Well?" Tom snapped.

"Yes, yes. He is here."

"Good."

There was a pause and then Tom heard a slight cough. He leaned forward onto his desk.

"What is it? Come on, out with it." There was another pause.

"The boy, sir. I don't know if he will cooperate."

Tom picked up his ivory-handled pen and spun it thoughtfully in his long fingers. He leaned back in his leather office chair.

"Don't you worry about that. He'll cooperate. He'll quack when faced with it. He's just a whelp."

"Do you want me to take care of it here, now?"

"No, your job was to let me know if they showed. I have experts I need to send in. These people are not as easy as you'd expect. You need to be set up for it."

"I could easily..."

"No, Abasi! Don't let them suspect anything. Just...find out what they are up to."

"Right, sir."

"Keep in touch." Tom clicked the receiver down and looked around. How dare Abasi question him. Nobody ever questioned him. He pressed a button on his intercom.

"You may come back in now, Suzie."

His personal assistant soon entered the large office. "Would you like your tea now, sir?"

"Thanks. Oh, and would you file these for me, please?" Tom passed the young woman a stack of paperwork as she smiled and walked from the room. His mask dropped as soon as she closed the door behind her. He stood and wandered over to the window. Hands clasped behind his back, he surveyed the view from the high rise. Why on earth were they in Mozambique? What was Sarah up to now? Did she know anything that could incriminate him? He rubbed his temples and returned to his desk. It was time to deal with his regular work, but perhaps he could kill two birds with one stone. Tom began to type out an e-mail addressed to the chief of police. He outlined his demand that they deal with the new threat to the National Parks safety. Freedom Fighters, as they aptly named themselves, were taking the law into their own hands by murdering poachers caught in the act. As a member of staff in parliament, one of Tom

Dawson's chief jobs was to address problems such as this within the national parks. Poaching was on the increase, but so also was the new threat of these murderers. It was this type of radical behavior that Sarah van der Merwe was responsible for starting. All when she did something different to save the elephants and blew open a whole poaching operation...Tom's poaching operation. While appearing to keep the parks safe from the top, Tom's personal priority was to protect his own assets and identity while running one of the country's biggest underground smuggling rings. This secret ran conveniently parallel to his work in parliament. Tom smiled to himself as he hit SEND on the e-mail. Soon Sarah and Mark van der Merwe would be out of the picture, and this would also send a powerful message to any freedom fighters. New and radical ideas to protect wildlife in South Africa would not be tolerated by the government...or the smuggling rings. Tom sniggered. The government. They were blind. The government was pro-wildlife and protecting their heritage. However, Tom knew if he were ever discovered, it would be the end of him. Opening his desk drawer and lifting a compartment, Tom checked that his fake passport and identification were still there and in order. If things went wrong, he would need to withdraw as much cash as he could and flee the country. He sighed and leaned forward to pinch the bridge of his nose. A headache threatened to return. He slid open his desk and popped two painkillers into his hand. Grabbing his glass of water, he threw his head back, taking the tablets.

CHAPTER
TEN

Kwanele glanced around the bunker-house as they entered. It was typical of the kind of office that he expected a park warden to work in. Posters lined the walls depicting maps of the parks, photographs, and details about each species of mammal, bird, reptile, and plant in the park. Computers sat on the desks, their screens already open on weather forecasts and radar maps. A doorway led into a larger room that housed a kitchen area, gun cabinet in the corner, with radios and other two-way devices. A large, wooden kitchen table and chairs sat in the center of the room. Abasi ushered Mark, Sarah, and Kwanele into the room and offered them a hot drink.

"If you please..." Mark held up his hand. "I think we might just head back. We were expected back before nightfall and—"

"But I thought you would stay for lunch, and then we could go back out and view the herd properly when the storm has blown over." A shadow crossed Abasi's eyes. "It's no trouble at all. I was told that if you ever came that I had to give you my best hospitality."

Sarah's smile was apologetic. "It's not that at all. We'd love to stay longer. It's just—" She sat at one of the chairs, looking washed out. Kwanele jumped as a loud clap of thunder rocked the bunker-house. The rain began to fall heavy upon the tin roof. Mark moved behind his wife in a flash, his hands on her shoulders.

"I think we may come back at a better time. This has been hard on my wife. That elephant at the graveyard. She meant a lot to Sarah." Kwanele watched as Sarah gazed up into Mark's strong face. A tear slipped from her eye and ran down her cheek. She looked over at the warden and wiped at her face.

"At least wait the storm out." Abasi took off his hat, giving it a shake, and hung it on the hook near the cabinets. He grabbed a couple of bottles of water from the fridge and offered one to his visitors. Sarah nodded and the bottle was tossed her way. Flopping down onto one of the chairs in the corner, Abasi ushered for them to sit as he cracked the seal on his water.

"So"—he took a long swig—"what brings you this way again? Have you been asked to move more herds over this way?"

Mark sat next to Sarah. Kwanele was awkward as he backed in the corner and stood watching.

"Not really..."

"I'll tell you what. The biggest problem at the moment is rhinoceros." Abasi took another swig from his water. "The numbers are low over here, too. If you could get some of those beasts across the border, it would help us out real nice."

Sarah looked puzzled.

"*Ja*," Abasi continued, his focus shifted to the mammal's poster on the wall. "It's safer over here in Mozambique. Not as many poachers this side."

"Right." Mark sounded bored to Kwanele, who shuffled with unease. He wanted to leave this place, right now, but he was powerless to say. He caught Mark's eye, trying to convey his discomfort. Mark blinked at him, then made a point to look at his watch.

"I think we might make tracks...before this storm softens the road too much." Kwanele let out his breath as he saw Mark flick his head in the direction of the storm outside. Abasi's expression tightened. Sarah stood and thanked the warden for his hospitality before she headed for the front foyer after Mark. Kwanele was quick to join them.

"Well, come back anytime." Abasi's face showed disappointment. "You are more than welcome." He shook Mark and Sarah's hands again before the three visitors dashed into the rain toward the Cruiser. Glancing over his shoulder, Kwanele saw Abasi wave to them from the protection of the patio. They shut themselves into the Cruiser and looked in dismay at how wet the short trip had made them. Rain hit the front windscreen in large sheets as Mark turned the wipers onto full strength. Headlights and de-mister turned on, Mark started the engine and with care, headed down the dirt track toward the border gate.

"Are you okay?" He glanced over at Sarah, who was rigid in the seat beside him. "I know we should have waited out that storm, but something felt wrong." She nodded as she fussed with her wet hair. Kwanele shuddered, and then looked up as he saw Sarah turn to him.

"How about you? Are you alright?"

Kwanele turned away from her and looked out the window.

"That wasn't what we thought it would be, Kwanele. I'm sorry. It was strange." He could hear the apology in her voice, but it did nothing to calm his fear. He sensed eyes on him and flicked a look up and away again. Mark was watching him through the rear vision mirror. He tried to concentrate on the view out the window. Rivulets of heavy rain had ruined that for him, too. He focused on the colors within the water.

"You're safe, Kwanele. You know that, right?" Pain reefed at his heart, and Kwanele turned to regard Mark's eyes in the mirror.

"Did you recognize that man?" Mark's brows lowered. Kwanele's eyes darted back to the window. In dismay, he tried to block out the emptiness that threatened to engulf him. They drove in silence until they went back through the gates into Kruger National Park. Kwanele sank into his seat. He could see Mark and Sarah throw each other worried glances. The road was slippery. Soon enough, though, it got easier as the rain eased up and the road went from slippery to sticky, then back to dusty. The clouds behind them rumbled as they headed from the storm. The afternoon sky overhead was still overcast as they headed back toward the bush camp and their bellies began to rumble with hunger from a missed lunch.

"Look!" Sarah squinted into the sky ahead.

"Vultures?" Mark confirmed. "But there weren't any carcasses on the way out this morning." Sarah grimaced.

"It's an elephant," Mark remarked as they got closer. "It's big." Sarah shook her head. Kwanele was sick to his stomach.

"It may not be poachers, Sarah, just relax. It could be anything."

Several hyenas skulked away as the Cruiser pulled up beside the beast.

"Okay, I'm sorry. You're right. Looks like a healthy adolescent male. The rest of the herd must have bailed. Look. Tire tracks." Mark and Sarah stepped out of the vehicle. Kwanele sat up and peered out the window as silence enveloped the Cruiser. He could see tears coming from Sarah as she circled the elephant, her hand covering her mouth. Kwanele was quiet as he slipped from the vehicle and leaned against the door. The top half of the young elephant's entire face cavity had been dug out to unearth the ivory that lay deep within. Mark shook and hung his head with grief. His face was flushed red with fury. Kwanele watched Sarah circling the animal, the color draining from her face. "How could someone do something so—" she cried out in anguish. "Mark. Mark, he's still alive!"

"What?" Mark's face twisted as the great beast groaned and heaved. It rolled over onto its side and the tranquilizer darts in its flank became exposed. Desperate tears gushed from Sarah as she ran and tugged at his arm, her voice shrill. "What do we do? Mark...do something! Help him! Please!"

Mark took off at a run to the back to the Cruiser, yanked open the boot, and lifted a wooden box from under the floor mats. He took out his Winchester rifle, loaded it quickly, and stepped up to the beast. Kwanele's eyes were wide as he shrank against the Cruiser. Sarah looked at Mark in horror.

"I have to, Sarah! He's almost dead! I have to put him down."

Sarah swept past Kwanele toward the back of the Cruiser, weeping.

Bang!

The blast ricocheted off the Cruiser. It was clean and swift into the forehead of the beast. Kwanele stood, his face wrenched in shock. Mark stepped back and lowered the rifle. He turned to regard the boy as smoke drifted in curly tendrils from the barrel.

"Not good, is it?" Mark stared at Kwanele, who shook his head. His stomach heaved and he thought he might vomit. He felt the same as when he was near the rhinoceros carcass near Olifants River. The fire in Mark's eyes drew his attention back.

"They're not nice people, Kwanele. This is what they do. They will use you and then spit you out. Don't ever get involved with them." The whites of Kwanele's eyes grew wide. Mark spat on the ground. "Well, you're safe enough now, anyway." Sniffing and wiping his mouth, Mark strode back to the Cruiser. Kwanele heard him murmur soft words to Sarah and heard the clunks as he stored the weapon again in the trunk. He gagged at the smell, a rough reminder of the warning he'd been given when last he smelt such as this. The emptiness had returned with more intensity as he slipped back into the car. Kwanele's mouth was dry as he fumbled with the seat belt. What was he going to do? He didn't want harm to come to these people, nor did he want to get killed. The trunk was still open and Kwanele could hear the couple as they stood at the back. He turned and peeped over the back of the seat. Sarah was crying and Mark was holding her.

"What can we do?" She looked at her husband.

"We can pray," Mark offered.

Sarah buried her tear-streaked face into Mark's chest and wrapped her arms around him. Kwanele felt intrusive as he saw Mark bury his chin into her soft locks of dark hair, murmuring something. He then stepped back, tilted her chin up, and kissed her. Heat rushed into Kwanele's face and he turned away.

Jacques pushed his warm muzzle into Kwanele's hand before he flopped over onto his side at the boy's feet. Kwanele giggled and bent to scratch the cheetah behind the ears where he liked it. "You are my friend." He sighed and sat cross-legged, edging close to pet the spotty beast around the soft fur of his neck. Jacques yawned and stretched out, batting at a stone with his large paws. His thick black claws were dull and worn down. Kwanele reached out and touched one, running his thumb over the smooth edges. They weren't sharp as he'd expected.

"You know..." A voice startled Kwanele, and he peered up. Mark leaned on the side of the building.

"...the cheetah is the only cat that can't retract its claws." He folded his arms across his chest. Kwanele's expression was blank. "Most cats retract their claws...they go into the paws when they don't need them," Mark explained as he walked over and squatted next to the boy and the cheetah. Jacques sat up and regarded the man with his somber eyes. Smiling, Mark settled into the shade with the pair. He leaned against the wall and stretched out one leg. "You still don't like me much, do you?" He chuckled. Kwanele shrugged and went back to stroking Jacques.

"Kwanele, I want to help you. I know you're scared about those people. When I found you—" He hesitated. "You said they wanted to shoot you." Kwanele glared at Mark, fear rising within. He had forgotten he said that. Mark shuffled closer. "Did you do something that made them chase you? Is that why you didn't want to talk to the police? Did they threaten you after you saw something?"

Kwanele's shoulders stiffened. Why was Mark here? Why was he quizzing him? Kwanele sucked in his breath as Mark moved closer to the pair. He touched Kwanele on the shoulder. Kwanele wanted to run, but fear kept him paralyzed.

"Hey. It's okay. You don't have to talk about it. I just want you to see that I'm on your side. Okay? We—" Mark stopped himself, and Kwanele couldn't help but wonder what he was about to say. He seemed genuine. Mark removed his hand and Kwanele relaxed a bit. They sat in silence, watching Jacques sleep flat-out. His flank heaved steadily as he breathed. "You're so much braver around him now. He likes you." Mark smiled.

Without reason, Kwanele experienced a rush of relief and decided in an instant to speak up.

"What is the Way?"

Mark blinked and turned to regard the boy, his face startled.

"Huh? What?"

Kwanele took a deep breath. "When we went to Lebowa. The man told you to teach me the Way." Mark raised a brow.

"You heard that, did you?" The man shifted to look squarely into Kwanele's face. "Well, I need to know something, Kwanele. If you want to learn about it, I need you to know that we are on your side. You need to trust us. You need to trust me…can you do that?" Kwanele ran his hand in long, slow strokes down Jacques's back contemplating the offer. Finally he gazed up at Mark. He was torn. It was a big leap of faith to trust in someone who he sensed didn't like him.

"How can I decide if I don't know what it is?"

Mark smirked and rubbed the stubble on his chin. "How do I know *I* can trust you?" Kwanele swallowed hard and waited. A frown flickered across Mark's face.

"Well, you don't. I have to prove myself, don't I? But the Way is a few steps further than you are ready for at the moment. First, you need to know the One."

"The One?" Kwanele tilted his head. Mark cleared his dry throat.

"When we face troubles in this world, there is a God we can turn to and He protects us." Kwanele's shoulders dropped in despair. He'd heard all about gods. They didn't do anything. They were children's fairy tales to keep kids from disobeying their parents. They were for weak people. Kwanele needed something real.

"I heard of gods. They do nothing." Kwanele sighed and went back to stroking Jacques.

"No, Kwanele. You're thinking of false gods. Idols that people chase after that aren't real. I am talking about the one true and real God. He is the only God, that's why He is the One. I'm talking about a God who heals the sick, sets the captives free, who does miracles. He is the One who can save you from those poachers. He is real, Kwan!"

"How do you know?" Kwanele felt an odd stirring in his chest. Mark smiled.

"Because He did it for Sarah when she was rescuing those elephants from the cull here in Kruger a few years ago. I saw things, Kwanele, things that made me believe when I didn't."

"What things?" Jacques was forgotten as Kwanele's full attention focused on Mark. Mark edged closer and went on in a quiet, secretive voice.

"I saw Sarah about to get attacked by a lioness, and an angel stepped in and sent it away. It protected her. She couldn't see it. Only myself and another man saw it. Actually, it was

Kgomotso who saw it! You ask him. It was a miracle."

"What's an angel?" Kwanele leaned forward, his voice just above a whisper.

"It's a creature from another world, from heaven. They are tall and some have big wings…like a bird…and white! They are all brilliant white like the light from the sun!" Kwanele's eyes grew wide.

"And you saw one?" He gasped. Mark nodded.

"It's real, Kwanele. If you call out to God, the real God, He will save you. You need to know one of His names, though. It's Jesus. If you call upon the name of Jesus, you will be saved."

Kwanele stared at Jacques in wonder, his overwhelmed mind spinning as it processed Mark's words. Mark stood with a grunt and his knee creaked. He leaned down and gave Kwanele's shoulder a squeeze.

"Please, I need you to know that I have your back. I am on your side." Mark looked at the boy. For the first time, Kwanele looked up at Mark and smiled.

"I know." Kwanele turned back to Jacques. As soon as Mark walked off, Kwanele stood and dusted himself off. Perturbed, Jacques stretched and got up, too, pushing his head into the boy's hand as they stood side-by-side. Smiling at the cat, Kwanele walked off, Jacques following close on his heels.

CHAPTER
ELEVEN

Sarah squinted at Jacob and Martha. "Are you sure you don't mind us staying longer?"

Martha rushed over and grabbed both her hands. "Honey, you are family. You stay as long as you want to." Jacob smiled and nodded his agreement to the statement. "We know how much this means to you."

"So, how did it go with your phone call to the parks board?" Martha looked at Jacob, before regarding Sarah.

"Okay, I think. They are really happy that I'm back on board and wanting to help. It's just that, I don't really know what I can do now."

"If I might make a suggestion, Sarah," Jacob ventured. She looked at him in question. "The first thing I would suggest is that you go and have quiet time with God and pray about what to do. It's dangerous to run like a bull at a gate with no backing from God. Here." He pressed one of their spare Bibles into her hands. "I know you didn't bring your own."

Sarah took the Bible, flushing red as she ran her hands over the worn leather. Jacob regarded her for a moment before she murmured her thanks. "Oh, I have an idea." Martha disappeared into the next room and return with a saddlebag. She took the Bible from Sarah, placed it snugly into the pouch, and went to retrieve a notebook and pen. Sarah watched her prepare the quiet-time pack with mild amusement before she understood the relevance of the saddlebag. They wanted her to ride again? "I'm sorry...I don't know..." Sarah hesitated and drew her hand away from the bag. Martha went and took Sarah's dusty Akubra hat off the hook on the wall. It had been there, untouched, since Sarah and Mark had fled to the city.

After dusting it off, Martha handed it to Sarah.

"Buster needs to get out. He's too fat," Jacob stated, hiding his smirk as he hobbled from the room. He soon returned, and handed her a rifle. "Be safe."

Sarah nodded and took the weapon, cradling it in her arms. The weight of the weapon brought back memories. Sweat began to leach its way onto her skin. They were forcing her to face the past again.

Martha grinned and left. Taking a deep breath, Sarah eyed the items in her arms. She had avoided horses too long. Maybe she could just go and check it out. Ducking back into the guest room, Sarah dug around in their luggage and pulled out her riding boots. She slipped them on and made her way out to the horse kraals, saddlebag tucked firmly under her arm. Buster was grazing in the corner with Mark's horse, Sniper. Sarah whistled. Both horses lifted their heads toward the sound. Sniper went back to eating, but Buster continued to watch with mild curiosity as Sarah approached him with halter and lead rope in hand. Even after years without riding, it took no time to catch, groom, and throw her good, old, faithful saddle onto the horse. Jacob and Martha had kept the gear in great condition. She had found it oiled and stored in a protective dust bag. Attaching the saddlebag to the front of the saddle, Sarah slipped the rifle into its sheath. She paused, running her hands over the fine leather of her saddle. The last time she'd touched this saddle was when it had been still attached to her now-dead horse, Honor. Sucking in a quivery breath, Sarah rested her forehead to the saddle. A rush of emotion overwhelmed her. Honor had been shot by poachers. They had deceived her. She thought they were from the parks board. Then they turned on her in the wilderness. It left her friend fighting for life and her horse dead. Sarah let the tears flow unhindered as she closed her eyes against the saddle. Honor and Sarah had been partners, so close they could read each other's thoughts.

Stepping back, Sarah wiped her face on her sleeve before she stroked Buster's neck. "Good boy." She tried to smile as she took a deep breath and mounted the steady horse.

Pulling her Akubra down over her face, Sarah wiped at her eyes again and trotted from the grounds as the guards held open the gate for her. It was midafternoon, and the waning sun was hot overhead. Sarah found Buster responsive and well behaved, despite not having been ridden for a long time. His movements weren't as lovely as the horses she was used to, but Buster was known for his consistency in being bomb-proof and great for beginners. Once out on the open track, she urged him into a soft canter. She relished the hot wind of the veldt as it whipped her face. A couple of giraffe looked her way as she cantered toward the tree line. Frightened, the graceful beasts broke into the lanky lope they were famous for, fearful that Sarah was chasing them. She pushed Buster into a gallop and passed the two giraffe, which wheeled away to her left. Storm heads, laden with cobalt rain, hung in sharp contrast against the azure sky. Sarah pulled Buster to a stop and breathed deeply through her nose. Tears of joy coursed down her face as she beheld the beauty of the place she'd fallen in love with many years ago when she arrived from Australia. "What do You want me to do, God?" She heard nothing for a moment. The beauty in the scene distracted her too much. Impatient, Sarah murmured louder into the fragrant breeze.

"What do You want me to do, God?"

Be still.

She felt it in her heart rather than heard it. Sarah closed her eyes against the warm breeze and waited.

Be still...and know that I am God.

The flutter of a delicate petal from a nearby blossoming native tree, borne up by the wind, brushed against her face. Her eyes flickered open. The sky seemed so big on this open landscape, the land so vast. The sky and clouds were so bold and dramatic, the blossoming tree so delicate and beautiful. The enormity of God's power and beauty was displayed in the natural juxtapositions around her. In an instant it struck Sarah and she gasped. Fresh tears of shame pricked her eyes. She hung her head and repented to God for not trusting Him, not giving Him her time, her all. There was an overwhelming impression in her spirit.

He is God!

She had fallen away from Him and allowed Satan to rule her life with fear. She thought back to the dreams. Declan, that evil man—the poacher who had once seduced her and tried to kill her. How had she allowed it to come to this? Not going to God with her fears, not rebuking the devil. She thought back to what Israel had said a few days earlier about spiritual warfare and that it was time to grow up in the Lord. Eat meat, instead of milk.

"I don't know what it all means, God. Please. I need help." She and Mark would need to get alongside Jacob and Martha more this week and learn what they knew. Buster sighed beneath her, and put his head down to graze. Sarah allowed him some more length in the reins. Pulling out the notebook and pen that Martha had packed into the saddlebag, Sarah jotted down what she remembered Israel had said about spiritual warfare.

Stowing it away again, she looked around for a decent-sized tree. She clucked at the horse, which lifted his head and meandered over to the nearby acacia. Sarah narrowed her eyes at the tree as they approached, searching for telltale signs of big cats. It looked abandoned, except for the odd party of birds occupying the branches. Sarah swung out of the saddle and tied Buster in the shade so he could eat. She scanned the tree a second time for leopards or other dangers. Nothing. Unclipping the saddlebag, she tucked it under her arm and hauled herself up onto the first strong limb. Several birds from the party on the lower branches panicked and took off higher as Sarah found a suitable branch, leaned against the trunk, and settled in. She sighed blissfully as she opened the saddlebag, retrieved the old Bible, and began to read the Word of God.

"What would You have me do, Lord?" She looked out through the leaves onto the veldt as herds of grazing wildebeest and zebra made their way closer to the tree, unaware of her and Buster's presence.

Look after My sheep.

Sarah again felt the still, quiet voice of the Lord in her heart.

"What sheep?"

Immediately Kwanele's face came into her mind. "Look after Kwanele?" She rested her head back against the cool trunk of the tree. Peace filled her heart as she contemplated the idea. Was that all? It seemed so easy. Her dreamy smile faded as she thought of her husband. He wouldn't be so easy to convince. Sighing again, Sarah gazed up toward the sunlight that streamed through the canopy of leaves. "If it's Your will, though, God, I'm sure You'll show me a way."

Mark opened the doorway wide to Jacob and Martha's home as Kgomotso stepped up onto the porch. "Motso! How are you?" Mark gave the man's hand a firm shake and pulled him inside, then slapped him on the back. "Martha, look who's here!" Mark called into the kitchen. Martha bustled out and with a cry of joy gave the tall swarthy Sotho man a hug. "Jacob is outside getting the fire ready. We have guests in tonight. You must go see him." She waved Mark and the bewildered guest back out the doorway. "Please, I must speak with Mark and Sarah." Kgomotso paused in the doorway. "Of course." Mark nodded. He caught the worry in the man's voice. "Sarah is out riding, but she'll be back before long. She left at three, and it's nearly sundown." Mark couldn't hide the elation in his voice that his wife was back in the saddle.

Kgomotso shrugged and followed Mark outside toward the campfire. Jacob waved his arms in the air as he saw them approach. "Kgomotso, my good friend! It's been too long! You must come back and work for us." Kgomotso bowed his head with respect, his brilliant white teeth lighting up his face as he smiled. "You are too kind, sir. But I must care for Uncle." Jacob nodded as he hobbled over and threw some more wood on the pile for the fire. "I understand. Can you believe it, Mark? We have a safari group in! It's the first one this month!"

"It's good." Mark cocked his hands on his hips as he surveyed the wood. Tours were few and far between lately, with nothing for the tourists to view except carnage from poachers. It was bad for business. Kgomotso sat on one of the log seats beside the unlit wood pile. "That is what I came to speak with you..." As Mark sat beside him, the large Sotho man appeared to struggle with where to begin. "Uncle. He did not tell you what happened with Koto."

Mark frowned and held his breath. The serious look on Kgomotso's face filled him with concern. "What happened? Are they alright?"

Kgomotso looked down at his feet and shook his head. "Do not know. Koto was angry with poachers. No tourism, no work. He could not feed family. Poachers started threats. They ask for Sarah." The blood drained from Mark's face.

"Yes?" He leaned forward, and a chill ran down his spine. Kgomotso went on. "They prayed. They still got threats. They got horrible things left at their door...then poachers threatened the children."

Mark gasped.

"It got too much. Koto felt God say to flee. They did not know where. They did not tell us."

Mark felt his face tighten. It wasn't fair!

"Oh Jesus, let them be safe!" Mark balled his hands into fists on his lap. Kgomotso nodded.

"I found out!" He sat up taller. "They went across ocean...to Sarah's land."

"They wouldn't have had the money to move overseas." Opening his fists, Mark rubbed his palms over his jeans.

"God!" Kgomotso had a matter-of-fact air about him. "They prayed, God gave them the way."

Mark blinked and shook his head in wonder. Could it be true? He sighed, dropping his shoulders.

Kgomotso smiled softly. "I wanted you to know."

"Why didn't Israel tell me that?" Mark scratched at his sideburns.

"He was too sad still." Kgomotso stared into the distance.

"Well, at least they're safe." Mark smiled, though he still felt a pang of regret. Pushing it aside, he slapped his hands together and stood up.

"Come on. Let's get your gear...you will stay tonight, won't you?" Kgomotso looked embarrassed.

"I did not plan to."

"You mean you came all this way, just to tell Sarah and me about Koto?"

Kgomotso inclined his head, a small smile tugging at his

lips.

Jacob hobbled up behind them. "Your old quarters are just the way we left them, Kgomotso. I think you still have clothes and other stuff in there you need to sort out, too. Go freshen up, and then you can come and help me get the pig on the spit for dinner." Kgomotso's countenance lifted, but then he hesitated. "Uncle." He shook his head. "He does not know I am here. He did not want me to talk about"—he cleared his throat—"Koto." His eyes fell downcast and Mark frowned.

"Why, Motso?"

"Because he wants you and Sarah brave in the Lord. Not in fear. He worry if you knew Koto had to flee, then you lose heart."

He straightened with pride.

Jacob was polite as he interrupted again. "Kgomotso, I will ring my a friend in Phalaborwa and get them to take a drive to see if your uncle needs anything, and let him know that you just wanted to come and visit."

Kgomotso looked unsure. Jacob put his hand on his shoulder. "He will be fine. You'll see. It will be getting dark soon, and our guests will be arriving. I could really use some help." He tapped his broken leg with a crutch. "I will talk with Israel when I am over that way next. If Mark and Sarah were going to be kept from fear, we shouldn't have told them our story, either. It's not stories that bring fear, it's the evil one."

Kgomotso nodded at Jacob's wisdom.

"Yes, sir." He smiled.

"Right! I'm off to make a phone call. Mark, will you help our guest settle in?" He inclined his head toward Kgomotso, a twinkle in his eye, and hobbled off on his crutches. Mark grinned at his Sotho friend.

"You can't argue with that."

"No." Kgomotso chuckled, but doubt flicked across his eyes as he followed Mark to the old car. Just as they got to it, Sarah came trotting in through the gates, the brilliant colors of the sunset behind her. Warding off the glare with his arm, Mark squinted and delighted in the sight. The vibrant colors of the sky shimmered against her dark curls of hair, which flew loose as she rode.

"I'm so proud of you, Sarah!" he exclaimed as she walked Buster past.

"I'm riding!"

"I know!" He lifted his hand and touched her arm as she brushed past.

"Kgomotso!"

"Hello, Sarah."

She returned her attention to Mark. "Could you please let everyone know that I saw the safari group on their way?" She twisted in the saddle to get his answer. Mark saluted her with a tilted smile. "Yes, boss." He laughed as she raised an eyebrow at him. Kgomotso snickered as he grabbed out a small bag, then slammed shut the old car's door.

Mark shook his head. "Is that it?"

The Sotho man considered his bag. "I was not thinking to stay, remember?"

They both laughed and the two men walked back toward the campsite, the twilight spectacular behind them.

Chapter Twelve

Mark couldn't get to sleep that night. He tossed and turned beside his restful wife, worried that he would disturb her. She stirred a couple of times until Mark realized he was going to wake her, so he got up. He sat on the edge of the bed, his head in his hands. He couldn't put a finger on what was disturbing him, but he felt a pull, an urge to go somewhere. Was it God calling him? Mark wandered into the living room. The crescent moon shone bright through the open windows. He'd forgotten to bring his Bible to the bush camp. They both had. Was it deliberate? He'd kept so strong for Sarah that he had indeed neglected to trust God. Hadn't he dealt with that already? How many times was he going to have to hand this thing over to God? He searched through Jacob and Martha's bookshelf in the semi-moonlit darkness. Finally, he put his hand on an old Bible. He returned to the bedroom, tugged a stretch cotton shirt from his suitcase, slipped it over his broad shoulders, and quietly snuck out toward the back porch. He settled into one of the old couches with a sigh and sat back watching the moon.

The clear night sky was marred only by the occasional low-flying cloud, which would creep its way as silent as a ghost across the blank expanse. A sliver of light filtered through the rondavel from the kitchen lamp he'd flicked on. This gave him a faint glow to read by.

The Bible was old and dog-eared in many places, several tattered bookmarks still stoically holding their place. Mark flicked through to Psalms and a red bookmark fluttered from one of the pages onto the ground. Quickly retrieving it, Mark tried to find the place where it had been. His eyes fell on Psalm 27, and his heart skipped a beat.

Is this what You want me to read, Lord?

His eyes began to move across the words with consideration.

The Lord is my light and my salvation—whom shall I fear?

The Lord is the stronghold of my life—of whom shall I be afraid? When evil men advance against me...

Mark stopped, rubbed his eyes, and skipped over to the next psalm. Psalm 28, and his eyes fell immediately on verse seven.

The Lord is my strength and my shield. My heart trusts in Him and I am helped.

He felt his heart quicken and he reached up to grasp his elephant pendant. This confirmed what God had shown him down at the waterhole. He needed to trust God to be his strength. Mark gave thanks that he was able to put this into practice by allowing Sarah some freedom to come out of her shell again. He could have so easily tried to hide her away from the atrocities of the current Kruger, but he didn't.

So, what do You need me to trust You with, Lord?

Just as he thought it, he saw Jacques pad across the courtyard below, the moonlight glistening off his shiny fur. He appeared blue and spotted in the dark. The cheetah stopped and gazed up at the porch, sensing someone watched him. Mark thought of Kwanele. He was entrusted to teach the boy the Way—to tell him about Jesus. Mark still couldn't entirely trust the boy, and that unsettled him. He was making an effort to befriend and help Kwanele, but deep down, he was skeptical. Mark watched Jacques when he felt a still, small voice in his heart.

The cheetah is a proud, strong animal...and yet Jacques is at peace with his life. He trusts that he is looked after by his master.

The cheetah sat and licked his paws, before stalking off again.

You, too, are like the cheetah, Mark. Strong and proud. But you needn't be. Trust Me with everything!

The bush camp was a-bustle with life the next morning with tourists everywhere. Three Jeep loads had come in the night before, many of the tourists from overseas. This was the bread-and-butter of the people who worked in the tourism industry. Jacob took one of the guides aside to ask how many kills they had come across and if the tourists were affected by it.

"There was a killing." The guide looked weary. "Just one, yesterday. Down near Olifants River. Rhinoceros again. That seems to be the latest flavor." He shook his head and kicked at a stone. "The people on board, they were angry. It made them want to donate to a cause. They wanted to help. I suppose that's good, but what can they do? There are no causes to stop this." The guide pressed his lips into a thin line as he looked over at the campfire. Breakfast sizzled away on a hotplate for the guests, and the smell of bacon wafted around the area.

Jacob raised his head toward the tourists in his bush camp and hope still stirred in his soul. Most of the guests were happily eating and sharing their photos with each other from the day before. Several took photos with Jacques. Jacob chuckled as he watched Kwanele by the cat's side, ensuring that they didn't overcrowd him. The cheetah loved most people, but he had never bonded to one person as much as he had with Kwanele.

When the boy deemed that Jacques's photo session was over, he simply walked away and Jacques, loyal only to Kwanele, was quick to follow. Indeed, the two could not be separated. Kwanele and Jacques disappeared behind a building, and Jacob turned his attention back to the main crowd. Kgomotso appeared and inclined his head with respect to Jacob. "Thank you for your hospitality, but I need to return to Uncle now."

Jacob shared a warm smile, giving his shoulder a squeeze. "You are most welcome here any time, my friend. And don't forget, we always have a room for you, and you are welcome to live here and work for us again anytime you want." The tall, swarthy Sotho man flashed his brilliant white smile. "Many thanks, Jacob!" He shook his hand, a chuckle in his words.

"Have you said good-bye to Mark and Sarah yet?" Jacob pointed over to the other side of the campfires, where the couple was chatting away with some tourists.

"I have, thank you." Kgomotso said a second farewell and headed back to his car.

Rounding the corner to go to his special spot against the wall, Kwanele rocked to a stop when he was faced with one of the tour guides. The tall white man with the thin black moustache leered and took a step forward. Kwanele dropped his gaze and went to pass.

"Stop." The man held up a palm. Kwanele froze and looked gingerly up at the man. Jacques nuzzled his nose into Kwanele's hand and sat next to him. The man glanced at the cheetah, then back at Kwanele, his eyes narrowed. He then squatted down to Kwanele's level and produced a piece of newsprint paper from his jacket. "Recognize this?"

Kwanele tried to stay calm as he saw the photo of Sarah leaning against the elephant. It was that photo. Why would this man show him that photo, unless— Fear gripped Kwanele as he tried to think of how to respond. His mouth felt dry as he nodded. "It's Sarah." Looking away, he tried again to walk past the man. A strong hand gripped his shoulder. Kwanele went rigid as he stared at the tour guide. The thin moustache quivered as the man appeared to rein in his own emotion. Kwanele was repulsed as he watched beads of sweat form on the man's upper lip.

"You were given a job to do, weren't you?"

Kwanele kept his expression blank, but he could feel his heart pounding against his chest.

"Answer me!" the man hissed. Jacques stood and stared at the man, his mouth gaped open. Kwanele nodded, putting his hand on the cheetah's head for support.

"There is a warehouse, back in Mozambique. You've been there. You will get Sarah and her husband back there."
Kwanele frowned in confusion. The guide's eyes darted to the cheetah then back again, before he suddenly grabbed Kwanele by the front of his shirt and pulled him close.

"Back to the bunker-house. Understand?" He shook

Kwanele, who let out a whimper. Jacques growled low in his throat, the hackles rising along his back.

"When?" Kwanele squeaked. The man shoved him back, and Kwanele nearly lost his footing.

"As soon as you can. The sooner, the better. They are set up. Get Sarah to want to go there and get her to call Abasi when you are on the way."

"You're not going to...hurt them?" Kwanele's voice stammered. He already knew the answer, but he had hoped that the plan might have changed.

"What interest is that to you?" The man glowered at Jacques with distaste. The cheetah was crouched over, the hairs on his back still bristled. He growled again, baring his teeth when the man regarded him.

"Calm him down," the man snapped. Kwanele attended to the cheetah. He kept his eyes fixed on Jacques until he felt the man's attention pass over him. He risked a look over his shoulder. The man had left them. The newspaper print was left on the dirt. Kwanele scooped it up and jammed it into his pocket. His heart beat so hard against his chest that it hurt. What was he going to do? Tears welled in his eyes as he staggered over to his hiding spot. He crouched down and nestled into the ferns, shuffling himself until his back found the cool stone of the building. Kwanele hugged his knees to his chest and wept. Jacques crawled in under the building, where the ground was cool, and kept watch. After a long while, Kwanele sobbed himself to sleep.

Long after the guests had left and the bush camp was empty, Mark watched Martha as she piled leftover food onto plates for lunch. There was always excess after a group left because of the way they cooked. Nobody minded, though, as it kept them fed for days. "Where's Kwanele?" Martha asked Mark and Sarah as they sorted through some pork bones for Jacques. "I haven't seen him since breakfast." Mark shrugged. Jacob walked into the room, rubbing his leg. "Last I saw of him, he was rescuing Jacques from another photo session." He chuckled.

Mark stood up. "I know where he is then." He took a large pork bone from the pile and made a show of spinning the greasy item in his hand. He lost his grip, fumbled for it, and caught it awkwardly midair. He failed to recover his dignity, though, as he felt his face flush crimson. Mark cleared his throat and took his leave to find Kwanele.

"Kwan! Jacques!" Mark called as he strode around the various camp rondavels. "Kwanele!" he called again, looking under the ferns and shrubs that were landscaped along the base of each building.

"Kwan—ah." He paused mid-name as he spotted the boy curled up on his side, asleep behind a fern. Jacques's tail was visible as it protruded from under the building. "Jacques!" Mark threw the bone, and the tail immediately disappeared as Jacques changed position. His muzzle appeared as he took the bone and dragged it back under the rondavel. "Kwan." Mark's voice was soft as he gently nudged his shoulder. "Kwanele."

The boy's eyes fluttered open in alarm. He sat up like a shot and looked around.

"Hey, hey. It's just me." Mark backed up from the panicked child. "You fell asleep outside...that's all."

Kwanele looked past Mark with wide eyes. Mark stood and dusted his jeans off. "It's alright, Kwan. It was just a dream. Do you want some lunch?" He smiled and held out his hand to help the boy up. Kwanele looked at the offered hand, got up himself, and bent to dust off his trousers. Mark started off and gestured. "Come on then."

Kwanele followed at a distance before he stopped. Mark turned around and frowned.

"What's wrong?"

"Nothing." Kwanele gazed at his feet. Mark shrugged and continued to the rondavel. They entered and the room fell silent. Kwanele hurried past, toward the bathroom. Mark saw the crease etch into Sarah's brow as she leaned to his ear.

"Everything okay?"

"I think so. I found him asleep. He's spooked, though. I think he had a nightmare." Mark squeezed her arm as he brushed past, also heading for the bathroom to wash his hands.

Soon enough, they all sat around the table and ate a lavish lunch. Pouring herself more juice, Sarah spoke up about her desire to go back through Kruger to investigate the poacher sites.

Mark nearly choked on his meal. "Not alone you're not."

"Well, no, I want you to go with me, Mark...and anyone else who wants to."

Jacob and Martha regarded her, their faces stoic.

"To what end?" Martha put her fork down and gave her full attention.

"Just to see what's going on..." Sarah stammered as she looked them all in turn. Mark saw that Jacob and Martha's expressions appeared just as tight as his face felt.

"I want to get an idea of how bad Kruger is being affected." Mark put his knife and fork down and placed his hand over hers, gloving it.

"Sarah, you can't stop things from happening out there. What will this prove?"

She pulled her hand away.

"I just want to know what's going on. I don't know what I can do, but I want to see it."

Mark sighed to himself, and then noticed Kwanele, who kept his eyes downcast on his food. The atmosphere in the room dropped dramatically. Jacob intervened.

"We just want to make sure you are safe. If you don't need to go looking for trouble, then why do it?"

"Whatever happened to, the Lord is our strength and He is our protection?" Sarah shook her head. "Have you all changed your minds?"

"Of course not. We just want you to use wisdom." Martha smiled, but her eyes were severe. Mark watched as his wife's countenance fell. Was she giving in? They could only hope. She sighed and pulled apart a bread roll on her plate.

"What about how you all encouraged me to go into the park on Buster yesterday?"

"We thought you wouldn't go too far. You're talking about driving all over Kruger looking for kills?" Martha's eyes flicked to Jacob. "Trusting in God doesn't mean to go and look for trouble."

"Okay, okay. You've got me. I was talking with one of the tour guides last night…" Sarah kept chewing on the bread as she spoke. Kwanele flicked her a glance. Mark noticed.

"…they told me about people out there. People who fight against the poachers."

"You mean the parks board?" Mark corrected.

"No, it's not the government." Sarah set her cutlery down and looked them all in the eye. "These are people who have formed groups that go and intervene in poachers' operations. They call themselves Freedom Fighters."

Mark concealed his emotion as her large green eyes turned upon him. Her long dark lashes worked their magic, but Mark remained unmoved.

"…and what? You want to go and join them?" Mark raised an eyebrow. Sarah shook her head.

"No. I want to ask them what they do. I want to find out how they plan to stop them…I just need to know."

Kwanele coughed. He fumbled to reach his glass and take a sip of water.

"Kwanele, did you talk to people last night, too?" Mark wanted to piece together his odd behavior. The boy shook his head, not making eye contact with Mark. Mark let out a long sigh, leaned across the table, grabbed some more potatoes up with the tongs, and dumped them on his plate. "Well, I suppose we'd better pack a decent lunch then and borrow some two-way radios."

Sarah grinned at her husband. "Thank you, Mark."

"Hey! I didn't say I agree. I just know you'll do it anyway. Someone's got to watch your back." A scowl crossed his face as he began to eat the potatoes.

"Stay safe," Jacob warned. "Are you going with them, Kwanele?" Mark scoffed inwardly. Kwanele would more than likely stay here with Jacques. He nearly choked on his meal a second time when he saw Kwanele nod from the corner of his eye. Martha and Jacob exchanged glances.

"We might need more ammunition, too." Sarah nudged Mark, who grunted in reply.

"You sure you're up for this? You might see more things like that elephant the other day." Mark half-teased, but his expression was serious. The only reason he was going was to protect his wife. He didn't need another life to watch. The boy nodded again.

"Okay then. We'll plan it for tomorrow." And with that Mark went back to the business of eating. The conversation was over.

CHAPTER THIRTEEN

A chill hung in the morning air of May as Sarah packed gear into the Cruiser. The sun, not yet risen, cast crisp shades of lavender and soft pink onto the edge of the African horizon. The cool colors were yet another sign that winter was on its way to the veldt. Jacques watched from his spot on a wooden ledge, like a concrete sentinel. He raised his head with interest when he saw Kwanele emerge from the rondavel. Mark threw a small backpack to the boy. "You might as well make the most of this, Kwan! This is a lovely day for a safari. I've put some field guides in the Cruiser, and I put a set of binoculars in your pack as well as a compact camera." The boy looked at him and clutched the bag to his chest. "It's all good!" Mark laughed, scruffing Kwanele's tight curls as he walked past. "I'll show you how to work the camera. You'll be a pro in no time!" Sarah rolled her eyes at Mark and headed back into the rondavel for more gear.

She passed Mark on his way inside as she returned. Kwanele placed the pack into the backseat of the Cruiser before he sank onto an outside wooden ledge next to Jacques. He leaned into the soft fur of the cheetah, and watched the scene. Sarah paused, a smirk on her face. She supposed it must look unusual to the boy: her bustling about as if preparing for war, and Mark, happy as a lark, about to go on a Sunday picnic. "Did you get extra ammunition for the rifles?" Sarah snapped back into work mode as Mark returned and placed the icebox into the rear of the Cruiser. He winked at his wife.

"I'm serious, Mark. If we find more animals like that elephant, you'll have to put them down." He spun, saluted his wife, and continued back into the rondavel. She shook her head and checked for sunscreen, hats, two-way radios, and other miscellaneous items. Kwanele sighed from the wooden ledge. Martha came next, from the rondavel, approached Sarah with an envelope, and pressed it into her hand.

"Don't forget to duck in to Letaba campsite for me and pick up some more fuel for us. You'll need the jerry can from the shed." Sarah nodded and pocketed the envelope of money.

"Honey." Martha grasped the girl by the shoulders. "Relax! You are all tense. Yes, I know you are on a mission, but please…take this time to enjoy the park, too. Take Kwanele to see the elephant museum at Letaba." She gazed over her shoulder at the boy. "It will give him a new appreciation. And teach him more about his own lands." She smiled, rubbing Sarah's arms, then left. Sarah could hear her call out as she got through the door.

"Mark! Can you get the jerry can from the shed? We need to mow the grounds again." Sarah smiled as she thought back to what she felt God tell her when she had been in the tree the other day.

Look after My sheep.

She gazed upon Kwanele, who leaned against Jacques, his red jacket wrapped tight about him. Yes, she resolved. They could spare some time and money to visit the elephant museum. As she contemplated, glare from the sun burst forth from its nightly confines and kissed the horizon. Sarah shielded her eyes and refocused on Kwanele and Jacques. The warm glow bathed Jacque's coat with a rich orange color as he lazed on the wooden bench. He sank deeper into the wood and soaked in the warmth as it hit his body. The Cruiser now packed, Sarah tipped her chin to Kwanele, indicating they were ready to go. Reluctant, he slid off the bench and got into the Cruiser. Soon, the three of them were headed down dirt track road, leaving the cheetah behind to enjoy the dawn. Sarah drove, as Mark looked over the map in the passenger seat. "Where are we headed?" he asked, as Sarah pushed her sunglasses down over her eyes. The glare from the sun was harsh at sunrise, especially when they were driving directly into it.

"We can go to Letaba later in the day, so let's cross the river, south toward Timbavati." She turned onto the main bitumen road that would take them past the large rest-camp of Letaba and onward down the track. Already as the sun got higher in the east, they spotted herds of zebra and springbok that meandered their way through the scrublands.

"Sarah, slow down." Mark put his hand on her knee. "Can you get around the bottom side of that herd and stop for a moment so we get a closer look? So Kwan can get a look."

Sarah sighed. They had only just left the bush camp. They had work to do today. She did as directed and pulled up the Cruiser under the shade of a large tree. Leaning on the steering wheel, she took off her sunglasses to scan the mopane. Now the herd was closer. They saw that egrets also picked their way through the shrubs, snatching up insects as they went. Several of these white- and caramel-plumaged birds also rode upon the backs of the animals, picking insects from their backs.

Sarah sighed as Mark urged Kwanele out of the vehicle and the two of them leaned against the side of the Cruiser. They proceeded to take photos and identify the sleek birds in the field manual. Kwanele had the oversized binoculars up to his small face, peering through them. Sarah lay her cheek down on her arms and smiled to herself. Why was she so impatient? This was what God wanted them to do. She looked at her husband, a sadness in her eyes—the trail guide, whose love for the wilderness of Africa had been squashed in the daily grind of city life. Out here, he was fulfilled, he was free. She watched as he explained the symbiotic relationship the birds had with the great herds of the veldt. Soon enough, the pair reboarded the Cruiser and they were ready to head off again.

"Okay." Mark grinned at his wife as she pulled the Cruiser into gear and retraced her tire-flattened tracks through the grass back to the road. They continued on, and as Sarah spotted more wildlife, she also noted that Mark resisted asking her to stop. She wondered if she was being selfish. Soon enough, they passed Letaba rest-camp. Sarah watched Kwanele through the rearview mirror. He kept his eyes glued to the window. She wondered how much of this he'd seen growing up. Probably none of it. It would all be a new and wondrous experience for him. They drove on past Olifants rest-camp, where Sarah turned off the beaten track again and headed down toward the river. There were several large water holes down here, and she decided that it was her turn to show Kwanele something. She drove along past the mopane shrubbery in low gear, squinting to see through the leaves down to the water. It was harder to hear where things were when in a vehicle than on a horse. Mark glanced at Sarah, and she caught his eye. He looked over his shoulder and smiled at Kwanele. A smirk grew on Sarah's lips as she knew that Mark was on to her plan.

"There is usually a lot to see down at the water."

Kwanele nodded and picked up the binoculars from the seat beside him. "Blast!" Sarah pulled up the Cruiser, pulled the handbrake up, and stepped out into the warm air. She moved past a large spindly shrub and looked around the landscape. Within seconds she hopped back into the Cruiser. Mark raised a brow at her. "Up there." She pointed as she pressed the accelerator. She navigated with care around the trees and bushes up to the other side of the waterhole. She killed the engine a safe distance away and motioned everyone to step out with her. She heard them before she saw them. A small herd of elephants was at the water's edge drinking. They picked the water up in their trunks and sprayed it over themselves. Others were rolling in the waterhole. Sarah moved in for a closer view and squatted next to a bush, her face hurting from the broad grin she wore. Mark ushered Kwanele over and held out his hand to help the boy over some rocks. Kwanele shrank back.

"Kwanele? What's wrong?" Mark frowned, but he continued to urge the boy. "Come on, I'll show you how to take a photo."

Sarah gazed over her shoulder at the scene. Why did Kwanele look so haunted over these elephants? He'd seen elephants in Mozambique. She brushed it aside as Kwanele stood. She could see that Mark would help him through.

"Kwan?" Mark came back over to the boy and knelt in front of him. "Kwan..."

The boy looked into Mark's strong but compassionate features.

"I don't know what you are going through...but...you don't have to do it alone. Are you thinking about the dead elephant we saw on the way home from Mozambique?" Kwanele's face screwed up, but he shook his head.

"Is it what happened at Mozambique?" Mark pressed further. Kwanele only frowned deeper and shrank back. He looked toward the shrub they stood beside. Mark narrowed his eyes as he looked beyond Kwanele into the brilliant blue sky. He ran his hands through his hair. Sarah stood crouched as she watched the scene with interest.

"Well...whatever happened, let's try and enjoy today, okay?" He held out his hand once more to Kwanele. Taking a deep breath and nodding, Kwanele touched the binoculars around his neck, then took hold of Mark's hand. Mark hauled him up the rocky incline, then released him to work his own way down the track toward the water. Satisfied, Sarah went on ahead. Her long strides found the elephants in no time. Cautious, she approached the herd. They were wary as they regarded her, but Sarah remained brave and calm. They began to respond in like. She heard a child's gasp behind her and realized that Mark and Kwanele had arrived and watched from a distance. The elephants had ceased their dust bath and were quiet as they stood lined up, watching Sarah with curiosity. She stood, her hand outstretched, palm open, a peaceful expression on her face as one of the elephants ventured his thick wrinkly trunk forward toward her hand. The elephant sniffed her hand, and then fumbled his trunk over it, grasping it. Satisfied with her scent, the elephant released his grip from her hand and turned its back to her. Without a fuss, it went down to the water to drink. The other elephants followed suit and ignored her presence, returning to their previous activities. Sarah turned her triumphant face toward Mark and Kwanele. "It's been too long." She exhaled deeply, tears slipping from her eyes with a long-held-in emotional release. Mark smiled at his wife, before finding himself a nice fallen log to sit on and watch the herd. Kwanele came and sat next to him and pulled the binoculars to his eyes. His view was blocked by massive leathery-gray hide. He took them from his eyes and frowned at them, turned them the other way and tried again. Mark laughed. "We're too close. You don't need them. But here..." He passed the boy the compact camera and proceeded to show him how it worked. After a few wayward shots, Kwanele got the hang of it and proceeded to take many photos, growing more delighted with each one.

"Steady up there, boy. Save some room for other places." Mark adjusted his sunglasses and watched as Kwanele put the camera back in its protective case.

Midday came and went with the trio exploring the region as far down as Nwanetsi. They spotted no unusual kills, bar for those made by wild predators. They had stopped and watched and photographed many game animals. Sarah noticed that Kwanele seemed to be putting aside his fears and enjoying himself. They had a picnic lunch at Timbavati, while watching giraffe pick from a thorny acacia tree as zebra grazed in the background. So far their journey had unearthed nothing sinister, and Sarah started to doubt if God really wanted her to find anything at all. Perhaps God had given her what she'd needed—a pleasant day out with Mark and Kwanele. They were driving back north now and intended to get off the main tracks and cut across some of the less used roads. They were tracking some antelope and a family of lions eating a fresh kill when a sudden movement in the tree line caught Sarah's eye. She saw Mark's head turn in the same direction.

"Sarah. There!" He pointed. She stomped her foot on the brake, jolting everyone forward.

"Sorry." She gazed back at Kwanele, who looked toward where Mark was pointing, his binoculars and camera at the ready.

"That's..."

Mark squinted.

"That's hessian!" Sarah gasped as she pulled the Cruiser into REVERSE and backed out of sight under the tree line. She didn't know if they should get out of there or call the police. She looked at Mark, excitement and fear in her belly as she flicked off the radio and struggled to wind down her window. Straining to hear, she pointed at her satellite phone, silently questioning Mark as to whether or not they should call someone.

"We don't know what it is, Sarah. It could be just a bird hideout."

Sarah studied the situation a moment longer before killing the engine.

"Let's check it out...but Mark...should we get..."

"No, no gun! Not yet. It could cause trouble." He put his hand on her arm a moment, before he hopped from the Cruiser.

"Are you coming, Kwan?" The boy shrank lower in his seat and shook his head.

"That's fair enough," Sarah whispered to Mark as they left the Cruiser. They snuck around the bushes and made their way to where they had spotted the hessian. They sighed with relief when it appeared nobody was around. Coming out into the open now, they explored the clearing behind the hessian and noted that it did, indeed, look like some kind of bird-hide, but what was unusual about this one was that it was equipped with radios and contained many large wooden boxes, all covered over with army-print hessian. "What do you suppose is in them?" Sarah wondered out loud. Grunting, Mark swept the hessian away with a flourish. "One way to find out." He squatted to examine the boxes, and noted that they were latched, but not locked. "Hmmm." Unclipping the latches, he swung open the first lid. Sarah stepped up behind him and gasped. AK-47s, elephant rifles, grenades, and several cruel-looking knives.

"I think we should get out of here," Mark suggested as he closed the lid on the box, "and call the police."

"Not before I take some pictures." Sarah produced her camera. "Open that box again, Mark." He smirked, but his expression soon changed as his brows hooded his face.
"I don't know, Sarah..."

She stood glaring at the box but made no move to open it herself. Mark turned away from her and she reached to touch the wood. That's when Mark jolted into it. She sucked in her breath, snapping her head up.

"Whoah!"
Mark's hands were in the air and a man stood with a rifle pointed at them. She straightened up with alarm as another dark-skinned man came and took her camera and shoved her

back against Mark. The other man with the rifle kept the nozzle trained on Mark, but looked at Sarah, jerking the rifle to indicate she was to follow Mark's lead. She lifted her hands.

"Who are you? What are you doing here?" The man with Sarah's camera had a thick African accent as he glared at them. The men were dressed in army uniform, but with several additions that showed they were not from the military.

"Well?" hissed the man with the gun.

"We could ask you the same thing." Sarah frowned but felt a boldness rise within her.

The man with the camera snickered. "Except I am not the one with a gun pointed at me now, am I?"

Mark cleared his throat. "We were sightseeing, and we just saw this bird-hide by accident. No harm done. We'll just be on our way." He flashed his most charming smile. The men exchanged glances and spoke in hurried Swahili.

"We already pulled apart your vehicle. Maybe you are just sightseeing...but your vehicle is not packed out like a tourist's. Who are you?" the man with the gun growled, and as he examined Sarah, as his eyes smoldered. Her lips tightened and she said a silent prayer. What should she say, or not say? Her eyes flicked toward Mark's. Kwanele!

"I know you." The cameraman rounded Sarah, looking her up and down as his smile grew wide. "You were in the newspapers. You worked for the parks board. You're the elephant woman!"

Sarah shrugged. "I worked with them, not for them." She wondered what bias this man would take.

"Quiet!" the gunman barked. Sarah raised her lowered hands again.

"Then you would know well"—the man with the camera continued to circle them. He smirked now like a lion stalking his prey—"you would know well, that we do not tolerate poachers."

Sarah melted with sudden relief. "You're the Freedom Fighters?" She let her guard down completely and dropped her hands. Mark stiffened next to her. The man with the gun shouted in Swahili at her, and she found the gun leveled straight at her face. Eyes as round as saucers, she threw her hands up again and backed closer to Mark.

"We're not your enemy." Sarah tried to keep her voice calm, but her hands started to shake. The man with the camera rested it on a ledge and hissed at the gunman, who lowered his weapon.

"And you were just photographing wildlife, weren't you?" He patted the camera. Mark shuffled nearer to Sarah and the man's smirk vanished.

"And you. Who are you?" He squared up to Mark and stared with challenge into his eyes. Mark's remained neutral.

"I'm Sarah's husband." Mark did not waver once at the close proximity of the man. Sarah could smell the stale tobacco on his breath. Glancing sideways, she saw Mark swallow hard, his Adam's apple lifting with the act.

"We're on your side, as Sarah said."

The man raised his brows at Mark. "The purpose of Sarah's camera is to get photographic evidence of poaching to take to the media and the government...so we can get something done about it. We mistook your hideout as a poachers' hideout." Mark looked Sarah's way.

"Ha! So the truth comes out now, you lied!" The gunman scoffed. "The government? What good will they do? While they sit and do politics and realize that they do not have money to help, many animals die." The gunless man sat.

"So...?" Mark's hands began to lower. Sarah felt it, too. It was becoming a strain.

"So? So it means we must do something about it ourselves!" the other man hissed impatiently and narrowed his eyes at the gunman. Sarah flashed Mark another look, but it was seen by the leader.

"I'm tired of this, just kill them."

The man with the gun smirked as he stood and leveled the rifle at them again. Sarah held her breath as the safety clip clicked off.

"Wait!" the boss ordered. Impatient, the gunman lowered his weapon. The boss circled Mark and Sarah once more. "If you are not poachers, tourists, nor one of us...then you are diplomatic troublemakers who will run and blow the whistle."

"What would you do if we were poachers?" Sarah lifted her

chin.

"You would be dead!" the gunman growled as he eyeballed Sarah.

"And tourists?" She arched a brow.

"Sarah." Mark's eyes went wide with fear.

"This is no game," the boss snarled at her. "I know who you are, and what you did, Sarah. I won't kill you this one time because of that...but we are not going to let you go blow the whistle and get us arrested, either."

Mark and Sarah exchanged glances.

CHAPTER
FOURTEEN

Kwanele heard the Jeep before he saw it. Someone was coming. Where were Mark and Sarah? He spun around, his eyes wide. On instinct, he launched from the Cruiser and scrambled beneath a nearby mopane shrub. The sharp branches dug into his arms and legs and caused him to suck in his breath. He squirmed around to find comfort. It wasn't long before he heard the vehicle pull up behind the Cruiser. He froze and peered out from under the shrub.

He saw the trousered legs of several men in army camouflage walk past. Sounds of items being tossed on the ground followed, as they began to ransack the Cruiser. Kwanele felt sweat prick on his body as he recognized the barrel of a rifle hanging down by one of the men's legs. The hairs on the back of his arms stood up. Were they here for Sarah now? Was he going to be killed for not taking her to Mozambique? He heard conversation as they found Mark's rifles in the trunk. They took them back to their Jeep. The sounds and voices started to fade as the men headed down the track in the direction Mark and Sarah had gone. Kwanele gasped. He shifted his position, relieved as the blood flowed back into his cramped legs. He felt a chill as angry shouts echoed in the distance. They found them. He needed to get out of here. There was a long silence and Kwanele strained to hear more. He was about to crawl from his spot when the crunch of footsteps appeared from nowhere, right next to his mopane shrub. He recoiled. It was the same men. He recognized the voices. Kwanele ducked low to the ground to see what was happening. One of the men dived in to the driver's seat of the Cruiser and his legs disappeared from view. The man cursed and reemerged from the Cruiser.

Kwanele smiled to himself as he put his hand on his pocket and felt the Cruiser keys tucked away.

"Where are you going?" a voice asked.

"Back to get the keys. They must have them on them!"

The second deep voice snapped, "Forget it. We don't have time. We need to go in case they called the authorities before we got here."

"But it's a nice truck."

"It's an old truck. Forget it. Let's get the hell out of here!"

"I'm going to torch it, then. There's a jerry can in the back."

Kwanele shuddered despite the heat of the afternoon. He didn't like the prospect of being in a shrub so close to a fire, but at least he knew the jerry can was empty. Just as he considered moving to a safer place, the rumble of a vehicle resonated in the distance.

"Sello, quick. Someone's coming. Let's go!"

There was a scuffle of boots as both men raced back to their Jeep, leaving the Cruiser untouched. He listened to the sounds of the engine disappear into the distance. The silence that lingered afterward was almost too good to be true. He crept out from his shrub and glanced around. The sounds of a close party of birds chirped as Kwanele strained for the sound of the other vehicle. It must have turned away, because he could no longer hear it.

Would those men be back to destroy the car? Did they know about him? Would they look for him?

Heart beating heavily in his chest, Kwanele crept toward the tree line and the hessian. He hesitated, as he tasted the bile rise in his throat. What would he find? Were they dead? He had liked Mark, Sarah, Jacob, and Martha. He had loved Jacques. Would he ever again see any of them after this? Taking a deep breath, Kwanele melted into the bushes and emerged in the back of a hidden clearing. There, tied against a tree in the middle of the hideout were Mark and Sarah, mouths gagged, but fully alive. They were bound back to back. The tension in Kwanele's stomach unfurled like a spring. Mark and Sarah twisted their heads toward Kwanele, a look of sheer joy lighting their eyes. Kwanele let out his breath, and with a broad grin, he rushed to their aid. His fingers began to work at the ropes, before he stopped in alarm and yanked the gags from their mouths.

"Kwanele! Thank goodness you are okay. We sure are glad to see you." Mark squirmed against the ropes as Kwanele resumed working at them.

"We were so worried that they found you." Sarah's face was drained of color. "Quick. I want to get out of here. I can hardly breathe!"

"I think they will come back." Kwanele looked over his shoulder, and dread crept over him once more. "They said they were going to torch your car." He tugged apart the last knot and loosened the coils. As one, Mark and Sarah wiggled their hands free and helped uncoil the rope.

"I thought they killed you." Kwanele felt his heart beat faster, and his voice came out as a squeak. He wondered what this meant for him. Either the job was forfeit, or these were not the people Kwanele feared. He wondered which it was. Shrugging off the last of the coils, Sarah leapt toward Kwanele and wrapped him into a tight hug. He trembled as the adrenaline still surged through his veins. Making their way back to the Cruiser, they collected up the items thrown in the dirt and shut themselves in, locking the doors.

"What a mess," Sarah groaned. "Are we missing anything?"

Sarah glanced out her window onto the dirt. "Doesn't look like it. Have you got the keys?" Mark held out his hand. She shook her head.

"You drove here."

"Yeah, but I think I left them in the ignition."

"Oh, what?" Mark ran his hands through his hair and groaned. Kwanele cleared his throat from the backseat. Sarah craned her neck to regard him, her face beaming as she saw him produce the keys from his pocket. She elbowed her husband. Mark grunted and looked in the rearview mirror. Kwanele felt a surge of pride as the man's frustrated features melted away into relief and respect.

"Kwanele, well done. You're a quick thinker." Kwanele watched as Mark gave him a thumbs-up before he held his hand out for the keys. He handed them over with a halfhearted smile, and then rubbed the back of his neck.

"I can't believe he got my good camera," Sarah grumbled as she bent to tidy the items scattered at her feet. Mark started the engine and waited. When Sarah straightened up, he looked her in the eye. "It could have been a lot worse, honey."

Kwanele saw Sarah shudder as Mark pulled into gear and got them out of there. Kwanele sat hunched in the backseat, fear stilling his heart.

They had driven for a while in silence before Mark turned to his wife. "I don't think we should be going after those people again, Sarah." Kwanele watched as the man almost shook with frustration. "They are just as dangerous as the poachers."

Sarah nodded. The color had not yet returned to her olive features. Kwanele frowned in the backseat. "They were not poachers?"

"No." Mark kept his eyes ahead on the road. Kwanele sank back, troubled. This meant that they were all still in danger.

The biggest rest camp in Kruger, Letaba rest camp was like a small town in itself. It contained the accommodations, just like the bush camp that Martha and Jacob cared for, but was much larger. Apart from that, it also had shops, fuel supplies, and an elephant museum. It was a lazily stretched out green oasis of manicured lawns and beautiful, tall shady trees that nestled snug beside the Letaba River and near to where Mark and Sarah had once worked. As they drove through the gates, Kwanele was briefly enthralled with the sight of tamed delicate impala. They wandered the lawns, grazing, in full knowledge that they were safe within the confines of the rest camp.

"Should we go and talk to the parks board guys in the museum?" Sarah touched Mark's arm as he went to get out of the Cruiser. He nodded.

"We should go there straightaway. Report what happened."

Kwanele shuffled behind as they walked into the Elephant Hall. Sarah attempted to dust off the scuff marks on her clothes, but to no avail. The two adults looked as if they'd just been in a tussle with a lion. Kwanele looked around the entryway to the hall in wonder as Mark asked the receptionist if they could speak with a park ranger. The woman went out the back. Kwanele peered through, into the hall. He sighed as he caught Mark watch him with interest.

"We'll take you in there in a bit, Kwan. It showcases some of the great tuskers of the past."

Kwanele blinked at him. Mark smiled. "Some elephants that were really old, grew some massive tusks. We call them great tuskers. Maggie, the elephant we saw dead in Mozambique— well, she was one of the first Sarah made contact with. Maggie was a great tusker." His expression fell as he looked into the distance. Sarah slipped her arm through his. A middle-aged man with salt-and-pepper hair and a neatly trimmed gray beard came out. He eyed them with suspicion from beneath his bushy brows. Kwanele shrank behind Mark and gripped his belt. They were all ushered out the back into a small office area, where Mark began to tell their story. The man leaned back in his chair, his face growing red.

"And why on earth were you off the beaten track? Don't you people read signs?"

"We told you." Sarah wrung her hands. "We were trying to find them."

"You said you were not part of the Freedom Fighters, so why were you seeking them out? Sounds like a stupid move to me. Don't you people know what we constantly risk to keep people like you safe?" The man's frown deepened. Exasperated, Sarah went to speak again, but the man held his hand up. She clamped shut her mouth. He leaned forward, and his chair creaked. He stared her down for a few heartbeats. "Sarah White." Sarah gasped.

"Yes, I know who you are." He leaned back again, smug.

"Actually, sir, it's Sarah van der Merwe now..." Her voice trailed off as the man's face turned a shade redder. Kwanele saw a vein bulge in his neck and he looked away.

"Do not make the mistake of thinking, Sarah White, that you are the only one out there who wants to stop poaching. We have been training our rangers double-time in military fashion for quite some time now. They are much more equipped than you are to handle this kind of battle."

"But..." Sarah stood, her face crestfallen.

"No buts. You did your part when you rounded up the D-12 herd over to Mozambique. Unless you have a team of horses and your magic touch now to do it again, then you can't do much to help. This is no longer your battle."

Mark looked at his wife and rested his hand on her knee.

"You're both very lucky you weren't killed." The man continued to glare them down. Particularly Sarah. There was an awkward silence. The old ranger sighed, his expression fading to one of sympathy.

"Sarah, you've done so much good in the past for us. We know you mean well. And you, Mark van der Merwe, is it?"

Startled, Mark sat up and nodded. "*Ja*, sir."

"You headed up that safari business from Brennan's, didn't you? Took the safari trail rides?"

"We both did, sir." Mark took his wife's hand and gave it a squeeze. "But since the court case, the place was shut down. The police put us into protection. We've been living in Polokwane, sir."

Kwanele's mouth dried up. They didn't know these people. Why were they saying so much?

"And got married, I see." The ranger's face strained as a smile tried to form. Sarah blushed. He studied them in thought for a moment. "Are you working now?"

"Well..." Mark looked at his lap. "I have work at Polokwane. At a travel agency."

"Bah!" The ranger leaned back again and waved his hand in the air. "A waste, that is." He looked up at the two again. "I have a proposal for you. If you want to help this much, maybe we should get you both some work in the industry. Tourism again, or conservation, but in the field this time." He turned to Sarah again, a bemused whine in his voice. "If you must get involved, for heaven's sake, do it right."

Mark's eyes lit up.

"But you may have to sit some extra courses." The man started shuffling through papers on his desk. Kwanele thought Mark looked like a kid in a candy store, but when he gazed at Sarah, he saw she was quiet.

"Can we think about it?" Her tone was quiet. Mark searched her face, a crinkle in his brow. The ranger cleared his throat and gazed down at Kwanele, who had so far remained hidden behind Mark.

"And what's your story, young man?" He knit his fingers together on the desktop as he regarded the stricken Kwanele.

"He's nervous of new people," Sarah cut in, casting a glance at them in turn. The ranger pursed his lips as he inclined his head.

"You know what?" He spoke to Kwanele as if he were a child. "There are many young men, with warrior blood in them...like you. And they grow up and become part of the action group against poaching. They train as rangers for the parks board." Kwanele shrank back at the man's bold words.

"Please." Sarah shook her head. "He is very shy."

"That's understandable." The man stroked his beard. "Well, enjoy Letaba," he said, standing with a flourish. "And if you change your mind about work, please give me a call."

He passed Mark a business card and ushered them all back into the foyer. Sidling up to Sarah, he reiterated, "If you want to help, you can join the cause properly. Please, no lone wolfing. I don't want the next body we uncover out there to be yours." He shook her hand and with that, left. Kwanele felt awkward as he stood next to them in the foyer. What now?

"He didn't even say they would do anything about the Freedom Fighters." Sarah shoved her hands into her jean pockets.

"Why didn't you let him tell us what he had available for work?" Mark rubbed his temples as they wandered into the free Elephant Hall exhibition.

"I think we need to think about it first. Are we meant to be coming out into the open again, or still hiding? I know what Naicker would say."

Mark shrugged. "Is it any different out here than back in the city? We're going to be hounded anywhere we go."

"But we haven't even told the police that we went away. We're not protected out here."

Kwanele had had enough. He pushed between them, grasped both their hands, and dragged them toward a massive elephant skull mounted on the wall.

It proudly displayed a set of massive tusks, even bigger

than Maggie's had been. The label read, ONE OF THE SEVEN GREAT TUSKERS.

Sarah glanced at Mark, an apologetic look in her eyes. He caught her puppy-dog expression and smiled. Kwanele rolled his eyes. Finally. They spent the next hour in the Elephant Hall, showing Kwanele the magnificent creatures that were part of his heritage. The butterflies in Kwanele's stomach had settled. They collected fuel in the jerry can for Jacob and picked up some extra supplies and groceries, as well, for the bush camp, before they returned to the Cruiser to head back. The drive back was a silent one. Kwanele felt tired but relieved as he sat back and enjoyed his very first ice cream. He wondered when this dream would end and cold hard reality would hit.

CHAPTER

FIFTEEN

Sarah groaned as Mark stormed out of the room. They had shared with Jacob and Martha what had happened over the evening meal. After another heated discussion, Sarah felt that the police who were managing their case needed to know that they had come out to the bush camp in Kruger. With Kwanele, who had been quieter than usual, tucked safely into his bed for the night, Sarah decided to ring the private number of the officer in charge of their case, Lieutenant Tim Naicker. She dialed her cell phone as she sat at the kitchen table.

"What was the outcome?" Martha wandered past her with a tea towel in hand, drying the last of the dishes. Sarah rolled her eyes. "He said that we are not prisoners, but we've put ourselves in danger and taken ourselves out from their protection. In a nutshell, now that he knows we're here, he has to relocate men to watch our backs. He also said something about us wasting their money, resources, and time." She sighed deeply. "Do you know where Mark went? I think I've upset him."

Martha raised her brows at Sarah with sarcasm before eyeing her tea towel in thought. "I think he said he needed to oil his saddle."

Sarah guffawed. Martha threw the towel at her and Sarah caught it with ease, throwing Martha a cheesy grin.

"I'm serious, Sarah. He forgot that he rode through the water last week and that it needed to be oiled." Sarah threw the tea towel back at the older woman, a wry smile tilting her features.

"Hmph!"

Sarah stood, slapped her hands on her thighs, and headed

toward the back door. Putting the dish and tea towel on the bench, Martha stopped her.

"Sarah, I think you need to consider what Mark told us the ranger said. God gave you a task to do a few years ago. It was a special one, I know. And you did it. He doesn't require any more than that. The chapter may be closed on that task now, and you can bet God has a completely new task. A new chapter. Have you asked Him?" Martha smiled with compassion. Sarah felt stricken. Despite all her efforts to stay strong, Sarah began to tremble.

"Oh, come here, child." Martha rushed over and pulled Sarah into a warm embrace. Sarah accepted the hug for a moment before she pulled back. She stared into Martha's dark eyes.

"I did. He does...at least...I think He does."

"You mean you don't know?" Martha frowned. "The sheep know the Shepherd's voice."

"I know, I know...because they spend time getting to know the Shepherd. I know."

Martha looked at her. "I think it's time you went back to visit your church family in Phalaborwa, too. It's time to reconnect to God's family."

Tears began to well in Sarah's eyes as she thought about her old friends—the people she had grown to love who had introduced her to Jesus. She was far away from them all, so far away from God. He wasn't in her dreams like He used to be. She felt lost. Martha patted her on the back and stood aside as Sarah stepped past her and out the door onto the back patio. The evening air was cool in comparison to inside, and the last colors of sunset clung to the horizon of star-lit skies. Sarah stood a moment and took in a deep breath through her nostrils, drinking in the bite of fresh air. She sniffed back tears as she jogged down the stairs and across the gravel path toward the horse kraals. As she rounded the dark corner of the buildings, she could see that the light was on in the shed. Wiping her sleeve across her eyes, she took a deep breath and entered the old wooden shed. Mark looked up when the floorboards creaked. He sat on a stool, hunched over his saddle, which was perched on the old sawhorse. His rag was poised in the air as

Sarah stepped lightly into the room. She sat opposite him and offered a meek smile. Maybe she shouldn't have interrupted him. Mark swiped his rag through the tub of saddle oil and continued to rub down the underside flaps of the saddle in a smooth, circular motion.

"I've been thinking about what you said over dinner." He concentrated on the saddle as he spoke.

Sarah blinked.

"You were right to call the police. It was foolish of me to just whisk you away without considering your safety." He stopped rubbing and regarded her.

Sarah leaned forward and rested her elbows on her knees, hands clasped as she sighed.

"I just want what's best for you, Sarah...and..." He paused a moment, his blue eyes locked on to her eyes. "I want you to stay safe. I think this poachers thing is too big for you now...and we don't have God's covering on it."

The tears threatened to explode from her eyes. Sarah wiped at her face and looked down.

"Sarah." Mark put his rag down and moved across to her. He crouched before Sarah and lifted her chin with his thumb so their eyes met. "I love you." His voice was husky. That was enough. The tears let loose. Sarah lifted her sleeve to wipe them from her eyes, but Mark took her hands in his. He stretched up and kissed the tears from her cheeks. Sarah closed her eyes for a moment, enjoying the intimate connection.

"I'm so sorry." Her voice was hoarse when she opened her eyes again. "You're right. God hasn't told me to save the elephants this time." She hesitated. "He's told me something else...and I've not been doing it wholeheartedly."

A muscle twitched in Mark's mouth. "Neither of us has." He gazed over at the wall of the dusty shed. There, covered in dust, was a cross on the wall. Sarah followed his gaze. They both stared at the ornament for a moment. "It's time for a change," Mark remarked. "But not our way, God's way. What did you hear from God?"

Sarah couldn't bring her eyes to meet his. "He said, *Look after My sheep.* But when He said it...I thought of..."

"Kwanele?" Mark finished in amazement.

Sarah nodded as their eyes met. "We have been looking after him, though." He helped her to her feet. Sarah shook her head and felt her hands quiver in his. "No, when I want to go out chasing dangerous people...I am not looking after him. He's just a child." She dropped her gaze. Mark tilted his head at her before he pulled her close. Sarah felt his hand on her head as she leaned against his shoulder.

"We all learn. God was looking after us, and no one was hurt. No harm done. From now on, we can move on."

She nodded and buried her face into the comfort of his strong embrace. "Martha said we should go to Phalaborwa, to our old church." Sarah pulled back and searched her husband's face for a response. He looked past her at the cross on the wall and nodded. "Tomorrow is Sunday."

"Church would be overwhelming to Kwanele. Especially when our friends see us, they will want us to stay and have lunch with them after church." Sarah frowned with concern.

Mark smiled. "It's okay. I'll talk to him." He tilted her chin and gently pressed his lips against hers. He was about to pull back, when she pulled him closer, kissing him deeply. Mark slid his hand around the nape of her neck and pushed his fingers up into her thick hair.

A powerful jolt rippled through Sarah as she felt him tilt his head to deepen the kiss. They were going to be okay.

Mark found Kwanele in his usual spot, but this time he wasn't in the shrubs. Mark raised an eyebrow, a smirk tilting his mouth as he found them. Jacques was sprawled out in the shade, Kwanele lying on his back. The boy's head rested on the cheetah's belly like a pillow. They both had their eyes shut, but Kwanele held a small stick in his hand that he fidgeted with. Mark chuckled as he approached. "You know, even tame cheetahs are still wild. It's a miracle he'll let you do that. Maybe you should sit up now, just in case he decides to grab your head or something."

Kwanele opened his eyes and rolled his head to see Jacques's face. The cat lifted his head, yawned at Kwanele, looked at Mark, then flopped back down and closed his eyes to sleep.

"Is he sick?" Mark furrowed his brow as he watched the docile cheetah. The steady rise and fall of the cat's frame seemed normal enough. Kwanele sat up and ran his small hands down the length of the cheetah's spotted flank.

"We were playing before—he was normal." Kwanele shrugged. "Is it time for dinner?"

"We just had breakfast!" Mark chuckled. "No, it's not time for dinner." He eased himself down into the dirt and leaned against the rondavel. "I...ah...I just wanted to come and talk to you." He went awkward. How was he meant to start this conversation?

"Oh." Kwanele hooked up the twig again and began to draw in the dirt.

Mark settled himself before he reached into the folds of his collared shirt and produced his leather necklace, with the wooden carved elephant pendant. Slipping it over his head, Mark held it out to Kwanele. The boy dropped the stick, and with care, took hold of the elephant. He turned it in his hands and ran his thumb over the wood, his eyes wide with delight over its smoothness and the delicate craftsmanship.

"That is really special to me." Mark cleared his throat as the words came out brokenly. "When I was struggling, and I didn't know where to turn, I met Koto. We became good friends. He showed me the Way. He introduced me to Jesus. Once, my heart was made of stone. I didn't think I needed anyone's help. I thought I could manage on my own. Then when I found Jesus, I discovered that I had turned myself to stone on purpose—so I wouldn't get hurt."

Kwanele continued to study the elephant, his expression somber.

"Anyway, Koto gave me this. He said that it represented strength. His people come from a long line of warriors. But warriors, too, must get their strength from believing in something. He wanted to remind me that I, too, was a warrior in God's Kingdom, but my strength needed to come from God. I haven't worn this for a long time, until now. I'd forgotten the important message that this represented. I'd forgotten what

God did for me." Mark closed his eyes a moment, unsure if he was getting through to the boy or not. Kwanele held the necklace back out for Mark to take. Opening his eyes, he stared at the necklace, then smiled at Kwanele in a warm way.

"I'm telling you this because...I want to give this to you."

Kwanele shook his head and tried to give it back to Mark. Mark put his hand over Kwanele's outstretched fist and pushed it back toward the boy's heart.

"You are from a long line of warriors, Kwan. You have true Zulu warrior blood beating through your veins. Do you know what that means? You can also get your strength from God, the one and only God. He will hear you, and He will save you. You are afraid of poachers that want to shoot you, but you don't need to be. God will be your strength and your protection!"

Kwanele held the necklace for a long time, and Mark wondered what was going through the boy's mind. Feeling awkward, he stood and cleared his throat again.

"We are going to town today, Kwanele. To Phalaborwa." Kwanele's eyes blinked with recognition. "We're going to go to a church." Mark tried to regain Kwanele's attention. "It's a place where you can learn more about God, and about what He did for you and what He can do now. It's a place to learn about the Way."

Kwanele looked at Mark, his deep brown eyes unblinking. After a moment, he stood and brushed himself off.

"Well, alright then." Mark stepped aside so the boy could emerge from his spot. "Let's see if Martha has any more of those clothes for you." As they headed back to the rondavel, Mark turned in time to glimpse Kwanele staring at the pendant in awe as they walked. He knew he'd made the right decision.

CHAPTER
SIXTEEN

Mark, Sarah, and Kwanele sat in the comfort of the Cruiser watching people file through the large car-park toward the Sunny Bank Christian Fellowship Church. The dirt car-park had been expanded and bitumen laid, with car spaces marked out in bright white road paint. "This has changed heaps," Mark gasped. Taking a deep breath, Sarah looked at her husband. "Why are we so nervous?"

"Because we don't know what we'll find." Mark thought about the friends whom he and Sarah had grown to love and respect at the church years ago. Would they still be there? Would they be okay with their sudden return? Kwanele clicked opened his door, making the first move. He looked so smart in his new church outfit that Martha had rustled up for him. Mark turned to Sarah, a twinkle in his eyes.

"Kwanele's coming out of his shell." He unclipped his seat belt, stepped out of the Cruiser, and flashed a grin at Kwanele. Mark had shaved off his stubble that morning and put on Sarah's favorite cologne. Straightening his red formal shirt, Mark slipped his wallet and cell phone into the back pocket of his denim jeans. Sarah appeared at his side and slipped her arm into his. She leaned into his ear. "He's out of his shell because you are starting to be what he needs." She eyed him. Mark cocked an eyebrow at her, and his breath caught in his throat for the second time that morning. She was wearing an elegant pale pink and floral dress that dropped to her knees in Spanish style. Her yellow heels matched the yellow floral patterns that flicked throughout the pink, breaking up the dominant color. "You know what I mean?" She grinned and squeezed his arm again. He couldn't follow her gist, however, as he was too captivated by her beauty. He nodded, and they made their way toward the auditorium.

The main foyer was streaming with crowds of people.

"I don't remember it being this big." Mark looked around in wonder. "I don't recognize anybody." He frowned.

"It is big. I guess that means they are doing well. It's attracting people." Sarah stretched onto her tiptoes and searched the crowds for one of their old friends. She guided Mark and Kwanele toward a visitor's desk and smiled at the neatly dressed woman.

"Good morning," the cheerful woman offered before Sarah could open her mouth. "Are you all new?"

Sarah laughed. "Sort of...not really, but recently 'yes'." She blushed. "We actually got married here four years ago."

The lady's eyes lit up. Sarah continued. "Does Brandi Mulherron still come here?"

The woman's shoulders dropped as she shook her head. "I'm sorry." A curious look crossed her face and she tilted her head as she examined Sarah's face. "Are you the one she used to talk about all the time? Sarah?"

Sarah swallowed hard, her eyes hopeful as she nodded. Mark's mouth dried up as he thought of Koto's family. "What happened to her?" He leaned forward. "She was one of Sarah's best friends."

The woman's expression shone with sad warmth. "I know. She often said that. She left town."

"Was she being harassed?" Sarah's brows pulled together. The woman appeared thoughtful. "I'm not sure. She stuck close to her friends, but she seemed happy. She got a job on the other side of the country. At a saddlery." Mark saw Sarah's shoulders drop with relief. "What about Max and Kym Sutton?" Sarah continued. Kwanele shifted at her side and Mark saw he was beginning to appear bored.

"Yes." The woman beamed and moved out from behind the booth. She pointed down a hallway. "Kym runs the crèche room. She'll be down the hall there signing in toddlers. Max is around here somewhere. He's the assistant pastor."

"Wow." Mark's jaw dropped open. "Things sure do change."

"Change is good," the woman chirped. "Especially if it's for the better." Her words lingered in Mark's mind as she sent them off down through the milling crowds of people toward the crèche room. Doors had opened and people had started to file toward the modern auditorium. Sarah reached out for Kwanele and urged him to take her hand. He appeared to be in a whirlwind of overwhelmed awe by the sheer numbers of people in such close proximity. Different people from many different African tribes and tongues all gathered in the same place in peace, as if they were all from the same family. In this place, black and white were equal—as it should be. It was like he was home for the first time in years. Mark was taken by surprise when Kwanele latched on to his hand instead of Sarah's. Mark closed his large strong hand around the cool, slender hand of the boy. Mark felt a wave of warmth when he spotted the elephant pendant just visible under Kwanele's Sunday shirt.

Sarah poked her head in the doorway of the crèche room. There was a small throng of mothers and fathers lined up to sign in their toddlers, who squirmed with anxiousness to escape into the colorful world of toys, puzzles, color-ins, songs, and stories within. A tall slender woman in jeans and a turquoise blouse gave directions to her younger assistants. Her straight brown hair was pulled elegantly into a clip. She glanced up at the line of parents, when her eyes came to rest on Mark and Sarah.

Mark chuckled as he saw her jump with apparent recognition. Her whole body lifted in delighted shock. She called over one of her assistants to ensure the parents were all greeted appropriately before she made her way through a sea of small children to the doorway. "Mark! Sarah!" She ushered them into the less crowded hallway and threw her arms around them both in turn. Tears glistened in her eyes. "Are you both well? Are you staying for church, or passing by?"

"We're here for church." Sarah smiled.

Two little girls that looked to be about two years old wiggled through the crowd and appeared at Kym's legs. In union, they began to tug at her clothes. Mark covered his mouth to stifle another chuckle. Their pretty apricot dresses were marred already with the biscuits they had just finished mauling. "Mummy, more?"

Kym beamed and lined the girls up in front of her. "These are our girls, Leah and Caitlyn! Can you believe it? I had twins for my first go."

"Mummy, more biscuit. Hungry." Leah tugged at Kym's blouse, leaving a mush of biscuit on the flowing fabric. None too frazzled, Kym pulled a Ziploc bag of crackers from her jeans pocket. "What do you say?" She held it up.

"Pu-lease!" The girls held out their chubby fingers, all cheeky giggles as Kym passed out one cracker each.

"Now go back inside and sit with Miss Lydia. I'll be there soon."

The girls ran back inside the room as Kym attempted to wipe at the biscuit mush on her sleeve.

"Busy, huh?" Mark stuck his hands in his pocket.

Kym sighed. "Apparently, twins for my first pregnancy mean a higher chance of multiple births next time. It's worth it, though." She gazed over her shoulder back into the crèche room. "I'd better go. The service is going to start soon. Will we see you after church? Lunch?"

"Sure." Both Mark and Sarah nodded. Kym grinned, waved, then flitted back into the room. Mark, Sarah, and Kwanele made their way into the well-lit auditorium just as the music started. The church here had grown in the years they had been away, and most of the rows were packed out with eager people, keen to hear the message of God. Ushers were putting out spare rows of chairs at the back of the room. One of them indicated the empty seats to the trio. Smiling his thanks to the usher, Mark directed Sarah and Kwanele to a new row on the side. The cool air-conditioner blasted from the wall behind them, and Mark noticed Kwanele shudder as the boy nestled in between them. Sarah put her arm around Kwanele's shoulder. "It is a little cold in here, isn't it?" Kwanele nodded and leaned in to Sarah. Mark's eyes met hers. He saw pleasant surprise in his wife's expression.

The music up front changed subtly and the congregants began to stand up. Words came up on the big screens, and everyone began to sing as the music began. Mark glanced down at Kwanele. The kid had his eyes closed, but he wore a large smile on his face as if he were drinking in everything. Before long, various speakers had come and gone, before finally the pastor rose to give the message. Mark kept glancing sideways at Kwanele, whose eyes were glued to the front in apparent awe. When the pastor was finished, he gave an invitation to anyone who was in need to come down the front for prayer. Mark and Sarah startled as one as they felt Kwanele jump between them.

"Come on!" He grabbed their arms. "Quick, or we'll miss it."

Mark frowned as he bent to listen to Kwanele over the music.

"What's wrong?"

"We need to get prayer." Kwanele tugged at Mark's arm. "We will miss out. We need to pray that the poachers don't find us."

"Hey. Shhh." Mark held up an urgent finger. He cast Sarah a worried look, and they all moved into the aisle. A muscle in Mark's jaw twitched—they needed prayer for this. Why would he be too proud to ask for it? It took the innocence of a child to jolt them to reality. They waited in patience with the other people who stood in the front. Various church staff moved around and prayed for various people.

Sarah nodded to Kwanele and the boy followed her example and bowed his head. They waited for someone to approach them.

"And what can I pray for your family?" asked a gentle male voice. *I know that voice.* Mark's eyes flicked up to the male face in surprise. Sarah smiled and looked at Kwanele, a twinkle in her eyes.

Kwanele jumped right in and addressed the man with boldness. "Please, sir, I do not know your God."

The man grasped Mark and Sarah by the shoulders. Mark smirked as he saw the recognition dawn on the man's face.

"Wait a minute. It can't be. Sarah? Mark?" Mark released a full-blown grin at Kym's husband, Max. Recognition registered for Sarah. "Max?" Tears welled in her eyes. Max had grown a full beard in the last few years and looked very regal.

They all embraced as one big group. Kwanele squirmed and pushed up into the middle of them.

"Listen. We need prayer. It is very important. Urgent, in fact." He stamped his foot.

Everyone stepped back from the boy. "Whoa there, young

man. We can definitely pray, right now." Max put his hand on the boy's shoulder, a patient smile lighting on his face.

"It's okay. What is so urgent that you need prayer for?"

Mark nodded when Kwanele looked up at him, his question in his face. The boy took a deep breath, and made his request known.

"We are all in danger of being killed by poachers. We need this God to save us. He must protect us from them. They will shoot us."

Mark's brows shot up at the forcefulness of the boy's words, and he looked at Sarah with concern.

"He's been through a lot," Sarah explained. Max nodded and crouched down, his hand on Kwanele's head. Kwanele reached up and took the hand.

"Not just me. All of us," he protested.

"Kwan—" Mark's face creased as he started to scold the boy, but Max shook his head.

"It's okay." He smiled, but gave Mark a firm look. "This is very important to the young man." He placed one of his hands on each of the adults' shoulders.

"Kwanele," the boy corrected, eager for Max to pray. Mark had never seen such forcefulness from him before, and he wondered what brought it on. Max prayed beautifully that God would keep them all under the hidden protection of the Kingdom of God, that He would work all things for good, and that Kwanele would get to know Jesus in a real and powerful way. Releasing his hands from them, Max gave a broad smile.

"May we talk after?" He indicated toward the people still waiting for prayer.

"We can do better than that." Mark grinned. "We're all doing lunch. We spoke with Kym already. We'll wait for you in the coffee lounge if you like."

Max nodded, then moved on to the next people in line. Kwanele seemed satisfied as he grasped both their hands and gave them a squeeze. "Can we get extra prayer from him at lunch?" He danced on the spot and Mark and Sarah tried not to laugh.

CHAPTER
SEVENTEEN

Sarah watched as Max swiped the remainder of a fried chip in tomato sauce, then popped it into his mouth, before searching his plate for his next bite. "So, you've been in Polokwane? How's that been?"

Mark put his fork down.

"Honestly?"

Max raised his brows. Mark shook his head, then collected more of his chicken dish onto the fork. "It's been hard. We've been cut off from everything we love."

He frowned as Kwanele giggled beside him. Kym fussed over the twin girls in their high chairs, who decided to break into a mini-food fight. Kwanele thought it was hilarious. Sarah grinned and directed him back to his meal of chicken nuggets and chips. She was glad to see him enjoying himself. Smiling up at Sarah with a mouthful of nugget, he returned to his meal. Sarah looked at her husband, who still wore that frown. She reached under the table and gave his thigh a squeeze. He managed a halfhearted smile in return. He looked drawn. Several years of stress and fear and being cut off had really aged the handsome Afrikaner man. He still carried himself proudly, and his wavy brown hair and broad-muscled shoulders still turned many women's heads. Sarah watched him as she remembered the pain of their past few years in the city. His strong, handsome features pulled like carved bronze as his jaw set. She knew that he was determined not to let it get that bad again.

"What about your church in Polokwane? Did you find a good fellowship?" Kym wiped tomato sauce from one of her daughter's hands with a disposable wet cloth.

"Well, ah...actually...." Sarah looked down and felt her face flush.

Max and Kym both raised their heads at the couple, concern written in their eyes.

"You didn't find a church?" Kym seemed surprised. Mark pressed his lips together as Max looked from one to the other.

"You have been running for your lives, and you didn't—" So shocked was Max, that he couldn't even finish the sentence. He shook his head. Sarah felt Mark stiffen beside her.

"We knew it was dangerous—we were afraid to make new friends in case they got hurt, too." Sarah gripped her husband's knee under the table again.

"But it was just an excuse." Mark voice sounded brittle as he cut in. "We know that now. We were afraid."

"We've really struggled." Sarah took up where Mark left off. "We know we have backslidden, and we need help and prayer to get back. We know all that now. It's partly why we've come back. We needed to break out of the bad pattern we've fallen into." She stopped and smiled at Mark. "I have Mark to thank for that. He made a bold decision."

Leah coughed on a chip, drawing Kym's attention back to the twins. She patted her daughter on the back and passed her a sippy-cup of juice before she turned back to the couple. "So you are at Jacob and Martha's at the moment, did you say?"

Sarah nodded. "So is Kwanele."

Kym smiled down at the boy, who was happy eating and talking to the twins. The conversation trailed into a lull as everyone ate more of their lunch. Sarah looked from the couple to Kwanele, then back to her food. The story of Kwanele and how he came to be with them had been explained earlier at church, but there was still a lot that Max and Kym didn't know. Kym reached out over the table and took one of Sarah's hands.

"Please. You both need to know that we are all here for you. We always have been. It's easier to fight this evil when we all stand together in prayer and support each other. Isolation will be the end of you—spiritually, emotionally, and physically."

Mark scoffed. "We've already experienced two of those three. I'm not ready to experience the third."

Max sipped his soft drink. "In all seriousness, though, it's true."

Mark and Sarah both sobered up.

"We know," Mark admitted. "We know, and we don't want to go back there. It's time to step out of the boat, change things." He gave Sarah a serious look. Sarah stared at him for a moment, trying to read his expression. What was he thinking? Suddenly she realized. That job offer from Letaba. The one she wasn't sure about. She took a deep breath and decided to lay the cards on the table. These were some of their closest friends, after all.

"We—well, more like Mark, anyway…were offered new jobs."

Mark jerked his head toward her, his eyes full of question.

Sarah tossed her loose dark curls to one side cheekily. She enjoyed shocking her husband. Max and Kym appeared to miss the subtle interchange.

"Hmm, do tell." Max pushed some more food into his mouth and listened attentively. Mark continued to eyeball his wife. "Yes, honey, do tell."

Sarah threw a coy smile her husband's way before she explained about the rangers offer at Letaba.

"Did you find out more?" Kym appeared cynical.

Mark propped his elbow on the table, rested his chin in the palm of his hand, and watched Sarah, his brows raised.

"We didn't," Sarah admitted. "I didn't want to. I got scared and wanted to leave." She cast him an apologetic look. "I'm so sorry, Mark." Sarah could feel tears well in her eyes.

"There's no reason why you can't go back, or ring him," Max interjected. Sarah nodded, then felt a jolt go through her. Of course. The business card. She spun to Mark. "We need to talk about this some more."

Mark put his hand up. "Whoah."

Sarah's shoulders dropped at the gesture. "I know, I know. Have you still got that card, though?"

"*Ja*," he said.

Max wiped his mouth with his napkin, then piled all the food scraps onto his plate. "How long are you planning on staying at the bush camp?"

Mark and Sarah looked at each other before they turned to Max.

"No idea." Mark shrugged. "We are living each day one at a time right now."

"Well, we have the number for Jacob and Martha's. Maybe we could come out and see you all there?" Max glanced at his wife and her face lit up.

"Oh, I could get some photos of the girls with Jacques. That would be so cute." Kwanele's eyes shot up at the mention of his beloved cheetah.

"Not too many photos." He finished his drink. "Jacques doesn't like photos."

Everyone laughed good-naturedly as Kym bowed her head to the Zulu boy.

"I will let you be in charge of it, then."

Kwanele's chest lifted as he nodded his consent to the idea.

Kwanele tossed and turned in his bed that night. His mind whirled with too much information. He'd learned a lot about this Jesus person through both Mark and church, and he struggled to get his head around it all. There was a tug at his heart, which made him both excited and agitated. He thought that to be one of God's children, he needed to accept Jesus into his heart. He'd also heard that God would listen to his prayers wherever he was and that he could talk to God about anything. He felt a deep yearning in his soul, telling him that it was all true, and that Jesus was the answer to his problems. There was also a twang of doubt, which hovered over his head like a dark cloud. It threatened to rain upon him if he chose the wrong path. If none of it was true, if God wasn't real, he would have put them all in more danger by being bold enough to try and defy the poachers. He clutched at the elephant pendant around his neck, hoping to glean some truth, some courage, some strength from it. The wood was cool beneath his fingers. There were no magical qualities in the pendant, it was just wood. Just as swiftly as the terrible thought accosted him, it fled into the recesses of the shadowy cloud of doubt that still lingered. No, the wood was not magical, but it wasn't meaningless, either. It represented a power, a strength far greater than his own. Was he really a warrior inside, or a coward? He tossed and turned in his bed, wrestling with his conflicted thoughts. Sweat leached onto his pillow.

Pray.

The word came into his head out of nowhere.

Who am I to talk to God? Only pastors can pray for you, can't they? he argued with himself.

No, a voice whispered on the wind. *If you want to be a child of God, you can talk to Him like you were His child.*

Kwanele sat up and shuddered. "But I'm not a child of God," he whispered back into the quiet of the night.

Pray.

The word echoed into the very core of his being. It drew him, called to him, he couldn't resist it.

"God?" His small voice sounded too loud in the small, dark room. "If You can hear me, I need to speak with You." Kwanele looked around the room, making out the outlines of the chair by the table with his jacket hanging over it. He looked toward the window. The curtains blew softly on a cool breeze.

"My name is Kwanele. I need Your help." He hesitated and listened to the chorus of crickets outside. The whispered words into his heart that urged him to pray earlier were silent, as if waiting for him to go on. A tingle went down his spine, and he felt a strange anticipation.

"I heard You know everything there is to know in the world, about everyone. If this is true, then You know about me. You know about the bad people. You know what they want. I need Your help. I need Your Son, Jesus, in my heart to save me. I don't understand everything about sin, or about why Jesus died, but I know people say it was to save me. All I know is that I need Jesus, and I am asking you to put Him in my heart...somehow. Please don't let it hurt."

He looked around and trembled. "God, if You are real, You can save me from the bad people, and Mark and Sarah, too. I have no home, but I know where I want to be. Please show me that You are real. Please help me." He laid his head back onto his pillow and clutched the corner of his duvet to his chin. Sniffling, Kwanele began to weep. "Help me, Jesus..." His murmurs faded away as he fell asleep. "Help us..."

A cool wisp of air blew in through the bedroom window. The thin curtain above Kwanele's bed shifted and brushed across his face. He shuddered in his sleep and pulled the duvet tight up under his chin. There was a rustle outside the window, then a loud *thump.* Kwanele startled awake, sat up, and looked around in fear. He squinted into the dim room. The nearly full moon was rising outside his window, and the blue glow now penetrated directly into even the darkest corner of his room. He studied his room for a moment.

Nothing.

With a sigh, he settled back into his covers. He wiggled himself deeper into the bed and rolled onto his side, tucking his knees to his chest in the fetal position. Slowly he settled again. His eyelids began to grow heavy and his muscles relaxed.

THUMP!...SCRAPE!

Kwanele sat up like a shot. That wasn't his imagination. And it came from outside. He rocked up onto his knees, batted aside the curtain, and peered out the open window. All he could see was the tall, wooden slats of the wooden perimeter fence that sat all but a meter from his window. Narrowing his eyes at the fence, his vision trailed up to the cruel, looped barbed-wire that lined the top. A sudden wheezy sigh reverberated from outside the fence. Kwanele froze. Then the shuffle noise again. All senses now on full alert, Kwanele strained, trying to peer over the fence. He couldn't get in the right position. He stopped and listened.

Nothing again.

There was no way he'd see over the fence like this. Carefully balancing himself up onto his feet, he lifted the glass pane of the window higher. It creaked as he secured it on the highest latch. He stole a glance over his shoulder into the dark room. Hopefully he wouldn't wake anyone. Returning his focus to the fence, he waited for a reaction to the creak.

Nothing.

Maybe it had moved away. Was it an animal? A bird? More curious and bolder by the second, Kwanele put one foot up on the windowsill. With care, he ducked his head and eased himself out the window. The air was cold on his bare arms and legs. The pajamas that Martha had rustled up were light cotton shorts and a button-down shirt. Goose bumps appeared on his limbs. Kwanele stood outside on the window ledge, his feet planted on the broad windowsill. He very carefully leaned forward, momentarily unbalanced before his hands scrambled and caught hold of the rough wooden fence. He stretched onto the tips of his toes, and peered through the barbed-wire into the wilderness beyond. An owl hooted in one of the trees above. It stirred up several small vervet monkeys that were nesting in the tree for the night. Kwanele could just make out their small gray faces as they peered back at him from above. Kwanele scanned beyond the fence. There was nothing unusual out here. He exhaled with a mixture of disappointment and relief. Kwanele leaned back and caught hold of the window frame. He looked toward the ground. It wasn't too high up, but if he did fall, he wouldn't find it easy to haul himself back in. He loathed the idea of having to knock on the door, wake people up, and then explain himself. A movement under the rondavel caught his eye, and he grappled at the window frame with fear. The shape emerged. It was just Jacques. He meandered out and looked up at Kwanele with expectation. A chuckle of relief escaped Kwanele's lips.

"Jacques, do you sleep there every night? Under my window?"

The cheetah yawned and sat to scratch behind his ear with his clawed hind foot. Kwanele eased himself down to sit on the window ledge. His legs dangled down above the cheetah. Jacques stood up and stretched so that his head just rubbed the bottom of Kwanele's bare foot. The boy smiled broadly. He wouldn't sleep in fear now, knowing his best friend guarded him at night.

"I love you, Jacques." The cheetah rocked down to lie on his belly. He tensed as his head locked on to something through the fence. Kwanele frowned. Maybe there was something after all.

"You heard it, too?" The hackles rose on the big cat's neck, and Jacque's lips curled back into a growl so low in his throat that Kwanele could barely catch it.

"There's nothing there, Jacques. It's just birds and monkeys." Kwanele tried to convince the both of them. He eyed the top of the fence. Should he stand up and have one last look?

A sudden urge to slip back into his room, slam shut the window, and hide under the blankets hit him. Kwanele swallowed hard and fought against it. He was worried that he could be heard from outside the fence. He kept his eyes trained on Jacques, gauging the danger by the cheetah's response. The cat rocked up onto his feet, crouched, and growled louder. His hackles rose up like the bristles on the back of a hedgehog. Kwanele felt his heart beat faster. Jacques stopped growling and lay back down. He licked his lips in agitation. Kwanele narrowed his eyes in confusion. Something was there, but it was coming and going. Kwanele tilted his chin toward the sky. A cool breeze had sprung up and rustled the leaves of the trees overhead. The little vervet monkeys murmured, their chittery voices whispering secrets on the wind.

THUMP.

There it was again. As if something had hit the other side of the fence, right in front of them. Kwanele leapt to his feet and paused. Should he look? If he didn't and he missed it again, he'd never get to sleep. He needed to know what animal was out there to put his mind at ease. Shaky, he gathered his nerves, leaned forward, and grasped the wood to peer over the fence.

Kwanele gasped and nearly lost his footing. A massive male elephant stood right there. Jacques was back on his feet now. He growled, his neck bristled. Panting in terror at the near fall and the sheer shock of what he just saw, Kwanele gripped the wood, eyes wide, as he tried to compose himself. With all caution, he peered again over the fence.

"Peace, be still."

A man's deep voice spoke. Kwanele blinked as he beheld the elephant again. There was a strange man sitting astride the elephant. How had he not seen this man before? He was tall and dark and wore the garbs of a great Zulu warrior king. The ostrich feathers on his headdress stood out brilliant white and black under the gleaming moon. He wore a necklace made from sharp teeth, a leopard skin around his loin, and he carried a spear in one hand and a great shield in the other. Kwanele's eyes widened. Jacques's growl grew louder.

"Be still," the man commanded in a quiet voice. He raised his hand, then lowered it palm down. Kwanele blinked with surprise as Jacques licked his lips, flicked his tail, and obeyed the voice. The cat then slunk back under the building, the gleam in his eyes apparent as he sat watchful. The great tusker elephant groaned and, ears outstretched, shook the dust from its head. Dust sprayed all over Kwanele. He coughed and covered his mouth with one hand as the great elephant knocked his trunk against the fence again.

THUMP.

The man said no more. Kwanele wondered, *Is he waiting for me to say something?* Kwanele swallowed hard and took a deep breath.

"Who are you?" His voice failed to give volume. The Zulu warrior smiled at Kwanele. His demeanor was calm, but also powerful and majestic. Kwanele sensed he was in a great presence. Had he not been hanging on to the side of a fence, he would have bowed in reverence. The man tilted his head, a look in his eyes as if he could read Kwanele's thoughts.

"Did you not ask for help?"

Kwanele frowned as he locked on to the man's eyes. Those deep, penetrating eyes. Could this man see into his thoughts, his dreams, and his soul? Was the Christian God a Zulu? Standing on tiptoes, Kwanele started to cramp in his feet as the questions reeled in his mind. He needed to move, even though it meant moving out of view of the pair. Inwardly groaning, he adjusted his feet and stepped down to ease the cramps. He rocked back on his heels and wiggled his toes to bring back the blood supply. The tone of the elephant's sigh shook Kwanele's attention back to the fence. He glanced up and sucked in a sharp breath as he saw the man now perched on top of the fence. There he sat, amid the barbed-wire loops, as if they weren't even there. Kwanele jumped backward. How did he do that? If he could get over the fence, anyone could. The thought sent a chill down Kwanele's spine.

"Be at peace," the man spoke. "No man can penetrate these walls."

"Then how?" Kwanele peered up at the man, his eyes wide. "I...I prayed," he stammered. "Are you...Mark and Sarah's God?"

The man smiled and shook his head. "He is the God of all of us. He is the God of all the world, all nations, tribes, and tongues. I have been sent to you, from the One whom you have called."

Relieved that he could keep his feet flat on the windowsill now, but still frightened, Kwanele blinked. He tried to sound out words in reply, but his voice only failed.

"So...you don't understand about what Jesus did for you?" The man's deep baritone words sounded like velvet. Kwanele made eye contact with the man and nodded.

"God has sent someone to help you with that—he's already started to help you."

Kwanele frowned. The Zulu warrior continued, "You must follow Mark van der Merwe. You must listen to his words. He has the key for you to understand the gift God has given to all men...though not all choose it." Sadness crossed the man's expression.

"How do I get Jesus in my heart to save me from the bad people?" Kwanele spoke up, worried that the man would leave without telling him the secret. He shifted on the fence and adjusted his weight and shield.

"You already do. You asked God to put Jesus in your heart. It is done." He smiled. Kwanele's eyes widened, then he frowned with confusion.

"But I don't feel different."

"It is a journey, Kwanele. You have only just started on it. God chose you. You must follow the Way of the Warrior!"

"But I don't know how to be a warrior!" Kwanele protested. The man pointed the spear toward Kwanele's heart. Kwanele shrank back.

"You already are one. It is inside your heart, your blood. You just need to train in the Way. Look!" The man leveled the spear up and caught Kwanele's elephant pendant on the end of the shiny metal. Kwanele grabbed it up and held the elephant in front of his eyes. He squinted in the moonlight. Had something happened to the pendant? It had changed color and one side of it now displayed a delicate etched cross. The boy held it close to his eyes in wonder as he examined the changes.

"When Jesus is in your heart, you have been washed clean in His blood. You are now a new person—the old is gone. Your past is wiped clean. All that matters now is what you do with your future."

Kwanele looked up at the man, hope in his eyes.

"You mean it? My past is gone?"

The Zulu warrior gave him a serious look. "You must now walk in truth. Walk in the light."

Still captivated by the elephant pendant, Kwanele nodded.

"You must ask God daily to protect you. If you fail to do so, you are still in danger. The evil one does not like people to choose God. Hear well, the words I have spoken to you this night."

Kwanele stared at the man and nodded. So much had been told to him. Would he remember it all?

"You only need ask, and you will remember." The Zulu answered the unspoken question.

Kwanele looked down, and with care, tucked the pendant into his pajama shirt again. He pressed his palm over the raised surface through his shirt. But when he went to thank the man, he was gone. One lone ostrich feather from the headdress sat in the top of the fence. Kwanele leaned over, retrieved it, and ran the black and white through his fingers in wonder. Climbing back into the window, he clambered onto his bed and then onto the floor. He padded over to the wide-brimmed hat Mark had bought for him at Letaba Rest Camp and pushed the base of the feather into the leather hat band. Quietly, he tiptoed back to his bed. Kwanele lay on his back and replayed the conversation he had just had with the man. Was that what Mark had called an angel?

"Please protect me as I sleep, God," he murmured to the night. A few minutes passed, and then Kwanele fell into a deep sleep.

CHAPTER

EIGHTEEN

A sharp rap on the door woke Kwanele.

"Kwan."

He rubbed his eyes as he sat up.

"Kwan. Wake up, Kwanele." Mark's deep voice resounded through the door. Kwan yawned as he blinked against the warm sunlight that streamed through his window. He looked toward the closed door. In an instant, memory from the night before flooded back into his mind with such force that he sprang out of bed. Did he dream?

"Hang on," he called to Mark and raced across the room to his hat. With a loud bump, he knocked over a large ornament that sat against the wall. Swiftly, he set it upright and turned his attention back to the hat. It was there. He reached out a shaky hand and picked up the hat. He stared, wide-eyed, at the brilliant black and white feather that was just where he'd placed it the night before. So it wasn't a dream.

"Kwan?" Mark rapped on the door. "Are you okay in there?"

"*Yebo.* I'm fine." Kwanele turned his attention to the pendant that hung around his neck. Nervous, he pulled it out. The wooden carved elephant had turned a brilliant tone of red, and the cross carved into the back was still as real as when he first saw it. He ran his thumb over the cross in wonder. The indentation was smooth, not like the scratchy marks that a knife would create. It was extraordinary.

"Mark?" Kwanele tucked the pendant away.

"*Ja?*" came the muffled reply.

"Can you come in here, please?"

The doorknob turned, and Mark stuck his head through the doorway.

"Are you alright?" He looked concerned. Kwanele took a deep breath and sat on his bed. Where did he start? Mark entered the room and sat opposite Kwanele on the old chair against the wall.

"What's wrong?"

Kwanele stared long and hard at Mark, and tried to gauge how the man would react.

"Nothing. But something happened." He took a deep breath, and his brow knitted together. Mark sat opposite him and leaned forward.

"What is it?" Mark's voice was barely above a whisper.

"Last night, I heard noises, outside. I thought it was nothing, and then I thought it was an animal. So I went out on the window ledge to see—" Kwanele rocked onto his knees and drew back the curtains so Mark could see the fence outside. "When I first looked, I found Jacques. He sleeps under my window now."

"He must love you very much." Mark's smile was genuine, and it took Kwanele off track. His eyes lit up as he looked toward the window.

"I know."

"So, are you okay now—he didn't frighten you too much?"

"I'm not finished." Kwanele's eyes grew wide as he turned and perched on the edge of the bed. He leaned close to Mark. "There was a loud *whoosh*, then a *thump*—"

"Uh-huh." Mark's attention seemed to waver as he glanced about the room.

"Mark."

"I'm listening." He refocused on the boy.

"I looked again, and there was an elephant!"

Mark blinked at the revelation. "An elephant?"

"With a Zulu man on its back."

Mark stared at Kwanele for a long moment, his brows raised. "It was just a dream, Kwan."

"No, it was no dream." Kwanele vaulted onto the floor and paced the carpet. "I saw him in real life. I was awake. He was a Zulu warrior. He spoke to me about your God, about the Way. About Jesus. He said he was sent by God to speak with me. I'm not lying, Mark." Kwanele started to jump about, his voice raised in protest. "He came. He was real. He said you were to teach me the Way, and he said I was a warrior and that I am safe from danger."

Mark's body language softened. "I'm sorry, Kwan. You're right. It sounds like God sent an angel to you." He shook his head, his expression crinkling. "Please forgive me, Kwan."

"And just to prove I'm not lying—" Kwan leapt over to the other side of the room and snatched up his hat. He pulled it snugly onto his head. "He left me one of the ostrich feathers from his headdress."

Mark narrowed his eyes. "That certainly is quite a feather."

"There's more." Kwanele's voice lowered and he held a finger to his lips. He stood in front of Mark and pulled the necklace from his shirt. "I didn't touch this at all. It changed by itself as the man spoke to me."

Mark's eyes grew wide. "May I see it?"

Kwanele slipped it over his head and passed it to Mark. He heard the man draw a sharp breath as he held the stained wood. He ran his thumb over the carved cross as Kwanele had, almost as if he had to feel it to believe it.

"That's amazing, Kwanele." Mark's voice was hoarse. "What an incredible encounter. Like Sarah used to have. God must have some big plans for you."

"But you have to teach me and train me in the Way." Kwanele looked deep into Mark's eyes. The man's focus became fuzzy, and it was as if he was in some sort of reverie.

Kwanele jolted him from his thoughts.

"So, will you teach me everything about the Way?"

Mark got up and ruffled the boy's tight black curls.

"Of course I will. Now—"

Kwanele had a sudden sense that Mark had another purpose in mind for the morning. He looked at the man with expectancy.

"I woke you up early for a reason. It's going to be a hot day later on, and so I figured we needed to do this earlier. You're going to learn something new today. It will take a warrior heart to do this, are you up for it?"

Kwanele raised his brows before he nodded slowly.

"But I need to learn the Way," he whined. Mark smirked at

him over his shoulder.

"Trust me, this is a starting point for you. I am teaching you the Way. Here." Mark ducked back outside the bedroom door and returned. He placed a pair of new riding boots in Kwanele's bewildered hands.

"Boots? To keep?" Kwanele couldn't believe it. "Thank you."

Mark nodded. "I hope they're your size. The size is different from normal boots."

Kwanele raised his brows again. "What type of boots are these, then?" He turned them over in his hands.

Mark threw him a coy smile. "Get dressed, put them on, and I'll show you." He began to leave the room, but then he turned to add, "Oh, wear those long blue trousers Martha got you. And get some thick socks." Mark shut the door behind him as he left. Kwanele held the boots in front of his face. The new, shiny leather smelt great. He drank in the scent as he held them up to his nose for a moment. He then placed them with care on the bed, and went looking for the appropriate clothes. Soon dressed, he sat on the chair and with difficulty squeezed his feet into the new boots. Re-donning his wide-brimmed, feathered hat as a finishing touch, he appraised himself in the mirror. Not bad. He strutted out into the kitchen. Mark was pouring some milk onto some cereal.

"Here. Get that into you, and we'll go." Mark took a bite from a piece of toast as he crossed the room and returned the milk to the fridge.

"Did you get the boots on alright? They're always tight to get on until you wear them in."

Kwanele held up one of his feet and his chest welled with pride. "They feel fine now that they are on."

"Good." Mark nodded his approval as he moved around the room putting away items that he'd gotten out for breakfast. Kwanele sat at the table and began to eat. He noticed that Mark wore similar clothes. Long blue jeans, brown leather riding boots, and a long-sleeved button-down shirt.

"What's all the noise out here?" Sarah wandered into the room in her nightgown and slippers, bleary-eyed. She surveyed the pair and put her hands on her hips.

"Do you think he's ready, Mark van der Merwe?" She

reached up to brush a stray lock of hair behind her ear and turned to Kwanele.

"Kwanele, could you please take your hat off at the table." Kwanele grinned, placed it beside him, and continued eating his cereal.

"I'm taking it slow, one step at a time, Sarah. You know how I am with beginners." Mark gave her a sardonic grin, and she swiped him across the shoulder.

"You and beginners?" she scoffed. "As I recall from our safari trail-riding days, I used to be the one out next to beginners on the trails fixing any basic problems that you missed."

He held his hands up in defense. "Honey, we don't have the same time restraints here. I will take it slow." He closed the distance to Sarah with speed and placed his hands on her shoulders. Kwanele tried not to look, but he couldn't help himself as he watched Mark look deep into her eyes. "Trust me."

"Okay." Sarah blushed. She moved away to the bench and flicked on the kettle.

"Are Jacob and Martha up yet?" She yawned and began to prepare herself a coffee. Mark nodded as he chewed his last bit of toast. "They had an early group arriving and wanted to get the catering area ready. I think Martha's supply truck was due with food for the cold room, too. She wanted to meet them to unpack it."

Sarah gave her husband a severe look.

"I offered to help," Mark answered the unspoken reprimand. "I even told her that we need to earn our keep. So I wanted to unpack the truck."

Kwanele watched the silent interchange between them.

"She told me I had more important things to do..." He grinned at his wife as he rinsed his plate and wiped his hands. He kissed her on the cheek as he passed by, a spark in his eye.

"I have to tell you something exciting later on."

"Oh?" She touched her cheek where he had kissed her, and Kwanele turned back to his food, rolling his eyes.

Mark stood by the shelf at the back door and squirted some sunscreen into his hands from the pump bottle. He began to apply it over his tanned features. "You need some of this, too, Kwan." Kwanele lifted his gaze to meet the Afrikaner's. "Just because you're brown doesn't mean you don't burn."

Kwanele pushed his empty bowl into the sink and leapt to attention in front of Mark. Mark took the bottle and squirted some of the oily cream into his open palm. He copied Mark's example and dabbed spots of it onto his forehead, chin, nose, cheeks, and chin. He then rubbed his hands together and rubbed it over his entire face.

"Ears," Mark directed as Kwanele mirrored his actions.

"Neck." He pushed another dab of cream into Kwanele's hand. Sarah chuckled as she watched the pair.

"Well, I might come out and watch a bit later." She sat at the table with her coffee and picked up the morning paper. Task completed, Mark and Kwanele waved to Sarah and left the rondavel.

Jacques met them at the bottom of the stairs. He immediately rubbed his head into Kwanele's hand. Mark reached over and scuffed the cheetah's coat.

"Morning, Jacques. You'd better stay here this time," he added as they walked off around the building.

"Why?" Kwanele jogged to catch up to Mark's long stride.

"You'll see." They rounded the corner and passed several staff members as they were preparing for the day's activities. Mark asked if one of them could attend to Jacques and ensure he didn't follow them. He more than likely needed to be chained up for a while, considering he was stuck to Kwanele like glue most of the time. Kwanele's eyes grew wide with apprehension as he saw they were headed for the horse kraals. Buster and Sniper nickered their greetings as they approached. Kwanele stopped in his tracks and shook his head.

"I know what you want to do...and I can't do this." Kwanele's voice quivered with fear as he stared at the kraals. Mark crouched down in front of him, level with his face. His face was filled with compassion.

"I know this is a fear of yours, Kwanele, one that I in part caused. I am deeply sorry for that, and I want to help make it up to you. We will take it one step at a time. I will promise you something right now, okay?"

Kwanele wasn't sure, but he nodded. There was genuineness in Mark's eyes.

"I will not push you further than you can handle. Your first lesson in warrior training today, though, is to face a fear—at your pace."

Mark waited; his eyes gentle but firm. Kwanele had seen that look before. He'd seen it in the eyes of the Zulu warrior king.

"Okay." He looked down, his voice a hoarse whisper.

"Pardon? Was that a warrior's voice?" Mark stood, a smirk on his face. "What did you say?"

"Okay." Kwanele lifted his chin and voice. Mark laughed.

"That's better. Come on."

Kwanele trailed along behind as Mark pulled open the shed doors and stepped inside. He took a deep breath. He hauled out a saddle and pad, passed by Kwanele, and hefted it over the rail on the fence. He adjusted the gear so it hung neatly before striding back to the shed. He returned with a halter and lead rope, bridle, and a box in his other hand. Soon enough, Mark took the halter and lead rope and slipped into the kraal toward his horse. After Sniper was moved to the next yard, Mark smiled through the wooden rails at Kwanele. He stood at the fence, his hands gripping the wood. Now the only horse left in the kraal was Buster, who stood in the corner and watched their movements with interest.

"Come on in," Mark ushered. Kwanele looked at Buster. He was a deeper shade of brown than Sniper and his mane was the same brown. He also had a small white blotch on his forehead. Kwanele noticed he had a scruffier coat.

"He won't hurt you," Mark assured him, then held out his hand. Swallowing hard, Kwanele climbed through the rails. He remembered his last encounter with a horse. That day, Mark had not been so patient.

"What are you thinking?" Mark stood in front of him, his hands on his hips. Kwanele stiffened and felt his heart beat harder in his chest. Mark softened and crouched to Kwanele's eye level. "Remember, one step at a time. Your pace."

Kwanele looked into Mark's eyes. He believed him. He gave a small nod.

"Good." Mark straightened up and headed toward Buster. In minutes, he had tied the lead rope onto the post.

"You're going to start just by getting to know him, okay? Pat him, brush him." Mark scooped up a brush from the box and handed it to Kwanele. He took the brush and stepped next to the horse.

"Oh, come on." Mark laughed. "You cuddle a cheetah and lie against his belly, but you won't come and meet a half-asleep horse?"

Kwanele looked up at Mark in shock. Was he angry, or playing? Kwanele saw the comical expression still in the man's eyes and began to chuckle. After his hand connected with the soft coat of the old brown horse and he began to work the brush in rhythmic strokes, Kwanele's nerves settled. This wasn't so bad. Buster exhaled loudly, and Kwanele stepped back warily.

"That means he's happy." Kwanele glanced at Mark, who had shifted away from him and was working on combing out the knots that had formed into dreadlocks in the horse's tail.

"Is this Sarah's horse?" Kwanele continued to brush in the same spot on the neck.

"Hmm? Oh…" Jerking his head in Kwanele's direction, Mark moved back next to him. "Like this." He modeled the short, flicking strokes to use with the hard brush and showed where it needed to also cover the girth and also up onto the back. Smiling and more confident, Kwanele began to work the brush in the new zones.

"So…?" Kwanele pressed.

"No, this is not Sarah's horse." A sadness crossed Mark's eyes. Kwanele tilted his head in question at the expression. Mark sighed and pressed his lips together in a tight smile. Kwanele looked toward the other kraal and pointed his brush.

"That one is yours, though, isn't it?"

Mark smiled and nodded, though his eyes no longer sparkled. He left the tail and moved up toward the neck of the horse.

"Did Sarah have her own horse once?" Kwanele pushed. Mark leaned against Buster's mane.

"She did, Kwan." He sighed. "She had a beautiful golden horse called Honor. They loved each other. It was just as special as you and Jacques, except that Sarah had known Honor a lot longer. That horse would have done anything for her. That horse almost knew her every thought. It would have followed her to the end of the earth." He paused and gazed with sadness into the distance. After a moment, Kwanele saw him snap out of it. He looked over at Sniper, and scoffed. "Not like him."

Kwanele raised an eyebrow. "You don't love your horse?"

Mark arched a brow. "I do. I do love my horse. But I just don't have that special thing with him like Sarah and Honor had."

"What happened to Sarah's horse?" Kwanele ran his hand down the horse's soft neck.

"Ahh, there was a bad accident. In the Kruger."

There was more silence as they worked until Kwanele went and placed his brush into the box.

Dropping the tail and mane comb into the box and pulling out a pair of battery-operated clippers, Mark checked the charge and turned them on. He moved up the horse's neck and began to clip a spot on the mane behind Buster's ears. Kwanele skipped around to see better and watched with confusion till the buzzing noise was turned off.

"Bridle path," Mark explained. "It gets the hair out of the way for the halter and also the bridle. Looks neater." He looked over at the boy, his expression clouded.

CHAPTER
NINETEEN

"Tell me the whole story." Kwanele scrunched up his nose. "What happened to Sarah's horse, Honor?"

He saw Mark's face cloud up. The man exhaled, put the clippers back in their case, and propped his elbow onto Buster's back.

"Was it poachers?"

Mark's face fell. "*Ja.*" He breathed. "*Ja*, it was. They didn't like Sarah in their business."

Kwanele turned away. "Oh." He then looked up with confusion. "But wasn't she a Christian?"

Mark dropped his arm off the horse and regarded the boy.

"She was," Mark agreed with some hesitation. "But being a Christian doesn't mean bad things still won't happen. God knows more than we know, and He has reasons why some things happen or don't happen, reasons that we will never know."

The light Kwanele had felt inside faded in an instant. Had he been tricked? He thought that having Jesus in his heart would save him. If what he heard now was different, then he'd been shortchanged. Kwanele stepped out from the kraals. Mark blinked as Kwanele passed him. He ran toward the rondavels, fear and emotion rising in his throat. He heard Mark come up behind him.

"Kwanele...Kwan, wait!"

The man skidded to a stop in front of him and pressed his palms onto Kwanele's shoulders.

"Come and sit with me. I'll explain."

Kwanele searched his face. He wanted to believe it was all true. What if it wasn't? Reluctant, he turned around and headed with Mark back toward the kraals. They sat on the bench outside the shed. Kwanele shuffled his backside on the hard wood.

"Can God help me or not?" He wanted a direct answer.

"Yes," Mark insisted. "That is definite."

Kwanele was confused. "But He didn't help Sarah?"

"Sarah is still alive, isn't she?" Mark pointed out. "Sarah's best friend, Brandi, didn't die, either. Many bad people died during that accident." Mark frowned. "But you know what? God doesn't want even bad people to die."

It was now Kwanele's turn to scowl.

"Is He on their side?" He shook his head. It didn't make sense.

Mark put his hand on Kwanele's shoulder. "Kwan. He's on *all* our sides. The trouble is, He gave us all something very powerful, and many people use it the wrong way—for evil. Even Christians mess up and use it the wrong way at times."

"Why would He give something powerful to bad people, too? That's just stupid."

"No, Kwan, it's not." Mark rubbed at his eyes. "This thing He gave us all is very important, but not all people use it wisely. There is a very important reason why He gave it to us."

"What is it?" Kwanele's eyes grew wide, as though he were about to receive a great secret.

"He gave all men free will. That means He gave us all the ability to choose for ourselves. To choose good or bad." Mark's voice was low. Kwanele waved his hand in front of his face to swish a fly away.

"We all have that. That's not special."

"But it is, Kwan. Imagine if people couldn't choose, if they all just did as they were told, like slaves."

They sat in silence for a moment as Kwanele tried to imagine a world without free will.

"If He is God, why did He do something so stupid?" He shook his head. Mark laughed. Kwanele's frustration surfaced even more at Mark's reaction.

"I'll tell you why." Mark grinned as he tried to control his amusement. "Because He loves us so much. He doesn't want to control us like slaves. You know what? If we have free will, then when we choose God and ask for Jesus to be in our hearts, it's even more special to God."

Kwanele shook his head again. He didn't understand. He sighed, his shoulders sagging.

"Let me put it this way." Mark leaned forward, his arms resting on his knees. "Would you rather Jacques spend time with you because he loves you, or because he is chained up and has no choice?" Mark sat back.

"I'd rather him be with me because he likes me. When I found out he slept under my bedroom window—it was special." Kwanele smiled as he thought about the cheetah's loyalty to him.

"That's it." Mark slapped his hand on his thigh. "God feels the same way about us as you feel about Jacques. We're not His prisoners, Kwan, or His slaves. We're His children, all of us, even the poachers. They just don't know it."

Kwanele was disgusted. He scrunched up his nose. Mark's lip curled. "But they have not chosen God, have they? If they had, they would not be killing God's creatures, or trying to hurt other people."

"So can God still save me, help me?" Kwanele cut to the chase once more.

"You are already saved if you asked Jesus into your heart." Mark turned to look into Kwanele's eyes. "Do you understand what that means?"

Kwanele shook his head. "I just want to know that I can pray and that God will save me and you and Sarah from those poachers."

Mark ruffled the boy's hair.

"A reasonable question." He tilted his head. "When you pray to God, He will always listen, and He will always answer you. But sometimes not the way you think He will. He is God, after all."

Kwanele looked long and hard at Mark. How much could he trust this God whom he had already put his faith in? He had nothing to believe in, and he desperately needed someone, something he could count on.

"It will be okay. You've prayed for that protection. You've been specific about it. God will help—if you believe He will do it, then He will." Mark removed his hand from Kwanele's shoulder and looked up at Buster.

"So..." Mark picked a stick up from the ground and started to draw in the dirt. "Would you like me to explain why Jesus came and died for us?"

Kwanele shifted on the bench.

"The Zulu warrior angel I met, he said that you would help me. You would tell me what Jesus did for me. He said the same thing you just said, that God gave a gift for all, but not everyone chooses it."

Mark nodded as he drew in the dirt. Kwanele tilted his head sideways to look at the image scratched in the ground.

"This is two sides," Mark began. "On this side is us"—he drew some squiggles to represent people—"and on this side, God." Mark pointed to the other side.

"Down here"—Mark pointed to the chasm between the two sides—"this is impossible to cross. Nobody can get from this side to that. No matter how hard they try, they will never be good enough to cross."

"Why is there a gap?" It made no sense to Kwanele to even have a gap in the first place. "Why are we separated from God at all?"

Mark tapped the side of his nose.

"Free will?" Kwanele asked at a guess. Mark chuckled.

"The first man and woman, Adam and Eve—they were the first to be given free choice. They were put in a garden with God."

"On this side?" Kwanele pointed at the God-side of the chasm.

Mark nodded.

"*Ja*, but there was no chasm then. So God said they could eat from anything in the garden, but not from the Tree of Knowledge. But the devil—the evil one—he was like a snake. And he also lived in the garden. He went to Eve and asked her why God had said not to eat fruit from the Tree of Knowledge. He talked her into using her free will to disobey God. It was the only rule that God had given them, but because of free will, they could still choose to disobey Him. Eve ate from the tree, and then gave some to Adam and he also ate. It became a curse—a curse that covered all people from that day on. When they disobeyed God, it created the chasm. It separated all the offspring of Adam and Eve from God. That's us."

Kwanele stopped him with his hand. "Wait. Why would God put the tree in the garden, then? It seems like God did a lot of stupid things."

"How well could free will work if there was nothing for them to choose to do or not to do?" Mark grinned. Kwanele thought he was starting to understand.

"Good question, Kwan. God is just. He made a law. Laws are stronger than rules. It's like the law of gravity. It's impossible to defy the law of gravity, isn't it? God couldn't break the law. So He couldn't bend the rule. But He still loves His children."

Now Kwanele was lost again. Gravity? But he barely had a chance to speak up, as Mark kept on.

"So He had mercy on us and came up with a plan. The plan was this: 'For God so loved the world, that He gave His one and only Son, that whoever believes in Him shall not perish but have eternal life.' Disobeying God is called sin. The curse is sin. Every single person born into the world, from Adam and Eve to now, is infected with sin. It's a sickness that no one can get rid of. It's the name of this chasm in the ground that separates us from God. Everyone in the world has sinned; we have all disobeyed God, done bad stuff. It's in our blood. It's the curse. We are all born, separated from God through sin. That's why we grow up and still make big mistakes without even knowing we do it. So now that no one is near God, we have to all choose God."

Kwanele looked over the sketch on the dirt, his eyes wide.

"So He sent His Son, Jesus?" he prompted. He wanted to know what happened next.

"Yes, and this is why. Jesus is from God; in fact, He is also God. I'll explain that another time. Because Jesus is God...He is clean from the curse of sin. No sin. He cannot sin. If we are to get back to God, it would take one thing, someone who has no sin, to take our punishment for us."

"What's the punishment?" Kwanele swallowed hard as he shifted on the hard wood bench. Mark continued, "It's death.

Not just your body, though, but your spirit. When your body dies, your spirit lives on. 'The penalty for sin is death.' But if someone sinless dies in your place, then you could be saved. But only if that person was perfect, with no sin...Jesus. He was the only person in the whole of history who ever had that power. It's because He is from God, and He is God."

"So, Jesus died for us?" Kwanele was still confused. "Does that mean God is dead?"

"It's not finished." Mark took the stick in his hand again and pointed to his sketch. "Jesus was killed—by people. They didn't know who He really was. It wasn't an accident, either. They did it on purpose, and it was horrible. He died on a cross." Mark drew the shape of the cross in the dirt next to the diagram. Kwanele's eyes went wide with recognition. He gasped and pulled out his pendant. He ran his thumb over the cross as he held it close to his face. When he looked up at Mark, Kwanele saw a sparkle in the man's eye. "That cross now represents Jesus to the whole world and what He did for us. It is a very important symbol to Christians.

"He didn't just die for one person. He died for all of humankind, everyone who was, who is, and who will be." Mark drew the cross again to bridge the gap from one side of the chasm to the other. "The only way to be saved from sin and death is to accept that Jesus died for you and ask Him into your heart. He gave us a way back to God.

"The thing is, Kwan, He didn't stay dead. No. After three days, He rose again. He is God. He proved He rose again in front of many people. Then He went to heaven, a place where our spirits will go when our bodies die. Jesus is preparing a place in heaven for all of us. If you have asked Jesus into your heart, that's a good start. But there is one final thing that goes with that. You need to say you are sorry that you were a sinner, tell Him that you understand, and then accept that gift that Jesus died on the cross so that you could be saved and have a bridge to get to God. Then, even if your body dies, you will live forever." Mark stopped. Kwanele's mind reeled as he tried to process it all.

"This is much bigger than a few poachers." Mark smiled softly. "We need to pray for those people. Pray that they will get to know the Truth. Then they won't keep doing bad things." Mark regarded the horse in front of them. "When you accept Jesus, your heart changes. You no longer want to do bad things—to sin." Mark looked down at his feet. There was a comfortable silence for a while. Kwanele finally leaned over and nudged Mark from his thoughts.

"Could you help me pray now?"

Kwanele felt tears prick his eyes, but he didn't care. Mark looked up at him, and a tender smile tickled the side of his mouth. His blue eyes softened.

"Of course I can." He reached over and wrapped an arm about the boy's shoulder. He bowed his head, his eyes shut. Kwanele had seen this done at church before and was quick to mimic Mark's actions. He bowed his head and closed his eyes as well.

"Jesus, we know You are real and that You can hear us. I want to thank You so much for sending someone last night to speak with Kwanele. For giving him courage and a purpose. You've heard his heart, Lord. You know that he wants to be saved, that he understands what that means now. I pray that You will give him strength, give him the words that he needs to be able to pray from his own heart." Kwanele opened his eyes and glanced over at Mark, who nodded softly. "Just talk to Him from your heart, just like you talk to me." Closing his eyes again, Mark bowed his head.

Kwanele heaved an emotional sigh. He sniffed back tears and immediately felt Mark's arm tighten around his shoulder.

"Jesus?" Kwanele's voice sounded raspy in his own ears. "You know my past. Your Zulu angel said You could wipe it away. I was born a sinner. I know sin. I have done it, I have chosen it, and I have had it chosen for me. I don't want it anymore. I heard the story Mark told, and I listened to his words like the angel said. If Jesus died for me, then I accept that. I want to cross the bridge and live forever. I want to know that I am saved. I want a new heart, a new life. I want to be one of Your children, and I want to..." He stuttered to a stop and wiped his eyes. Mark looked at him questioningly. When Kwanele offered no more, Mark sealed the prayer.

"Amen."

Closing his other arm around Kwanele, Mark embraced him into a warm hug.

"You did it."

A tingle ran down Kwanele's spine.

"So you and Sarah are saved, too?" Kwanele sat up and eyed Mark, who nodded.

"And Jacob and Martha."

Kwanele smiled, and a peace washed over him. Mark studied the sketch in front of him and started to doodle with the stick.

Kwanele jumped to his feet. "What's next in warrior lessons, Teacher?" He slipped through the fence back to Buster's side. Mark laughed and stood.

"Let's finish this grooming." He slipped through the fence to join Kwanele. "Then see where we go from there."

CHAPTER TWENTY

Over the next few days, Mark worked on Kwanele's horsemanship skills. Sarah came down often to watch. Mark was sure that she had started to miss this part of her life. A door in her wounded heart that she had not allowed anyone to open had started to reveal itself. Was the door locked? Had she blocked God out from this room, too? He pondered all these questions as he watched her slip through the fence one day. She caught Sniper and put him in the other kraal before Mark had a chance. He tilted his head at her. He didn't want her to feel any pressure from him. She jutted her chin in the air toward him.

"Hey, I got in the saddle again recently. I rode Buster a couple of weeks ago." Her defensive manner caused Mark to stare before she broke into a coy smirk. "Okay. Mark, may I have your permission to ride your beloved horse?" Mark's eyes lit up.

"Of course, m'lady." He made a show of bowing. Sarah giggled as she went to get her gear from the shed. Kwanele looked on with curiosity from where he had just caught and haltered Buster. He led the docile horse over to be tied.

"Remember how to saddle?" Mark quizzed as his eyes darted back toward the gear shed.

"Yes, sir." Kwanele smirked as he followed Mark's gaze toward Sarah. Mark caught the look and laughed, waving his hand toward the boy.

"Hey. Focus. Well, come on, show me then."

When Kwanele paused, he waved him again into action. He tore his attention away from Sarah and back to the task on hand. It was so good to see Sarah get back into horses again. It helped her to heal. Mark considered their future. When they found a job and a place to live, he would look into buying her another horse, if she'd allow it. Would he find a palomino mare again? He gazed at Kwanele, who was busy grooming Buster. They might need two extra horses yet. Mark wondered how they would afford it all. Where they would live? Mark's thoughts came to a screeching halt. What was he thinking? He blinked in surprise at the direction of his thoughts and pushed them aside.

"Hey, I can do it myself, remember?" the boy protested as Mark tried to assist. His mouth stretched in agreement. As he placed the brush back into the box, a scripture verse popped into his mind. He could remember the words, but not where it came from. Jesus had said about not worrying, "Look at the lilies of the field, the birds of the air—"

He raised his eyes heavenward. *I get it, Lord. Don't worry. I remember. You will take care of all of our needs.* Mark leaned against the fence and folded his arms across his chest as he watched Kwanele with Buster. The boy had progressed well. Kwanele pulled over the mounting block and, stepping up, began to fling the saddle up the special way Mark had shown him. He swung it from his hip, and it came to rest in place on the horse's back. Mark wandered over to help him girth up. He reefed it up two more holes before he stood back again and refolded his arms.

"Okay, what next?"

"Bridle." Kwanele walked over and unhooked the bridle from the fence. He passed it to Mark.

"Go grab your helmet." Mark slipped the bridle over Buster's face, pushing the bit into the horse's mouth. It was amazing how far the boy had come in just a few days. The clink of a gate latch caused Mark to raise his eyes. Sarah had ridden through the far gate. She waved.

"Hey," he called, laughter in his voice. "Don't get too used to him. You'll be back on Buster when we get a date to ride."

She chuckled at his warning. "Bye, guys."

"Stay safe," he called again after her.

"Always." He heard her reply from a distance. Kwanele returned and adjusted the helmet.

Mark took immense pleasure from seeing this shy boy who had been so scared of these big animals begin to show courage and grow into someone who not only had faced his fear, but was now learning a skill and enjoying it Before long, Kwanele was back in the saddle, riding the drills he'd been taught. Time flew by, and soon enough, Sarah returned.

"How's he doing?" she asked as Mark leaned back on the fence to join her.

"Great. He started a bit of the trot today." He gazed back at her and screwed up his nose.

"What?"

"Go take a shower." He snorted.

"Ha. Always the charmer, aren't you?"

"You didn't flog my horse, did you?"

She pushed his shoulder and wiped some of her sweat onto his neck.

"Agh!" His sour expression broke out into a grin as he shoved her back and pulled the brim of her hat over her eyes.

"He's unfit," she pointed out with a smirk. "They both are. They need work." He looked at his wife sideways, brow raised. This was progress. She was back in her horse-trainer mind-set. Sarah sighed and gave an apologetic smile. "I'm sorry."

"Don't be." He reached around and rubbed the back of her neck. "I'm happy to see you like this again." He leaned over the rail and kissed her before turning his attention back to his student. He was reluctant as he slipped his arm away.

"I'll see you inside for lunch." Sarah's words were soft as she turned to leave. Mark nodded, but his focus was now back on the job as Kwanele began to trot Buster again.

"Remember, up on the balls of your feet, Kwan. Up, down, up, down. Don't let him get lazy. He just cut that corner." Kwanele was strong in his poise as he rose to the trot. He was going to make a good rider. "That's it, deep into the corners. You're such a natural. We'll have to get you your own pony one day."

Mark cringed as he realized what he'd just said.

"What about this one?" Kwanele patted the old horse on the neck as he slowed to a walk. Mark felt a pang of regret.

"We gave him to Jacob and Martha. But as long as we are

here, I'm sure they will let you use him as your own."

Kwanele dismounted, then took the reins over Buster's head and led him back to the fence.

"Is it lunchtime yet?" His big brown eyes pleaded.

"Yes, it's about that time." Mark chuckled as he looked toward the sun. They untacked Buster, and Kwanele helped to carry the unsaddled gear back into the shed as Mark let Buster go into the paddock with Sniper. He watched as Buster, light with sweat, groaned and eased himself into the dry grass, rolling luxuriously. Sniper wandered over and sniffed the air, buckling his knees to join his paddock buddy in rolling in the soft, dry grass. Kwanele stepped on to the bottom rail and rested his arms on the top. He smiled as he watched the two horses. Saddle-shaped sweat marks glistened on their backs as they finished their roll. Then, lurching to their feet, they strained their necks toward the ground and gave stiff, full-body shakes. Buster snorted several times afterward and settled in to grazing. His tail flicked at the last bits of loose grass that were caught up in his long, thick hair. Mark patted Kwanele on the back.

"Come on."

Sarah looked up as Mark and Kwanele entered the rondavel, grubby but satisfied. Martha had prepared a late lunch for them in the kitchen and waved them on into the bathroom to clean themselves up. Soon they joined Sarah and Martha at the table to eat. Martha put down her drink after a long sip and looked up at her guests, smiling. Sarah caught a strange expression in the woman's eyes.

"What?" She swallowed her mouthful of sandwich and laughed.

"Oh, nothing." Martha exchanged looks with her husband, who had also just joined them. Sarah narrowed her eyes at Martha, and a smirk formed on her lips.

"Sarah?" Martha stood and topped up all their glasses with more juice to divert the matter. "Have you heard from your family in the last year?"

Sarah screwed up her nose in disgust.

"You know who I meant, girl. I mean the lovely family that adopted you in Australia."

Sarah relaxed as she took another mouthful of sandwich. She chewed it in thought.

"I got a letter from them a few months back," she remembered, smiling.

"How's the farm?" Jacob took a sip from his glass. Sarah smiled at the word *farm*. Farm insinuated a neat block that ran several dozen head of cattle and other animals. Sarah's stepparents owned two great cattle stations in the Outback of Australia. She understood that Jacob and Martha didn't comprehend the enormity of what that meant. One of the stations took a day to cross from one side to the other by car. Combined, they were bigger than the whole of Kruger National Park.

"They are holding up, just. They've been in a drought for a long time. They find it hard. They have had to sell a lot of the horses now. They keep losing animals to disease. It's easier to use motorbikes and protect the cattle as best they can. Last year they had bad heat waves, and they have been worried about bushfires again." She took a long swig of juice, and her brows raised at all the expectant faces around her.

"They are okay, though, I think." She hesitated. "Nothing they couldn't fix. They are really resilient people. There's nothing left to burn anyway." She looked off to the distant window. They'd taken her in as one of their own—that family. Taught her how to ride and train horses, taught her how to muster. What were they all doing now? What about the things they didn't share in their letters? Were they still upset with her for running away to South Africa when she had turned nineteen? She felt a warm hand slip into hers under the table, and she allowed their fingers to knit together. Turning toward her husband, she leaned in to him.

"You miss them," Mark observed. A shadow crossed his features that Sarah couldn't read. She hadn't told him of her family's pain. Last year, when she had gotten the letter, she had answered it and then thrown it away. She didn't share it with Mark. She didn't want him to feel guilty that she was with him, here. It was a time when she had retreated into her own thoughts, her own pain. She'd endured it alone. When she looked at Mark now, she saw that he was aware of her pain, but he took it on the chin. She could see that he was hurt. She was only trying to save him from more pain, but keeping him in the dark appeared to cause even more. She squeezed his hand three times and tried to give him an apologetic look. He studied her for a moment, before he squeezed her hand back and then released it.

"I'd like to meet them all someday." Mark smiled sideways at his wife as he took another bite of his sandwich. Sarah stopped chewing and looked at him, but his focus was back on his plate. Martha cleared her throat and poured herself a second drink.

"Well, Sarah. We have a computer in the office, and we have that new satellite Internet now. If you want to e-mail them, you are welcome to do so."

Sarah picked up a bit of cheese that had fallen from her sandwich and popped it into her mouth.

"Thanks. I appreciate that."

"Well, with Mark and Kwanele doing lots of horse lessons these days, we thought it might help distract you a bit." Jacob smiled. Maybe she could. Sudden emotion rose in Sarah's chest. She breathed and pushed it down.

"Anyone want more to eat?" She buried her thoughts. When everyone shook their heads, she began to stack up the plates, and swiftly carried them toward the sink.

"I could use some coffee, though." Mark glanced over his shoulder at his wife. Sarah didn't respond immediately, and she felt him brush past as he flicked the power on the jug. Sarah cast a scowl over her shoulder at him, and he gave her a cheeky grin. He placed his hand on the back of Sarah's neck as he reached up with the other hand and pulled down the coffee tin from the shelf. Their eyes locked for a moment. Sarah saw love and warmth in those deep blue eyes. She tilted her head into his hand and smiled before mouthing the word *sorry*. His hand slipped down to her back as he grabbed down the sugar in a fluid motion.

"There's no need," he murmured. Mark turned to scan the

room. "Anyone else up for a hot drink?"

Kwanele was already gone, presumably outside to be with Jacques. Martha was up and filling the sink to wash the dishes. Jacob leaned back in his chair and shook his head as he rubbed his sore leg. Sarah touched Mark's shoulder.

"I'll have one, hon." Her hand lingered a moment before she turned to the sink to help Martha.

Kwanele, comfortably full after lunch, sat under the shade near the horse kraals with Jacques by his side. He knew that Mark had told him not to let Jacques near the horses because the cheetah made them nervous, but he couldn't help it. He wanted to be close to both. The horses were turned out into the one of the small paddocks now where they were happily grazing on the remainder of the wet season's long, dry grasses. With winter fast approaching, Mark had mentioned that Jacob would need to get some hay in for the horses. He had volunteered to take the old truck to pick it up from town. Jacob, who still struggled with his leg, had agreed. Jacques finished licking his paws after he polished off the meat Kwanele had brought him. He stood and turned about several times before he flopped onto his side in the sun-dappled dirt. Kwanele smiled and stretched out on the grass, folding his arms behind his head. He sighed deeply. If only his life could stay just like this forever. Mark had shared with everyone what had happened with Kwanele and the angel the night before, and also about the decision that he'd made when they had their talk at the horse kraals. He began to feel that life was good—except for one thing. Jacob had mentioned a book called the Bible. Kwanele frowned as he wondered how he would ever be able to hear God's Word if he couldn't read. Nobody had ever taken the time to teach him to read or write.

Kwanele sat up and squinted out into the paddock. He shielded his eyes from the sun. First things first, he needed to have closure on this job business. He needed to know for sure that he and the people he was growing to love were free from the danger and fear that went with it. Despite the freedom and lightness that Kwanele felt from giving his heart to Jesus, a dark cloud of doubt hung heavy over him. Kwanele thought about Mark's story of the devil, Satan.

Could Satan try to undo the good that God had just done? In his heart he felt an immediate answer. Of course he would and was doing so. Kwanele sat forward, crossed his legs, and propped his elbows on his knees. He rested his chin in his hands. He needed to learn how to become a warrior, to become brave, to know how to fight the evil one. He would need Mark to teach him the Way, all of it, so he could fight like a warrior of God. Jacques lifted his head to regard the boy. His eyes touched Kwanele's heart with love. At that moment, the cheetah got up and rubbed himself against Kwanele's back. He then lay down beside Kwanele so they were still in contact. It was comforting. Kwanele reached out his hand, and his fingers disappeared into the thick, rich fur as he massaged the cat. Kwanele thought about Sarah. She had laughed at the way Jacques followed Kwanele around, like he was his personal protector. He was rarely out of his line of vision. "I think that cheetah would do anything for you, Kwan," Mark had said. As Kwanele looked at the cheetah, he thought about past conversations. He believed Mark and Sarah were right. Jacques had tried to protect him from the guide when he came, and then he also tried to protect him from the angel. Jacques had gotten upset, but how much more would he protect Kwanele if it came to the crunch? Sighing, Kwanele hoped he'd never have to find out. He bowed his head and began to pray for all their safety and protection. Jacques stretched and gave a low, luxurious growl as he changed positions to get out of the sun. The sun had moved. Kwanele felt it burn into his right arm. He gazed over at the horse paddock, got up, brushed off his trousers, and wandered over to the fence. The two horses lifted their heads and watched him with curiosity before they returned to their grass. Kwanele felt Jacques bump into his leg. The cat leaned in to him as they watched the horses. Sniper lifted his head again, wary of the cheetah. Jacques flipped his head around to lick at an itch. Sniper appeared as if frozen, not taking his eyes off the cat. Jacques swiveled his head back and flicked his tongue in and out to drop loose fur. "Silly cheetah."

Kwanele obliged as Jacques rubbed his head into Kwanele's hand. Any perceived danger that the cheetah had drawn had ceased to exist as Sniper returned to his grass and even edged his way closer to the pair. Kwanele grinned. They weren't nervous of Jacques now. He knew Mark would have scolded him if he'd known that Kwanele had brought the cheetah through the gate down to the kraals. Maybe if he snuck him down here a little bit each day, they would grow to accept each other. Maybe Jacques would even be able to tag along one day when Kwanele rode. Dreaming of all the possibilities, Kwanele found another soft patch of grass and settled onto his back to savor the afternoon. His only worry with learning the Way of the Warrior was that he was not entirely sure that Mark knew what he was doing, either.

CHAPTER
TWENTY-ONE

Sarah hung up her cell phone as she tipped her mouth at Mark. He was reclined on a chair in the bedroom, his feet up on the bed as he read the Bible.

"So, are they coming?" He flicked a thin page over.

"Yep." She spun to regard him. "They'll be here a bit earlier in the afternoon, so they can show the girls the place. Apparently the girls haven't been to Kruger. They want to see Jacques and some other wildlife if they can—and the horses will be good for them to see, too. Max said they've prayed for us." She pulled her hair tie out and let her long black locks cascade down her shoulders. She shook it out and combed her fingers through it as she searched for her brush. Mark laid the Bible face down in his lap and watched his wife, a calm smile on his face. Sensing his eyes on her, Sarah stopped and turned to regard him, her shapely eyebrows arched.

"What?" She chuckled and warm color flooded into her face at the tender look he gave her.

"It's just you." He smiled, stood, and walked over to her. He brushed his fingers lightly through her hair and tugged at a loose strand.

"I've missed you." He rested the palm of his hand on her cheek. He cleared his throat and smiled at her, a twinkle in his eye. "I feel like I'm getting my Sarah back."

She closed her hand over his and gave it a squeeze.

"*Ek is lief vir jou.*" Her Australian tongue still struggled to enunciate the Afrikaans as she murmured the words.

"I love you, too." Mark drew her into an intimate embrace. "I don't want to go back to Polokwane." Sarah barely heard Mark's breathed words.

"What are we going to do?" Sarah pulled back from him and searched his face. He broke eye contact and ran a hand through his hair.

"I don't know." He shook his head and sat on the edge of the bed.

"I know how you feel, Mark. I feel the same way." She sat next to him and rested her hand on his forearm. "But we can't stay here forever."

He looked up at her, and she could see that he had a sudden thought.

"What if we could stay in Kruger, though?" Mark held her gaze as he waited for her to respond.

"The Letaba man?" She searched his face as he nodded.

"Do you want to ring him?" She tried to read his thoughts.

"Do you think I should?" He pushed the question back to her.

She hesitated. "I don't know."

He touched her chin and turned her face toward him.

"Sarah, we are dying in Polokwane. Look how alive we are back out here, with friends and family, the wilderness. We need to make a change."

"I know. You're right." She blinked against the tears as they fell. "I'm just scared, that's all."

He wrapped his arm about her shoulder and drew her close. He slipped his other hand around the back of her neck and pushed his fingers up into her thick hair. He then guided her head down into his chest. She wept for a long while, years of pent-up emotion released as thoughts of her stepfamily were brought to the surface. Mark held her and kissed her hair.

"We'll think of something. We'll talk to Max and Kym about it when they come, get everyone to pray with us, pray about what to do."

She nodded and buried her face into the comfort of his embrace. She could feel his chin as he rested it atop her head.

Sarah heard the giggles and screams of Max and Kym's girls from the rondavel as they were released from the car. Coming out onto the top step, she smirked as she watched Jacques cower behind Kwanele's legs. He was only there a few moments before he skulked under the building instead. Caitlyn's bottom lip dropped with disappointment, and she held out her stubby fingers toward where the cat had just disappeared. Leah ran past her sister, grabbed her hand, and spun her around in a dance before she ran off toward the unlit campfire area. Giggling, Leah clambered up onto the wooden bench seats and balanced her way along as Caitlyn watched.

"Careful..." Max warned them. "Come on, girls, come on back here." He waved them back. Kym wore a tired smile as she first hugged Sarah, then the others in turn. The twin toddlers ran, laughed, and giggled as they took off around the inside perimeter of the bush camp. Sarah tilted her head as she figured they probably needed to burn their pent-up energy after the long drive. Sarah grinned as she saw Jacob step out from behind a building in front of the girls. The girls skidded to a stop, looking up at the dark man with wide eyes before they spun about and ran back to their dad. They hid behind his legs, suddenly shy.

Jacob sauntered over and winked at Max.

"Long time, no see." He thrust out a hand to Max, who shook it readily. "Energetic kids." Jacob nodded at the girls, who ducked their heads back behind their father.

"You have no idea." Max tugged at the girls to come out from behind him. "This is Mr. Jacob. You need to be polite to him. This is his place." The twins stopped fussing and nodded in unison.

"Welcome back. You have gorgeous girls. And twins." Martha bent down to give the girls a warm smile. "How old are you both?"

Leah held up three fingers.

"Tree," Caitlyn butted in and held up three chubby fingers.

"Do you have any toys?" Leah's bright eyes searched Martha's face. Martha straightened and looked upward in thought, her finger to her chin. "Hmmm." Jacob touched his wife's shoulder.

"That old box of your sister's in the spare room. The one that she gave us for when we have guests with kids."

"I thought we donated those to charity." Martha frowned. Jacob winked at the girls. "We have toys."

"Yay," they cheered in unison as Martha ushered them all up the steps into the rondavel.

"Did you want afternoon tea, or do you want to have a look around first?" She smiled. Kym stuck her nappy bag down in the corner of the room and pulled out a camera.

"Could we show the girls some animals first?" She smiled, straightening up. "Then we can pull out the toys in the other room while we have coffee and cake."

Mark grinned, slapping Max on the back. "Sounds like a plan." Max turned to help the girls back down the steps and retrieve their hats from the car. Sarah stood and regarded how motherhood had altered Kym. She seemed at peace and content with life in general, even if she had adopted a militaristic way of organizing people.

Soon enough, they were all down at the horse kraals. Mark held Buster by the lead rope, while Kym took photos of the girls one at a time as they sat on the placid animal. Max hoisted Leah down from Buster again and patted the animal on the neck.

"Thanks, Buddy. Thanks, Mark." The huge animals had put the toddlers back into their shells, and they returned to sit next to their mum on the bench, who handed them drinks in their sippy cups.

"Can we go play with the toys now?"

They tugged at Kym's shirt. Sarah gave a nodding smile to her husband, who shrugged and released Buster.

"Thanks for your trouble." Kym smiled at Mark and Sarah. "Sorry, they seem less interested in seeing animals now and more interested in some old toys."

Mark chuckled. "It's all good. They're kids."

Sarah slapped him on the shoulder.

"Hey." He frowned, but his eyes danced as he rubbed the spot. They returned to the rondavel, where Martha had laid out an extravagant afternoon tea. Leah and Caitlyn's eyes lit up, and they climbed up onto a seat each, their eyes wide as they beheld all the sweets on the table. Kym rinsed and refilled their sippy-cups with the jug of juice.

"May I?" She looked at Martha as she indicated the food on the table.

"Of course." Martha passed her two plastic dishes. There were not enough chairs at the table for everyone, so most of the adults chose to stand, leaning against the benches as they ate and talked. Kwanele sat at the table with the girls, where they all tucked in to generous servings of cakes, biscuits, and rusks. By the time the girls announced they were full and Kym wiped their grubby hands and faces, everyone took their mugs of hot drink and settled onto a freshly wiped table. The instant they were cleaned up, Kwanele had shown the girls into the next room, where the box of toys had been laid out. Sarah gave him a warm smile when he returned.

"Come and sit with us." Mark dragged over a stool from the kitchen bench and added it to the table of six. "I was just telling Max and Kym how you have decided to become a warrior in God's Kingdom." Mark put his hand on the boy's shoulder as Kwanele sat.

"Well done." Kym smiled.

"Have you started reading the Word to him, Mark?" Max asked with interest. Mark shook his head.

"Not yet."

"The Bible?" Kwanele's head perked up. He held the man's gaze.

"We will start doing that tonight," Mark assured him.

"Promise?" Kwanele's look was severe until Mark nodded.

"I will." He reached out for a jam drop biscuit. "You've outdone yourself here, Martha."

Martha gave a small nod as she stood and collected their empty mugs.

"Round two?" she offered and received several nods.

"You drink too much coffee." Sarah gave Mark a gentle elbow in the ribs.

"Never." He looked hurt, but Sarah knew it was in jest. "I drink tea at night—occasionally."

"Doesn't count."

"Actually, Mark, tea is just as bad, if not worse for caffeine." Max smirked at his friend.

"Hey. Whose side are you on?" Mark laughed with Max as

Sarah pointedly poured a glass of water and placed it in front of him.

"Yes, ma'am." He scooped up the glass and downed the contents in several chugs.

"All jokes aside now." Max grinned. "You said that we needed to pray for something important. Does this have anything to do with Kwanele's request at church for safety?"

The atmosphere in the room changed in an instant. Mark cleared his throat. "Yes, we were hoping you could help us pray for direction, if that's okay?" He glanced around the table at everyone, who nodded their approval to the idea. The soft clinking of Martha fussing with the next round of hot beverages was the only sound that could be heard for a moment.

"To answer your question, though, Max, yes, it does have a little bit to do with that." Mark flicked his attention to Kwanele for a moment. Sarah saw it, too. The boy had a strange light in his eyes.

"We also want to pray for our future." Mark took the fresh coffee from Martha and nodded his thanks. "As you all know, we've been in hiding for the past few years. The police wanted us to change names and everything, avoid the press, avoid the parks board–everything."

Sarah saw the sympathy etch across Kym and Max's features as they listened. She didn't want their pity. She wanted practical solutions. She sighed and looked toward the ceiling. *Please, God, don't abandon us.*

"It must have been hard." Kym reached across the table and placed her hand over Sarah's. Taken by surprise, Sarah bit her lip, trying to hold back the tears that sprang to her eyes.

"It was like they asked us to give up our whole lives, our identity—who we are." Her voice quivered, and Sarah regretted that she'd opened her mouth.

"At least you had each other." Max's voice was quiet.

"Sort of..." The words slipped out of Mark's mouth, and he flicked his focus to his wife and back. She saw him bite his tongue. She didn't respond. She was emotionally drained. So was he. She knew she should have offered him a smile, just to let him know he was okay, but she felt despair threaten to crush her spirit again. She took a sip from her coffee and looked down at her lap. Mark sighed and ran his fingers through his hair.

"I don't know if we told you or not, but Sarah has been struggling with depression since living out there." Mark choked up as Sarah frowned at him.

"They're our friends, Sarah. If we don't share, how can they know how to pray?"

He was right. She felt numb as she reached out for him. The emotion in his voice had caught her by surprise. She had been so consumed by her own grief that she had not noticed Mark's. She knew the pain was more than her depression. She'd been so selfish not to realize that he was in pain, too.

"We lost a child." Sarah's voice was barely above a whisper as she regarded their stunned faces in turn. "We—" She gazed at Mark and saw the emotion roiling just under the surface.

"I can't have children." Sarah pushed aside her rising emotion. She set her jaw and couldn't make eye contact, but she could sense that there was nothing but sympathy. These were people she could trust. There was a strong silence for a while, and Martha eased herself into a chair. Sarah saw her cringe when it creaked.

"It's okay." Sarah wiped her eyes as she allowed the tears to fall. "It's okay." She excused herself, got up, and found a tissue box on the bench.

"That's not what we want to pray about." She chuckled through her tears and felt her face heat up self-consciously. Sarah sat next to Mark, and warmth flushed through her as his leg pressed up against hers under the table. It was comforting.

"We want to confess our sins, pray for forgiveness, and pray for direction."

Max nodded, even though he looked confused. Mark exhaled.

"Out at Polokwane, we didn't try to connect with believers. We were justifying it by saying that we didn't want to hurt people by getting close to them, that we were afraid people we got close to would get stalked and hurt if we did. I think we may have convinced ourselves of it, when really, isolating ourselves seemed like a tonic to our pain." He stopped, trying to gauge a reaction and bring order to his thoughts.

"That's not a sin."

"No, but we became backslidden…lukewarm." Sarah felt his leg start to jiggle with nerves. "We got caught up in trying to fight the fight on our own strength. We neglected ourselves by neglecting our support networks, neglecting God. We realize all that now. It was wrong, and I repent for my part of it. I repent on behalf of the two of us."

"But you hardly had a choice, now did you?" Kym shook her head, appearing just as confused as Max. Sarah clasped Mark's hand and knitted their fingers together.

"But we didn't even try to make new friends. And I am sorry, too. We should have come back sooner."

There was a long silence again before Max shrugged and bowed his head. He began to pray.

"Lord, You have heard the confession of these, Your children. We know that what they have endured in the past few years has not been Your ideal life for them, but in Your great plan You can use them through all things. They will be strong people because of what they have endured. We know that You work all things for good and that we cannot possibly fathom the depths of Your heart. We know that You love us, and that You forgive us. Please, Lord, take Mark and Sarah into Your protective arms, along with anyone else that You would entrust to them."

Sarah exchanged glances with Mark.

"Lord, You know that they have been in hiding from a great enemy for many years, an enemy that people in our congregation have also had to deal with. But You are stronger, Jesus. You have already defeated the devil, and it is up to us to walk in that and accept that. Give us faith to pray, Lord, faith to move, and faith to do Your will. Please protect Mark, Sarah, and Kwanele from their enemies. Cloak them and shield them so that they cannot be harmed. Show them what Your will is and what they should do to restore their lives to what You have planned for them."

"Help them to grow closer to You and to hear from You," Kym added when her husband paused for a moment.

"Bless them beyond their wildest dreams and prosper them greatly," Martha prayed.

"Lord Jesus, surround them with Your Holy Spirit and teach them the way. Teach them spiritual warfare," Jacob finished.

Silence encircled the room as everyone waited for someone else to speak. When nobody else did, Max closed the prayer. "Amen." They all looked up at each other. Sarah saw how intently Mark stared at Jacob. Spiritual warfare? This was something that was very foreign to them both. She remembered when Israel had spoken very similar words. He'd also said to eat meat and move away from milk. Sarah recalled this was from scripture, a reference to growing up in your faith. She watched Mark close his eyes and put his head into his hands.

"You will learn. We know how to teach you. You will also receive visitors who also know." Jacob gave Mark and Sarah a knowing smile. Mark raised an eyebrow.

"Who?" he quizzed.

Jacob leaned back in his chair.

"Try this shortbread. Martha made it. It's great." Jacob passed the plate around.

"We need to pray about what to do with Polokwane, too." Sarah accepted a piece of shortbread.

"Well, where do you want to live?" Kym grabbed up a piece of shortbread and stuck it on her plate next to a half-eaten biscuit. Mark and Sarah looked at each other.

"We want to be close to the wilderness again, close to our friends, close to church. I guess another trail-riding place would be great, but there aren't really any others that run in this area." Mark finished his second coffee, but he kept his hands cupped around the empty mug, as if enjoying the warmth that still emanated from it.

"We were offered work," Sarah began. "Well, it was more like Mark." Max and Kym raised their brows with interest. "It was the park ranger from Elephant Hall at Letaba," she clarified.

"Doing what?" Max chewed on his shortbread.

"You didn't tell us this." Martha frowned at Sarah, who gave her an apologetic smile.

"We didn't tell you because...well, it wasn't important...it wasn't an option at the time."

It was Mark's turn to frown, but Sarah continued to explain

herself before he could cut in.

"It scared me...the idea of being in the thick of danger again. Part of me wants the excitement, like I did a few days ago trying to find those people out in Kruger. But another part of me was...well...terrified. We hadn't prayed about it, and we hadn't really talked about it." She turned to Mark, who gazed at her with understanding. "I'm sorry."

Max cleared his throat.

"What was the job offer? Where was it?" He coughed again and took a drink of juice. Mark shrugged at Sarah.

"We don't know. We need to ring him, find out details."

"Well, that might be the answer to your prayers." Max tilted his head before he turned to his host. "Martha, your shortbread and your cakes are delicious."

She inclined her head. Kwanele asked for another glass of juice, and Kym, being the closest, gladly complied.

"And what's going to happen with you, young man?" she asked in a conversational tone. Kwanele stiffened and looked around the table for help. Everybody looked at each other, not sure how to answer. They needed to wait and see what the outcome would be with the investigations. How long would the police allow him to stay with them?

"Kwanele is welcome to stay here with us all as long as he wants. Until we know any more, this is his home." Jacob flashed his white teeth in a brilliant smile. Kwanele's shoulders sagged, and he tilted his lips in a half smile.

"We just have to pray that things go smoothly and that Kwanele adjusts to whatever happens." Sarah gave the boy a brave smile. She hated to think what could happen.

"I want to stay with you forever." Kwanele looked around with wide eyes. Mark put an arm around the boy's shoulder.

"We want that, too."

The adults all regarded each other. Nobody knew what would happen with Kwanele once the case was settled. He would most likely be put into the custody of the state. Another orphan. Mark stood and cleared the air with an exuberant stretch, and his fists almost touched the ceiling.

"Well, you are all here for a while, aren't you? Let's all go for a drive and see if we can spot some wildlife." He looked around the room. Kym stood and said she would get the girls.

CHAPTER
TWENTY-TWO

"A strange man called today for you." Jacob frowned as Sarah returned from the horse kraals.

"The ranger who wanted to offer Mark a job?" Even as she said it, she knew that wasn't it. He didn't have their contact details. Heaviness formed in her stomach. Jacob shook his head and would not break eye contact. She raised her brows in query. The way he was staring at her, sober, not a hint of jest, suddenly hit home.

"What?" She stiffened, and a chill ran down her spine. "No, this can't be happening. Nobody knows we're here except for the people we trust." She cocked her boot up on a chair and tugged at the Velcro to loosen her riding chapettes. She slipped the leather hide from her calf and leveled her gaze back at Jacob. "Did they say who they were, what they wanted?" He shook his head.

"What?" Sarah lowered her leg from the chair.

"Sarah, I think it's time."

She frowned and cocked her other leg up, ripping at the strap to remove the other chapette.

"What, to leave?"

"No." Jacob waved his hand at her. "It's time to stand and fight. Not your way, God's way."

"Well, what did he say?" She arched an eyebrow. "Was it Mark's boss?" Sarah wanted to rule out any other possible explanations before hitting the panic button.

"Sarah, you're not listening. Why would Mark's boss call for you?" Jacob stood in front of her, and his expression pierced her. She regarded him a long moment before she felt a wave of nausea and became unsteady on her feet. She steadied herself on the back of the chair, then eased herself into it. Jacob joined her at the table.

"There's more." He sighed. She raised her eyes to meet his, waiting for it to come.

"He asked if Sarah White was here."

There it was. That sign that it was real again. Sarah tried to push away the fear that threatened to rise in her. So they used her maiden name. It could have been the media. It could have been a coincidence that they called the bush camp, here and now. She didn't realize how long she'd stared at the table until she heard Jacob shift.

"I said no. I didn't lie. Sarah White is not here. I didn't tell them Sarah van der Merwe was," Jacob continued. "They started to get upset about that. I repeated that you weren't here. They asked if you had stayed here recently. I told them that I wasn't authorized to disclose information on guests."

Sarah paced her breathing, trying to remain calm.

"Then what happened?" Her voice trembled.

"They hung up." Jacob pushed out his lip matter-of-factly. Sarah's mind reeled.

"Sarah, we are not pushing you out. Don't ever think that." He leaned toward her—his voice grew quieter, more secretive. "But people have worked out that you are here, that much is true. They will keep at it, Sarah. We need to plan to fight. Spiritually and physically, if it comes to it."

"But that's the police's job. We should never have—"

"Nonsense, girl. I'm not saying to not put your faith in local law enforcement, but I am saying that you need to put your faith in God, too."

"How?" Sarah whispered, her eyes wide. Jacob thumped a leather-bound Bible upon the table in front of her.

"Using our weapons." He had a strange glint in his eye. "I didn't tell you everything the other night, but I have contacted Lebowa village. I got in touch with Israel and Kgomotso. They are coming to help us."

Sarah sat back in her chair, uneasy.

"Maybe we need to leave. I don't want to put you all in danger." She looked toward the window. Jacob shook his head, and his voice rose with authority,

"You cannot run from this anymore, Sarah. This has got to be the last stand." She locked eyes with him and saw he was not going to budge. They were going to stick this out as a family of God. Stand together. She rested her hand on the old leather Bible and gave a weak smile.

"Okay."

Mark burst into the back door with Kwanele and hung his hat on the hook.

"What's going on?" He frowned when he saw the serious expressions on Jacob and Sarah's faces.

"Err..." Sarah hesitated. Her eyes flicked at Kwanele, then to Mark. He pressed his lips together. Whatever it was, it was something she didn't feel he could hear. Mark saw her exchange looks with Jacob. The old African shrugged and rose from his chair.

"Saturday night."

"What's Saturday night?" Mark poured himself and Kwanele a glass of water. Cocking a hand on his hip, he emptied the contents of the glass in one hit.

"Israel and Kgomotso are coming. They're going to pray with us." She gave a weak smile, but Mark missed it.

"Ah." Mark smiled and wandered into the next room. Jacob jerked his head at Sarah, indicating that she should follow Mark. She then heard the man raise a cheerful voice to the boy. "Come and give me a hand, Kwanele. We'll fix Jacques some dinner." Jacob indicated that Kwanele should follow him. Eager, the boy disappeared out the back door with Jacob. Sarah took a deep breath and went to track down her husband.

"Mark?" She found him in the bathroom, drying off his hands.

"Hmmm?" He frowned. "What is it?" He rehung the towel, then turned and touched her arm.

"Someone's found us." The quiver in her voice rose as she watched his eyes grow wide.

"How do you know?" He jolted and gripped her by the shoulders. "Did we tell the ranger where we were staying?"

Sarah shook her head. "I thought the same thing, Mark, but someone rang Jacob asking for me. They were asking for Sarah White." She watched as his expression registered.

"Great," he spat. Sarah could see his mind whirl. He paused a moment before his face relaxed and he smiled at her. "It's fine, honey. We'll pack our stuff and leave in the morning." He turned and straightened the hand towel on the rail.

Sarah reached out, cupped his face in her hands, and turned him to face her.

"Honey, we can't."

"Huh? What?" He took her hands from his face and held them tight as he searched her face.

"Jacob and Martha want us to stand and fight this." She saw the doubt cross her husband's eyes.

"Fight? This puts everyone in danger, not just us. Jacob, Martha, Kwan..." His expression was dark as he stormed into their room. Sarah hurried after him.

"Mark, I know this is scary, but we can't run. We need to trust God this time."

"Irresponsible, Sarah."

"You're one to talk."

"What's that supposed to mean?"

She saw him fight against anger as he stared out the window, hands on his hips. She didn't know what to say. He crossed the room and threw their suitcase on the bed. "What if God's will *is* to run, Sarah?" He unzipped the case. Sarah closed the gap and then closed the lid on the suitcase.

"Did you ask Him?" Her gaze was steady, and he stopped.

"No." He sighed and sat heavily on the bed. "Sarah?"

She sat next to him, trying in vain to calm her nerves. His face was puzzled.

"Why are you not scared about this, Sarah?"

"I am scared about this." She wrung her hands.

"Sarah, they have police for a reason. Have you ever considered that they are God's hands, too?"

"I know that. I just—feel—that it's time to end this once and for all."

"You don't understand." He exhaled and leaned forward onto his knees. "I'm your husband. You are my life. It's my job to keep you safe. All I know to do is run. Standing and trusting God to fight for us, well, it scares me to death, Sarah. I don't want to fail as a husband."

Sarah slipped her arm around him. "You have never failed me as a husband. But you don't have to do it alone."

"How do you know that to 'end this once and for all,' as you say, is not going to be the end of us?"

"I don't know that. But I know we need to trust God."

She saw him cringe. She didn't have all the answers. She silently implored God for direction. A thought struck her, and Sarah crossed the room to her handbag. She returned with a business card and offered it to her husband. Mark considered the card in her fingers.

"Sarah, I don't think this is the time."

"Of course it is. A step of faith—the perfect step of faith." She waved it in front of his face again, a playful spark in her eyes, before Mark grasped her around the wrist. She gave a bewildered yelp as he rose to stare her in the eye, a smirk pulling at the side of his lips.

"You're very chirpy for someone who just found out some very bad news." He tilted his head and rubbed her wrist. Sarah locked eyes with him.

"Believe me, I'm just as worried as you are, but we need to do something." She swallowed, a sliver of doubt threatening to push up her throat. She tried to ignore it. "We need to pray, trust, and have some faith." She sat next to him again. "Ring him, find out the stats. Get the information at least."

She flicked her head toward the card. The smirk tugged at his mouth again, and Mark patted her cheek playfully. "Okay." He took a deep breath as he pulled his cell phone from the back pocket of his jeans.

The corner of Sarah's smile twitched as she left the room. She was trusting God, trusting Jacob's judgment. Was she was wrong to do so? Was this the right move? The enemy still plagued her mind with doubt as she breezed out onto the back deck. She was determined to put her faith in God.

Please, Lord, keep us all safe. Help Mark to be strong in You. Above all, Lord, show us Your will in all of this and give us the strength to follow it.

It took a huge step of faith to convince her husband to take that step she'd been afraid of. The enemy had just lost round one—they *were* taking this step of faith. She jutted her chin into the air in defiance. Closing her eyes, she focused on the warmth of the sun as it hit full upon her face. Voices. Sarah's eyes flew open and fell to see Jacob and Kwanele in the courtyard below. They were cutting up meat from the cold room for Jacques on the outdoor stainless-steel bench. Jacques sat a little off to the side, waiting for whatever tidbits would be thrown his way. Compassion filled Sarah's heart as she watched the boy. It had only been a few weeks, but Mark and Sarah had grown to love Kwanele as their own. The thought of what would become of him in the future filled Sarah with dread, sadness, and a fierce protectiveness. But if the authorities allowed Kwanele to stay with them, how could they take him away from Jacques to live somewhere else? Sarah looked up at the soft clouds, which hung low overhead, her head full of questions.

Only You know what will happen, Lord. Only You know how to resolve all these questions. She became aware of a new confidence. No matter what happened, it was all in God's hands. From below, Kwanele looked up and spotted Sarah. He gave a cheerful wave. Sarah chuckled and waved back, wondering if they would have all the necessaries to consider adoption.

Adoption?

The thought caught her by surprise. She turned away and pushed the thought aside. It was time to focus and pray on present issues. The sound of the door behind her startled Sarah from her thoughts. Mark emerged, excitement in his eyes.

"So?" Sarah took a brave breath.

"He's going to check some things out, get back to me." Mark tucked the phone back into his pocket.

"And?" Sarah pressed. Mark joined her at the rail. He leaned his back against it, arms folded across his chest as he regarded her.

"Well, he said there were several places that could use both of us, as a team, if you want to. Otherwise, they are happy to take one of us. The main position available is at a bush lodge on the Sabi Sabi Reserve. They run horse-riding safaris. James is making inquiries for me."

"James, is it?" She quirked an eyebrow. A thought struck her. "Sabi Sabi? Down near the Paul Kruger Gate?"

Mark nodded. "*Ja.* They have a small setup, but it's still good. Apparently they let staff live on-site, too." He stopped at the expression on Sarah's face.

"What's wrong? You're the one who said to ring." He cocked his head to one side. Sarah concealed her expression.

"It sounds good." She lifted her chin and tossed a smile at him.

"But...?" Mark lowered his brows, and moved his face closer to hers. Sarah crumpled under that smoldering gaze.

"The distance. It's all the way down the bottom of Kruger."

"Sarah." Mark softened. "Our friends will always be our friends, and we can always come and stay with them. But if this is what God wants for us, then we must make sure that we still find a new church, build up our support networks again. We can't make the same mistakes again. That is what really matters."

"I agree." Sarah went and sat in the cane couch, and the cushions sank beneath her. "It would be great, wouldn't it?" She stammered as her husband joined her on the couch. He took her hands in his and bowed his head. Seeing he was about to launch into prayer, Sarah swallowed hard. Her mind still reeled with too much worry.

"Lord Jesus, You've heard the offer that we could have at Sabi Sabi. Please let Your will be done, Lord. If that is what You want us to do, make it clear to us and make straight the path. If not, please let us know, and give us both peace, Lord." He opened his eyes and squeezed Sarah's hands. She flushed as he then brought them to his lips and gently kissed them. "We'll work it out, okay? It will be okay." His reassuring smile put Sarah at ease.

"I'm sorry I worried." He brushed the back of his hand across her face. It tickled. He glanced back into their room at the suitcase still on the bed. "I know you're still worried, but if you want to stand and fight, if you believe that is God's will for us, then I will support that. Don't stress about the job. If it's right, God will give us both peace."

Sarah gazed at her husband with deep affection. "You're right. Can I ask one more thing, though?"

"Anything."

"Can we do the right thing and update the police on this?"

He gave her a coy smile. "I thought you were against the police thing?"

"I was never against it." She scoffed and pushed his shoulder.

Mark chuckled before he fell into thoughtful silence.

"Now I overreacted a bit too much there. But we don't even know if there is a real threat yet. Maybe before we do anything, we should just wait a bit longer and see if it's real or not. Okay?"

"Okay." She screwed up her face, not quite sure.

"Can you please start on the carrots?" Martha directed when she saw Sarah walk into the kitchen.

"So Israel is coming tomorrow night, then?" Sarah took up the cutting board, peeler, and knife.

"And Kgomotso." Martha smiled over her shoulder as Sarah dug into the crisper in the fridge and retrieved the bag of carrots.

"Of course." Sarah crossed the room and glanced at the clock. It was going to be a late dinner tonight. Sarah figured that was the price you paid when everyone was outside with guests and riding horses.

"We also have guests in tomorrow night, so you may not see me or Jacob for some of the night," Martha continued absently.

Sarah peeled the carrots with dismay.

"Please listen to what Israel has to say." Martha looked her way with concern. Sarah tightened her lips and nodded. How hard would it be to learn about spiritual warfare? Waltzing across the kitchen, Martha opened the oven door and checked on the chicken she had cooking. "Now, tell me about this job."

"We don't know a lot," Sarah admitted. "The man has to call

Mark back. But it's down at the Sabi Sabi Reserve." Sarah put the scraps from the carrot peels into the compost bin. Martha glanced sideways at her, her brow raised.

"And you're not happy about that?"

"Yes," Sarah wavered, "and no." She cut the carrot into rings and popped them into a pot of water. "It's a long way from here." Sarah began on the next carrot, sadness in her eyes. Martha stopped and considered Sarah's words for a long moment.

"Sarah, there are much farther places than Sabi Sabi. It's not like it's all the way across the world." She glanced sideways at Sarah, a chuckle in her voice.

"I know." Sarah sliced into the carrot, her focus on the task at hand. "I also know all the stuff about God's family and how we are all part of it wherever we go. I know we'll find a new church family, and that it is just a bigger part of the whole body of Christ. I know all that. It's just that, we've just found you all again in our lives and we'll miss you."

Martha's face lifted. She chuckled again as she stepped over to the young woman, grasped her shoulders, and turned her around. Martha gave her a warm embrace.

"Of course you will." She held her for a long moment. "But wherever you go in this world, you will always have us." Martha held Sarah at arm's length and looked deep into her eyes. "I mean it—anywhere in this world."

Sarah's brows drew together in confusion at Martha's cryptic words. "Wha...?" Martha patted her shoulder and clucked. "But you don't have to worry about that at the moment. Your job at the moment is to stand and fight the evil that keeps chasing you." Her eyes gleamed with both an inner peace and hunger for adventure.

"I know." Sarah swiped the rogue tendril of hair back from her face with the back of her hand and put on a brave smile. "I know."

Martha left her to the carrots then, wandering to another room to collect clean tea towels. Sarah gazed at her back as she left the room, curiosity burning within her.

CHAPTER TWENTY-THREE

Sarah backed up against the cold surface of the wall behind her in terror.

"What do you want?" Panic was nearly closing her throat. The white man's silver business suit shimmered metallic under the fluorescent lights above, and his blue eyes were so wild and vivid that Sarah wondered if he wore contacts. His stare was heartless and cold. Sarah shuddered and watched with horror as another man stepped from the shadows and stood beside the businessman. His ginger hair blew malevolently.

"What do you want, Declan? Can't you just leave me alone?" Tears of rage burst from her eyes. He sniggered at her fear and nodded at the man beside him.

"I want what I've always wanted." He narrowed his eyes at her. Sarah shrank back in fear against the cold metal wall, and her skin crawled at the cruel hunger in his eyes. Declan laughed at his effect on her and stepped closer. Like a trapped bird being cornered by a cat, Sarah let out a shrill scream.

"Jesus, help me." She looked around and suddenly felt a burst of courage. Glaring at the men from hooded eyes, she stood up straight, stepped forward, and shouted, "In the name of Jesus, leave me alone." She had a fierceness she hadn't felt before. They hesitated, a look of confusion on their faces. The face of the man with the white hair screwed up with hatred, and he tensed to step toward her.

"Jesus, help me," she screamed again and clammed shut her eyes, cringing as she awaited the white-haired man to close in on her.

There was silence.

She felt a change. A warm breeze. She scrunched up her

face and flicked open her eyes. She blinked into brilliant sunlight. She stood on open lowveldt. Grass swayed gently about her legs. She felt an immense peace flood over her, and sighing with relief, she threw herself down into the surprisingly soft grass and lay there at complete ease. A weight lifted off her as if she'd just won a major battle. She smiled and closed her eyes, rejoicing in the warmth of the sun on her face. "Thank You, Jesus. Thank You, Jesus," she murmured into the breeze before she fell into a blissful sleep.

Sarah rolled over in her sleep and sighed. Her eyes blinked open. She was in a darkened room—the bush camp guestroom. It had been a dream. The curtain shifted against the window, and she slipped out of bed and shut the window. Sarah hugged her arms to herself in the cool night air and turned to watch Mark as he slept. All he was wanted to do was find a better life for them. They would stay and fight this out until they knew what would happen with Kwanele, and then they would look at moving on. Martha and Mark were right. They would always be able to visit.

Kwanele. She thought about him again as she slipped into her slippers and dressing gown. She padded in silence out into the main part of the home. She grabbed a glass of water from the kitchen and crept into the darkened office. Careful to keep quiet, she booted up their computer as she searched around in the dark and flicked on the modem. Martha and Jacob said she could e-mail her family back in Australia, after all. She wanted to check something else, too, though. She brought up the search engine.

After several clicks to various links, Sarah started to wane. She yawned and rubbed at her eyes. Her gaze flicked over to the clock on the bottom right-hand side of the screen: two a.m. Was it nearly time to end her search? She jotted down a number on a scrap of paper she found in the waste-paper basket. A shuffling noise startled her as Mark appeared at the office door. He leaned against the doorjamb and blinked back his sleep.

"Honey?"

She slipped the scrap of paper under the keyboard and shut down the page. Mark frowned and tried to lean to see around her onto the screen.

"What are you up to?"

She shut down the computer. A guilty smile tugged the corner of her lips as she rose to meet him.

"Oh, just stuff. I couldn't sleep." She scooped up the empty glass and brushed her fingers across his hair as she passed him.

"Did you have another bad dream?" Mark's exhaustion fell away as he followed her. "You haven't had one since Polokwane." He appeared thoughtful.

"I did." Sarah tilted her mouth. "But it ended better this time."

"Oh?"

"I'll explain later on, when I'm awake and Israel and Kgomotso come tonight. I have an inkling it might relate somehow." They walked back to the bedroom, but he pulled away from her gentle grasp.

"I'll meet you there." He appeared to stifle a yawn. "I want a drink." Sarah nodded and moved back to the guestroom.

Mark went to the kitchen and filled a glass from the jug in the fridge. He glanced over his shoulder back down toward the office where Sarah had been. A nag tugged at his heart. She'd looked guilty when he found her. What was she hiding? He slipped into the room and clicked on the lamp. Nothing seemed out of the ordinary. He didn't want to boot up the computer again. What was he even looking for? He rubbed the back of his neck and was about to click off the lamp when he spotted the corner of a piece of paper, partially hidden under the keyboard. He drained the last of his water and tilted his head to read it as he pulled it out with care.

Adoption authorities. SA.

As he pulled it further, he saw a phone number scrawled onto the paper in Sarah's elegant hand. Brows pulled together in thought, Mark slipped the paper back under the keyboard. He flicked a glance over his shoulder before he wandered back to the kitchen, dropped off his glass, and returned to the guestroom. They had only known Kwanele a few weeks. Who knew what would happen? He stood in the doorway for a moment and regarded his wife with concern. Sliding back into the bed behind Sarah, Mark draped his arm around her and cuddled in. She murmured something he couldn't understand. He stared toward the wall, unable to settle. He didn't like the fact that she'd tried to keep that from him, as well. It was far too soon for her to be thinking of adoption. He hadn't even liked the kid at first. Mark found himself begin to grow irritated. What else had she hidden from him? He removed his arm and rolled away from Sarah. He bunched his pillow up under his head and stared toward the window. As he lay there, struggling to find peace, the devil ate away at the one thing that could bring them down harder than any poacher ever could: their trust in each other. Their marriage.

"So, is that what you mean by spiritual warfare?" Sarah asked the people who sat around the room. Israel opened his Bible. He began to direct them to various passages. Kwanele sat wide-eyed as he listened to the stories of Jesus' followers who had cast out demons in the name of Jesus.

"But you must be careful. Not everyone who casts out demons in Jesus' name is one of His. You must know Him," Israel warned.

"Well, no problems there." Mark slapped his hands on his knees.

"So you think the figures in my dream could represent Satan?" Sarah wondered aloud.

"Definitely," Israel confirmed. "But in some cases, your dreams will also reveal the identity of people who are real,"

"I know. I dream of Declan quite often. He was real," Sarah confirmed as Israel nodded.

"He was the poacher who pretended to help you, and then tried to kill you?"

Mark put his hand on Sarah's as she shuddered in memory.

"From what you've said this Declan has said to you in

dreams, I believe he represents the devil." Israel confirmed what Sarah and Mark had already guessed. "As for the other one in your latest dream? Only God knows." Israel rubbed his chin in thought. "God gives us gifts. We know this from Sarah. The story of her gift is a living testimony. But God also gives other gifts, discernment, prophecy, words of knowledge." He looked around the group, his eyes narrowed. "What if God gave Sarah an insight into someone else?"

"Maybe." Mark appeared to weigh it up. "But we don't know anyone like that."

He gazed at Sarah, and she shook her head.

"That is what I mean. A gift of knowledge—something that nobody except God knows."

Sarah and Mark exchanged glances.

"Prayer is your strongest weapon," Israel continued as he jerked his head toward Kgomotso, who rose to retrieve a long, zipped-up leather bag. "But the Word of God is stronger. If you pray the Word of God, the words from the Bible, and pray them with authority, then you can beat the enemy. The real battle happens in the heavenlies before it ever happens physically."

He nodded, and Kgomotso unzipped the bag. With care, he pulled out the same twisted kudu horn that had been mounted on his wall at Lebowa village. Mark and Sarah frowned at the item. Kwanele leaned forward with interest, his young eyes bright. Israel looked up at Mark and Sarah, his expression shrewd.

"Now, I know what you think. Don't. I got this by proper means." He took the horn from Kgomotso and rested it on his lap with care. "The Messianic Jews in Israel believe that if you blow the shofar, it shouts into the spiritual realm that you are declaring war on the enemy. The war, however, is already won, and you are simply stepping out with the banner of God. It is a powerful spiritual weapon, though not as much as prayer and the Word. This is a spiritual tool of warfare."

He turned the horn and passed it to Mark, who examined it with distaste as if it were poached. He looked up at Israel, a look of confusion on his face.

"It okay," Kgomotso assured them. "The kudu had been eaten by lion already. Already dead. Salvaged, not poached."

Israel scrunched up his face at the young couple again.

Mark raised his brows, "Okay, okay." With care, he handed it back to Israel.

"It great tool to call for help." Kgomotso grinned, his white teeth lighting up the room.

"Except that you couldn't hide that in your back pocket for a rainy day." Mark chuckled.

"Would you like to hear?" Israel stood on his ancient, wobbly legs and raised the massive, twisted horn. He put the small end to his lips, inhaled deeply, and then released a mighty blast. The sound sent shivers down everyone's spine, as if it could slice through an unseen substance in the atmosphere. Mark saw Kwanele shudder with the force of it. The air reverberated with the sound for a full five seconds before Israel put the horn down and looked around the room, triumphant and out of breath.

"The battle is in the spiritual realm." It was at that moment that Martha and Jacob entered the room.

"I thought we heard one of those," Jacob exclaimed. He rubbed his hands together as he sat in one of the lounge chairs.

"Now, we pray." Israel laughed. "The whole body is here, well, our part of it." He sat down, and his dark face flushed with satisfaction. It was at that moment that the house phone rang, loud and clear from the kitchen. Sarah looked at Jacob and then stood to answer it. She knew in her gut that this was it. She wanted answers. It was time to face this. Mark frowned and went to stand.

"No, Mark." Jacob stilled him. "It's time for us to pray now. Let's do battle in the heavenlies. Perhaps it's nothing to worry about."

Sarah hesitated as she reached for the receiver, her hands clammy with sweat. *Please let it be nothing, Lord.* She grabbed the receiver from the wall and held it to her ear.

"Hello?"

"Ah, hello...is Sarah there?" The voice sounded muffled, and it had the accent of a dark man. Sarah held her breath and changed the phone to her other ear.

"This is Sarah. Can I help you?"

The group stopped praying the instant they saw Sarah enter the room. Her face was pale as she confirmed the phone call.

"It was the same caller."

Everyone stared as they waited for her to go on.

"I think it was the Freedom Fighters." She sat, bewildered.

"What?" Mark frowned. She saw the muscles in his neck tighten. "How did they get the number?"

Sarah shook her head.

"I forgot to ask."

"They are dangerous people, Sarah. What did they want?" Mark stood and paced the room, his arms folded across his chest, fist to his lips in thought.

"They asked me to join them." She cringed as she waited for his response. "It wasn't a threat." She took in the worried faces around the room. "I said I wasn't interested and that I thought there was a better way they should tackle it."

"You said what? You can't engage with these people, Sarah. They won't listen. What about last time?" Mark reefed his hands through his hair. Israel stood on shaky legs and raised his hands to silence them all.

"It was not poachers." His voice was full of authority. "Therefore, we have won the first battle." He held his hands up to God, giving praise. Mark rubbed his hand across his jaw.

"What did they say?"

"They wanted to meet." Sarah's throat constricted at the sight of both panic and anger as they exploded on Mark's face.

"I said no," she assured him. "I explained about the ranger's men and how they are recruiting." She looked around at the confused faces, and her words fell into a determined hush. "I said they should look into that, and then they wouldn't get arrested all the time for murder. Then I told them about my faith. I told them about what God did for me when we moved those elephants. Then I offered to pray for them, and the man let me."

Mark turned to regard her in bewilderment.

"Wait a minute. You said all that to them? And they listened?"

She nodded. Mark closed his gaping mouth and shook his head. "Let me get this straight. These dangerous people called, wanted you, and you shared the gospel with them?"

Sarah nodded, her eyes wide. Mark slapped his leg. "Well, let's just hope they don't show up here next."

"Hallelujah. That was a wonderful move of faith, Sarah." Martha beamed. "I think our prayers helped." The room hummed with murmured agreement, except for Mark, who continued to stare at his wife in bewilderment.

"Mark van der Merwe." Jacob tore his attention from Sarah. "You just passed a great test."

"What?" He rubbed the back of his neck as he sat down beside Sarah.

"You left the protection of Sarah to God just then, and an amazing thing happened. Who knows what will happen with the seed that Sarah just planted." Jacob clapped his hands together with glee. "Thank You, God."

Mark leaned in to Sarah and murmured into her ear, "You have no idea how hard that was." She intertwined her fingers into his and squeezed his hand.

"I'm sorry." She was genuine. Jacob took control of the room, and they finished the night with more prayer. Around nine o'clock, a tired group of people retreated into the kitchen for late coffee and tea while Mark carried a sleeping Kwanele into his bedroom. Sarah walked with Mark and stood in the doorway watching as Mark pulled the sheet and duvet up to his chest.

They had seen such a dramatic change in the child in the weeks he'd been with them, from a starved, frightened, and untrustworthy child, to a boy at peace with his surroundings and safe and secure in a place where he was loved and provided for.

CHAPTER
TWENTY-FOUR

Mark slipped his cell phone into his back pocket and jogged down to the campfires to find Sarah. He found her sitting with Kwanele and Jacques on a bench under the shade of an acacia. She had the Bible open and was explaining some of the Old Testament stories to the boy.

"Sarah." Mark slowed to a walk, a twinkle in his eye. "James rang me back. Sabi Sabi wants to take us both on. They have a rondavel for us, and a spare paddock for Sniper. They pay a good wage, too."

Sarah closed the Bible onto her thumb to keep her page.

"When?" The question caught in her throat.

"As soon as we are ready. They're expanding, and the owners who run the trails want to pass the job on to employees. It's a three-bedroom cottage, Sarah, bigger than the flat."

Sarah's eyes lit up with a little more interest, but then Mark thought he saw the doubt cross her face again. He narrowed his eyes. Did the doubt have anything to do with the child who sat by her side and the scrap of paper he'd found in the office? His eyes flicked over the boy, and Sarah responded in likeness. They would need to discuss this later, when Kwanele wasn't around.

"How soon do they need an answer?" Sarah kept her expression steady. Mark rubbed the back of his neck again.

"We've got plenty of time to talk about it." He hesitated. "I need to go help Jacob cut some firewood." With that, he stalked off.

Mark eased the bit into Sniper's mouth and hung the reins

over his saddle. Feeling the strain in his neck, he grimaced and turned toward where Kwanele was ready to saddle Buster.

"Not that one, Kwan, the thick one. Notice how the girth point is higher up under the saddle flap. The thin one is the surcingle, that gets done up last."

Mark watched a moment as Kwanele untwisted the leather and connected it with the girth.

"Go as tight as you can, and I will fix it in a second."

Mark returned his attention to his own horse, tightening the girth with a grunt.

They were about to go on Kwanele's first trail ride into Kruger National Park. Kwanele ran his stirrups down and clicked on his helmet. He maneuvered the horse and stepped onto the mounting block. Reins correctly gathered and boot cocked into the stirrup, Kwanele stepped up and into the saddle with ease. He grinned with pride like a Cheshire cat as he sat astride the placid animal. Mark slid a rifle into the leather sling on his saddle with a thud and tilted his head to regard the boy.

"You didn't wait for me to tighten your girth, Kwan. Very dangerous. Your saddle could slip." With a flick of his hand, Mark left Sniper and directed Kwanele to cock his left leg up onto the saddle while he pulled tight the girth and surcingle.

"Right." He returned to Sniper, unclipped the lead rope, yielded his head toward him, and mounted up.

"Ready? Did you hook on your water bottle?" Mark swiveled in his saddle to examine Buster and Kwanele again. The boy patted the drink bottle holder attached to the front of his saddle. Mark grunted with satisfaction and sidled Sniper over to the gate, where he opened it with ease. They rode out for quite some time, stopping every now and then to observe various small herds of gazelle and zebra that picked their way through the mopane.

Mark looked back over his shoulder. "Trot up next to me, Kwan." The boy grinned. A proud expression spread across Mark's features as the boy caught up. The kid was a natural. Spurred on with Kwanele's solid control of Buster, Mark eased Sniper into a steady trot and followed the track that would eventually loop back around to the bush camp.

"You're a good rider, Kwan," Mark appraised when they slowed back to the walk.

They came out into a clear lowveldt section, and Kwanele pointed into the distance, his eyes wide. A pride of lions lay in the sun near a tree. There were eight of them in all, several lionesses, a very old male whose jaw hung wider as he panted in the afternoon heat, and three young males. Mark tensed in the saddle for a moment as he surveyed the situation.

"We'd better steer clear, but it should be okay, Kwan. They've just eaten their fill. No interest in us. They'll sleep the afternoon away." Mark gave a tilted grin to the stricken boy whose brows widened in query.

"How do I know?" Mark chuckled at Kwanele's expression. Kwanele gave a slight nod, his eyes locked on the pride.

"See their paws? Blood. And look at how their bellies are all pushed out from stuffing themselves, and..." Mark pointed beyond the lions. There was a zebra carcass on its side in the sun. Most of it had been consumed to the bone, except for the once noble, striped head. Several vultures danced around, impatient as another lioness with two cubs continued to have their fill.

"Nice-sized pride," Mark observed idly. The lioness with the cubs worked loose a black and white hind leg and, followed by her offspring, began to drag it back to the company of the pride. The vultures dove in as she abandoned the remains. The old lion raised its head as she approached, gave a massive toothy yawn, and then dropped his head back onto the ground.

"Let's get out of here, though. Lion country can be very dangerous, Kwan. If you're ever faced with lions, pray that there are people with you, for one, have a rifle handy, but in your case, you face them up."

"Face them up?" Kwanele tilted his head.

"*Ja*, balk at them. Face your horse toward them and pretend you're going to run them down. It puts them off most of the time—but never come out alone."

Kwanele's face flushed as he was about to speak. Mark grimaced. "I know, I know. Do as I say, not as I do. It's fun, isn't it, though—coming out here on a horse?" Mark's face lit up with a half-smile as they turned their horses back onto the track headed toward the bush camp.

"Patience, Abasi. They will come." Tom Dawson strode with confidence over to the long mirror mounted on the wall and straightened his jacket. "I came out to make sure you had all the arrangements in place for when they get here."

Abasi stammered as he went to the cabinet and pulled out a vial of liquid.

"I have more." He held it up to Tom, who narrowed his eyes at the reflection in the mirror of the Mozambique warden.

"You don't need a lot, Abasi. Just enough and it will send the elephants mad without leaving any traces. Too much and it will kill them. You don't want the autopsies to suggest residue from that stuff, nor do you want ten dead elephants. The key, Abasi, is not to leave any evidence. Vials, canisters, they must be disposed of. It must look like an accident. Remember the time frames? Do not forget them, they are vital. Do not call anyone until the effects wear off the elephants. Have you lined up your veterinary team?" He put special emphasis on the word, in the hope Abasi would understand the subcontext. The warden stowed the vial back in the cabinet and turned the key in the lock.

"Yes, they have been paid. They will verify what we tell them to."

"Which is...?"

"The elephants went mad."

Tom clasped his hands behind his back and rocked on his heels.

"And if people ask why they were in such a small enclosure?"

"They volunteered because they are elephant whisperers?" Abasi seemed unsure of himself. Tom spun on his heel and glared at the man.

"No room for doubt, Abasi! Sarah is the whisperer. Mark is her husband, and he was in there to help her. Make sure you remember that. This will be all over the press. She is high profile—no room for mistakes. She was against using tranquilizers and insisted on using her magic touch, there was no time to move the elephants to safer quarters because they were all in danger."

"Of course, boss, I meant to say that," Abasi stammered. Tom glared at him again, his cold eyes hooded.

"And the boy? He knows why we want them. He'll end up a witness." Abasi wrung his hands. Tom turned to look at his reflection again and straightened a piece of white hair.

"Make sure he is in the enclosure with them. He's so keen to be their friend now. He wanted to assist them." He waved the issue away. Abasi frowned as he wiped sweat from his brow.

"He is slippery, boss. What do I do if he gets away?"

"He won't get away." Tom's voice was flat. "He is not high profile. If he tries anything, do whatever you need to do to remove him from the situation."

Abasi nodded, and his gaze fell to the rifle cabinet.

Tom sighed with impatience and turned to him. Putting his hand into his jacket, he produced a handgun and pushed the side of it into Abasi's chest.

"Don't lose it," he grated, his cold eyes full of threat. Abasi nodded his thanks as he slid the handgun into a drawer on his desk. Tom's vivid blue eyes widened in horror at the misuse of the weapon.

"Carry it on your person at all times. Do not leave it lying around," he growled. "Get a holster or something, I don't care. Just don't lose it. Has your woman made afternoon tea yet?" Tom strode through the doorway from the offices into the living quarters.

He worried about Abasi's incompetence. If he didn't stick to the plan or got emotional, it could ruin everything. Mildly satisfied that his alibi was secure, however, Tom breezed into the modest kitchen area. If it went wrong, it would be Abasi who took the heat, not him. Just like Brennan had taken the heat all those years ago.

Kwanele passed the long metal rod to Jacob as directed and watched with interest as Jacob used it to maneuver, prod, poke, and otherwise check the pork on the spit as it dripped above the spitting campfire. The smell drifted around the whole courtyard as guests held their plates and breathed it in with longing.

"Nearly done." Jacob stood back and wiped his sleeve across his brow. The safari group had arrived earlier than expected and were ravenous. "Okay, Kwan. Come and help me get these spuds off the other fire."

Kwanele looked over his shoulder as he followed the head chef across the pavers. This was the same company that had been here when that man had harassed him, given him the photo.

"Kwanele."

His heart skipped a beat as Jacob touched him on the shoulder with his gloved hand. He took the large tray offered to him and held it outright in two hands as Jacob fished the foil-wrapped potatoes from the fire.

The heat from the flames licked up as a soft breeze pushed oxygen into the fire, and Kwanele felt a trickle of sweat run down the back of his neck. It tickled him and he longed to put the tray down and wipe at it, but he held strong. So far, the tall white man with the jet-black hair and a thin moustache was nowhere to be seen. Kwanele scanned the crowd to his left, looking for the people dressed in khaki safari uniforms. He had missed their arrival. Maybe the man didn't come. Kwanele thought back to that day and wondered what had happened to the newspaper clipping that had been left thrown in the dirt. It had been weeks now, and Kwanele hoped it had found its way to the garbage or been destroyed when his clothes were washed. The tray in his hands began to weigh heavy as it piled up with more foiled spuds.

"Kwanele," Jacob chided in a quiet tone as Kwanele's gaze strayed once again over his shoulder toward the campers. The tray-load of potatoes began to pitch.

"Kwanele, keep your mind on the job."

"Sorry." He balanced out the tray again. Jacob finished loading up the last potato for this round.

"That will be too heavy for you if we add more. Let's put this on the table and get another tray."

Without a word, Kwanele followed the old African to the table.

Outside the compound of the bush camp, Stephan stood aloofly leaning against the safari Jeep. The passenger door was open, and a cell phone glued to his ear.

"I don't know why you don't just deal with this yourself. You already know he won't cooperate." Stephan wiped at the beaded sweat that formed in the dark hairs of his upper lip with the back of his sleeve. "Well, don't tell Dawson that you took things into your own hands. He'll string you up in that thing, too." He rolled his eyes as the man on the other end of the line ranted at him. It had been a long day, and this had grown tiresome. If they had dealt with it themselves ages ago, maybe he could have quit his job by now and left for Europe with his cut of the bounty. He clicked open the lid on a box on the passenger seat and proceeded to pack away the tourist binoculars that were still scattered on the open-seated tray of the Jeep.

"Yes, well, I have to go now, Abasi. Nice talking with you." He tried to end the conversation abruptly but groaned as Abasi continued irately. He couldn't listen to this a moment longer. Swapping the cell to his other ear, he snapped.

"Look. I'm not scared of Dawson, but if I were you, I would be. I'll see what I can do. No promises." He ended the call before the warden could argue further and shook his head. "I'm getting too old for this..." he muttered under his breath as he finished packing away the equipment that the tourists had scattered over the Jeep.

CHAPTER
TWENTY-FIVE

Kwanele sat huddled between Mark and Sarah, his plate resting on his lap as he ate the pork. His eyes flicked up to the man who sat across the fire from him. It was him. That same trail guide who had pushed the newspaper clipping of Sarah at Kwanele the last time they came. The man who'd threatened him. The bush camp didn't seem like such a safe place anymore. He couldn't risk telling Mark and Sarah about the man. Not unless he told them his part in the job. And he could never do that. A sharp fear rose in the pit of his stomach. It threatened to push him into hysteria at any moment. The man had a large pork bone in both his hands and ate at it hungrily. His cold gaze focused suddenly on Kwanele. He held it for a moment. Kwanele blinked and looked away, bile rising in his mouth. The bitter taste made him want to gag. He wasn't hungry anymore. He knew the man would find a way to speak to him later. If Kwanele stayed within range of the people he knew, then he might be able to avoid a confrontation. He glanced over at Mark, who steadily worked through his jacket potato, fully laden with melted cheese, ham, sauce, and cream. He determined that he would not let Mark out of his sight. Mark made him feel...safe. Glancing down at the boy, Mark raised a brow and pointed his fork toward the cob of corn on Kwanele's plate. "Try the corn. It's delicious."

Kwanele tilted his head back toward his food and pushed the vegetables around with his fork. He kept his head bowed, but risked the occasional peek toward the man opposite him. Kwanele watched with relief as the man's attention was diverted to the woman next to him as she started to speak. Perhaps he could get through tonight without an encounter. All too soon, the tourists began to disperse to their various rondavels for the night. As the crowd thinned out, Kwanele stayed glued to Mark and Sarah as they helped Jacob and Martha clean up. He threw himself into washing up with Sarah and putting various things away as directed. Back in the safety of his home rondavel again with the people he trusted, Kwanele finally began to wonder if he'd escaped the attentions of the man. He relaxed and with utter relief, finally retired to his room for the night. Tucked safely into his room, Kwanele thanked God for His protection as he snuggled deep into the covers of his bed. He rolled over and stared at the open door to his bedroom. Maybe they had given up. Maybe they had not. How would he know? Overthinking the situation planted new seeds of doubt in his mind, and Kwanele struggled to settle after that.

He woke with a start in the early hours of the morning. There was a noise under his window. A scraping. Was it Jacques? Was it another angel of God? At the thought, Kwanele's vision snapped into focus and his heart began to beat faster with excitement. *Oh Jesus, if You have another message for me, it would be so wonderful.*

A rough voice stopped his train of thought.

"I know you're in there," someone hissed under their breath. "I saw that elephant woman reading to you last night. Now listen up. I know you're awake."

Kwanele sat up and clutched his blankets to his chest. Hysteria threatened to choke him.

"How?" He tried to stop the drum of his heart in his ears.

"It doesn't matter," the voice snapped. "I'm giving you a message from the warden at Mozambique. If you don't do your job, it will be done for you, and to you."

A growl rumbled from under the rondavel, and the man cursed explosively. Kwanele could hear the rustle of leaves as the man left the window. He heard the soft footfalls as the man hurried away. Kwanele trembled as he broke out into a cold sweat. Jacques—he must have scared the man off. They would still kill Sarah, Mark, and him. What was he going to do? His breath came in short, sharp pants as he tried to control his nerves. He resisted the urge to call Mark and Sarah. They might be angry, throw him out. No, they weren't like that. As he wrestled with his thoughts, Kwanele's eyes darted around the room. Adrenaline coursed through his veins as an idea started to form in his mind.

The stars overhead blinked in the cool night air as Kwanele wrapped his red coat tight around his body. It would be daylight in an hour or so, and he wanted to put as much distance between the bush camp and himself as he could. If he could get to the police somehow, get some help, perhaps they would all be saved.

He hadn't wanted to cause alarm to everyone, nor had he wanted to face the inevitable questions. This was something he needed to do on his own. He cringed as the light from the shed flooded out onto the horse kraals. Sniper and Buster nickered in greeting and wandered over to the fence. Kwanele made quick work of it, hauling out the saddle, pad, and bridle from the shed. He dragged over the mounting block to outside of the kraal. He slipped into the kraal, rope and halter in hand, and caught Buster. He worked quickly, throwing the saddle onto the moderate-sized horse. Kwanele untwisted the girth and surcingle and worked to get them as tight as he possibly could. He knew he'd never get it as tight as Mark, but he had no choice. Breathing heavily from the exertion, Kwanele struggled to open the sides of Buster's mouth to slip the bridle in. He almost cried out with relief as he buckled on his helmet and mounted up. The girth wasn't tight enough, and so the saddle slipped a little. Finding his seat, Kwanele stood and put all his weight into the right stirrup, and shoved it level again.

As they made their way toward the back gate, Kwanele inwardly cringed as Buster's hooves clopped and echoed around on the grounds. He was faced with a locked gate. Time for phase two. Kwanele twisted around in his saddle and searched for the keys he'd borrowed from the key hook in Jacob and Martha's rondavel. He fished them out from his pocket and held them up in the dim light. The gate latch was lower than the horse, just a little out of his reach, and he had to strain in order to pull the padlock into a position to click the key. He stretched for the latch and groaned as Buster stepped away from the fence. Kwanele struggled to reposition the horse. Sweat beaded on his brow as the horse stepped too far forward and needed to be backed up a step. Finally, it was right. He took a deep breath and lurched down. Straining, his fingertips hooked the padlock. A yellow stream of light crossed his line of vision. He gasped and snapped his head around. A torch beam moved around the buildings. The guards. Panic rose in his throat, and Kwanele willed himself to stay calm. Slipping the key into place, he jiggled it with urgency. His back began to cramp from the unusual position. Buster swayed beneath him, and the saddle began to slip to one side. Oh great. The torch beam was closer. Kwanele's breath came out ragged as he fought with the key. *Click.* It found its home, and the padlock sprang open. They didn't have time to waste. He pulled back the latch on the gate and pushed with all his strength. The hinges were flung forward, clanging as they bounced. Excited voices rose nearby, and beams of light danced about as the guards jogged toward him. With no time left, Kwanele kicked Buster through the gates and broke into a fast trot as he righted his saddle level again. He peered over his shoulder and disappeared into the night. Kwanele could see the distant torch beams as they scoured the immediate area for signs. Had they seen him? He didn't have time to wonder. He heard distant shouts. The bush camp floodlights came on around the whole facility, and more beams of light began to dance off the silhouettes of people as they ran out the gate. There was no turning back now. Face turned into the breeze, he pushed on, eyes watery against the wind as he tried to get his eyes accustomed to the darkness. Buster's blood began to heat up, and he surged into the bit. Alarmed and not prepared for a faster gait, Kwanele pulled the horse up to a walk. He risked another look over his shoulder. The darkness of the wilderness had swallowed him up. He gulped and urged Buster on again, careful to balance how much speed the animal gave him. Kwanele turned off from the main track and skirted thorny bushes as he trotted Buster deeper into the bushveldt. Relief washed over him at the same time as realization hit. *I made it. I escaped. What have I done? Will this even do anything to save anyone?*

Kwanele sighed and pulled Buster back to a walk as he thought of Mark and Sarah. He'd just stolen a horse and keys like a common thief. Would they catch him and turn him over to the police without letting him explain? Guilt washed over him as he wandered his way into the darkness. They would soon all be out in their vehicles searching for him. Buster snorted beneath Kwanele several times in a row. He was well hidden now, deep into the thicket of bushes and trees. It was then that he began to worry about the dangers in the bushveldt. Shuddering, he squinted into the heavy foliage of the trees above. They meandered and wandered through the maze of foliage with no idea of which direction they were headed. It was difficult to make out anything among the dark shapes of the night. Which way was Phalaborwa? Perhaps he should have stayed on the main road, but then he would have been caught. Buster slowed to a stop in response to Kwanele's indirection and began to graze. Kwanele looked around in confusion. He couldn't even remember which direction he'd just come from.

"Some warrior I turned out to be." Emotion began to sweep over him. "Let's go home." He turned Buster around and began an attempt to retrace his steps. They wandered for some time, Buster compliantly following Kwanele's lead. But when Kwanele supposed they would exit the thickets and emerge onto the road again, he found that the mopane shrubs grew thicker and he had to turn back. Buster began to snort with nerves as they continued into the thick of the bushes.

A sudden rustling noise startled Buster, and he leapt into a trot. Kwanele yelped and lunged forward to grip the reins. His breath came in short gasps as he tried to pull the horse to a stop. Buster wouldn't obey. Frantic now, Buster grabbed the bit and pulled his head around, snorting and jig-jogging on the spot.

"Buster. Stop," Kwanele pleaded as he tried to right the saddle that had slipped once again. A dark shadow slinking low in the mopane caught Kwanele's eye. Buster's reaction was explosive. He grabbed the bit and leapt into a canter. The dark shadow sprung from the shrub and bounded after them with frightening speed. That was all Buster needed. Panicked, he threw his head down and bolted. Horrified, Kwanele gripped the saddle in front of him and screamed for the horse to stop, but it only set him into a greater frenzy. They were being chased, and whatever it was, was gaining. One hand locked onto the saddle, Kwanele reached out and grabbed for the flapping reins. He caught them and closed his eyes. All he could hope to do was endure the ride. The saddle felt uneven. He lost his balance. The next few seconds flew by in slow motion as Kwanele was airborne from the now-sideways saddle. Reality jolted him fair in the tailbone as he landed in a thicket of thorny bushes. Kwanele cried out in pain and called for Buster. The only reply was the echo of hooves disappearing into the distance. Buster was long gone. Kwanele kept still in his awkward position as he tried to gain his bearings. The cold, hard reality of his new predicament hit him as the chorus of crickets resumed their song around him. Even though he'd gained his night vision to some extent, without his horse the darkness seemed to crowd closer around him, threatening to smother him for intruding on its territory. As the adrenaline ebbed away, it was replaced with the reality of pain. A dull throb wound its way up his back from his tailbone. Thorns bit into various parts of his body. He needed to move away from the prickling bush. He reached out his arm to find solid ground. A sharp pain shot up it as he tried to bear weight on it. Not good. He recoiled his arm and cradled it to his chest as he became aware of a strong metallic taste in his mouth. Blood. He put his hand to the corner of his face and felt the warm liquid that ran from his nose. His body ached as he used his other arm to pull himself to his feet. The cruel, thorny bush left behind, he stumbled onto the compacted dirt track and attempted to dust himself off. The snap of a twig underfoot caught Kwanele's attention, and he spun, his wide eyes scanning the mopane bushes. The outlines of the leaves were clearer in the dim light. He glanced up. He could just make out the hint of color as it crossed the horizon. A dark shadow moved from under the mopane, and Kwanele stiffened. He was not alone. He was injured, and he was in the dark in the wilderness of Africa. A lump rose in his throat, and he struggled to control his sudden panic. He needed to think. He looked skyward in desperation. Suddenly a voice filled his heart.

You are a warrior!

He sniffed back the blood that ran from his nose as he let the words sink into his spirit. Boldness filled him as he squared up to the shadow that appeared to stalk him from the bush.

Please, Jesus, give me Your strength, Your protection. Your peace.

"I'm ready." Kwanele's voice came out as a squeak as he stared into the bush. The mopane bush rustled, and the shadow emerged fully. There was no threat in the cat's body language as the cheetah sauntered over to Kwanele. It rubbed itself against Kwanele's hip.

"Jacques!" He collapsed onto the dirt, hugging the cheetah around the neck. Jacques always knew where he was. Of course he would have followed him. Emotion rose up as he clung to his one safety net, the loyal cat.

"Okay, I can do this now. Thank You, Jesus." His gaze swept skyward again, and tears glistened in his eyes. "Where to now?" He straightened and looked around. To his right, the line of mopane bushes continued along a dusty thin goat track. It was dense and dark. With Jacques to protect him from the wilds of the wilderness, Kwanele began to step out with renewed determination. Daylight was near as Kwanele sought to stick to the dense parts of the mopane. They wandered for a while before Kwanele paused and rubbed his leg. Jacques looked at him expectantly and rubbed his head into Kwanele's hand. Then, without warning, the cat stiffened, the hair on the back of his neck bristling. He ducked his head low and surveyed the area. Fearful, Kwanele grabbed at his collar. Jacques let out a low rumble deep in his throat.

"What have we here?"

A deep voice behind Kwanele startled him, and he spun in panic. Jacques moved to curl protectively around Kwanele. A man stood before them, swarthy, tall, and well-muscled in an army camouflaged outfit.

"*Oi!*" the man hollered out. "Check this out, man."

A few more men in similar attire emerged from the bushes, and stared. Jacques's whole body stiffened as he continued emitting low growls. Kwanele wriggled his fingers tighter around Jacques's collar.

"He's hurt," one of the men observed stepping closer. "Come." He waved Kwanele to follow them back through the bushes. Kwanele shook his head and backed away. The dark-skinned men all formed a semicircle around him, their arms folded across their chests, their faces cold and hard. Two of them held heavy guns at the ready.

"Come," the first man repeated in a stronger tone. Kwanele's eyes flicked to the guns, then back to the man. He was trapped. Fearful, he stepped out to follow the man, not letting go of his grip on Jacques's collar. The others continued to flank him. They walked on for quite a while, down the thin goat trail deeper into the mopane scrub. Soon enough, they broke out into a small, hidden clearing, where several more men in army fatigues sat around a small fire.

"Eh, Sello. Look what we found."

Of all the men by the fire, an older man with thickset lines creased into his jawline looked up at the newcomers. His eyes narrowed. He bit into a hunk of chicken drumstick, and then spat some gristle onto the ground.

"Who are you, boy?"

Kwanele stared at the ground, his breath coming short and sharp. His body ached even more, and he longed to be back at the bush camp in his warm, soft bed. He began to tremble.

"He's bleeding, man, help him first," someone reasoned in a compassionate voice. The man, Sello, grunted and flicked his head toward them. Kwanele kept his eyes lowered as he heard several men shuffle off. Moments later, a wad of wet cloth was held out to Kwanele. He took the cloth and wiped at the caked blood on his face. Sello watched him in silence. Kwanele's knees began to wobble, and he nearly stumbled on the spot. Sello jutted his chin out toward the other men and snapped at them. He spat another chunk of gristle.

"Sit, boy," he commanded. Supporting his weight on Jacques still, Kwanele sank to the ground. A tin mug of water was then offered to Kwanele.

"Thank you." He raised his eyes and saw Sello staring at him.

"Why are you here?" Sello grabbed more chicken from the dish on the ground in front in him.

"I need to get to Phalaborwa." Kwanele looked around the men in the circle. One of them let out a hearty laugh.

"Phalaborwa? Like that? You and a cheetah, walking to Phalaborwa?"

Sello narrowed his eyes as he moved next to the fire, crouched, and began to prepare a hot drink.

"I'm interested. Tell us your story, boy. You are all alone except for your, er"—he waved a hand in Jacques's direction—"guard dog here." Several men laughed, and he glared at them. "You're all scuffed up, wandering the Kruger in the dark." He flicked a half-burnt stick back into the fire with his foot.

Kwanele regarded the man for a long moment. Would these people help him?

"I was riding a horse..."

"Riding a horse?" They roared with laughter before Sello snapped at them.

"Yes, sir. I have learned how to ride at one of the bush camps. I left because I was trying to find help."

Sello narrowed his dark eyes.

"I was threatened."

Sello's focus moved to his mug as he filled it with hot water.

"By whom, the caretaker?"

"No, sir. A trail guide...well...I think he might be a poacher."

"A poacher taught you to ride?" Sello chuckled as he scooped sugar into his mug. The other men behind him laughed. Kwanele's brows pulled together.

"No, a man threatened me. He was a tour guide. He has a black moustache. I think he's a poacher." Kwanele's voice rose in pitch, and Sello raised his hand to stop him. Kwanele clamped his mouth shut, but the men kept laughing.

"Stop!" Sello spun to glower at them all. Kwanele's eyes grew wide as Sello turned again to him. "A poacher? How do you know he's a poacher?"

Kwanele could feel sweat drip down his back as he examined all their faces. *Please, Lord, what do I do? What do I tell them, Lord?* He worked his hands over the leather of Jacques's collar, his palms itchy. Jacques had settled beside him now and watched the scene intently. That still, quiet voice that Kwanele was growing to trust daily penetrated his heart again with words that made him tremble.

The truth will set you free.

Kwanele's heart thundered in his ears as he considered the words. Tell the truth? He trusted God. He knew that. What would happen if he revealed his part in the job? His hand ached, and he realized that he'd gripped Jacques's collar way too tight. He deliberately released his hand. *It makes no sense, but I trust You, God.*

He swallowed hard and looked Sello square in the face.

"Please, sir, if you will please listen to my story... It's a long one..." He hesitated. "I might be able to trust you."

Sello leaned forward with interest and waved at Kwanele to continue. The men began to murmur behind him.

"Uninterrupted," Sello barked. Instantly, they were silent and shuffled off to attend to other duties. It was now just Kwanele, Sello, and a few other quiet men left. The lump in his throat began to hurt as Kwanele spoke up.

"You called my friend not long ago. Maybe you can help us."

Sello narrowed his eyes. "I thought this was a story, not a plea. Who is your friend?"

"Sarah van der Merwe. I think she used to be called Sarah White." Kwanele sucked in a breath. Did he do the right thing? Sello's eyes widened.

"Tell me your story," he snapped. Kwanele was uneasy.

"I was threatened by poachers many weeks ago. It was my job to make friends with Sarah White and take her to them so they could stop her from saving the elephants. They said if I didn't do it, they would kill me. They already killed the man who used to look after me.

"I tried to run away so I wouldn't find Sarah. I didn't want to be killed, so I ran. But Sarah and her husband, Mark, they found me. I tried to get away, but they have cared for me. Now poachers have found us. I am afraid. I am afraid for her. There is a poacher at the bush camp now—that way." He pointed down the track. "The man with the moustache. He threatened me at my bedroom window last night. I took a horse and tried to run to find help." Kwanele searched the man's face for a hint of aid.

"I know who you are," he added against his better judgment. "You rang Sarah a few days ago and"—he swallowed—"you tied up Mark and Sarah and left them in your camp. I was there that day. Someone was going to torch their car, but didn't." Fear crept up his throat, and Kwanele looked down at the mug of water in his hands. He could sense Sello's eyes as they bore down on him.

"So it was you who let them go." The corner of his mouth lifted into a slight smirk. "You are bold. Brave. I like that."

Kwanele looked up in sudden hope, but Sello's hooded expression darkened. "Why do you think that we would want to help you? Or her, for that matter?" Tipping his head back, he drained his mug.

"Because I thought you stood against poaching?" The words tumbled from Kwanele's mouth in a heap. "I thought you might like to know where all the poachers are going to be meeting— where they want me to take Sarah. I want Mark and Sarah to be safe. I want to be safe. I need help. Please, I've already lost everything."

Sello paused, and his brows rose with interest. Kwanele lowered his gaze. Had this been a big mistake? Did he hear right from God?

Sello rubbed the stubble around his creased jawline as he considered Kwanele's request.

"Poachers' meeting, eh? Where?"

Excitement threatened to burst, but Kwanele gathered his words with care.

"There is a warehouse behind the bunker-house at the ranger's center just across the border into Mozambique. I've been told to take them there. They're going to kill them."

Sello arched an eyebrow as he regarded the boy. His expression suddenly lightened.

"What's the story on the cheetah?"

"He—he's my best friend." Kwanele touched his hand to the watchful cheetah's head. Jacques lifted his head and licked Kwanele's hand. Sello leaned back, his eyes aloof.

"You might be telling the truth...your horse?"

"I fell off, sir. I don't know where he is," Kwanele admitted honestly. Sello sneered as he scratched his head.

"Well, I don't know, boy. You need to tell the truth to your friends, then they can call for help."

Kwanele felt as if he'd been struck across the face.

"How do you know that I didn't tell them?" he gasped. The smirk on Sello's face widened, and he leaned forward.

"If they knew the truth, you would have awakened them and told them to call the police. You wouldn't have stolen a horse in the middle of the night and rode off into the Kruger at risk to yourself—am I right? I know, because you have the same stubborn spirit as the rest of us."

Kwanele dropped his gaze.

"Am I right?" Sello repeated.

"Yes, sir," murmured Kwanele.

"So, here is what I am going to do. First, I am not going to kill you. It looks bad for me. Second, you are going to take your guard dog and walk back to the bush camp to tell your friends the truth. Third, if you mention where you found us..."

He let the sentence hang in the air. Picking up his knife, he began to chisel away at a chunk of wood in front of him. "I think you get my drift..." He waved the boy on. "Joe, show this kid which way to go home. I think someone will be looking for him on the road by now. Abdul, clear the fire, we need to move on."

Kwanele was crushed. After he'd revealed his heart, they were going to do—nothing? Dejected, he stood as the small camp became a flurry of motion. Water was doused on the fire, tarps removed and packed up. Weapons collected. Another tall, swarthy man appeared in front of Kwanele and grunted for him to follow. The thought of the long walk made him weary. He ached all the way to the bone. Kwanele limped his way after the man, Jacques at his side. He was led back out of the bushy maze and onto semi-open lowveldt. He shuddered as he looked into the dawn. He was being left for dead to wander home on his own. Anger broiled deep in his heart at the injustice.

"That way." The tall, dark man pointed into the distance, then turned and disappeared back the way he came. Kwanele stared after him in dismay. He sighed and looked at Jacques. The soft pink hue on the horizon reflected off his orange coat. "Let's go then, bud."

Chapter
Twenty-Six

Kwanele headed in the direction toward the bush camp, Jacques padding silently at his side. He was grateful for the company of the cheetah, and it was encouraging to know that he might be able to protect Kwanele from predators in the wilderness. The darkness retreated as pink lit up the sky. Dew seeped up Kwanele's trousers and made his legs cold and wet as he trudged through the long lowveldt grasses. His jacket was ripped and bloodstained at the elbow, but he tugged it closer about him, grateful for its warmth in the cool air. The hum of an engine some time later stopped Kwanele in his tracks. He squinted into the distance and could just make out the shape of one of the tourist's Jeeps as it drove along the track, headlights on full beam. The last thing Kwanele needed now was to see that tall, white poacher man again.

He crouched low into the long grass and scurried over to a thick mopane, tugging Jacques with him. His red jacket! With sudden realization, he shrugged it off and pushed it down into the grass. His tan-colored shirt would blend in much better. After a while, the sound of the Jeep disappeared. Kwanele rose with caution and shivered as he pulled his jacket back on and zipped it up to his chin. He felt like he'd walked for ages, each step heavier than the last, when he saw a flash of white in the distance and heard the gentle roar of a familiar engine. His breath quickened with excitement. It was the Cruiser. This time he stood up straight and, shucking the jacket off once more, he held it above his head, waving it around like a flag. In no time, the yellow headlights turned his way, and Kwanele heaved with relief when he saw the Cruiser slow down. The passenger door flew open.

"Kwan!" Sarah ran and pulled him into her arms. Mark pulled out of gear and leaped out, jogging over to them, worry etched into his features.

"What happened, Kwan? Thank God you're okay!" He knelt in the wet grass and wrapped his wife and Kwanele into a strong embrace.

"We were so worried." Sarah pulled back to examine him. "You're hurt."

"What on earth were you doing riding, by yourself, in the dark?" Kwanele could hear the mixed emotions in Mark's voice, and tears sprang to his eyes. He explained about the trail guide being a poacher and how he had been threatened.

"Why didn't you tell us about him earlier?" Mark's eyes were clouded with concern. "If he threatened to hurt you last time, you should have said something."

Kwanele bit his lip—he needed to tell the whole story, including his part in it, but now was not the time. Mark had already slipped back into the Cruiser and was alerting Jacob and Martha on the radio. Sarah glanced at Jacques and ran her hand over Kwanele's hair, laughing with relief.

"Kwan, you brought a bodyguard?"

"I didn't mean to," Kwanele protested. "He followed me. It was him that spooked Buster, and I fell off." His voice trailed off as he thought about the events that followed.

"So, that man was at your window? Why did you run off on Buster? Why didn't you wake us?" Sarah wrapped an arm around him and steered him toward the Cruiser.

"I was scared—I wanted to go for help." Emotion hit Kwanele, and he began to hiccup with tears as he slid into the vehicle. He scuttled over and made room for the cheetah to climb in.

Jacques sniffed the interior before he jumped with ease into the seat beside Kwanele. He tucked himself down and rested his head on Kwanele's legs. Sarah sighed with exhaustion as she climbed into the passenger seat next to Mark.

Kwanele saw Sarah turn in her seat to regard him, and his body began to shake.

"We might need an ambulance, hon." Sarah touched her husband's arm, and Mark gazed in the rearview mirror. He nodded and passed his phone to Sarah.

The bush camp looked like a different place when they returned. It echoed with emptiness, even though the place crawled with people. All laughter had been replaced by somberness as the guards conferred with policemen who had arrived an hour later. Kwanele would need to be checked over by medics once they arrived. The current group of tourists was in lockdown mode until everyone had been questioned. The guards confirmed Kwanele's story to the police about the man at the window, saying that they thought they heard something there, but when they got there, it was gone. They had found footprints that matched the brand of boot worn by the trail guides, though. Buster and Sniper were safely in their locked kraals; Buster had returned home a bit shaken up and riderless. The biggest piece of evidence was the fact that the trail guide in question, Stephan Venter, had fled the scene in the Jeep during the search for Kwanele, and he had left his disgruntled colleagues to answer awkward questions and organize the transport of all the tourists back to their base center in Phalaborwa without the use of the third Jeep. Much to Jacob and Martha's dismay, the bush camp was to be closed to visitors while investigations took place. Investigators needed to talk with Mark, Sarah, and Kwanele about events since they left Polokwane leading up to today and why they had chosen to defy the rules. Though Sarah's phone call to the police a few days earlier seemed to placate them for a while, the new developments had started a spark of fresh concern. Why hadn't they mentioned the boy? Why hadn't they mentioned to the other police who they were so that it would all be connected up with the relevant people? Now things had developed, and the police that had protected them in Polokwane were all over it. The bush camp was in a complete whirlwind, and Kwanele worried that he'd been the one to cause it. What would the poachers do to him now, once they got their hands on him? He needed to tell Mark and Sarah the truth, but he wanted to tell them alone. It seemed impossible to get anywhere near them alone right now. Sick to his stomach and numb, Kwanele allowed himself to be led by a police officer over to the medic vehicle, which had just arrived at the grounds. He shuddered and turned to regard Mark and Sarah as they appeared to be tied up with another policeman nearby. He could see their mouths move, but he couldn't hear over the throng of voices that milled and moved about the campgrounds.

Lieutenant Tim Naicker turned and scrutinized Mark and Sarah as he slipped the receiver of his two-way radio back into the lock on his holster. He was in his midforties, clean-shaven and fit, but worry lines etched his face. His eyes were red-rimmed from countless sleepless nights spent working recently on their account. Tim exhaled deeply and cocked his head to one side.

"Guys, how can I keep you safe if you keep giving me the slip and gallivanting all over the country—and in the Kruger no less?"

"But I rang." Sarah feebly stepped forward.

"You rang way after you'd already been here for way too long." Tim snapped and rubbed the corner of his left eye. "After it was too late."

Mark reached out a hand to Sarah, and she slipped in beside him.

"Now I find out that you've been here for over three weeks, including involvement with a murder and the discovery of this boy?"

Sarah's mouth dropped open, but Lieutenant Naicker's hand shot up. He wasn't finished.

"Yes, I pulled the files. I heard how you avoided giving statements, but it was all still recorded, somewhere. Did you think that we don't communicate between districts? Our systems are all linked." Tim shook his head with irritation. He closed his eyes and pinched the bridge of his nose. Mark and Sarah stood silent. Sighing, Tim lifted his gaze, and looked the two over.

"I realize this has been hard on you both." He hesitated and looked toward Jacob and Martha's rondavel. "Can we talk inside? There are developments I need to share with you."

He saw them both nod and followed them toward the building. Sarah grabbed Mark's hand for support and leaned in to him. He couldn't blame them for being shaken. But it was, after all, their choices that had led to this. He glanced over to the right and saw the Zulu boy being interviewed by the sergeant as medics were working on his wounds. He looked just as shaken up, as he held up his arm for the ambulance officer to take his blood pressure. Tim's attention returned to the present as Mark nodded toward the open doorway. They all entered Jacob and Martha's main office complex instead of the rondavel. Once the screen door creaked shut behind them, they all shuffled about the small room and sat at the small table. Sarah glanced sideways at Mark as they sat. Tim saw her stiffen as she watched him. Naicker opened the file in front of him, his expression closed. He had known the couple for several years since he took on their case after the elephant ordeal. It was he who had relocated them, hidden them, and protected them. They owed him their very lives. Tim cleared his throat and spun a file around so they could view the front page. There was a line-up photo of a middle-aged, gray-haired black man holding the placard with his name on it. Mark narrowed his eyes, and Naicker saw recognition. He cleared his throat again.

"Do you recognize this man?"

"This is the man found dead at the rhino crime scene," Mark observed.

"Joseph Ngubane," Tim confirmed. "Convicted of theft, breaking and entering, assault, laundering money, and just an overall general con man. More recently, he was wanted for his involvement in the ivory smuggling trade."

The lieutenant leaned back in his seat and watched as Mark and Sarah read through the first page. Satisfied after a few minutes, he reached under the first page and tugged another photo loose from a paper clip. The small glossy printout showed Kwanele, his gaunt expression vacant, clothes tattered. Tim conceded to himself that the image was a shadow of the happy child they now found outside. Tim leaned back in his chair and waited for their responses. Mark screwed up his face. Sarah sighed. Interesting.

"We know Kwanele was involved with this man. This man was using this poor boy for his own benefit. It wasn't by choice. Kwanele was forced to do the things he did. He should not be held accountable for the crimes of this man." Mark jutted his finger onto the photo of Joseph. The lieutenant leaned forward, his elbows on the table, and steepled his fingers together.

"So…?"

"So, we have just had word that among poaching rings, there is a very large price on both of your heads. Sarah's price is higher." He waited for that information to sink in. They held it together.

"What has this got to do with Kwanele? Besides, hasn't there been a price on our heads for three years or more? What's new about that?"

"Now that you've left Polokwane, it's tripled." Tim's tone was flat as he turned the file back to himself. Mark and Sarah's eyes widened.

"But…"

"Don't you understand?" Tim rose from his chair and glared at them. "They had tabs on you right from the beginning. Until you were a threat, they weren't going to move. We had it staked out. We could have had them. We were about to move. You have no idea what you undid by leaving Polokwane. I had men undercover who put their lives at risk." He controlled himself and sat down again. The color drained from Sarah's face.

"We have reason to believe that Joseph Ngubane and his presence with the boy in the Kruger is connected somehow with you both leaving Polokwane. We also believe we may have found the mastermind behind the elephant attack three years ago."

"But you arrested John Brennan. He's in jail," Mark protested. The lieutenant grimaced.

"Yes, but he was not the mastermind. He was working for someone else. We think it's the same person. But the fact is, you were being watched in Polokwane. We've known that for a year. That's why we had our undercover guys staking out the place. Somehow, security in town wasn't as tight as we first believed."

"You think?" Mark's brows drew together. "You knew for a year, and you didn't say anything? So you put us at risk, too."

"We didn't think it necessary to alarm you."

"Necessary?" Mark slammed his hands on the table before shoving himself backward. Sarah touched his arm, and when he looked at her, his face screwed up with emotion. He glared at the lieutenant.

"I've busted my guts to protect my wife for four years. And I've had to watch as she slowly sank into depression. We lost everything, everyone we love and hold dear, and for what? So you—" Mark threw his hands in the air and made a noise at the back of his throat. Naicker watched as Mark clasped his hands to his head and paced the room, breathing through his nostrils like a steam train. His breathing eventually evened out, and he turned with quiet malice toward the lieutenant.

"When are we going to be free of this?"

"Mark." Sarah's voice was quiet. Mark looked at her, and Tim saw him relax. Unsteady, he lowered himself back into the chair beside Sarah and waited for Tim to go on. Naicker sat stone-silent through the outburst. When he was sure Mark wasn't going to speak again, Tim continued with control.

"Nevertheless, people have worked out that you're here now. We have set up security around the bush camp, and you will need to remain here until we clear you. No one enters, no one leaves without consent." His thin lips tightened into a hard line as he saw Mark wind up to retaliate again.

"You're putting us under house arrest?" Mark slammed his hand on the table with fury. The lieutenant narrowed his eyes at Mark.

"For the time being, yes. This thing is about to break wide open, and I don't want the people in my protection killed." He wasn't going to engage with Mark again. He stiffly rose, adjusted his police hat over his thick hair, and stepped outside the small offices. The clink of the screen door as it fell into place roused the couple from their shock.

Mark tried to calm down as he regarded his wife, but to no avail. He was furious.

"What will they do with Kwanele?" Sarah's body was taut with fear. Mark's brows pulled together as he slipped his arm around her. Despite the heat of the morning, her skin was cool and clammy, and he thought he felt her begin to tremble.

"I don't know." The crease lines eased from his face as he looked on her with renewed concern. Jerking himself to face her, Mark held the back of his hand to her forehead and frowned. She had a slight fever.

"Sarah? Are you alright? You have a temperature." Renewed lines of worry etched into his face. She shrugged it off.

"It's not important —I need to know about Kwanele."

He gripped her shoulders and looked deep into her green eyes. Why hadn't he noticed before? Her eyes were puffy and red-rimmed. Had she overdone things? The last thing she needed now was to come down with a virus.

"Sarah, look at me. It is very important. *You* are important. We will get through this. We'll get you to a doctor." He stopped himself as he remembered. "House arrest." He spat the words. "This place will be a target now. What if they did something crazy like rigged the whole bush camp with a bomb?"

Sarah tilted her head at him in disbelief.

"Okay, okay, maybe not a bomb." He shook his head. "I feel less than safe here now, that's all." He got up from her again and paced like a caged lion. Sarah slumped in her seat and managed a half smile.

"Remember what Israel said, Mark. The battle begins in the heavenlies. There is something we *can* do."

He stopped pacing and looked at her. The thought of prayer when action was needed unnerved him. The door creaked open and Martha popped her head in.

"Kwanele is allowed to stay here." Her smile was reserved as she wrung her hands. "We all have to—"

"I know." Mark didn't mean to snap at her, and he instantly regretted it.

"Mark." Sarah stood, stepped in front of him, and rested her hands on his chest. "Please. I'm scared, too." She ran her fingers over his set jaw. His gaze softened.

"I'm sorry."

"I don't think you will be stuck for long." Martha smiled encouragingly. Mark hmmphed loudly before he examined Sarah's pale features again.

"Martha, is that medic still here?"

Sarah shook her head. "It's fine, Mark. It's just a head cold. I'm just tired and in shock still. It'll wear off. I promise."

Mark looked at Martha for an answer. She flicked her eyes toward Sarah, who smiled and lifted her countenance. "Sorry, he left a few minutes ago," she murmured.

"Could you call him back?" Mark's eyes leveled with worry on his wife, studying her for signs of weakness.

"I'm fine, Mark. Really." Waltzing over, she grasped his hands in hers and brought them to her lips. Doubt clouded his eyes.

"You what?" Tom crunched the phone onto his ear with his shoulder as he jotted something down on a notepad. "Why the hell didn't you contact me before you made a stupid move like that? Now, it's up to you. You get them out there in the next twenty-four hours, you hear?" He crossed the room and stood before the large window as he listened to the groveling on the other end of the phone.

"The vets? Well, get them organized." He thundered across the floor to his desk and slammed the phone down with a loud *clunk*. He stood a moment, hunched over the desk, before he inhaled and composed himself. A gentle knock sounded on the door. Straightening, he pushed a piece of wayward hair back into place, adjusted his jacket, and smiled.

"Enter," he directed.

An attractive woman in a business suit and pencil skirt poked her head into the doorway.

"Sir? Is everything alright?"

"Quite." Tom waved her away. She turned to leave.

"Oh, Trudy?" he called after her.

She stopped in her tracks and turned to look at him in query.

"Tea, please."

Inclining her head, she left as Tom sat lightly in his chair. He needed to calm his nerves. He worked his hands into fists, furling and unfurling them—trying to release the tension. Why on earth did he let incompetent fools do this job for him? He began to realize that he'd have to deal with them next before they were caught and squawked to the police. His alibis were not as secure as last time.

Chapter
Twenty-Seven

Kwanele looked up as Sarah's cell phone vibrated in her handbag. It jiggled all the various pens and bits and pieces that cluttered the elegant accessory.

"Your mobile stationery shop is screaming." Mark's tone was flat as he glowered and left the room. It was obvious to everyone that he was angry at being under house arrest—he paced the rondavel like a lion, and no one could say or do a thing to persuade him to calm down. Sarah frowned and retrieved her bag from the dresser. Sitting on the bed, she rummaged through it. By the time she located her phone, it had vibrated its way to the bottom of the bag among all the loose *biros* and other paraphernalia. Kwanele turned his gaze out the window. He sat on a chair, his chin rested on his folded arms as he leaned against the windowsill. He sighed and closed his eyes. Sarah flipped open her cell phone just before it stopped ringing.

"Hello?" There was a long pause. "Abasi, hi, how are you?"

Kwanele spun his head toward Sarah at the name, his eyes wide with alarm. She pushed a piece of hair aside from her face as she murmured her replies. Kwanele stiffened as he watched her begin to pace the room.

"It's a bit hard at the moment, we have stuff going on and we can't get away." She frowned, sat heavily on the bed, and tapped her fingernails on the bedside table. Kwanele got up and crumpled to his knees before her. Sarah jolted backward. He waved his hands in front of her face and shook his head, mouthing the word *NO*.

Her brows pulled together as she covered the speaker on the cell with her hand. "Hang on, Kwanele. I'll be just a minute." Kwanele shook his head.

"Is it that bad, Abasi?" Concern now wrenched her features.

Kwanele stormed out of the room. He reentered the room, an irritated Mark dragged by the sleeve. Mark folded his arms across his chest and waited for the call to finish.

"Look, I know you are trying to help her, calm down. I need you to stay calm, or we won't be able to help her." She raised her eyes to regard Mark and Kwanele.

"Abasi, can you ring me back in ten minutes? I'll talk to my husband about it. Okay?" She pressed the hang-up button and opened her mouth to speak, but Mark held up his hand to silence her.

"Did I hear right? Kwan tells me Abasi wants us to go to Mozambique. Did you explain our situation?"

Sarah crossed the room and closed the bedroom door behind them.

"An elephant calf has broken its leg—they can't get the vets close enough to tranquilize her to operate. The other elephants have crowded around her—they don't want to put her out because she'll get trampled. They need me to come and calm them all down."

Mark looked at her, his expression torn.

"I did explain we can't get away at the moment. He got hysterical. He's saying that the other elephants are already going to injure her if we don't remove her from the herd." She began to pace.

"Odd. Elephants usually rally around an injured animal to protect it, not hurt it," Mark pondered.

"I know. Something's not sitting right. He's a ranger, he'd know that, too. That's why I'm worried." Sarah began to get upset. Kwanele groaned in frustration as Mark moved toward the window. Suddenly he turned to Sarah and Kwanele, a sparkle in his eye.

"I hate being trapped here. This place is a target now. Mozambique would be one of the safest places for us anyway. No one would look for us there if they think we're here." A grin spread across his face. "Let's escape."

"No!" Kwanele grew hysterical.

"Why not?" Mark raised a brow. "Isn't this the kind of

adventure you always wanted?"

"They will get us." Kwanele's voice became a shrill squeak.

"They will if we stay here," Mark countered. "I need to keep you both safe."

Kwanele swallowed hard. Mark's tone intimidated him, and lowering his eyes, Kwanele backed into the corner. Years of learned compliance kicked back in. Mark seemed very emotional right now—one minute angry, the next minute happy. Kwanele had seen adults like this before. They were unstable. He was afraid to explain everything to them now. Mark would be so angry with him. He bit his lip as fear formed in the pit of his stomach like a heavy rock. He needed to keep them from going to Mozambique somehow.

"The police will stop us." Kwanele looked out the window as two constables walked past.

"We could do it tonight," Mark whispered. Eyes wide, Sarah nodded.

"Thank you, Mark." She put her hand on his arm.

"It's an emergency. Tim will understand. Better to get his forgiveness later with no harm done than to ask his permission." As Mark reasoned, Kwanele thought he saw a shadow of doubt cross the man's features. He hoped that God would speak to the man and keep them from making a big mistake. No...realization hit Kwanele. God was relying on *him* to be His hands and feet. He was the messenger now. But he was afraid. He watched with dismay as Mark sat on the bed with notepad and pen. He murmured out loud as he started to plot out when he knew the guards changed shift. Sarah sat next to him.

"Don't forget there are extra people on duty now. Police."

"I know. We'll work around it."

"What about the Cruiser? We'd never get it out." Sarah frowned. "I don't know about this, Mark."

Kwanele watched the conversation unfold as he slid into the corner of the room. In his head, he began to pray. *Please, God. Please, Jesus. Stop them. Help me stop them, Lord...please.*

Mark paused. "The old bakkie, in the shed outside." His eyes lit up, and Sarah tilted her head in confusion. "You know? That old bakkie that was put into retirement? We use it for bush-bashing sometimes. It's outside the compound in the old fallen-down shed for a reason. It may still have life in it." Kwanele thumped the palm of his hand onto his forehead. The adults didn't notice.

"And what if it didn't? We'd be busted in no time."

"We'd think of something."

"If you want to escape, you need to think of something now." Sarah wheezed as a cough caught her off guard.

"Sorry." She cleared her throat skeptically. "Mark, that thing would wake up all of southeast Africa if we by some miracle got it started."

Mark frowned as he thought for a moment.

"I could pull in a favor with Carlito?" he wondered out loud. Sarah stood up.

"The caretaker of Shimuwini bush camp? That's still about fifteen kilometers away. Are you sure you want to involve other people?"

"I'm up for it. You?" He grinned. Sarah sat and propped her elbows on her knees.

"What? Walk there?"

Mark nodded and turned to Kwanele. "You coming? You've walked farther than that when you were weak. You're strong now. A warrior." Kwanele looked stricken. Mark sighed. "Okay, I'll ring him. Maybe he could pick us up halfway."

"What's the bet we'd be caught by then?" Sarah slipped her cell phone into her jeans pocket. Just as she took her hand from it, it vibrated again. She pulled it out and pressed *answer*.

"Sarah here."

She looked at Mark, and he nodded, silent affirmation that she could answer in positive to Abasi's request. She pressed her lips together before she spoke.

"Yes, we'll try to get there somehow. We'll be out by morning, but don't be surprised if we arrive earlier in the night. Can you swing passage with the guys at the border? No, we won't be out the normal way. Why?" She rubbed her eyes. "Just circumstances. That's all." There was a long pause before Sarah rounded up the conversation.

"Thanks, Abasi, you're the best." She pressed *hang up* on the mobile and took a shuddering breath. "I don't know why we are doing this, but it's set now. We have to do it." She wrapped her arms about herself. "Do you guys mind if I lie down? I'm a little tired." Mark nodded and guided Kwanele from the room. As he closed the door behind them, he pulled out his own cell phone. Kwanele silently allowed himself to be led away. He wiped his hands on his trousers repeatedly.

The waning moon started to rise on the horizon like a sliver of light, barely touching the dark ground below. A cool breeze had sprung up in the early hours, and Kwanele stood numb as Sarah fussed about him being wrapped in his still-ripped red jacket, long pants, and boots. He was beyond protest now. His pleas had fallen on deaf ears the night before as they planned out their strategy. His only hope now was to go with them and somehow steer them from harm's way, or somehow convince them to not follow through with their plan. Perhaps once they were out, Sarah would listen to him. Could he tell her the whole story without her getting angry? She didn't seem herself, and he didn't want to burden her.

Putting a finger to his lips, Mark led the way, careful as he took the same key from the hook that Kwanele had taken the night before for the gate behind the horse kraals. Mark passed Sarah the Winchester rifle he'd borrowed from Jacob's cabinet, and lit up the LCD on his wristwatch, checking the time. Almost 2 a.m. In three minutes the police that patrolled the grounds with the guards would change shifts. He had gained knowledge of their shifts from the roster that Tim Naicker had pinned on the temporary command center at the bush camp. They snuck down the back stairs and headed toward the horse kraals, their breath visible in the chilled night air. The end of autumn was fast approaching. Mark took the rifle back as they moved in the shadows of the buildings. Mark would signal for them to halt at times as a policeman or guard passed by. The shade from the acacias and mopanes down at the horse kraals would provide a little more shelter as they darted between the pale shadows that the moon cast over the landscape. Mark held his hand up once more, and Sarah clasped his shoulder, her rapid breath light. They made their final sweep to the kraal. The horses lifted their heads. Everyone held their breath and prayed the horses wouldn't make a sound. Sniper nickered softly, followed shortly after by Buster. Everyone froze. Nothing.

Thankfully the people on duty had not heard them, or if they did, they didn't register the significance of it. Sarah accepted the weapon again as Mark firmly choked the lock and worked to stifle the sound as he clicked it undone. Success. He pulled back the gate latch and cringed when it still creaked a little. He created a neat gap, and they all slid through. Mark then returned the gates to their original position and reattached the latch. He dummy-locked the padlock. As one, they moved toward the nearby scrub, where they all began to move at a steady pace, keeping greenery between them and the view of the bush camp. After about a kilometer of sneaking through the dense mopane, Sarah nodded at Mark, and they all broke into a light jog, putting as much distance between them and home as they could.

Dave came onto duty at the 2 a.m. shift, and he breathed in the cool night air. He enjoyed the early morning jobs. They always gave him that rush of adrenaline, to be on the field in the dark. He adjusted his headlamp. The constable nodded toward his comrade with a lopsided smile. Dave didn't care that they all laughed at his headlamp. It freed up his arms, and that was all that mattered. He saluted his comrade, who waved wearily and headed in to catch some sleep. Rolling his shoulders to let his blood flow after a light sleep, Dave began to meander through the peaceful grounds. He'd jumped at the chance to come out to Kruger on this job. Not because of the "babysitting," but because of the possibility of excitement or danger. Aside from that, he enjoyed the wilderness of Africa— the beauty, danger, and mystique of it all. It was something he'd rarely been able to enjoy with the high demands that work put on him. A noise caught his attention.

He frowned as he stopped to listen for it again. Which direction had it come from?

There it was again, lighter but still there. A scuffle. He craned his neck toward the sound. It came from near the kraals and sheds down to the west of the complex. Horses? He knew there were horses down there, but they didn't scuff along the dirt. His senses on full alert, he signaled to his partner. The other constable gave him a thumbs-up, and Dave began to scan beyond the perimeter fence line. If someone was out there, they needed to be ready to hit the alarm. Dave moved stealthily into the shadows and flicked off his headlamp. It took a moment for his eyes to adjust to the darkness around the trees and sheds. A rustle stopped him in his tracks.

He waited. The gate behind the shed? There it was again, a scrambling noise now. He pressed his back against the shed, and adrenaline started to kick into full gear. He slipped the safety catch off his gun and held it flush against his chest. With care, he rolled his head around the corner of the shed and stared out through the wire of the double gates. He heard it again, a scuffling noise. It came from beyond the gates. Dave braced himself, then flicked his torch onto maximum and aimed the gun.

"Stop. Police."

There in his torchlight, he spotted a cheetah, five hundred meters away outside the fence. Dave's shoulder's sagged. The big cat paused and squinted into the beam. His eyes gleamed fluorescent green as the light reflected from his pupils. He regarded Dave for a moment, before turning and trotting off into the darkness beyond. Dave chuckled at himself for his nerves and let out a long sigh of relief. Wildlife. He left his light on and strolled back past the horse kraals. The horses nickered in question as he passed.

"At ease, boys." He smirked and returned to his post. The other constable appeared a moment later and looked at him in query.

"It was just a cheetah outside," Dave confirmed. The officer gave another thumbs-up and returned to his post. A while later, Dave would rub at the back of his neck with confusion. Was that cheetah wearing a collar?

"Stop." Sarah grabbed on to Mark's arm to steady herself as she gasped for breath. "We need a rest." She bent over and locked her arms onto her knees, the sharp pain in her side unbearable. She glanced over at Kwanele, who threw himself on the ground dramatically. Mark laughed.

"Come on, you two. Sarah, straighten up and put your hands behind your head, it will fill your lungs better."

Sarah followed the direction and felt that, with each breath, the stitch in her side subsided. Grateful, she accepted the small bottle of water Mark held out to her. She took a swig and then passed it to Kwanele, who got to his feet and drank deeply.

"How far do you think we've come?" Sarah squinted into the distance behind them. Mark pulled a compass from his pocket and checked their bearings. "I'd say roughly five kilometers." He stretched out. They had kept up a steady pace for quite some time. Mark gazed around in concern and clicked off the safety latch on the Winchester. He held it at the ready.

"What's wrong?" Sarah's eyes grew wide.

"Nothing, I hope..." Mark's voice trailed off.

"Where is Carlito?" Sarah wheezed and her chest grew tight. She doubled over, her fist to her mouth as she began coughing. Mark's brows creased.

"I'll be okay." Sarah held up a hand at the look on his face. She tried to control another fit of coughs, but failed.

"I'll give him another call. In the meantime, let's just keep to a steady walk."

Too tired to answer, Sarah and Kwanele began to trudge onward. Mark pulled his phone and rang his friend, who was already out in his Jeep on the lookout for them. When they heard a rumble from up ahead and saw the headlights, Mark held up his arm against the glare.

"*Ja*, I can see you now, Carlito. See you in a bit." He slipped his cell phone back into his pocket and turned on his small LED light torch, waving it toward the vehicle. Within moments, the Jeep pulled up beside them.

"Mark van der Merwe, you are a strange man." Carlito laughed. "Wandering around a National Park in the dark, you could get mauled, man." He shook his head in wonder. "But your lady here, eh? She can calm the wild beasts for you, eh?"

Sarah managed a weak smile as she climbed into the Jeep and collapsed on the seat. Sarah beckoned Kwanele to slide in the backseat with her as Mark took over the driver's seat and Carlito settled into the passenger seat.

"Just drop me off at home, please. My wife, she worry," Carlito directed. Mark grunted and pushed the Jeep into gear.

"Wait!" Kwanele cried out, his door still open. Mark slammed his foot on the brake.

"Eh, watch the merchandise," Carlito protested as Mark turned to see what the commotion was. Kwanele pointed outside. Sarah shook her head in confusion.

"We've got to go, Kwan."

The boy shook his head, unclipped his seat belt, and jumped from the open doorway back outside into the night air.

"Kwan?" Mark frowned as he squinted into the darkness.

"Just wait. Look!" Kwanele pointed. He whistled. Everyone's eyes went wide with recognition as Jacques trotted into the beam of the Jeep's headlights.

"Oh great," Sarah groaned as she thought about the elephants.

"I'm not taking him back, we'll be busted," Mark protested. "Sarah, is there room in the back?"

Sarah shook her head and squirmed over. She pushed her small frame against the door and cringed. "I hope so. He's not exactly small."

Kwanele slipped into the Jeep in the center seat and patted the spot next to him for Jacques. It was the second time within two days that the cat had taken a ride in a vehicle. Kwanele snuggled back into the seat and stroked the cheetah on the head, a tender smile on his face. Jacques stretched in typical cat fashion and took up all the space that was offered to him. Kwanele snuggled closer to Sarah. Sighing, she settled back against the door and watched, helpless, as Carlito leaned out and closed the door on Jacques's side.

"Do you think he pushed the gate open?" Sarah queried as Mark set off down the track toward Shimuwini bush camp. He scratched his head.

"That or he crawled under the fence. I just hope it was the latter. I don't want a search party sent out for us yet."

Carlito frowned at his friend. "Just leave me out of it." He was tense. "Don't get my Jeep lost, and don't say I helped you." He pressed his lips together, arms folded across his chest. "If anyone asks me, I'll tell them you stole my Jeep."

"Thanks, Carlito. I knew I could count on you." Mark laughed at his friend. The young African man threw his hands in the air.

"I'm not joking, Mark. I owed you a favor, but nothing like this. That debt is well and truly paid now—with interest. You now owe me big-time."

"Deal." Mark pulled into the Shimuwini bush camp gates. They waved good-bye to the man, who just shook his head as he crossed the track and shut the gates behind him and hurried over to his home. Sarah then moved into the front of the Jeep with Mark. As soon as Kwanele shifted over, Jacques took up the slack. He repositioned himself, taking up almost the whole width of the Jeep, his head resting on Kwanele's lap.

Sarah smiled at the sight. "That cheetah really loves you, Kwan."

Mark pursed his lips. Daylight would hit soon, and they needed to get out of the open before security at the bush camp caught on that they were gone. He turned the Jeep onto the road that headed past Boulders Bush Lodge. If they were stuck on the main roads now, it would reduce the tracks that police could follow. Mark pushed the Jeep into fifth gear and coasted along the bitumen road. They would hit the border before daylight at this speed. Abasi would get them in, and they could catch a few hours' sleep before Sarah needed to do her job for them. She knew Mark would then ring Tim and explain what had happened. Tim would be bound to agree with the logic in it. They were safer away from the bush camp. A tug of doubt pulled at Sarah's heart, and she leaned against the window, biting her lip.

CHAPTER TWENTY-EIGHT

It was 4 a.m. when they pulled up at the bunker-house. Mark stepped out of the Jeep and stretched as he saw Abasi wander out to meet them. Abasi had been true to his word, and the guards at the border had let the Jeep through at the odd hour. The warden waved them over, his eyes settled a moment on Sarah as she stepped out of the vehicle. Mark looked at his wife. She appeared exhausted.

"Come, you all need some sleep?" Abasi gestured for them to follow. "There are spare bunks in the quarters. Get a few hours' rest before the vets arrive. Follow me." He stopped short when he saw Jacques leap out of the open back door of the Jeep. A nerve twitched in Mark's mouth as he saw Abasi's attitude transition from alarm into annoyance.

"Sorry about the cheetah." Mark stepped over the cat and touched his head. "He followed us halfway to Shimuwini, and we couldn't take him back. He is tame."

Abasi hesitated but then nodded. Mark shrugged. It was too bad. It was just the way things happened, and the warden would just have to accept it.

"He can sleep in the foyer?" Abasi scratched his head. Kwanele grabbed the cheetah's collar and pulled the cat close.

"He sleeps with me." He knelt down and murmured to Jacques.

Abasi was about to protest, but Mark put his hand on the man's shoulder.

"It's okay. He won't damage your home. I take full responsibility."

Abasi eyed the cat as Jacques sat and licked a paw.

"Okay, he is like the ones at the place that has the cheetah conservation project, yeah? You know, the captive ones they breed to help the wild numbers. They are tame." He gazed over his shoulder at Mark as they followed him into the bunker-house. Mark grinned.

"He's even better than those cheetahs."

Abasi showed them into an open-plan room with several bunk beds that lined the walls.

"The vets will be here at six, which gives us all a couple more hours to sleep. I will wake you later on for breakfast."

Abasi left them and trudged back down the hall to his quarters, leaving the three disoriented.

"Okay, come on, crew." Mark took charge. "It's been a long night. Let's get a bit of shut-eye." He watched with satisfaction as Kwanele curled up under the covers of a bottom bunk, Jacques on the floor below him. Sarah tossed him a weary smile and climbed into another bottom bunk.

"I hope we made the right choice," she murmured, coughed, then closed her eyes.

Mark blinked and found the last bottom bunk. He eased himself into it. The old, weathered mattress was thin beneath him, and he felt the slates of the bed beneath his aching back. Mark rolled with discomfort onto his side and punched the thin pillow into some semblance of a cushion. He finally tucked it in half and slid it beneath his thumping head. He hoped a few hours' sleep would ease the headache. He lay on his side and watched Sarah sleep across from him. Her thin frame heaved back another cough, before she cleared her throat instead. Crease lines formed between his brows. What was he thinking? Sarah had gotten worse—she was in no state to be out in the night, let alone trekking through the Kruger and helping to wrangle elephants. But they'd done what they'd done, and she would be too stubborn to go back now. He sighed and resolved that they would do the job, then get out of here back to the bush camp so Sarah could rest up in safety.

Mark's phone rang shrilly at 5:30 a.m. His eyes flew open. He grabbed the phone and checked the caller ID on his phone.

Jacob and Martha's place. It had started. They'd be discovered missing. He ran his thumb over the button and toyed with the idea of turning the phone off. They weren't ready to come home and be confronted by Naicker yet. Perhaps Jacob and Martha could stall the search for a bit. Mark pressed *answer*.

"Morning."

Jacob sounded relieved, but he whispered into the phone.

"Mark, where are you all? The police are furious. They saw signs of a break-in and thought you were in danger. They came here, and we discovered that you weren't home. They have sent out a search party. That lieutenant has been calling Sarah's phone. It's in the guestroom, going crazy. Where are you?"

The headache swiftly returned as Mark swapped the cell phone to his other ear and propped himself up on his elbow.

"We're okay. We're in Mozambique. An emergency came up with an elephant calf in D-12 herd, and they asked if Sarah could help. It's okay. After all, the bush camp is a prime target. We're safer out here in Mozambique. No one knows we're here. Listen, we'll do the work when the vets get here in half an hour, then we'll come straight back. I promise."

There was a long pause on the other end of the phone.

"I don't know about this, Mark. You should have told Tim Naicker."

Mark cringed and shifted his weight onto his hip. He swung his legs off the bunk bed onto the cold floorboards.

"Be careful out there. Get it done and get home as soon as you can. They are really upset that you might be in danger. You have no idea what a panic you've caused."

Mark sighed heavily.

"I know. I'm sorry, Jacob. Maybe we were wrong to do this, but we'll get it done and then get back as soon as possible, okay?"

"Just fix the elephant thing and get home." Jacob mumbled something else and excused himself.

Mark heard the hang-up tone. Rubbing his face, he eased himself out from under the bunk, crossed the room, and touched Sarah's shoulder. She murmured in her sleep and rolled over. Her eyes blinked open, and she regarded him vacantly.

"Is it time already?"

Mark nodded.

"As soon as the vets get here, you help them isolate that calf and then we need to get back. They are all going nuts back there."

Sarah yawned and looked over at Kwanele. Jacques was already out from his haunt under the bunk. He stretched and regarded them as he yawned.

"Kwanele?" Sarah touched the covers over the boy lightly. The boy startled, suddenly on fully alert.

"We have to leave this place now." He rubbed his eyes as he sprang out of bed and slipped his socked feet into his shoes. Jacques mirrored the boy's alarm, tensed, and looked about. He licked his jowls in concern. Mark put a firm hand on Kwanele's shoulder.

"We will, as soon as we help this calf."

Kwanele gazed into Mark's deep blue eyes, concern etched in his small face.

"You don't understand. It has to be now," the boy hissed through clenched teeth. Mark frowned at Kwanele's forcefulness and knelt down at his eye level.

"Is there something you know that we don't?" he whispered, searching Kwanele's anxious features for the first time since they'd left the bush camp. The door behind them creaked open, and they saw Abasi dressed for work, a broad smile on his dark face.

"Good morning, all." His countenance was cheerful, and Mark noticed Kwanele shrink away. He stood stiffly and kept his hand on Kwanele's shoulder. He thought he felt the boy start to tremble under his fingers as he let go and smiled at Abasi.

"Morning. Are the vets here yet? Something urgent has come up, and we need to get back home as soon as possible."

Abasi inclined his head with respect.

"I understand completely. We will not keep you long. They are on their way now. Come. You can all have some breakfast while we wait."

"Thank you so much." Mark wrapped his arm around Sarah's waist as they followed the warden into the small kitchenette. He could hear Kwanele shuffle along behind as if his legs were heavy. He glanced over his shoulder and saw both Jacques and Kwanele pause in the doorway, looking at each other. The ghost of a frown passed Mark's brow, but was interrupted by the scurry of the warden.

"There's bread in the fridge, toaster over there. If you want cereal, there is some in this cupboard and milk in the fridge also." Abasi darted about opening the appropriate cupboards. "I have eaten already. Help yourselves but please clean up after yourselves as well."

He paused, and his gaze locked on Kwanele. Mark rubbed his face as he spotted the exchange. Kwanele gave his head a slight shake and backed into the corner of the room, his hand clutched about Jacques's collar.

"You are not hungry?" Abasi asked the boy in a childlike, cheerful way. Kwanele's eyes were hooded and dark. Mark felt an eerie dread tingle up his spine. What had the boy been trying to tell him before?

"I'll put the coffeepot on." Abasi tore his gaze from the boy and set out some coffee mugs. Mark and Sarah skirted around one another as they grabbed breakfast for themselves. Finally, they settled at the small wooden table. Coffee in hand, Abasi leaned back in a chair by the doorway and let out a long sigh of contentment as he savored the beverage. Sarah beckoned for Kwanele to join them at the table.

"Come on. Come and have some brekky."

Reluctantly, the boy stepped over to the table and sat. Mark noticed how he kept a watchful eye on Abasi. An awkward silence filled the room as they all ate. Mark was desperate to pick up the conversation that he'd started with Kwanele, but he felt too much at risk to bring it up now. There was something going on with the boy, and Mark felt that whatever it was could be pivotal to everything. Sarah crossed the room with their soon empty dishes, and filled the sink to wash up as Abasi had directed. A crackle hissed through Abasi's radio.

"Vets are on site." The warden pushed himself from the chair and deposited his mug in the sink.

"Let's go." He clapped his hands together. Sarah paused over the sink of soapy water.

"I thought you said to clean—"

"Never mind that now, this is urgent. You said so yourselves." He waved them to go out the door in front of him. Mark grabbed Sarah's hand and gave it two squeezes. She shot him a quizzical glance. Something was suddenly strange about Abasi's behavior. If it were that urgent, wouldn't he have had vets here already, so that they could have done it when they all arrived? Kwanele stepped out further in front of the group, Jacques at his side. It was clear he was putting as much distance between him and Abasi as he could. Mark pressed his lips together as he glanced at Sarah. New people, presumably the vets, met them at the car-park.

"Dennis." A white man in denim jeans and a casual sweatshirt offered his hand to first Abasi, then the others in turn. Mark nodded as he received a handshake equally strong to his own.

"Mark."

Sarah smiled as she shook hands, but she was quick to pull away when the man turned to Abasi.

"We'll try again this morning then, shall we?" He grimaced.

"These are my two assistants, Gabby and Ben." The other two vets bundled equipment from the 4WD and swiveled their heads to nod acknowledgment.

"We left them where we put them yesterday," Abasi explained as they all walked around the corner of the large shed complex.

"Them? You mean the elephants?" Sarah frowned as she waited for clarification.

They rounded a corner of the warehouse, and Sarah gasped with shock as they beheld a huge caged-off area. Ten adult elephants and two calves had been pushed into a space that was way too small for them. Their expressions were bleak, and they looked dehydrated and starved. Mark calculated that from the look of their conditions, they had been here longer than twenty-four hours. His composure crumpled into fury as he stepped forward to protest, but it was Sarah who beat him to it, her eyes wild with anger.

"How long did you say they were like this? Since yesterday? This is unacceptable, Abasi!" Stepping close to the enclosure, she searched the mass of gray bodies and located the calf with the broken leg. The leg hung limply inside the stretched skin, well and truly messed up.

"No wonder you feared the calf would get trampled. It's a wonder she's not dead now and the healthy calf with her—they are too closed in. They're going to be trampled, Abasi." She shook with anger. Mark glared severely at the vets and frowned at their doleful expressions. They seemed oblivious. It was an animal welfare issue. Anyone could see that.

"And you." Sarah turned to the vets, rage in her eyes. "You say you were here yesterday? You should know better."

It was Mark's turn to step forward. He placed his hand on Sarah's shoulder.

"What was your plan, Abasi? Get Sarah in there with them to calm them down?"

Abasi hesitated.

"Let them out now, Abasi," Sarah commanded. "They need to be released to help those calves—you can't help the injured one with all those in there. I can't work in those conditions."

Abasi stepped backward and looked at the vets. Sarah had run out of patience. She strode toward the man.

"Give me the keys." She held out her hand. Abasi glanced back at the vets, who had positioned themselves behind him, and shook his head with apprehension.

"Come on, Abasi." Sarah's open palm shook urgently. Abasi reached into his coat and instead of keys, produced a handgun. It took Mark a moment to register what he'd pulled as Sarah blinked with confusion. She rocked backward. He leveled the gun toward her, his expression dark.

Mark didn't think.

His reaction was explosive, driven by fear. With panic in his eyes, he launched himself forward to block his wife from the line of the gun.

"Sarah!"

The next few seconds flew by in a blur.

Abasi turned the gun toward Mark and pulled the trigger. The sound of the shot as it echoed off the buildings was deafening. Mark pushed Sarah down with force into the dirt, the bullet ripping across the top of his shoulder. They fell to the ground with a crash, and Sarah gasped as the wind was knocked from her lungs. Kwanele cried out, then lost his grip on Jacques's collar as the cheetah hissed and leapt forward to attack Abasi.

Fear in his eyes, Abasi swiveled the handgun and his second shot ripped through the air, hitting the cat square in the head. The elephants panicked at the sound and rumbled over the top of each other in sudden terror to escape the danger. Jacques skidded and crumpled to the dirt in a limp heap, instantly dead. The blood began to seep through his fur in the dirt. Sarah wheezed and struggled to get out from under Mark, but he placed a hand on her shoulder and stopped her.

A whimper issued from Kwanele, and he stared in frozen disbelief at his best friend, who had just died trying to defend them. A cruel smirk curled Abasi's lips as he turned his triumphant expression toward the boy. Mark grimaced and saw the drawn and haunted look in the boy's face. With eyes only for Jacques, Kwanele didn't see the danger he was in as he rushed forward and collapsed in the dirt. He cradled the cheetah's limp head in his arms and cried out in anguish. The sound sent chills up Mark's spine. He feared for worse.

"Shut up!" Abasi ordered as he glanced over his shoulder at the vets, who all stood with smirks of approval. Sarah gagged as she struggled to cough. Mark shifted in agony and moved aside. He twisted his mouth at the vets. They obviously weren't who they had said they were.

Abasi seemed to grow confident and swiveled the weapon at the couple on the ground, then back to Kwanele. Mark sucked in his breath as the pain grew worse. He clutched at his ripped jacket. Warm blood seeped through his fingers at an alarming rate. He was lightheaded. Sarah kicked her legs fiercely to get out from under him. Mark felt awkward as he rolled over in pain. She squirmed and coughed as her ribs were released from Mark's weight and she sucked in oxygen. With a wild look in her eyes, Sarah swiveled onto her knees to check on Mark. He watched her face contort at the sight of the scarlet patch that grew rapidly on Mark's clothing.

Abasi cleared his throat, suddenly drawing their attention. Realization at their predicament set in. They had been set up.

Abasi waved the hand-gun toward Kwanele.

"Back up. With them." He signaled Kwanele to join the couple on the dirt. When the boy didn't immediately move, Abasi started screaming at him. "I said, back up!" He cocked the gun, his eyes cold. Kwanele tore himself away from Jacques and swiped at his tear-streaked face. He scooted toward Mark and Sarah and dropped to his knees. He watched, eyes wide, as Mark gasped, trying to move to a better position. He grasped at his pulsing wound, blood seeping onto the dusty ground. The female vet assistant, Gabby, threw a wad of medical gauze toward Mark, her expression neutral.

"Cover it!" Abasi commanded Sarah. He flicked his head at Mark. She hesitated.

"Cover it!" he screamed with even more force. Shaking, Sarah reached for the gauze and pressed it against Mark's wound. "Can I have some water?" She kept her eyes averted. Abasi ignored her and turned to the vets.

"Write this down. Make sure you get it right. The cheetah turned wild, and we had to put him down in self-defense." Dennis casually flipped out a notepad and biro. Tilting his head, Abasi regarded his prisoners again.

"Get up." He waved the gun at them. They got to their feet, their hands in the air, except for Mark, who was too badly injured to comply. He stumbled to his feet and pressed one red-streaked hand firmly against the gauze on his shoulder. Waving them onward, Abasi directed them away from the elephant cage, back around to the front of the warehouse, and into the great doors, as the vet, Dennis, slid the roller door open. The air in the warehouse was heavy with dust as they drew into the darkness. Sarah doubled over, racked with coughs.

"Shut up!" Abasi yelled at her.

She struggled to swallow her coughs, choking and wheezing as she tried to clear her throat. Mark could hear her short, raspy gasps, and it broke his heart. When he gazed into her eyes, they were filled with tears.

"You're not going to win, Abasi." Mark kept his voice controlled and steady. "The police are already looking for us."

"Shut up!" Abasi screamed again. He waved the gun at them furiously. They were directed to the back of the warehouse into a moderate-sized inner room. Abasi regained his composure, cracking his neck from one side to the other.

"Welcome to where we lock up our...treasures." Abasi leered as they looked around the room, horror in their eyes. The room was filled with all kinds of trafficked poached goods. Cleaned elephant tusks were stacked against one wall, rhinoceros horn against another. The room was also filled with various antelope horns and skulls, and skins from big cats and zebra were rolled up neatly on a bench, covered in protective plastics. Sarah's knees went weak, and she staggered. Mark caught her with his good arm and held her firmly under her elbow.

"No one will hear you in here." Abasi snickered. "Not that anyone would turn up here looking." He laughed and flicked the weapon toward the posts in the middle of the room. Dennis grabbed Kwanele, who cried out in terror as he was dragged to a pole. His arms were twisted roughly behind his back as he was wrestled and tied to the post. The other two vet assistants shoved Mark and Sarah, forcing them to stand back to back against the other pole. Mark cried out in agony as the man, Ben, yanked his arms behind his back. The gunshot wound was stretched taut and suddenly gushed with fresh blood. A wave of dizziness threatened to black out Mark's vision, and he swayed on his feet with nausea as his wrists were bound together behind the pole. Something warm brushed against his hands and he knew that Sarah was being put in the same position behind him. She gasped in pain as the rope cut into her wrists without mercy. Mark set his jaw with fury. The assistant, Gabby, tied a sling into place around Mark's injured shoulder, staunching the flow of blood.

"Leave it," Abasi ordered. "It doesn't matter now. Not in here."

Mark scoffed. The sloppy first-aid effort was meaningless in the midst of their situation. Gabby hesitated, glared at Mark, and then left it as it was. Mark glared at her in return for a moment before he strained his neck to the left, and saw Kwanele sink to the floor.

Mark tried to think, but the agony in his shoulder made it hard to concentrate. Jacob knew they were here, that should count for something. As he thought of it, the cell phone in his pocket rang out. Mark held his breath. It echoed shrilly against the cold walls. Abasi cursed and signaled to Gabby, training the gun on Mark.

Gabby sneered at Mark seductively as she slid her hand into the back pocket of his jeans and produced the offending cell phone. Mark was revolted as he turned his head away from her. Abasi waved Gabby over to him, snatched the cell, and looked at the caller ID on the screen.

He cursed again and threw the phone to the floor. Stomping his heavily booted heel onto the screen, Abasi silenced it forever.

"Don't try anything." He jutted his chin into the air as he glared at Mark. Mark stared from beneath his brows, fury in his heart. Abasi flicked his head for the others to follow him, then he took one last look around the room and latched closed the soundproof door behind him. There was the click of a key in the lock as Mark, Sarah, and Kwanele were plunged into a thick darkness. The silence that fell over them was as suffocating as the dark, and Mark began to squirm at his ropes until he and Sarah were able to ease themselves down into a sitting position on the cold cement.

"Kwan?"

"I'm okay," Kwanele murmured softly in reply. Mark turned to his wife.

"Sarah? Are you okay?"

She rolled her head around the pole, and Mark thought he heard her stifle a whimper. She took a deep breath and spoke barely above a whisper.

"I'm doing better than you. How's your shoulder?" The smell of blood lingered in the musty air. Mark was well aware of it.

"I don't know," Mark admitted. "It's deep. Will need stitches when we get back." He grunted and left the comment to hang in the air.

"I'm scared, Mark," Sarah whispered into the darkness. Mark unfurled his fists and tried to connect with her fingers, to give her a touch of hope. Silence clung in the air before it was replaced with quiet sobbing.

"Kwan?" Mark spoke softly into the dark room. "We'll get out of this, Kwanele. It'll be okay." Mark hoped he could keep his word. The sobs continued unabated.

"Kwan, listen to me." Mark's voice was firm. "You are a warrior, Kwan. In the Bible, there was a story about Paul and Silas. They were locked up in a jail, just like us. God helped them escape when they prayed and sang praises to Him." The sobs subsided a little. "I know this is hard," Mark continued, "but I need you to be brave."

Mark heard Sarah sigh behind him. He knew what she was thinking. He'd just lost his best friend, and he was afraid of losing even more. He was already the bravest kid they had ever met. Sarah coughed and gritted her teeth as her body began to tremble with shock. Soon the sobs subsided completely and they were plunged into a vacuum of silence. Mark grunted to break the quiet. He felt Sarah slump against him, her body heaving as she coughed again. Mark frowned. Was that his imagination? He thought he'd just heard footsteps. He strained to listen. Sarah made a little noise.

"Shhh, hear that?" Mark startled when he felt something cool brush against his hand. Someone was there, working on untying their bonds. Mark recognized the rapid, shallow breaths.

"Kwan? You got free?" Sarah's voice was hopeful.

"I can't get these ones loose. They are tighter than mine."

"Try the door," Mark urged quietly. He listened as Kwanele scuffled across the floor of the dark room with caution. There was a sudden hollow crash, and the sound echoed through the room long after the items ceased to fall. Everyone sucked in their breath. No response from outside. They all breathed again.

"Horns?" There was amusement in Mark's tone, despite their circumstances. He heard a stifled grunt in reply, before settling back to listen for Kwanele's progress.

Chapter
Twenty-Nine

Tom tapped his foot, his fury growing as he listened to Abasi's excuses.

"So, sir, they refused to comply, and then they demanded I let the elephants out. They said that police were already looking for them. I had to change the plan, and I wasn't sure what you wanted. What do I do, boss? Shoot them?" Abasi clung to the phone, sweat beading his brow.

"You fool! Did you know they caught Stephan Venter out in Kruger? Why did you ring him? They are on to us now. You've left a messy trail. You should have locked them into the enclosure and followed the plan."

Abasi swiveled his head toward the vets as they waited in the other room.

"I can do it now. What do you want me to do about the cheetah and the bullet wound in the man? Police will find it when they find them with the elephants? They will know he was shot."

There was an audible sigh of frustration on the other end of the phone.

"Damn it, Abasi, I'm not an imbecile. Can't you do anything? Put the cheetah in the cleaning room for de-furring, and as for Mark van der Merwe—"

Tom hesitated. It was difficult to hide evidence when he wasn't sure what else Abasi had messed up. Abasi was an incompetent fool. He would miss things.

"This has to all be sorted out now, Abasi, the police are on the trail! You know what, just keep them where they are and wait for me. I'm coming. I'll do it myself."

"But, boss, Kruger is crawling with cops. It would look

suspicious for you to be driving."

"I'm not stupid," Tom snapped. "Expect me to turn up within the hour. I'm flying into Mozambique direct in the private jet." Abasi lowered the phone, his eyes wide. If Dawson turned up to the scene this angry with him, things didn't bode well.

"I found something," Kwanele whispered into the darkness. His voice sounded too loud in his own ears and he cringed.

"What?" Mark's voice was strained.

Kwanele wasn't sure yet. He shouldn't have voiced it. Was it just his imagination, or had he smelt that waft of fresh cool air? He felt around with care and shifted some more horns as his fingers found them.

"Hang on."

He laid the horns on the ground and felt through the darkness along the wall with his hands. He crawled into the space under a leaning bulk of elephant tusks and ran his fingers along the cool surface of the wall. There it was again. He paused, stuck his nose in the air, and inhaled deeply. Fresh air! He was certain of it. His fingers caught on a ridge, and hope stirred within. It felt like package tape. Kwanele moved his fingers, following the ridge until he'd mapped out a square, half a meter in length. Another texture was in the center. It seemed to be fabric. Fabric taped securely to the square?

"Kwan. What have you found?"

"Just wait." He used his nails to ease back the tape from the surface. It lifted easily. Kwanele peeled back the corner of the fabric, and a cool stream of air and dim light blinked back at him though a grate. He squeaked with joy.

"Kwan? Put us out of our misery." Mark groaned in the background.

It was a sealed-up ventilation hole. Kwanele ripped all the layers of tape away with the black fabric and let the light penetrate the darkness. In Kwanele's excitement to tell Mark and Sarah, he forgot he was hidden under the elephant tusks. He spun around and slammed his forehead into one. The great tusk creaked, and Kwanele clamped his fist around the smooth surface to steady it. The weight was too great for him, and it got away from his small hands. The massive treasure tipped and clunked into the rest of the pile of tusks. Kwanele watched in horror as the whole pile of them fell against one another like dominoes. He expected to hear a second enormous crash through the inner room of the warehouse. Kwanele heard gasps issue from Mark and Sarah. He braced himself for an imminent crash. It didn't happen. The horns caught and creaked to a stop. Kwanele's heart beat hard as he sighed with relief. The pile of massive tusks had stopped short against a cupboard, cushioned by rolls of furs. Kwanele heard a nervous chuckle come from Mark. He should have realized that there would be enough light now for them to see some of what occurred.

"Too close for comfort, Kwan, but we can see what we're doing now. Well done! Where's the light coming from?"

"I found a covered over air vent."

"Why do you think it was covered?" Sarah frowned.

"More than likely to help preserve the items in here." Mark grimaced as he tried to shift his weight again. "Kwan, think you can get out of that vent?"

The boy turned back to examine the grate. His hope faded as he saw the screws and found how tightly imbedded into the corners of the steel they were.

"Not without tools." He got up and began to search the tabletops. Nothing but labeled horns and other atrocities filled the space.

"Screwdriver?"

"*Yebo.*"

"Kwan?" Mark raised an eyebrow. "What type of screws are in that thing? Phillips head or flat?"

"What?"

"Never mind. What does do the holes in the screw look like?"

"A line."

Mark's eyes lit up. "Kwan. Come here. In my right back pocket. The car keys. Try those." He adjusted his angle, so the boy could worm his way into the pocket easier.

"The light. I can see your ropes better now." Kwanele placed the keys on the ground and began to work on the ropes that bound Mark and Sarah's hands to the pole. He grimaced at the effort, clawing at the rope without success. He snatched up the keys and attempted to work the keys between the loops of rope but to no avail.

"Forget it, Kwanele. Try and get out, get some help." Mark's breath came in short rapid gasps, and Kwanele could see the agony in his eyes.

He nodded and quickly padded back to the grate. The tusks were moved now, and he was able to look back at Mark and Sarah as they watched him intently.

"You're doing so well, Kwanele. I know how hard all this has been on you." Sarah's voice caught in her throat as she tried to encourage him. "Poor Jacques." Tears welled in her eyes. She blinked several times and put her head down. Kwanele regarded her a moment, a lump in his throat. He'd lost his best friend. But he wasn't going to lose more friends. He was a warrior. He could do this. He felt a surge of hope and determination as he turned back to the adults.

"We can't let them win!" He clenched a fist fiercely, shaking it at the ceiling. Sarah's eyes brimmed with more tears, and a happy laugh escaped her lips.

"That's my boy!" Mark's face flashed with pride as Kwanele locked eyes with him.

My boy? Kwanele let the words wash over him like a fresh wave of strength. Fatigue leached away, replaced with determination. He pressed his lips together and tried the keys to turn the screws. He needed to find just the right surface and angle, and then he needed the strength. After trying several keys, he discovered the curve from the back of one of the keys fit perfectly and held. He pushed in to the key, trying to turn the screw. It was stuck hard. He grunted as he tried again.

"You can do it." Mark and Sarah both encouraged him in low voices. Jaw clenched, Kwanele shook against the effort until the first screw twisted loose. He squeaked with joy again, twisted it out with his fingers, and dropped it on the ground. The first success was swept away with the reality that he needed to work loose three more. He knew he could do it, though. After a few moments, there were four screws on the ground and he carefully pulled the grate free.

"Go, Kwan. Find help," Mark urged. Kwanele looked back at them, hesitation in his heart. How could he leave them like this?

"Kwan, there's no time. Go, go now."

Mark was right. He nodded firmly and disappeared through the grate.

Mark tried to strain to hear the last of the boy's footfalls through the grate, but only the labored sound of his own breathing greeted him.

"He's in God's hands now." Sarah leaned her head back against Mark's. She was right. They could do nothing now but wait. They sat in silence. All the worry and suspicion that had hounded Mark regarding his wife fell away in light of their predicament.

"Sarah..." He felt an undefined burden rise in his chest. "I'm so sorry."

There was a noise as she shuffled her weight.

"No. It was me. I pushed to come and help. I was blind." She rolled her head back so it rested lightly against his thick head of brown hair. The subtle touch warmed his heart.

"Do you think we'll be alright?" He could hear the fear in her voice. He needed to be her strength, now more than ever. But he needed to draw his strength from God. It was a lesson he'd learned the hard way.

"All we can do now is pray and trust God to help." Mark sighed. He still hated the fact that he couldn't do anything more. Sarah lowered her gaze to the floor.

"We haven't been too good at that lately." She sighed. "Mark...?"

"Hmmm?"

"When we ran away, I felt something, deep in my stomach, like a warning not to come. It tugged at my heart, and I felt guilty. But I ignored it." Her voice faded into a whisper as tears began to roll down her face. Mark's mouth twisted.

"I felt it, too. I think it was the Holy Spirit."

He heard her sniff back tears in response, and his heart ached for her.

"We've been so stupid." She tried to subdue her emotion. "I'm so sorry, Lord." She raised her head skyward. Mark found her hand with his and latched on to two of her fingers. He squeezed them three times.

"I love you, too," she whispered under her breath, before she wheezed and another coughing fit took hold of her. Mark winced.

"Sarah..." He hesitated. He didn't want to hurt her, but he needed the chance to clear it up. "I want to ask you something."

"Anything." She sighed. He watched the dust dance in the shaft of light that emanated from the ventilation shaft.

"That night, when you were on the computer..." He wrestled against the hurt the moment had caused him. It all seemed so irrelevant now. "I found the paper under the keyboard, for the adoption agency."

A chuckle bubbled up her throat.

"I was checking it out. I didn't want to mention it until we got through things. I think it's important that we think about his future—"

"And I agree," Mark cut across her explanation. She stopped, and he thought he heard a gasp. The ghost of a smile traced up Mark's mouth. "I was just, surprised that you tried to hide it from me, that's all."

He felt her shoulders relax against the pole, and she stretched her fingers and found more of his through their ropes.

"I didn't intend to keep it from you, Mark."

There was a moment of awkward silence. She rolled her head around again.

"How's your shoulder?"

"Burning." He adjusted it. "I wish I could get this arm to the front. It cramps like nothing else."

"Hopefully Kwan won't be long." She sighed.

"Sarah. That night. The computer..." Mark whispered. "I think it's a marvelous idea."

Sarah was silent, but Mark sensed that she would be smiling.

"Thank you," she murmured after a long moment.

Silence engulfed them again, but there was no longer any tension. The cool air rushed in through the vent and stirred the dust around the room. Sarah struggled not to cough too much, afraid that the sound would now travel through the vent to outside and attract attention. She failed often. Writhing against her bonds, her slight body heaved with deep coughs.

"We should pray," Mark suggested after Sarah finished. She was silent, and he wondered what she was thinking. He began to murmur prayers of protection. He asked the Holy Spirit to do something miraculous to save them. He also acknowledged that it was God's call, and if it was their turn to go, then they just had to accept that, but not before they did everything in their power to prevent it.

Kwanele climbed out through the side window of the great warehouse, careful not make a sound. Afraid his shoes were noisy, he slipped them off and hid them under a mopane shrub. He crouched low and scanned the area. He needed to go past the main office bunker-house in order to get out the front gates. He was just about to launch when he realized his jacket was on. He thought about when he'd hidden from Stephan in the Kruger. The jacket was a dead giveaway. He shucked it off and shoved it under the shrub with his abandoned shoes. He would need to blend in now, be stealthy. His white socks muffled his steps as he scooted around the building, and then hid behind another bush. Mark and Sarah depended on him. He needed to use the skills he'd learned with Joseph to escape this place in broad daylight and make his way somehow back over the border and into Kruger. Wild animals no longer worried him—he felt safer with animals than he did people. Mark's words reverberated in his mind.

You are a warrior!

That's my boy!

Kwanele clasped his fist around the elephant pendant around his neck. Somehow he would find a way. He ducked out from hiding and raced across the dirt. The dark red patch stopped him in his tracks. This was where Jacques— He couldn't think on it now. Kwanele swallowed the emotion, lined up the bush ahead, and sprinted onward, sliding under the scratchy plant. That was too close. He chided himself for not keeping his mind on the job. The new job—the rescue mission. He was outside the main bunker-house now and crept close behind the foliage that landscaped the walls. He heard footsteps creak on the floorboards and heard murmured voices from the window above. They were all up the kitchen end of the bunker-house. Kwanele seized this opportunity and snuck quietly around to the front. He squatted low behind a sign and calculated his next move. He had to cover an open area of about five meters to reach the open gate—three meters beyond that to find his next hiding spot within Kruger. Kwanele regulated his breaths and began to psych himself up for the dash. The window of opportunity was small.

One, two, three...go!

He sprinted as fast as he could toward his target. He nearly slipped over as he rounded the short garden fence. He was almost to the gates. Hope filled his heart as he skittered onward. Then he saw it, from the corner of his eye. A car turned the corner, heading straight for where he was. There was nowhere to hide. Kwanele put his head down and powered on, praying that they wouldn't see him. He couldn't see the driver yet. Up ahead he spotted a dense little scrub. Pushing harder, he skidded onto his hip and slid under the shelter of a low shrub. His breath was heavy as he rolled onto his stomach. He wiggled and tucked himself deeper into the protective shelter of the foliage. He'd made it just in time. The expensive car pulled into the driveway. The door opened. A tall white man stepped out and adjusted his suit as he gazed toward the bunker-house, his sunglasses dark. Kwanele nearly choked and shrank back into the shrub. It was him! He recognized the businessman with the cold blue eyes. He hadn't seen this man since he'd given the job to Joseph. Fear coiled in his stomach like a venomous snake ready to strike. This was the man who wanted Sarah dead. Bile rose in his throat as he watched the man enter the building and the vehicle pull away. Kwanele started to hyperventilate. How was he going to stop this? How could he possibly hope to get help and escape from these powerful people? As the snake of fear started to grip his heart, a ray of sun broke through the despair. He clutched at the elephant pendant around his neck. He was their only hope now, he and God. He was God's warrior. Kwanele felt a rush of faith sweep into him at the thought of God.

Please, Jesus. In the name of Jesus. Help me get away and find someone to help us in time. Please, please, please, God. He emerged from the bush and skulked around some more signage before he broke into a run, down the main road toward the border gates. It was only five hundred meters away. Kwanele thought hard. Did the border men work for Abasi, too? He positioned himself behind a new shrub near the gatehouse and observed the layout. Beyond the gates were open road and open lowveldt grasses—no shelter to hide in for a few kilometers where the bushveldt line would start. He would have no hope of hiding once he was through the gates. They would catch him, question him, and then it would be a gamble as to whether or not they could help him. He frowned. It was too big a chance to take. The rumble of an engine startled him. He peered out toward the gate as a small, steel gray hatchback pulled up and wound down the window. He heard a muffled conversation and watched an arm extend through the window to offer ID and park fees. Was it time to open the gates to the public already? Kwanele cringed—the man in the suit was already at the bunker-house. Mark and Sarah were rapidly running out of time. They would be done away with and the evidence hidden or arranged before the police got onto the trail. Another rumble of vehicles sounded behind him, and he spun around to watch a convoy of three bakkies, their trays covered with canvas canopies. They slowed down as they approached the gate.

An idea struck Kwanele, but he would only get one chance at it. The three vehicles pulled up at the border gate, the third stopping right next to Kwanele's shrub. No time to hesitate. He sucked in a nervous breath and sprang from the bush. Kwanele ducked behind the bakkie and jumped. Gripping the tailgate, he swung up and slipped under the canopy. He gasped with disbelief and almost laughed. He'd made it. Adjusting his eyes to the semidarkness of the bakkie tray as it rumbled into action again, he noticed it was full of bales of hay. These people must belong to a reserve park that had animals, or they owned horses, he reasoned. It didn't matter. It was a soft ride and it was his answer to get through the gates. He lay back against a bale and prayed about what to do next as he rattled with ease into the Kruger.

Chapter
Thirty

"How long does it take to mix the gas?" Tom glared at Abasi with wrath. "You should have had it done before they woke up this morning."

"Ten minutes, Boss. It takes ten minutes for the chemicals to react with each other in the shot." Abasi glanced at him nervously. "I'll do it now."

"Hurry up. The police may already be on their way," Tom snapped and headed for the door.

"Where are you going?" Abasi's head jerked up in fear.

"You worry about the gas and the enclosure. What I do is my business."

A loud, metallic screech resounded as the large roller-doors to the warehouse were opened outside the inner room. Mark and Sarah blinked with fear. Someone was coming. They heard a key in the door before it swung open. Bright light from outside flooded into the room. Mark squinted against the brilliance.

"So, what have we here?" a tall figure gloated. Mark frowned as he watched a very self-assured white businessman stroll into the room, his hands folded behind his back. Moodiness crossed his face at the sight of Mark's injuries as he circled around and stopped in front of Sarah. Mark felt her shrink against the pole. He strained to see what was happening as he could just see the man lean down, his face close to hers. Mark shuddered.

"Sarah White. Or should I say, Sarah van der Merwe, now?" The man sniggered before he cocked his eyebrow at Mark. He straightened up and circled them again, a smug look pasted onto his features.

"Do you know how long I've waited to have you in my grasp?" They remained silent. "Too long," he snapped and stopped in front of Sarah again. Mark heard a sharp intake of breath from his wife.

"What?"

"That face!" Her breath was ragged.

"What?"

"My...dream..."

"Shut up!" The man snapped.

Mark struggled to catch his face as he passed. It was twisted into a hateful expression as he moved back in front of Sarah. "You nearly ruined me, Sarah, stopping the culls so you could move my precious ivory over the border." Mark twisted to try to see what was happening. He could just imagine the glower Sarah would have given the man.

"Ahh, yes, you know of what I speak, and now you've started a trend. Everyone wants to conserve the wildlife, save the elephants, save the rhinos, save the cheetahs." He waved his hands in the air, his tone mocking.

"No more! When Africa sees that you are no more, they will be afraid. They will stop their crusades—things will go back to the way they were."

"You're wrong," Mark growled through gritted teeth. His feelings toward this man were hard to contain as his voice quivered with anger.

"What did you say?" The voice was like ice. He stopped to regard Mark with mild interest.

"Whatever you do to us will fuel the fire of the nation," Mark spat. "They won't stop till people like you are behind bars forever."

The man sneered. "Ha! You really think you're that famous?"

He looked over at Mark with disdain. Mark held his gaze until the man rolled his eyes. "Bah, a pittance. The name of Sarah White will grow dim, and people will forget why they cared."

He circled back around, and Mark spat on his polished shoe in disgust. Tom's reaction was swift. He struck a blow to the side of Mark's face. Mark grunted and sucked in his breath. The trickle of blood was warm as it ran down his face from his nose. Tom rubbed his knuckle before he adjusted his suit and clasped his hands idly behind his back. He glanced over his shoulder as a sudden thought came to mind. He smirked when he saw the loose coils of rope where Kwanele had escaped. He turned back toward Sarah, his grin wide.

"Stupid acts of bravery." He glared at Mark. "So, you still think you will escape, do you—that your precious little Zulu boy will come back and rescue you?"

Mark wanted to punch that cocky smirk off the man's face. Had they caught Kwanele? Mark felt Sarah strain to make contact with him. Her fingers brushed against his, and he latched on as best he could.

"Do you think it was an accident that the boy got free? Or that by his sheer determination, he was able to get away?" Tom stopped spitefully in front of Mark before he continued his monologue. Mark narrowed his eyes, grave concern for Kwanele's safety his only thought.

"Oh, don't worry about Kwanele. He is completely unharmed." The man appeared to toy with them, like a cat with a mouse.

"Yesss—" He drew it out slowly, torturously. "I know his name. I have known him for a while longer than you, I would think."

Mark concealed his rising emotion as he glared at the man. Tom strolled around the pole casually as he delivered his next line.

"I just wish he'd done his job for me sooner, like I paid him to." He spun and glared at Mark.

It felt like he'd been punched in the stomach. Mark's face twisted with anguish as he lowered his gaze.

"Oh yes." Tom drew out his words with precision. "It was his job to bring you here. Bring you here so I could deal with your meddling in my ivory business once and for all."

"You lie!" Sarah burst out, as a fit of coughs caught her off guard.

"Do I now?" Tom leered. "Was it by chance that a random city kid was found in the middle of Kruger, at a crime scene, so close to your precious bush camp? A kid linked to a life of crime, smuggling, theft, con work. He is a master of deception." He shook his head with mock amazement and chuckled. Mark's features wrenched with anger, and he struggled to turn his head to follow Tom's movement.

"No! We don't believe you!" Mark's neck flushed red as he tensed against pain and fury, and he had to grit his teeth against the pulsing throb of pain that shot through his shoulder. Exasperated by the movement, Mark felt fresh blood begin to soak through and dribble down the gauze.

A muffled voice called Tom from the warehouse door outside. Casting a final contemptuous leer at them, he disappeared, clicking the door closed behind him.

Silence.

"It's not true," Sarah gasped. "He's lying. Kwanele wouldn't do that. He's changed—he accepted Jesus."

Mark sighed heavily behind her, silent for a long time.

"Mark? You don't believe him, do you?" Sarah's voice quivered with emotion.

"A master at deception?" Mark hung his head in defeat. "How do you think he got out of those ropes so easily?" His words were barely audible. "Sarah...I'm sorry. I think we've been had."

"No, I don't believe it!" Sarah shook her head, and he could hear that she was overcome with tears. In pain, he set his jaw and hung his head. He tried hard to suppress the emotions that reeled in his own heart. He needed to concentrate now. He had grown to love Kwanele as his own, just as Sarah had. Sarah squirmed in her bonds.

"I don't believe it!" She writhed against the pole. "I need to get free! You watch! He'll prove himself. He'll be back with help." Her passionate remarks fell into the cold silence.

"Mark?"

"What?" he shot back with anger. "I failed us—we're going to die, Sarah! Don't you get it?" His frustration melted as he felt the words cut into his wife. "I failed you..." he whispered hopelessly. There was a tense silence for a moment before Sarah finally spoke.

"No, Mark. You have put your trust in God. He will not fail

us."

The silence that followed was the most deafening so far as the words cut into Mark's spirit.

He felt rocked. His faith had just been so easily crushed in an instant. Did he really put his complete faith in God? Was he really using God as his anchor in the storms?

Lord, my faith and my strength are weak. I have nothing left. Please be my strength and our salvation.

He hung his head. Sarah sighed.

"Mark, maybe Kwan will come back. Then you'll know you were right to believe in him."

"Maybe..." Mark felt the full weight of exhaustion overtake his body, and he heaved against his bonds with discomfort. The dizziness had returned, and he thought he might black out. How much blood had he lost? Sarah murmured prayerfully under her breath. The scent of the words caught in Mark's ear, pricking up his senses. Sarah cleared her throat.

"Well, I believe that God won't leave us nor forsake us, therefore I believe in Kwanele. We showed him the Way! *You* showed him the Way!" Sarah lifted her chin and continued her murmured prayers with renewed vigor. A strange sensation washed over Mark and ebbed away at his doubts. His heart began to fill with clarity, faith, and strength. He began to join his wife in prayer, whispering words of thanks in dire circumstances under his breath. As he continued to pray words of faith straight out of the Psalms, his words grew bolder, louder, and more convicting, and he felt his faith begin to ripple with power.

"Thank You, Holy Spirit," he burst out and threw his head back. "Thank You, Jesus, that You have a plan and a destiny for our lives. Thank You that You are already preparing the way for our freedom!"

Sarah laughed as joy bubbled from her, and picking up when he left off, she continued the heartfelt prayer.

"Thank You, Jesus, that You are showing us what we need to do! Thank You that we have an opportunity to pray and praise like Paul and Silas did in the old days and that we will see Your glory shine from this situation!" Pausing, she allowed Mark to now tag-team with her.

"Thank You, Lord, that Kwanele is one of Your children and that in Your hands he is a powerful weapon against the enemy!" Mark declared. "Keep him safe, Lord. Thank You, Jesus, that we still have the ability to praise You even when we are tied up in the darkness." He lifted his head high and laughed as Sarah grasped for his fingers, tightening her grip with love.

They sat in silence for a time, before Sarah started to sing, her soft voice chiming through the room like a dream. Mark closed his eyes to the sound and drank it in before he added his rich, deep voice to the simple melody. The praise filled their hearts with strength and joy. For that moment, their hearts soared in a way that was unexplainable.

A gunshot rang out in the distance not too far away. Startled, their song was cut short as they strained to hear more sounds.

"Kwan?" Sarah choked in shock.

"No, that's a different sound. Someone's here." Mark gasped with relief. A short time later, they heard two more shots fired. They heard a voice again, this time different. Mark's eyes lit up with recognition.

"Naicker!" he gasped. "That's Tim! He's just outside, Sarah! Tim!" he cried out. His voice reverberated around the room. "We're in here, Tim!" He waited.

Nothing.

"He can't hear me!" he muttered in annoyance. Mark looked around the room and a thought struck him. Israel! The antelope horns. *Shofar!* Gritting his teeth against the pain in his shoulder, Mark wriggled himself down the pole so that he was almost lying on his back as he stretched out his feet. He tried to lever one of the fallen horns toward him with his foot.

"Mark?" Sarah's voice was hoarse. "What are you doing?"

"Getting a horn." His breath strained over the angle of his body as his arms pulled taut behind him. A rush of fresh blood began to pulse from his shoulder. Gasping through the pain, a chortle of relief escaped his lips when one of the horns rolled his way. He was in luck—this one had a crack in the top that had chipped away to form into a nice little hole, ready to use as a horn. If only he could just break off a little more. He got the leverage needed by maneuvering the horn so it was tucked firmly under one knee. Mark positioned the top of the horn just right and slammed the heel of his boot down on it. It snapped off nicely. Not a neat hole, but the right size to get a decent sound like Israel had done that day.

"Ma-ark." There was concern in Sarah's voice, and he paused. He heard it, too. Footsteps.

"Trust me." His eyes sparkled as he grunted and manipulated the position of the horn with his legs and feet. He only needed a minute, and he would get it just right.

The mysterious bakkie had traveled for quite some time into Kruger when Kwanele reasoned that he needed to get out before he went too far in the wrong direction. He had missed the fact that two police vehicles had passed them earlier, headed in the opposite direction at high speed.

He peered out of the canvas flap and saw the road rush past under him at alarming speed. He wouldn't be able to get off at this rate. He grimaced. Could he push through the bales, knock on the front window, and get their attention? Fear gripped his stomach. What if they were angry with him? What if they were dangerous?

He pushed his anxiety down. He needed to help Mark and Sarah at all costs. Kwanele shoved through the bales. He had nearly pushed through when he felt the vehicle lurch to a sudden stop. He frowned and squirmed to the back of the bakkie again and peered out of the canvas. He was in luck. Leaning out farther, he saw a Jeep that was parked up alongside the bakkie. The two drivers talked animatedly, and he caught snippets of the conversation.

"Be careful—many police in Kruger today... Something big going down."

Kwanele's heart almost skipped a beat. He recognized that voice. Sello, from the Freedom Fighters. Holding his breath with joy, he slipped out the back of the bakkie just as both vehicles started to move. He scrambled out in front of the Jeep, his hands waving about. He saw Sello slam on the brakes, his eyes wide with shock. His expression was quick to darken as he pushed his head out the window.

"*Oi!* Where did you come from?" His threatening features altered with recognition.

"You! Ah...come here, boy." He beckoned Kwanele over and directed his off-sider to open the front door. They ushered Kwanele to slip into the middle of the Jeep between them. Sello slammed the door and pushed into gear. Kwanele had a sudden impression of being trapped, and he wondered if he'd made a mistake. What if they didn't help him, or worse? He steadied his nerves. Sello seemed relaxed, so that had to count for something.

"What are you doing? Wandering in the middle of Kruger again? Did you tell them your secret?" He cut straight back to their previous conversation. Kwanele burst into tears of relief and frustration.

"I tried. They wouldn't listen. The poachers rang them and tricked them and they went to them. Now they are tied up, probably going to be killed, any minute. I went to find help. There are many elephants trapped in a cage, and they are going to kill them. They're going to kill everyone!"

"Whoa! Slow down, little man! Kill who?" Sello slammed on the brakes again. The Jeep screeched to a halt in the middle of the road. Sello turned a warning glower at his comrades before turning back to Kwanele.

"Both!" Kwanele squeaked. "They are killing the elephants and Mark and Sarah today...and they already killed Jacques!"

Sello frowned deeply. "Jacques?"

"My cheetah!" Kwanele's eyes were wide and burned from the tears and dust.

"Aah, the guard dog?"

Kwanele dropped his gaze a moment and nodded slightly. Sello frowned in thought a long moment before Kwanele looked up at him. What was the man thinking? In a flash, Sello's expression turned as hard as rock, and Kwanele felt as though he'd been kicked in the stomach.

"Where?" Sello peered over his shoulder at his men. Raising a shaky arm, Kwanele pointed out through the windscreen down the road ahead of them.

"Mozambique, sir. At the warden's bunker-house. There's a warehouse, and a caged-off area."

Sello turned to face the men again, his face grim.

"The police went that way," he reasoned. One of his men spoke up.

"No, Boss, bad idea. We get arrested if the police see us."

Kwanele bit his lip.

"But the police don't know where they are being locked up. He's going to kill them. Please!" Kwanele grasped Sello's arm, anguish wrenching him. Sello reefed his arm from Kwanele's grip.

"Stop it! Let me think." Those moments of silence ticked away slowly for Kwanele. Every moment counted. "You said there were elephants there, too, lots?"

Kwanele shuddered as he nodded.

"No, Boss! The police!" his off-sider protested. Sello turned to his men, and his eyes flashed.

"Who are we? Are we cowards? Do we run from a fight when lives are at stake?"

No one dared to answer him. He nodded with satisfaction, set his jaw, and pushed the Jeep into gear. Sello slammed his foot on the accelerator and released the clutch at the same time. Kwanele yelped with fear as the Jeep leaped into action, fishtailing along the dirt track until it gripped and sped toward the border.

"Boss. They won't let us in!" One of his men pointed out as the border gate came into view. There were no gates, just guards who manned the gateway. Sello narrowed his eyes and pumped his foot down harder on the accelerator. Kwanele felt adrenaline surge through him as they sped toward the gates, and he braced his arms against the dashboard. They sped through before the guards even had a chance to slip out from their offices and protest. Sello threw his head back and laughed heartily.

"If we go to jail this day, boys, we will go as heroes!" He waved his hand in the air as they headed in the direction of the bunker-house.

Tom stormed into the bunker-house in fury.

"Abasi! Where is it?" he growled. Abasi fumbled with the vials as he tried to mix the correct portions and insert them into the gas bomb. "You haven't done it yet?" He spat with disgust. "Give me my gun back!" Tom held out his hand as he looked at his watch. They were out of time. It had to be now. If it came to the worst and they got cornered, he would still make sure that Sarah was finished. He had waited too many years to let her get away again. He yanked the gun from Abasi's shaky fingers and slipped it into his coat pocket. His expression was haughty as he watched the African man work on the gases with trembling hands. Tom tapped his fingers on the bench, his patience thin. He couldn't be here when the police arrived. He needed to ensure the couple was finished and get out of there as fast as he could. Abasi's frightened wife stood in the corner wringing her hands. It irritated him.

"Watch the door, woman! Let no one in!"

Terror in her eyes, she darted away toward the front door. The pseudo-vets watched the windows and loaded their own handguns. Tom's chin lifted slightly at the sight of them. At least he had three decent mercenaries with him. They were professional. That made up for Abasi's lack. He pulled his own gun. Abasi heaved a great sigh behind them and went to complain, but Tom swiftly moved to his side. He tucked the gun back into the jacket. He had to do everything himself. He watched Abasi place the vials on the bench before he roughly shoved the man out of the way. He shrugged off his jacket, hung it on the back of a chair, and rolled up his sleeves. Tom snapped some gloves on and finished preparing the vials himself. He clicked the mixed glass dropper into the housing and pocketed the secured item. It wasn't hard. He glared at Abasi. He now had his weapon. Once it was smashed on the floor, it would send the elephants crazy enough to trample anything. If that failed, the lethal dosage would kill Mark and Sarah without leaving evidence. Either way, they would already be rendered a mess from the elephants. Tom looked at his watch.

"Get them into the enclosure—we need to do this now!"

The vets nodded and moved toward the door when Abasi's

wife hissed from the front room. "Police."

"Damn!" Tom shoved a chair, and it skittered violently across the floor with a loud *clank*. They would need another plan. He needed those people dead at all costs, and he needed to disappear.

Lieutenant Tim Naicker pulled up in the unmarked squad car behind the patrol vehicles. He stepped onto the dirt and crossed to the main bunker-house. He needed Mark, Sarah, and the boy back at the safe-house now. They had heard reports that the suspects were moving today. They had caught Stephan Venter from the Safari Tours the night before, and he'd confessed to them that there was a plan somewhere over in Mozambique. Once Tim had filled Jacob and Martha in on the situation, it hadn't taken Jacob long to tell them that he'd heard from Mark and that they had crossed the border in the early hours of the morning, lured out by a mercy mission to save some elephants. Tim had been furious that they would have so easily fallen for it. The bunker-house seemed quiet as he stepped onto the front porch and knocked on the door. A waif of a dark woman opened the door and looked at them in question. Tim flipped open his ID badge.

"Tim Naicker. South African Police. I believe that Mark and Sarah van der Merwe arrived here sometime this morning?"

She shook her head, her expression clouded. Tim saw a flash of movement inside the building as someone ducked past his line of sight.

"Do you mind if we speak with the warden for a few minutes?" Tim cleared his throat. The woman looked over her shoulder, and her eyes flicked this way and that. Tim narrowed his gaze.

"Sir!" An officer raced up the steps behind him, out of breath. Tim turned to regard the man.

"We found something. Around the back." Just as Tim turned to speak to the woman, she slammed the door in his face. He heard a gunshot echo off a building. That was all he needed. He vaulted from the porch in one leap. Tim broke into a protective stance, pulled his Glock, and held it up in two hands as he put his back to the wall of the building. It didn't take long to cross the grounds toward where the shot had sounded. He nodded toward two other officers who were backed up against another building. His radio blared on his shoulder holster.

"Ten-thirty-two, sir. Swahili—Warden Abasi Baridi. He took a shot at an officer—on the run toward the east side gate. Ten-eighty. Over and out." The radio crackled. Tim compressed the button. "Ten-four." He nodded at the other two and turned the volume low on his radio. He waved for the others to cover him. Quickly, he slipped toward the direction indicated. Two more shots rang out, and they broke into a run. They rounded the corner and saw two figures in white coats disappear around the corner of a building. Tim and another officer launched toward the next set of buildings and flattened their backs against the large warehouse doors. Tim turned to the officer. Sweat beaded the man's face.

"Mike, you cover me. I'll swing round this side as Meg and Pete approach the west side. Mark and Sarah have got to be here. Hopefully we're not too late."

Tim's radio crackled in undertones to life again, and he looked at Mike grimly as they listened to the muted report.

"You'd better come see. Elephants locked in a small enclosure. They look malnourished, and I think there is a dead calf underneath it all." Tim picked up his radio and pressed the speaker.

"We'll deal with it once we've secured the area. There are still shooters on the loose. Over and out." He nodded at Mike, and the two of them slipped around the building toward where they'd seen the shooters disappear.

CHAPTER
THIRTY-ONE

Sarah opened her eyes as she heard someone approach. The door opened, and in stepped a tall man in a white suit. The antelope horn Mark had been working with clunked to the floor near Mark's feet as he jumped with surprise. Sarah barely noticed as she stared with loathing. It was him alright. The man from her dreams. Sweat beaded on the man's brow. She stared in dread as he turned his vivid blue eyes toward her. A cold chill wrapped its clawed fingers around her heart, threatening to crush it. Her breath came in rapid gasps, and Mark tried to twist to look at her. A piece of his perfectly groomed hair came loose and hung limp against his forehead, giving him the appearance of a madman. He pushed it back, and his face twisted. One look at the businessman's wild eyes told her two things. He knew he was cornered. And he was acting on impulse. The man went to reach for an invisible pocket. He felt around and looked down at his clothing, cursing explosively. Sarah looked from the ruffled man to the open doorway. She wasn't going to let the opportunity slide.

"Help!" she screamed as loudly as she could. The man snapped into action. He crossed the floor and struck her across the face, stopping her screams. He leered and watched with apparent pleasure as her eyes welled with stinging tears. Mark struggled against his bonds.

"Get away from her! You filthy, no-good—" The sound of the door as the man slammed it halted Mark. The man flicked on an overhead light and looked around with spooky calm. He moved to the benches with the rolled-up furs and rummaged through the piles. "Aha." He produced a thinner sample of a cheetah cub pelt. Ripping the fur into two long strips, he returned to the couple, and one at a time, he pulled their heads back by the hair and tied the pelt gags into their mouths.

"Try calling for help now!" He snickered, arrogance in his eyes. Sarah tasted bile rise up her throat at the smell and taste of the skin. Tears slipped down her cheeks as she wept at the atrocity.

"Right. That will fix you while you wait." He smirked as he produced a small vial from his pocket. Sarah's eyes widened, and cold dread leached into her stomach.

A gunshot reverberated off the side of the warehouse, and the man turned in panic. The fray was too close for comfort for him; he had that desperate, haunted look in his face. Regaining his composure, he cast a menacing glare down at them one last time. In a blur of motion, he lifted his arm and smashed the vial onto the cement. Glass shattered from the cracked housing and a loud *whoosh* hit the room as the chemicals reacted to the exposure to oxygen. A noxious pale gas seeped into the room. The man covered his mouth and nose, then turned and fled. He pulled the door closed behind him, but in his hurry, he didn't see it bounce against the horn and fall back open. It was now slightly ajar. Still, the room filled rapidly with the gas, and Mark and Sarah both struggled desperately against their bonds. *God help us! God help us!* They had only one chance. Sarah heard Mark scramble to use his feet and legs to try to retrieve the dropped antelope horn.

Mark's breath chuffed in short bursts through his nostrils as he struggled to position the horn near his face. With each breath, the sour fumes leached further into his system, burning his nostrils as it entered. His head began to thump with an overwhelming pain.

The toxins began to penetrate his bloodstream, and his muscles twitched, the nerves reacting violently to the chemical. He felt Sarah's body tremor behind him. No time left—they would die if he didn't succeed. Violent spasms racked his legs as they held fast to the horn. Sweat ran in rivulets down his face as he worked to pry the tip of the horn under the fur gag in his mouth. The pelt was firmly tied, and he could taste stale blood and leather. He fought against heaving of his stomach.

No time. No time.

The room started to spin. Mark worked the sharp edge of the broken horn around his face, trying to find leverage under the pelt. The broken edges ripped into his chin and bottom lip. He grunted as shooting pain bit into his face, but ignoring it, he continued to work. No time. He was going to choke on a combination of fur, blood, and gas. Mark's stomach heaved as he tried to control the sensation of rising bile.

Sarah's writhing stopped, and she went limp. Panic took hold of him. Bracing against the pain, he gave a sharp shove with his legs. The horn ripped under the fur at the corner of his mouth. He moaned in pain and relief as he used his knees to push it further under. Was it too late? His muscles ached from convulsing, and his legs had started to grow numb. Grimacing against the sting of the cuts to his face and the throbbing in his muscles and now chest, he was able to place the rough shofar into his mouth.

He struggled to breathe. Blood began to clot up the damp fur in his mouth. Mark spat out blood and fur and coughed. He inhaled deeply and blew into the horn as hard as he could.

Please, God, let someone hear!

A long, loud blast penetrated through the gas haze and reached out into the warehouse. He blew long and hard, over and over, until he could go on no more. He gasped for breath. The combination of the gas and the blowing made him lightheaded, and his breath came in short, rapid pants. His body shook violently. Finally, his pain eased and he fell into the dangerous calm of unconsciousness.

Sello pulled the Jeep straight into the bunker-house grounds and followed Kwanele's directions toward the warehouse.

"That's him!" Kwanele pointed as he saw Tom run from the warehouse and down a causeway between buildings. "That's the big boss!"

Sello and his men didn't need a second invitation. A chance to get one of the people at the top was an opportunity too good to miss. The four men sprinted after him as Kwanele slipped out of the Jeep and ran for the warehouse. He pushed open the sliding doors as he heard a long, loud drone, as from a horn. It came from the inner room. He knew he couldn't undo the ropes himself. He ran outside again to look for help, but everyone had run off after Tom. The horn sounded long and loud behind him until it faltered and stopped. Kwanele gasped and sprinted into the warehouse. He swung open the inner door. The pale yellow light of the bulb overhead emanated through a strange fog, and a strong smell like sour eggs seeped from the room. It stung his nostrils. He glimpsed Mark and Sarah through the pale haze. They were lifeless; their heads drooped to the side. Terror ripped through his heart as he pushed through the offensive fumes. He crouched by their limp bodies and shook Mark's shoulder.

"Wake up! Mark! Please!" Reaching out, he touched Sarah's arm. "Sarah?" Her skin was warm. They were still alive—just barely.

He jumped to his feet and sprinted outside screaming for help. His eyes lit up as the policeman, Lieutenant Tim Naicker, materialized seemingly from nowhere. He put a firm hand on Kwanele's shoulder.

"Quick!" He pointed toward the warehouse. Tim was already on his way. Kwanele followed after him and saw the alarm register in the lieutenant's eyes. Covering his mouth with his sleeve, he ordered Kwanele to get help. He shook his head, wanting to stay.

"Go, Kwan, or they will die!"

Eye wide, Kwanele complied. He raced outside and found more officers. They all raced into the building to find Tim carrying Sarah from the room. "Quick, in there!" he barked and raced past them into the fresh air. Kwanele watched as the two officers hauled Mark's strong frame from the building next.

Emotion rose in Kwanele, and he folded his arms about himself, tears falling from his face as they were laid down with care and their gags removed. Mark's face was butchered, and Sarah had a large bruise under her eye. Everything became a blur to Kwanele as he saw officers perform first aid on the couple, Tim barking that they weren't to stop until the medics arrived.

Naicker's radio crackled to life, but Kwanele only had care for Mark and Sarah. The voices became a blur to him. He picked up snippets that the men had been caught and that they were arresting Sello and his men. Kwanele's ears and eyes snapped back into focus. He went and tugged on Tim's arm as he watched the people he loved most lying on the ground.

"Those men. The Freedom Fighters. What will happen to them?"

"That's none of your concern."

"But they helped you."

"Did they?"

"They brought me here in time. You wouldn't have known where Mark and Sarah were. They saved them."

"They're not out of the woods yet." Tim looked at the couple, grave concern reflected in his eyes.

"Will they die?" Fresh tears sprung from the Kwanele's eyes, and his small frame began to heave with sobs. Tim crouched down to his level.

"Let's hope not." He squeezed Kwanele on the shoulder, got up, and turned his attention elsewhere.

"Sir?" Kwanele tugged at him again. Tim paused, his brows raised wearily in question.

"Please do what you can to save them. They are like a mum and dad to me."

Kwanele's hopeful eyes bore into Tim's, and he saw the lieutenant's features melt in sympathy. A muscle twitched in Tim's jaw, and he shielded his eyes against the sun. Kwanele followed his gaze. An ambulance was approaching. The ambulance pulled up, and the scene became a flurry of people as the ambulance officers hauled out the stretchers and applied oxygen masks to the couple. Tim ducked back into the warehouse and brought out the vial. Kwanele listened with horror as Tim explained the components of the gas to the paramedics as he bagged the cracked housing of the gas bomb for evidence. Kwanele felt the blood drain from his face. Tim gazed down at him and gently squeezed his shoulder. They watched as the ambulance roared away, sirens blaring.

"You can see them later, Kwanele. We need to get your statement now, and then we'll take you back to Jacob and Martha. They can take you back out to the hospital."

Kwanele stared down the road to where he'd seen the ambulance head. Life wasn't fair. He'd been too late.

Kwanele didn't know what to expect when they arrived at the hospital. What if it had been too late? No one wanted to tell him anything. Even if they were alive, what if they had been crippled for life? It would all be his fault for not speaking up sooner. A heaviness lay in the pit of his stomach as Jacob and Martha drove to the hospital in Mozambique. After what seemed like an eternity, they pulled into the car-park and Kwanele launched himself from the vehicle. He sprang lightly up the cement steps, looking behind with frustration as Jacob and Martha took longer to follow. After Jacob spoke with several people, they were directed into the rooms where Mark and Sarah had both been placed on the ward. Kwanele paused outside, afraid of what he would find. He needed to know, though, but he was afraid. He took a deep breath and peered into the room.

"Kwanele!" Sarah's eyes lit up as she gasped out his name. She rose with some effort to a sitting position and pushed off her oxygen mask. Mark's head rolled toward the door, his blue eyes softening when he saw them all enter. His breath sounded short and painful under the mask. Kwanele ran first to Sarah and allowed the woman to wrap him in her arms and kiss him on the head, before he pulled away and approached Mark. The man struggled slowly to a sitting position. He beckoned for Kwanele to come to him and then wrapped him into a tight embrace. Kwanele saw tears form in his eyes as he lightly scuffed his hair.

"Hey, champ!" His voice was hoarse, but Kwanele still saw a small smile behind the cuts on his face.

Jacob and Martha looked at Mark in shock, and Sarah chuckled at their expressions.

"It's okay, you can say it. He looks messed up!"

Mark quirked a big, cheeky grin, but he winced as the cuts on his chin and lower lip pulled. He had a bruise on his cheekbone, and his bullet-ripped shoulder was in a sling.

"Ten stiches." He nodded toward his shoulder when he caught their line of sight. His voice slurred under the medication they had given him. A doctor wandered in and smiled warmly, shaking their hands in turn.

"They should be well enough to leave by tomorrow. We just need to observe them one more night to give them final clearance."

"When do we lose our sexy husky voices?" Sarah pouted, before grinning at her husband.

"A couple more days should clear that up." The doctor checked their charts again. Mark feigned annoyance.

"Awwwww!"

Sarah threw a pillow at him, and he caught it, just before it hit his shoulder. The doctor glowered with disapproval. He cleared his throat and looked apologetically at Jacob and Martha.

"Like I said, they are discharged tomorrow morning. Any time after ten a.m. On the dot, would be lovely." With that, he strode from the room. Sarah and Mark exchanged glances. Kwanele giggled at them, supposing they were just happy to be alive. Martha and Jacob pulled up two chairs between the beds and sat down. Mark patted his hand on the end of his bed, inviting Kwanele to sit there. He hopped up and looked around their faces. The lighthearted mood in the room had suddenly turned sober.

"Thank God you are both alright." Martha had tears in her eyes. "If it weren't for that phone call and Kwanele escaping..." She let the thought hang in the air. Jacob cleared his throat.

"So, Tim told you what happened when he came yesterday?"

"Yes." Sarah nodded in wonder. "He told us that Kwanele found those Freedom Fighters and convinced them to come and save us. They ran off after Tom Dawson, and it was Kwan who found us, calling for help." She looked at Kwanele, and her eyes sparkled. "You saved our lives, Kwan."

He shrugged. He was just overjoyed to see them alive. Jacob

shifted in his chair.

"The bush camp is still full of police and the bunker-house is now closed as a crime scene. Tim Naicker needs to talk with you again when you are ready—for your statements, I believe."

"I bet he does. But at least they found the main ringleader, Tom Dawson. They made over six arrests." Mark lifted his chin in the air. "The threat is gone. God delivered us, and we can move on with our lives now." No one agreed with him. A quiet tension mounted in the room. Sarah swung her legs off the side of the hospital bunk, looking thoughtful.

"Whatever happens, it's no use getting upset about it until we know all the details from Tim. Is he waiting for us to be released tomorrow?"

Jacob nodded. Sarah glanced at Mark, her face set with confidence. "God got us through some pretty heavy stuff yesterday. I'm sure we can handle anything now, Mark." She smiled encouragingly. Kwanele looked down at the floor. Why did he feel dread that a new chapter was about to end to this story?

Chapter
Thirty-Two

Tim Naicker took off his hat and tucked it under his arm as he entered Jacob and Martha's home. Martha closed the door.

"They're in the living room—it's much more comfortable there. Can I bring you a coffee?" Nodding his thanks to both offers, Tim headed in without another word. He entered the living room and saw Mark and Sarah next to each other as they enjoyed a cup of coffee each.

"How's the shoulder?" He pointed toward Mark's injury.

"*Ja*, it's good. Very tender still and starting to itch like crazy."

"That's good—it means it's healing." Tim took a seat opposite them and perched on the edge.

"So I've been told." Mark looked at Sarah.

"Did the elephants get let out? The calves in there..." She shook her head, and Tim could see her fight the emotion. She was pointed as she took another swig of coffee. Tim hesitated. He knew she wouldn't like the news.

"They were let out, and one of the calves was treated for a fracture wound to his front leg and shoulder."

Sarah leaned forward. "But it was a female calf with a broken back leg."

Tim cleared his throat. "The male was treated for his front leg. The little female with the broken back leg didn't survive." He looked down. Mark put down his coffee and grasped her hand.

"Could we really expect anything else?"

She shook her head. Tim's eyes burned with fatigue, and he nodded his gratitude as Martha entered. She handed him his steaming black coffee. After a week at the bush camp, the woman had learned how he liked it. He took a long, slow sip.

"Tom Dawson, what's happening there?" Sarah choked up. "He nearly killed us, Tim."

Mark slipped his arm around her shoulder and tugged her close.

"At least he was arrested, hon."

"Yes, but what will happen next? Will he go to jail, or get away with it?"

Tim pulled the coffee away from his lips and nodded.

"I assure you, he won't get away with anything. He didn't cover his tracks well enough this time. He left evidence everywhere. We have his prints on the device and both your testimonies. He's left a trail of evidence that leads to several deaths."

"Witness testimony." Sarah rolled it off her tongue like it tasted sour. "That's means—"

"Yes. It means you are still targets." Tim looked at them dolefully.

"I made a huge mistake coming out here, I know." Mark rubbed at the cut on his face.

"That may be so, but at least it forced a move by their hand. Helped us to catch them."

"But look at what it almost cost. I don't know if I can forgive myself for putting Sarah and Kwan in such danger." Mark picked up his mug and ran his finger around the rim of it. Tim stopped him with his hand.

"I don't doubt you're sorry...and I will get a full statement from you in a moment, just to wrap everything up and get ready for trials. But that's not why I'm here now."

Sarah and Mark exchanged concerned glances.

"I want to talk about your future—and Kwanele's."

Mark sat back heavily.

"What about Kwanele?" Sarah narrowed her eyes. Tim gave a halfhearted smile, trying to work out how to word what he was about to say.

"The thing is, I heard along the grapevine that you were both interested in adopting him."

Sarah looked over at Mark with surprise, but he just shrugged smugly. She stared. He flicked his chin toward Tim, redirecting her.

"Anyway, I realize you don't have the funds to adopt at this stage, so we took the liberty of filling in an application to give you guardianship of the boy." He paused, waiting for that to sink in.

"You what?" Mark tilted his head. "You didn't have to pull strings. I said we'd work it out."

Tim held his hand up once more. "It's done. I have more to say. There's a reason it's being fast-tracked."

"Wha—"

"If you please, let me get to it, Mark."

Mark shook away his curiosity as he gazed at his wife. Her eyes were lit up, brimming with tears. He gently took her mug and set it on the side table. She grasped his good arm, joy dancing in her smile. Tim took a deep breath.

"Here's the catch."

Mark looked at him with confusion.

"You didn't tell me there was a catch."

"Ahh, but I did just say that there was a reason it was fast-tracked. Let me explain. I am still in the process of making inquiries. You still need to be hidden."

Mark plunked his mug into his lap with a little too much force.

"You caught the top dog! You made all those arrests? Are you telling me there is another one lining us up?"

Tim shook his head. He detested informing them just as much as Mark hated receiving the news.

"There is no one that we know of at this stage."

"Then what's the problem? Can't we just live our lives now?" He locked his eyes on to Tim, whose face hardened.

"You will never truly be safe."

"So...witness protection for the rest of our lives?"

"I don't like it, either. It costs the state money."

"So...let us go."

Tim ignored Mark's remarks and continued in a calm voice. "You have some options, but they are fairly major and you have some big decisions to make. You have both made such a major contribution to the conservation efforts in the Kruger, and the government has agreed to grant the funds to help with what I am about to propose."

"We were offered work, down south —at another safari trail riding park. Are you going to say that this is not an option?" Mark protested.

Tim leaned forward, a vague smile on his face. "You can do what you want if you choose, but I strongly suggest you look at the options I am offering... Look...I know you are both believers in the Bible, so pray about it. Pray for your answers. I'll give you forty-eight hours to think about it."

"Well, what is it? What's the proposal?" Sarah jumped to the point.

"What we can offer you all—all three of you—is this. Funding and papers to move to Australia. Start a new life somewhere completely away from the dangers here." He sat back, waiting for the information to sink in. Martha wandered in again with a tray full of biscuits and gave Tim a sad smile. Mark caught the exchange.

"Martha?"

She paused as she collected their empty mugs.

"You and Jacob knew about this, didn't you?" Mark eyeballed her with amazement. She turned to regard him, an unusual expression in her eyes. She smiled and walked out of the room.

"How come you told her and not me?" Mark was incredulous.

"I assure you, I did not tell her anything. And no one else knows this." Tim was just as shocked as Mark at the exchange. Perhaps it had been their God that spoke to her. He was the only person at the bush camp who was savvy to that information until now. The woman clearly looked to have had some understanding. Never mind, it was out now. Tim stood and excused himself.

"I'll be back in ten minutes. I still need separate detailed statements of the events of Mozambique, but I want to give you both time to digest what I just said." He cleared his throat again and awkwardly stepped out into the kitchen to have his coffee there and leave the couple to process his offer. Heavy silence sat in the room as Mark and Sarah regarded the incredible turn of events.

Sarah turned to her husband. His face was forlorn.

"I wanted to look into the job down south." Mark hung his head. "I've never left Africa before…"

Sarah touched his shoulder.

"I hadn't left Australia when I came over here. It was a huge leap of faith, and I didn't even know God then. We don't need to make a decision yet. Let's just get ready to give our statements now."

He gazed into Sarah's soft eyes, and her heart skipped a beat.

"You want to go…don't you?" He searched her face.

She sighed and looked away. Mark turned her face back toward him. "Let's call our friends over later, and we'll pray about what to do next. What did Tim say? Forty-eight hours? In the meantime, we have some exciting news to tell Kwan." His eyes twinkled as he took her hand and squeezed it.

"I'll stay and give my statement first. You go. But don't tell Kwan until I'm with you." Nodding, she stood, leaned over, and kissed him softly before breezing out of the room.

Sarah found Tim in the kitchen, rinsing his coffee mug in the sink. "Mark will do his statement first."

Tim nodded and went to move past her.

"Wait." Sarah gripped his forearm urgently. Tim paused and frowned at her lack of protocol. She removed her hand.

"The Freedom Fighters. Sello, and his men." She looked into his eyes intently.

"What about them? They have been wanted for quite some time. We have them in custody now." He turned to face her fully, the intensity in her eyes drawing his attention.

"They saved us, too, Tim. Kwanele led them to us. I know you would have found us, but if it weren't for Kwanele finding them, you wouldn't have caught Tom Dawson."

He frowned.

"I only ask that you think about giving them a chance. I know they are ready to change. They risked arrest to save us on the word of a boy." There. She'd said her part. Sarah pressed her lips together, then swept past him and headed for her room.

CHAPTER THIRTY-THREE

Two vehicles in convey rumbled down the dirt driveway into the bush camp, tearing Kwanele's attention away from the leather collar in his hands. He blinked as the cars stopped at the front of the bush camp. His gaze dropped back to his hands. He rubbed his thumb over the worn leather of Jacques's collar. Tim had found Jacques, and at Kwanele's request, they had returned and buried the cheetah at the bush camp under the tree near the horse kraals. Jacob had given the cheetah's collar to Kwanele.

He tucked his knees up to his chest and shuffled in among the shrub next to the building—his and Jacques's special place. This had been his hidden place with Jacques on many an occasion. It was a place where he could think and confide in his best friend. Only one other person knew about this spot. Mark. A tear slipped down Kwanele's cheek, and he hugged his knees tighter, his face resting on his arms. A soft, warm breeze brushed against his face, and a still, quiet voice filled his heart with warmth. *You can still confide in a new best friend.*

"Thank You, Jesus," Kwanele murmured as more tears slipped from his eyes. The relief of being free from such an evil burden was overwhelming. Now that he was no longer in danger, he felt lost. Would Mark and Sarah turn him away now that the police had told them the truth? He buried his head in his arms. He loved them like parents, and now he felt like he was going to lose them.

He sniffed back his tears. Only hours ago, Kwanele had been walking outside, underneath the living room window, and had overheard Mark give his statement to the policeman. The policeman had told him Kwanele's secret. It had cut Kwanele to pieces to hear the pain in Mark's voice when he learned the truth. He couldn't bear to hear how it ended. He had run away to his hiding place, unable to stay and listen to more. He clamped his eyes shut against the agony of what he was going to now face and sobbed. They would know now. They would hate him. He would be sent away with the police. Bitter tears swept over Kwanele as he huddled in close to hide among the plants.

"I thought I'd find you here." A soft voice drifted across his consciousness. Kwanele snapped his head up and wiped his eyes. Mark crouched down, his shoulder still awkward in the sling. Sarah quietly stood behind him, a strange smile on her face.

"You alright?" Mark squeezed his shoulder. "We need to talk to you." Kwanele turned his face away. Sarah came and squatted in the dirt close to them both. Kwanele looked up with such a deep sadness in his eyes that Sarah blinked in surprise. Mark glanced back at Sarah with concern, before reaching out and squeezing Kwanele's shoulder.

"You're upset. Why?" Mark frowned.

Kwanele buried his face deep into his arms. He didn't want to talk to them.

"We're sorry about Jacques, Kwanele. We know how much he meant to you," Sarah ventured. The use of his full name instead of the pet name they'd given him drove the wound deeper.

"We have some important news for you, Kwan." Mark's voice was soft. Kwanele shot him a strange glance.

"What? That I need to leave with the police now?" he muttered, burying his face again. Sarah and Mark both exchanged bewildered expressions.

"Where did that come from?"

There was an awkward silence for a long while before Kwanele slowly lifted his tear-streaked face and gazed at them wordlessly, the whites of his eyes red raw from grief.

"I heard the policeman tell you what they made me do." He rested his chin on his arms. "You know about my secret. Nobody would want me now, least of all you."

Pain crossed their faces. Sarah crouched closer and rubbed

Kwanele's back with the flat of her hand.

"Yes. We know the story. We heard how you were treated, and used. But you know what? It made us love you even more."

Kwanele looked up at her with a distrust that ran deep in his veins.

"Why do you love that?"

"No…we don't love what happened. We love *you*. With what you've been through, it's God alone who has saved you, given you a new hope. It's given us a new appreciation of how strong you actually are. You are a new person now, Kwanele. And you truly are a warrior."

He stared into Sarah's bright emerald eyes for a long moment and fought against his heart to hope, lest he get hurt again.

"Kwan." Mark waited for him to look him in the eye. "We know how far you've grown. You truly are a warrior, and we are so proud of you." He tried to pull the boy into an embrace, but Kwanele pulled back. He stared into both of their faces in turn.

"How can I believe you? How do I know you won't abandon me?"

His heart twisted in anguish. It was too good to be true. It was a cruel trick. Mark and Sarah smiled lovingly at him.

"How would you like to live with us? Permanently?" Mark grinned. "We love you, and we don't want to ever leave you. We would like to be parents to you, Kwan."

Kwanele's eyes clouded in shock. Had he heard right? Sarah nodded.

"We'll be a family. The three of us." She touched his cheek lightly with the back of her hand. In his heart, Kwanele felt God's tender stirring. He looked into their eyes in earnest, and suddenly his focus cleared. They meant every word. He could see it in their eyes. He leapt to his feet and launched himself into both their arms, nearly knocking them backward. He hugged them so tightly he thought he would burst with joy. They all lingered there, savoring the moment.

"Come on, Kwan, our friends have arrived to pray with us. We're family now, and we have some serious decisions to make." Sarah smiled as Kwanele positioned himself between the two. He grasped their hands tightly as they all walked to the rondavel.

Everyone sat comfortably in the living room. Max and Kym were there, without the girls. Israel and Kgomotso had also traveled out to see them. Jacob and Martha were settled. For once Martha wasn't bustling about serving everyone. The dilemma had been presented, and now all that was left was to pray.

Max cleared his throat. Taking the lead, he launched straight into prayer as he had done several weeks ago in this very same room.

"Thank You, Lord Jesus, so much that You've delivered Mark, Sarah, and Kwanele out of the terrible danger they were in two days ago. You are the God of second chances, and You never turn Your back on us. Thank You so much for the hospitality of Jacob and Martha and how they've completely embraced all people into their care as their own. Lord..." He stuttered over the words. "Lord, You are good. You've heard the choice the Van der Merwes face today. We pray that You continue to wrap them in Your love and protection, and we pray, Father God, that You will give them direction. You know how little time they have to choose. Please make straight Your path before them."

Silence filled the room as no one else volunteered to pray. Mark and Sarah opened their eyes, and Sarah rocked her head back, gazing up at her husband. It was Israel who lurched forward in his chair, staring at them closely.

"I think you already know the answer," he said simply, and picking up his coffee, he took a casual sip. Kym leaned down and rubbed Sarah on the shoulder.

"Whatever you choose, we'll always be here for you. We're your family, even if you are on the other side of the world."

Sarah smiled at her friend. "We know."

Kwanele hugged his knees to himself again. Mark looked around in bewilderment as everyone reflected Kym's sentiment. *God? Do You really want us to go to Sarah's homeland? What would I do there?*

Kym piped up again. "Mark could get a job with horses again over there. He is very talented in tourism. I hear that many people from here are moving over to Australia. It's a great land of opportunity."

Max elbowed his wife, gently stopping her train of thought.

"How do you know that's what they were thinking?" he muttered under his breath. Kym covered her mouth with her hand, not wanting to sway them either way. Mark chuckled at her.

"It's fine, Max." He looked to Sarah and Kwanele.

"I'll follow whatever you decide, hon," Sarah remarked. His gaze settled on Kwanele. Mark wanted the boy's thoughts to count.

"What do you think, Kwan?"

The boy looked up at him, his eyes hopeful.

"Do I get to go on a plane or a boat?"

Laughter erupted into the room as Kwanele looked around at everyone in confusion. Mark reached out with his good arm and ruffled the boy's hair.

"We sure will." He chuckled.

"When?" Kwanele pressed, raising his head with keen interest. Mark looked around everyone, excitement growing within him.

"I guess that settles it." He stood and clapped his hands together. Mark caught Israel's eye. The elderly Sotho man nodded, a satisfied smile on his face. Sarah rose to Mark's side and wrapped her arm around his waist as the others stood.

"We'll miss you." Kym held out her arms and embraced them both. Kgomotso grinned as he approached the two. "You can find Koto and his family now." He shook Mark's hand. The news hit Mark like a pleasant shower of rain on a hot day. They were going to Australia.

Sello grimaced as he sat in front of the lieutenant in a private police station interview room.

"I know, I know...guilty as hell. Just tell me how many years do you think I'll get." Sello stuck his hands out, expecting to be cuffed and thrown into prison. Tim cleared his throat as he reviewed the files.

"You and your team will be on trial, but you may get an offer that I think you'll find appealing."

Sello leaned forward, a frown marring his features. Tim went on, "I might be able to get a lighter sentence as long as you do your probation with the parks board."

Sello raised his brows in surprise.

"They were very impressed with your initiative and skills catching our top suspect. They want you on the Ranger force—you and all your men."

Sello leaned back and folded his arms across his chest. He could handle that, but he was still suspicious.

"Wait. You've been trying to nab us for years. What's the catch?" His brows furrowed deeply as he examined Tim. Clearing his throat, Tim grimaced as he gathered the paperwork.

"There is no catch. And don't go thanking me—it was Sarah Van der Merwe who twisted my arm for your sake."

Sello leaned forward, his eyes wide.

"Sarah van der Merwe? You mean Sarah White? She did what?"

"She talked me into giving you all a second chance—said she thinks you've changed for the better, so you'd better prove it."

"Yes, sir!" Sello grinned from ear to ear. He could barely believe it.

"It is subject to the court hearing and jury decisions, though," Tim explained. Nodding his understanding, Sello smiled and stuck out his hand to the lieutenant. Perhaps they could all work together after all.

Epilogue

Mark pulled Sniper back to a trot, the heat from the harsh sun breaking his brow into a sweat. He took off his new Akubra hat—a gift from his wife at starting their new life—and wiped his brow with his sleeve. He looked over his shoulder. Kwanele and Sarah brought their horses up beside him, their faces flushed from cantering and laughing. They surveyed the spread of Murray Grey Cattle, as they all meandered idly.

"I told you you'd love my family's property." Sarah chortled. "Come on, I'll show you the river." Sarah urged her chestnut mount into a canter and left the other two to catch up with her. They all trotted with care down the steep bank of the river, and then plunged their horses into the cool brown waters. The tall ghost gums overhead shaded them from the intense heat. Mark sighed. They had made the right choice. Staying at the family homestead with Terry and Linda had been quite an adventure, but it was also wonderful to settle into their own house on the second cattle station.

Running a beef cattle property was a complete mystery to Mark, who was only familiar with tourism and conservation, but he was enthusiastic and ready to learn. Grateful that he wasn't being thrown in the deep end with management, Mark followed every instruction that Sarah's older brother, Jack, threw his way. Jack ran the second property with an iron fist and was eventually going to claim sole ownership of it, but he had no qualms with Sarah and her family living onsite on the second homestead. At the same time, both Sarah's parents and Jack had loved Mark's proposal to eventually set up a trail-riding business. He didn't have African animals to show off, but at least he could show tourists a "fair dinkum" Aussie experience out in the bush.

They had found a new church family in the nearby township an hour away. Mark and Sarah had determined that it was more important than ever to stay close-knit in a church family and to never isolate themselves from God's love again.

Mark moved Sniper over next to Sarah's chestnut in the waters. He reached out and took her hand.

"This is perfect." he sighed. They both broke into laughter as Kwanele grabbed on to an overhead branch and let his horse slip away from under him. After hanging for a moment, he threw himself, giggling, into the cool waters. Sarah regained her composure and gazed at her husband, a twinkle in her eye.

"Yes, it is perfect."

The End

ABOUT THE SERIES

Sarah's Gift is the first book of Skye Elizabeth's *Dare to Follow* trilogy about a group of friends who find God and themselves in the midst of adventure, danger, and beautiful vistas. *Mark's Strength* is an extension of that, with a focus on finding God through despair and leaning on His strength instead of our own.

Sarah's Gift (Book One)

Mark's Strength (Book Two)

Kwan's Choice (Book Three)

of the

TRILOGY

Kwan's Choice

Starting a new life in Australia should have been a dream come true for the Van der Merwe family. But when trouble comes from close quarters, they need to learn to lean on one another, God, and friends from unexpected places. Kwan is a grown man now, but can he learn to be what God has called him to be? A leader.

About the Author

Skye Elizabeth lives in Queensland, Australia, with her two children, Daniel and Rachel. She is an artist and a secondary high school teacher, who has a love for horses. Skye is passionate about helping people discover their dreams in life and strive for them.

Acknowledgments

Again, a novel isn't what it is without all the hard work and input that goes into it before it even hits the printers. To make something like this happen requires support and patience from so many sources. I want to personally thank the following people for all their support in this process.

- First and foremost to God, my Lord and Savior, who has carried me through the valley during the production of this book.
- To my wonderful family and friends who are always there to offer guidance, support, and prayer.
- Catherine Hudson, for all her hard work helping me with the edits and pushing me along to meet deadlines.
- To Kathy Bosman, who is my wonderful critique partner in South Africa.
- To SANParks, for all their continued hard work.
- And finally, to all the various people who have helped me with information, proofreading, and general tidbits along the way – especially, Heather Ashcroft, Len Robinson, and Michelle Evans.

Letter from Skye

Dear Readers,

Thank you so much for reading *Mark's Strength*. As I've been on the journey of creating and distributing this story, I've discovered that many questions have cropped up from the themes within the pages that readers would like to know more about. I have created a blogsite (http://www.daretofollowtrilogy.blogspot.com), where I will endeavor to answer as many of these questions as I can and steer people in the right direction for the answers to any other questions they have.

If you have just read *Mark's Strength* and have decided that you want what the characters have found in Jesus and you've realized that sometimes the burdens in life are just too much for you, then the next step for you is to say "yes" to Jesus. All you need to do is read the following prayer aloud, and the confession of your mouth will do the work in your heart.

> *Dear Jesus,*
> *I acknowledge that I can't do everything on my own. I confess that I have sinned in both my own ways and also by putting myself above others and You. I ask now that You forgive me, Lord, and I invite You into my heart to be my Lord and Savior. Thank You for the work that You did on the cross for me. Amen.*

I encourage you to visit my blog site to follow up on your decision and to start the journey of finding out more about this marvelous God we serve. As an author, I also love hearing from my readers. If you would like to leave any comments, or if you cannot find an answer to a question, feel free to e-mail me on the link provided. Thank you again for your support, and I look forward to hearing from you.

Blessings,
Skye Elizabeth
Email: skyeelizabethauthor@gmail.com
http://www.daretofollowtrilogy.blogspot.com